TITHE OF THE SA

TITHE
OF THE
SAVIOURS

A J DALTON

GOLLANCZ

LONDON

Copyright © A J Dalton 2014
All rights reserved

The right of A J Dalton to be identified as the author
of this work has been asserted by him in accordance
with the Copyright, Designs and Patents Act 1988.

First published in Great Britain in 2014 by Gollancz
An imprint of the Orion Publishing Group
Orion House, 5 Upper St Martin's Lane,
London WC2H 9EA
An Hachette UK Company

A CIP catalogue record for this book is available
from the British Library

ISBN (Trade Paperback) 978 0 575 12322 9

1 3 5 7 9 10 8 6 4 2

Typeset at The Spartan Press Ltd,
Lymington, Hants

Printed and bound in Great Britain by
Clays Ltd, St Ives plc

www.ajdalton.eu
www.orionbooks.co.uk

To Rob, Stella and Malcolm Blake

Acknowledgements

With thanks to Paul Leeming, Phil Sharrock, Becky Unicorn, Marcus Gipps, Dr Siouxsie Cooper and Oliver Flude

Bargain struck and bargain made,
Let our foes be ever afraid.

Prologue

The crow flapped tiredly onwards. There was precious little air movement in the desert, meaning the bird had to labour fitfully through the sky. Its dark feathers absorbed the ferocious heat of the sun. It knew it wouldn't be long before it simply dropped out of the sky. It knew it shouldn't be there. The land of the sun god was no place for a creature of blood. It was a blasphemy of sorts to venture uninvited into the kingdom of the Court of Light, a blasphemy that would all but guarantee the bird's death. After all, the crow was not only a creature of blood, but also black in colour – and that was anathema to the glorious sun god. Only those who reflected Sinisar's glory were truly welcome here. All others were punished by the hot and waterless environment until they overheated, their blood boiled, their flesh withered and was destroyed, and all that was left was white glistening bone, bone that would shine in the sun and be another jewel in the sun god's crown.

Yet the crow continued to flap on. It had come too far to have any hope of going back. And the *force* that had possessed it would allow it no other choice but to continue, even unto its end. Images of clouds and a water valley somewhere in this vast emptiness were imprinted in the mind's eye of the crow. The *force* insisted all would be well if the crow could but keep going. It would reach Haven. It would never want for anything again. It would be like coming through death and finding paradise. It but had to keep its mind and eye fixed on Haven. It must see all, watch all. Nothing in Haven must escape its gaze. The *force* would spy on all that went on.

Flap. Flap. The ground was a meaningless maze of broken boulders. *Flap.* Were its eyes misting over? Those couldn't be low clouds. Not here. The sun god would never allow such an occlusion of his majesty and bright heaven. *Flap. Flap.* There must be an imperfection in its eye, yet everything seemed clear when it looked away from the clouds. *Flap.* A false image born of being forced to hold so obsessively to the picture of the valley in its mind? *Flap.* They came closer. Then it was above the clouds. It descended rapidly, stretching its beak wide to catch blessed drops of moisture.

The crow tried to go into a long spiral to slow its descent, but it caught a downward draught and was suddenly tumbling, wrapped up in its own wings. Utterly exhausted, it did not have the strength to save itself. Yet where it should have slammed into the ground and been undone, instead it fell into the very valley it had envisioned the entire way across the desert.

Now it caught a thermal and righted itself. It desperately flared its wings and tail, but it continued to tear through the air at an alarming rate. Several feathers were ripped free and it screeched in panic.

The crow tried to pull itself up and away from the ground hurtling towards it. It was impossible. It tilted forward and went into a swoop, spearing downwards even faster so that it could then pull up gradually in a smooth arc. It feared it was too late. It was going to drive its beak and head straight into the ground and turn itself into the sort of wreckage other crows would come and pick over.

It skimmed between two rocks, the tips of its feathers brushing perilously close to the rough surfaces. Up! Yet it was still in the downward part of its arc. It stuck to the trail towards the valley floor, so that it had a better chance of levelling out. Nearly there! The ground raced up towards it, stones like teeth looking to tear out its guts. At the last it despairingly flung itself to the side and bounced twice on the surface of a fast-flowing river, before being dragged under.

It flailed back up and was swept round a bend and into a shallow. It thrashed and hopped, one damaged wing making it pirouette in the wrong direction for a moment, before it finally clawed its way up onto the relative safety of a flat rock.

It cawed in anger and pain as the *force* demanded it get moving again. The crow wanted to take its time drinking and lunging for a few of the water insects here. It needed to nurse its wing. But the *force* would not relent, and drove it up the riverbank.

This young human. See him, crow! Find him. Bury your beak in his eye. Mix the blood you carry with his. Drink his blood. It will restore you more than anything else can. Then you will return to me, crow, and bring me that blood. Move, crow!

The crow knew it was being ruined by the *force*. It hated the *force* but had no way to fight it. The crow wanted to die now, but was denied even that choice. It held its wing awkwardly off the ground and skipped towards the place that had the scent of humans. It would find the young human and hopefully be killed by it. Humans liked to kill, didn't they? They killed each other in huge numbers upon battlefields. So much carrion for crows and their ilk. Better to come near a human than to be captured again by the terrible thing that had created the *force* that commanded it. The thing had eclipsed the heavens so that the crow had been unable to tell up from down. It had plucked the crow from the sky, forced blood into the crow's mouth and then drawn blood from the crow in turn. The *force* had then compelled the crow to enter this living nightmare, and now the crow only wanted its own death. The crow prayed to the Geas for death, if the source of life would allow – or could gift – such a thing. Better to find this young human.

As if in answer to its prayer, jaws suddenly clamped around the bird and dashed it against the ground, killing it instantly. The large black wolf spat the bird out and backed away, hackles rising. It snarled, drawing back its muzzle to bare its teeth. There was something *wrong* about the bird. It was tainted with the magic of the *enemy*. The wolf had thought Haven would hide them, but the one predator both humans and wolf feared had found them once more.

Every moment of existence in this realm was a nightmare for the Speaker and his small tribe. The nature of the place forced them to adopt a permanent and meaningless form. As meaningless as that form was, however, it somehow engendered fear in the other creatures of this realm, particularly the humans, and this saw the humans harass and attack the Speaker's tribe with unexpectedly harmful bits of shining metal. The humans were so primitive and limited! Even communication with such base creatures was nigh on impossible – the ugly gurgling and gesticulation that seemed to be the language of the humans was a torture for the Speaker's tribe to endure. 'Desert giants!' was the most often repeated sound that the speaker could discern when confronted by the aggressive humans, but whether it was a form of question, command or accusation, the Speaker had no way of knowing. He suspected it was a challenge of some sort, for conflict had invariably followed when, in the early days, the Speaker's tribe had rushed up to the humans in an attempt to welcome them.

Now his tribe hated them. Yet these humans were by no means the most dangerous beings of this realm – there were half-images and ideas of things known as *Saviours* in the simple minds of the humans. It was these Saviours who seemed to direct the humans, in part through force of will, and in part through establishing a wider dynamic of community and behaviour among them. At first the Speaker had thought these Saviours a mere fantasy or necessary delusion of the humans, but after millennia of the tribe battling the humans here, in the land of this realm's sun god, the one who was Ba'zel had found them. The whole issue had been forced by the one human the Speaker had ever encountered who would not or could not yield to the Saviours. That human could never excuse the nature of the rest of its kind, of course – especially when he had led Ba'zel to the Speaker's tribe! – yet that one human did cause the Speaker to wonder how different the humans might be if they were free of the Saviours. It hardly mattered, though, for Ba'zel had found the Speaker's tribe.

Those known as the Saviours were precisely the sort of threat to the realm of the Speaker's tribe that the Believer had foreseen. The Believer had long ago divined that there would be those seeking to transcend their own nature at the expense of the existence of other realms. As per his nature, the Speaker had questioned the truth of the belief, as had other Speakers. They had asked for evidence, logic and meaning. Inevitably, that had seen the Deliberator and Convocation rule that the various tribes of the Speakers be exiled to the adjacent realms so that they could find that evidence, logic and meaning, on behalf of the Convocation, and guard the way into the Convocation's realm against any threat.

And with the coming of Ba'zel, the threat was made real. The exile of the Speaker's tribe to this realm had manifestly been as wise as it was deliberate. The Speaker and all other Speakers would say so on behalf of the Convocation forever more, or as long as they were permitted to exist. They would speak the reality of it and give the realm greater definition, meaning and substance, all the better to stand against the threat.

The Speaker looked up into the heavens of the sun god. A ragged shadow moved across the sky above the blood oasis that was the way into the Convocation's realm. An idea that was *crow-seeking-Haven* came to the Speaker. It was a harbinger or herald of the coming conflict. It was not just an omen – it was material sign of the conflict beginning. The Saviours approached. It did not matter, therefore, if that one human would not or could not yield to those Saviours, for all human existence would be ended in the coming conflict. It was inevitable now, all too real and soon to be made manifest. A shame, in a way, for that one human had made the Speaker wonder, the only moment of surcease in the nightmare that was this realm.

Lhara picked her way through the twisted forest. She stayed close to the path she had taken before, for everyone in the village knew there were hidden drops and partially covered sinkholes hereabouts, although the eldest in the village liked to tell stories to scare the children about individuals occasionally being snatched by malevolent forest wights or being bewitched by the dark fey. Most of the villagers avoided this ancient warren because they did not understand its sacred nature and thus, in their ignorance, feared it. Ludicrous stories of child sacrifice conducted by the pagans in the time before the Saviours were even whispered between the old men who sat nursing flagons of ale in the village inn all day. Lhara thought such tale-tellers and rumour-mongers were simply addle-brained, or were jealously looking to undermine the status of Old Sheela, the village wise woman who understood the mysterious whys, ways and workings of a man's heart, childbirth, fertility, nature, remedies and the forest. For as they advanced in years men became increasingly self-possessed and full of themselves. They did not like to be beholden to, guided by or instructed by any woman, even if it was a woman who had brought them into the world and more than likely overseen their upbringing. It was just the essential nature of men, Old Sheela had explained to Lhara when the young woman had made the trip to the wise woman's hut deep among the trees. And of course Lhara wanted a love charm to win back the heart of Jol, the handsome carpenter's apprentice who had drunkenly betrothed himself to the conniving baker's daughter, Wilhemina! It was a tale as old as time. Even so, Old Sheela had smiled with compassion and told Lhara to seek out the old altar to the god of love, which was to be found in a grotto in the twisted forest.

'Who is this god?' Lhara had whispered in fearful excitement.

'Pasca the Passionate, dear one.'

'Pasca? I have not heard that name before.'

'No surprise, child!' Old Sheela had snorted. 'The jealous Saviours commanded that they be the only object of the People's love. All word and thought of the Passionate One was stricken from the minds of the People. The Saints sought out those of the Unclean who had knowledge of the old god and silenced them for ever.'

'Then how is it you ...?'

'Old Sheela has her ways, child, Old Sheela has her ways. Now, the way to the old altar is as indirect, wild and full of misstep as love itself can be, so attend closely.'

Lhara had found the secluded grotto and the intricately carved altar, some of its lewder depictions making her blush. She'd then prayed fervently, baring heart, soul and bosom, as Old Sheela had directed. She'd begged and promised, prostrated herself and writhed in misery, offering all she had. Finally she was spent, and lay panting with a hand resting against the long shaft of the shrine.

'Well, I don't know about you, but I enjoyed that,' murmured a male but otherworldly voice with a timbre that set Lhara's insides vibrating.

Lhara gasped and looked up into sensitive violet eyes. A diaphanous youth wearing a glorious helmet of sun-metal stared down at her and drank in her soul. His face and barely concealed body were drawn in firm strong lines, but his beauty was so impossible that she did not believe she truly saw it, even though she looked upon it. She could not hold it properly in her mind.

'I will give Jol to you, Lhara, if you will vow to worship me and me alone for the rest of your days. You will constantly offer up thanks to me and never hesitate to do what I ask. Otherwise, I will be unable to guide you and lead you to your heart's desire.'

'I swear it, holy Pasca, oh, how I swear it! Instruct me, radiant lord, for I am yours!'

'Then hear me, Lhara, and do as I command. Take this candle of runes and black blood and light it tonight as the flame of your love, passion and lust. Set it outside the wall behind which Jol sleeps. Its heat will gradually overwhelm and consume him. It will burn away all other preoccupations and distractions he might have. Trust me in this, Lhara, for all will be well. When it is done, return to me and I will instruct you further.'

Lhara had hurried away and done all precisely as the god had directed. She'd placed the green-flamed and sickly sweet candle by the wall and retreated back to her own home. In the early hours of the morning the whole village had been awoken by terrified shrieking, shouts of anguish and a loud crackling roar.

'Fire! Help!'

'Blessed Saviours, protect us! Bring water!'

'Save her!'

'Hold him back! Jol, there is nothing you can do in there.'

'You don't understand! I love her!'

'More water!'

The carpenter's workshop had become an inferno, and the villagers had only just managed to prevent the fire spreading to other adjoining buildings and then the whole village. It transpired that Wilhemina had chosen to bed with Jol that night. He'd been woken by the sound of the growing blaze and run to fight the flames while assuming the stirring Wilhemina would get herself to safety. Yet, tragically, the baker's daughter had been overcome by thick smoke before she'd been able to escape. It was only when Jol had been forced out of the building by the conflagration that he'd realised his beloved Wilhemina had not made it out with him. He'd been devastated. Lhara had run to console him, but in his grief he'd hurled her away from him. Lhara had been ushered away by well-meaning neighbours and Jol had fallen to his knees to scream his heartbreak and rage to the heavens.

As the sun had risen on that terrible morning, it had revealed all the villagers standing silently before the blackened ruins of the carpenter's workshop. They stared, or bowed their heads as mourners at a graveside.

Old Sheela moved among the older members of the community, making sympathetic noises and whispering here and there, eliciting nods of agreement.

'So awful. Only tragedy can come of an unsanctified union between a man and a woman. They were not married, eh?'

'The baker's daughter should have been tending to the bread ovens, not stoking Jol's own fire.'

'Consumed by their own sin, undone by their waywardness.'

'Her parents should have kept a better watch on her.'

Rejected, horrified, feeling confusion and guilt, Lhara had fled back to the twisted forest. She entered the grotto now, tears streaking her cheeks and at a complete loss as to what to do.

'Sweet lord, what have I done?' she wailed. 'I never meant to kill her. Never!'

And he was there, wrapping her in his strong arms, comforting her, crooning to her. 'Lhara, remember the oft-spoken truth that all is fair in love and war. If what you have done is crime at all, it is only a crime of passion, and none are condemned for such. You did not properly know what you did. You were innocent. You were true to yourself and your heart. You were true to your love for Jol, true to him. You heard the elders pass their judgement that the fire was the price the baker's daughter paid for her sin. It was she who erred, not you. She should never have been there. It is an important lesson to the whole village. Once Jol has remembered himself and his love for you, it will all be as if it never happened. It never happened, Lhara, it never happened.'

She sniffed hard, and hiccuped. 'But he cast me aside. He wants no part of me, holy Pasca!'

'There, there, Lhara. Do not take on so. He is not himself right now. He hates himself for what he has helped cause, and does not think himself worthy of your love. It will take him time to earn that love. Yet do not fear, for I will whisper in his ear and all too soon he will be keen to press his suit. You must be gentle with him and show him understanding, Lhara. Can you do that? For then you will be married.'

'Truly, lord?' she dared hope, looking up into his eyes. 'You will do all this for me? Oh, thank you, holy lord!'

'You will have children. You will be happy and fulfilled, dear Lhara. How could I treat those who worship me any differently?'

'Can it be true?'

'And in return your firstborn will be mine.'

8

She shrank back from him. The blood had drained from her face. 'No,' she whispered.

He loomed over her, eyebrows lowered and a self-satisfied grin upon his face. She had never seen anything so hideous in its perfection. 'Oh yes, Lhara. You have sworn to do precisely as I ask, remember. A vow made to a god is no small matter, you know. It is as binding as your need for air and sustenance. It is as binding as your love for Jol, and his future love for you. It binds you absolutely.'

'Have mercy, lord, I beg you.'

The god tutted in disappointment. 'None of that, dear one. It would be bad faith on your part. Jol would want nothing to do with one who is so unfaithful, now would he?'

'I will forswear myself to you.'

The god's face became wicked with displeasure. 'You must know I cannot allow that, dear Lhara. If one follower was permitted to forswear themselves, where would it ever end? Pretty soon every follower would be at it, wouldn't they? Would you have the gods exist to serve the whims of mortals? That is against the natural order of things. At best it is utter madness, at worst the most unforgivable blasphemy. You will doom yourself, Lhara.'

The young woman shook in terror. 'Old Sheela will protect me!'

The god laughed humourlessly and shifted into the guise of the wise woman. 'We are one and the same, child.'

'You tricked me!' Lhara pleaded. 'It is all false. My vow was not a true one. I unsay it!'

'Come now, be reasonable, child,' the avatar croaked. 'I have given you all that you wanted. Be grateful that I do not ask for more than your firstborn. The child will be well looked after, far better than you could look after it yourself. It will become a demigod of sorts, in my name. You should rejoice that it is your own offspring that has been chosen. You are blessed by the god of love. And think of the consequences otherwise. Think of what would happen if people found out what you had done.'

'I have done nothing. It was all you!'

Old Sheela shook her head sadly. 'We both know that is not the case, don't we, dear one? Imagine what would happen if Old Sheela let it slip to the elders that you had come to see her just before the fire and asked about ways of winning Jol's heart and removing all impediment to the fulfilment of your selfish desire. Imagine what would happen were they to find the remains of the black candle among the ruins. They would know you for a witch, would they not, Lhara? What then? Jol will be lost to you. There will be no wedding. You will never have children, for I will also see to it that your womb withers inside you. The villagers will either burn you for your crimes or brand you and drive you out of the community. None will ever help you once you are marked. You will die alone and in misery.'

'You are evil!' Lhara cried, hands pulling at her hair in distress.

'You are hardly one to accuse others of evil after what you have done, are you, dear Lhara? Mortals are only ever victims of the evil that they themselves do. How can I be evil when I only want you to be happy? Believe me, I want none of those terrible things to happen to you. I would truly be a monster if I did. No one would grieve more than I if you were to be condemned by your own kind. You see, I am compassionate. Lhara, remain faithful to me and I can offer you forgiveness, for such is within the power of the gods. Repent and all will be as it was before. Obey me as your god and your life will be blessed. Jol and happiness will both be yours. Genuine and wondrous love like you have never known. Your world will be a paradise. Never will you have known such joy and contentment. I can offer you all of this if you will just speak to others in my name and spread my holy word. You will be a high priestess of the god of love. Simply repent your crimes here to me now, Lhara. Do not be too proud. Do not hate yourself either. Simply love yourself, your life, Jol and me, for they are all the same. Will you repent?'

Eyes wide, the trembling young woman spoke the words. 'I-I repent, lord.'

Her legs collapsed under her, but the god – who became Pasca the Passionate once more – caught her and held her up. His smile was infinitely kind and reassuring. 'See now, that wasn't so bad. Return to the village, dear one, and all will be well, you'll see. Know that you are much loved.'

Shaking, Lhara turned away.

'Oh, and Lhara?'

'Yes, lord?'

'You don't think you should be thanking me for all that I have done for you? A god could get to feel quite unappreciated otherwise.'

'Th-thank you, lord.'

'And Lhara?'

'Yes, lord?'

'Remember to worship me regularly, won't you?'

'Yes, lord.'

'That's a good girl. Run along, then. Remember, I'll be watching over you, always.'

The god watched and nodded to himself as the girl fled from the grotto. Another community of followers would soon be his. 'Alright, you can come out now, whoever or whatever you are. I knew you were there the whole time.'

A fearsome being emerged from the back wall of the grotto and the god turned to face it. The eavesdropper was statuesque in bearing – an overly large and crenellated skull supported by a frame of spindly and stone-like limbs.

Pasca's expression became schooled and then shifted into the mischievous visage of Anupal, Lord of Mayhem. 'Why, Thraal, you old sweetheart, there you are! You don't know how I've missed you. Really. The sleepless nights I've had. I've been beside myself with worry about what might have happened to you, truly I have.'

Elder Thraal became preternaturally still.

The Peculiar winced and took a cringing step back. Through gritted teeth he said, 'Thraal, be a dear and suppress the power of your presence, would you? Even with this helmet on, it's quite a strain.'

'You have stolen a Disciple's helmet. You are crowned by your own sin. You betrayed us, did you not, Peculiar?'

'Look, just reduce it a little, yes? I'm your biggest fan, you know that, but sometimes there's just no talking to you. Ow!'

Thraal abruptly reined in his presence. 'Speak.'

The Peculiar pulled himself back up and took several long moments to straighten his helmet and smooth down his robes. 'There, that's better. Honestly, Thraal, there is no need to be such a grump. You're just sore that the mortals gave you a kicking and brought your fancy Great Temple crashing down upon your big heads, aren't you? Don't worry,

I understand how disappointed you must be with how things turned out, especially after all the effort you put in. And for your information, the Disciple I *borrowed* this helmet from no longer had any use for it. Of course, should he, she or it require the helmet again in the future, I will not hesitate to return it. Alright?'

'You sought to claim the Geas for yourself rather than fulfilling your agreement with us. Do not deny it, for it was seen through the being Ba'zel.'

'So!' said the Peculiar huffily. 'I hear nothing from you for an absolute age – not a missive, or a letter, or a token of affection, or even an omen in the sky – when I've been frantic with concern, and then I get this! One accusation after another. Not a single *How have you been, Peculiar?* or *You're looking well, Peculiar.* No, just harsh recrimination and talk of fulfilling agreements. Did it never occur to you that if I was trying to claim the Geas then I might have been doing it for you? Did you not stop to think that I might have wanted to gift it to you, because I knew how important it was to you? After all we've meant to each other, as well. How could you? Quite frankly, dearest Thraal, I'm hurt. I'm not at all pleased with you. No, I'm not.'

'Your words are meaningless. You seek to obfuscate, misdirect and confuse. You do this to hide the truth of your betrayal.'

The Peculiar's mouth hung open and his hands covered his pained heart. 'You haven't heard a word I've said to you, have you? So cruel! I see it now. I mean absolutely nothing to you, do I?' His bottom lip quivered for a second, but then he tightened his exquisite jawline and squared his shoulders bravely. 'Very well then, elseworlder, if that's the way you want it, that's the way it will be between us from now on. If you wish to speak of betrayal between us, then it is of that we shall speak. There was *no* betrayal on my part, for as per our agreement the boy and rock woman were brought to you at the Great Temple. In the process, the plague was ended. My end of the bargain was completed. It is *you* who has not delivered on your end. Where is my seventh chamber of sun-metal, eh? All was lost, including my other six chambers, when you succumbed to the mortals. By your failure, it is *you* who has betrayed *me*. I am hugely disappointed, elseworlder. In fact I am livid and demand to know when reparation will be made.'

'Nothing has been lost, Peculiar. The chambers remain and are easily uncovered. We did not fail in any way. The location of Haven is now revealed to us and we are closer than ever before to claiming the Geas of this realm as our own. All is as we planned and willed it. These are the final moments of the convergence. There is nothing of consequence that stands in our way.'

The Peculiar's eyes narrowed. 'And did you plan and will it when Samnir the Sand Devil decapitated four of your kind in front of all humanity?'

Elder Thraal blinked slowly. 'It was of no consequence to us.'

'I still demand reparation.'

'As do we,' came the smooth reply.

Without turning his head at all, the Peculiar sprang backwards and landed lightly atop a tall stalagmite. He folded his conjured wings against his back and crouched like a gargoyle. 'What manner of reparation? What would you have of me, elseworlder, and what do you offer in exchange?'

'The terms of the agreement made when we first came to this realm still stand. You will ensure that the pagan gods remain divided.'

A shrug. 'Shouldn't be too difficult. In return, you will grant me the freedom to move through the world as I see fit.'

'As long as you do not interfere with our plans and intentions.'

'Perish the thought. And you will supply me with the seventh chamber.'

Elder Thraal nodded his assent. 'And you will give me egress, Peculiar, to the nether realm.'

The Peculiar paused. He tilted his head. 'Nether realm?'

'You thought we did not know of it? *All* is known to us.'

'Elseworlder, if such a place existed, you would not want to go there, trust me.'

'*Trust* you?'

'Alright, alright! But why the nether realm? Even I avoid it as far as possible. Spend more than a few moments there and it will draw all life energy from you. It is death and ending. Surely you elseworlders, ancient as you are, have more to lose by it than most. Some gates are not meant to be opened, even by beings who have travelled the cosmos! Some spells should never be cast. Some words should never be spoken. Some thoughts never thought. Some ideas never conceived. They will destroy everything.'

'The nether realm was used temporarily to prevent our will. We will not permit that to happen again. Now we are properly aware of the nether realm, our will becomes manifest and inevitable there. It will be ours and will be defined by us.'

'Well, rather you than me.' The Peculiar shuddered. Then he pursed his lips, a glint in his eye. 'Elseworlder, do you think I would make a good Saviour?'

Elder Thraal was caught out by the question for an instant. 'You are corrupted, Peculiar. Illogical and flawed. You could not be a Saviour.'

'What you call corrupted, illogical and flawed is what the rest of us call having fun. Learn to live a little, elseworlder. You know, let your hair down … if you had hair. Try not to be so pompous and stuffy. Laugh when someone calls you baldy or something like that.'

'Fun is the symptom, sickness and expression of inner conflict. If our young display this *instability* for too long, they are executed and returned to the Geas.'

'Wow. Tough crowd to please, eh? Alright, forget that. What will you offer in exchange for me taking you into the nether realm?'

'Lead me into the nether realm, Peculiar, and we will not consider you our enemy in the longer term. When we are done with Haven and its realm, we will leave its rule in your hands.'

'Let me guess. When you're done with Haven and its realm, there'll be precious little left to rule.'

'What remains will be yours.'

The Peculiar sighed. 'Better than nothing, I suppose. Very well, elseworlder, take my hand and I will lead you into the nether realm. Remember, it was you who wanted to go there in the first place, so no complaining that I never take you anywhere nice and that I don't know how to show a girl a good time. And don't go getting any ideas just because I let you hold my hand. No kissing when it's our first time stepping out together, and I have to be home before dark.'

'Your words are—'

'Meaningless, I know, I know. You could try saying something nice sometimes, you know. Also, have you ever thought of experimenting with colour more? A pretty blue scarf worn around your head would help frame and set off your features. Perhaps even wear it over your face entirely, so that you don't scare anyone we meet. I've got my reputation to think of, you know. Ow! What have I told you about suppressing the power of your presence? I'm already beginning to regret this. I just knew you'd be trouble.'

CHAPTER I:

From the end, the beginning

Something was wrong, very wrong. He'd woken up in his small bedchamber in his parents' house in Godsend. Although the child in him was glad to be back, the rest of him was sure – no, certain – that he shouldn't be there. He saw his collection of coloured stones in the niches of the wall. He reached for a red one and, touching it, felt better somehow.

He heard movement in the kitchen and smiled despite himself. His mother Maria would be making breakfast already, boiling water for the tea and laying out bread and honey, his favourite. He quickly got out of his pallet.

Beware.

He froze. He could not have heard the taint speaking. The taint was gone. It no longer existed. It had surely been a fading whisper of the dream from which he'd just woken, an impossible dream about living in Haven. Nothing more.

This is the dream, Haven the reality.

Jillan splashed ice-cold water from a jug onto his face and washed with a flannel. It brought him fully awake and allowed him to shake off the last of the lingering dream. Shivering, he hurriedly dressed and left his bedchamber.

'There you are, sleepy head.' His mother went onto tiptoe to kiss him on the cheek. 'Why, you get taller every time I see you. To the table, Jillan, or you'll be late for school.'

Jillan frowned. His mother seemed smaller than he remembered.

There were dark hollows around her eyes. When had she grown so old? And there was something different about the kitchen too – it was as warm and cosy as usual, but more cramped somehow.

Jed looked up from the table and smiled at him. 'Hurry up or there'll be none left for you. A hunter needs to keep up his strength, you know.'

Jillan went to his chair and sat down, gazing at his father. The man had a full beard and seemed just as bear-like as ever, but he didn't fill the whole room in the way he once had. There was something more grizzled about him too. With a start, Jillan realised he wasn't having to look up at his father – their eyes were level.

'No appetite, dear? Jed, his forehead's warm too. Maybe he's ill. He should stay home with me today.' There was a mixture of maternal concern and desperate hope in her voice.

Jed hesitated. 'You might be right. Besides, the school's not going anywhere, is it? It'll still be there tomorrow. Would you like to stay home today, Jillan?'

That wasn't right. His father should be telling him that the fresh air would do him good, that he didn't want to stay in this stuffy little house. That he should stretch his limbs and see his friends. That he shouldn't mope around with his parents, who were, after all … were …

Dead, Jillan.

Jillan swallowed hard. Jed could no longer meet his gaze. 'Mother, Father, I do not think I can stay here. I love you, but there are things I must go and do.'

'It's too dangerous,' Maria pleaded.

'Mother, Hella is out there, you know that. How can I not go to her?'

Maria began to sob quietly, but nodded in acceptance, even attempting a smile through her tears. Jed rose and put an arm around her. 'You're right, lad. You should go. Your mother loves you too much, is all. She wants to protect you. But if we kept you here with us for ever more, the Empire would go unchallenged and would win. We'd never be able to forgive ourselves. So you go, lad. Go on, and make us proud.'

'Take something and have it on the way then,' Maria encouraged.

As Jillan started to help himself to a generous piece of bread and honey there was a heavy bang on the front door. They all jumped.

You've already spent too long.

'Who is it?' Jed demanded.

There was a moment of silence. The hairs on the back of Jillan's neck rose.

'He's here,' Maria whispered, and was suddenly pushing Jillan towards the other bedchamber, where there was a small shuttered window.

Flee!

A barely human but sickeningly familiar voice came through the door and filled the house, the speaker's mouth apparently right against the wood. 'Give him to me, Jedadiah, and I will not snuff out the spirit of you and your life mate.'

'Go!' Jedadiah mouthed urgently.

'What about you and Mother?' Jillan begged.

'We will hold him here while you escape out the back,' his father said firmly.

'We can face him together. I've beaten him before!'

Stupid.

'No, Jillan!' his mother said fiercely. 'He is far more powerful here than when you knew him. As one of the living, you can have no hope of standing against him here. Go, for this place is not meant for you. Escape and find Haven once more.'

Jillan was bundled into the back bedchamber, and then he was squeezing through the narrow window and into the murk beyond. He fell head first to the ground, just about saving himself from serious injury but jarring nearly every bone in his body. His right wrist was agony. He shut his eyes against the pain and then fought his way up …

… and came awake in the small dwelling he shared with Samnir in Haven. The wolf loomed over him. It had his right wrist in its jaws and was shaking it.

'Ow! Alright!'

The wolf released Jillan's arm and sat back on its haunches. It licked a drop of blood off the side of its muzzle and seemed to grin as it watched him with glowing orange eyes.

Jillan cradled his wrist and lay back on his pallet for a few seconds to gather his thoughts. The dream – or nightmare – lingered at the edges of his mind. It faded, but he could not shake the deep sense of disquiet it left him with. He sat up. The wolf was gone, and now there was only a dull ache in his wrist. He struggled to separate memory and dream.

Hear me! came a dying whisper.

Then there was nothing. Just as there should be. Kathuula was gone. Azual had died long ago. The Great Temple had fallen. They were safe now, here in Haven. All the same he felt he should tell someone of the dream, even if it was just to have them reassure him it was nothing.

'Samnir!' he called, but there was only silence from the other rooms of their simple stone dwelling. What time was it? He couldn't tell from the dingy light in his bedchamber. And it was never too late or early for Samnir to be keeping his vigil among the upper crags of Haven, so the commander's absence did not tell him anything either.

He got out of his pallet, splashed water from a bowl onto his face and dressed. As usual he left his rune-inscribed leather armour where it was because it only caused people to stare and whisper when they saw him wearing it. He didn't want to be special or different any more. He just wanted a normal happy life with Hella. Once they'd been through the wedding ceremony – he shuddered at the thought of it because Hella wanted everyone in Haven, if not beyond, to attend – they'd hopefully be left alone to get on with setting up a home, perhaps having children one day, looking after Jacob in his old age, tending a garden, preserving fruit and vegetables to see them through the winter, and doing all the other trivial things that constituted sharing their lives together and finding contentment based on fitting themselves to the rhythm of the seasons and the way time passed in the world. It wasn't an unreasonable ambition, was it, after everything they'd been through?

Ash would smile knowingly and shake his head whenever they shared an ale of an evening and Jillan spoke of his plans to the woodsman.

'Jillan, my lad, there's about as much chance of you finding a quiet life for yourself as there is of us not having more after this first drink. One thing always leads to another, you see, surely you've learned that by now. Everything's connected, isn't it, thanks to the Geas. Take this wedding of yours—'

'Please, let's not!' Jillan would groan.

'You think you're going to get away with an intimate affair among friends, do you? No chance. Hella understands everyone will want to be a part of it, partly because they all owe you something, but partly because it will help bring everyone even closer together. With the Empire gone, the People need celebratory events like this if they are to rediscover a sense of community and belonging. In a way, you owe it to them, having taken everything else away from them.'

'B-but—'

Ash would laugh. 'Yes! That means you'll have several million people coming to the wedding. Look on the bright side – it'll mean a lot of presents – although how you're going to feed them all, and where they're going to sleep, I have no idea. I'm not sure my brewery will be able to cope. It'll be good for business, though. I've got Jacob bringing in as much extra ale as he can on that wagon of his every week. And you don't think the gods will let anything this big pass without them getting in on the act, do you? I can see Wayfar wanting to conduct the ceremony himself, Gar being your usher and Sinisar being in charge of decorations and entertainment. As for Akwar, I was thinking we could put him in a bridesmaid's dress. What do you think? It'll be wonderful. There'll be all sorts of squabbling and drama.'

Jillan would try to share the joke but would find himself feeling sick. 'I need another drink.'

'You see? It's just like I said. One thing always leads to another.'

Jillan stepped into the main room. It was empty. The fireplace was cold. The bread that Jillan had left out the night before had not been touched. Apparently Samnir had not come home at all, which was fairly unusual even for him. Jillan worried for his friend, who – although restless at the best of times – had seemed especially troubled or preoccupied of late. Jillan had tried talking to him about it on the few occasions they'd exchanged words in recent weeks, but the commander had waved all questions away. Thus far Jillan had respected Samnir's privacy, but this latest dream – and his every instinct – told him it was probably time he forced the issue.

Jillan took the stale bread from the table and then lifted his bow and quiver from their place by the door. During their early days in Haven there'd been little need to hunt, for curious deer and rabbit had wandered right up to them, but now the valley's wildlife had learned to make itself scarce whenever there was a human around.

He ducked beneath the door frame and stepped out into the early morning. He breathed deeply – the clean air usually refreshed him and put a spring in his step – then coughed for the amount of woodsmoke in the air. With new people coming to Haven all the time, and the onset of autumn introducing a chill to evenings, the number and size of the cooking fires in the valley was increasing. A sawmill of sorts had even been established to ensure there was a steady supply of wood for fires and for building shelters. Where once there had been swathes of trees upon the upper slopes of this part of the valley now there were only rows of stumps, like the crooked teeth of a giant.

'Something needs to be done,' said a gruff voice.

Jillan turned his head and saw Tebrus, head of the group of Unclean that Jillan had invited to join the people of Godsend before the town's fall, climbing up the slope towards him. 'Good morning to you too, Tebrus,' Jillan replied. His stomach rumbled discontentedly, so he bit into his heel of stale bread. Between mouthfuls: 'Let me guess, when you say something needs to be done, you mean you want me to do something about it.'

'Unless you want my people to take things into their own hands.'

'Alright, what is it?'

'You know the deep pool down a-ways, where my people put out their fishing lines? Some of the newly arrived Heroes have built lean-tos at the side of it and taken to washing their clothes and bathing there. I even caught one relieving himself at the edge.'

'Did you politely explain—'

'Aye, there was much polite explanation, and polite pushing and shoving, and then Bruban politely broke the head of one of the Heroes. If Hella hadn't happened along—'

'Hella got involved?'

'Aye, she did. If Hella hadn't happened along and used her Geas-given power to command an end to the scuffle, then who knows where things would have ended up.'

'But the matter's now resolved, yes?'

'Nay, lad, nothing of the sort. The Heroes are still there befouling the pool. They give evil looks to all that come close. Something has to be done about them. My people came to Haven precisely to escape such men and their Empire! We fought and lost many a loved one because of those stinking Heroes—'

'Tebrus!' Jillan interrupted sharply. 'Don't speak like that. You know full well that these Heroes were not responsible for what the Saviours forced them to do. Saying otherwise is just the sort of prejudice the

Unclean have always suffered because of the Empire. You should know better!'

Tebrus ground his teeth. 'Not responsible?' he said quietly. 'They knew what they did. How is it that the commander managed to make a stand where others did not, eh? I'll tell you how, Jillan. He is a man of conscience, that's how. Not like these animals who are now being allowed to desecrate Haven with their filth. They are ruining everything Haven should be.'

Jillan struggled to keep an even tone. 'And have you spoken to Samnir about this?'

Tebrus hesistated. He became uncomfortable. 'I am loath to bother him with such a matter.'

'Tell me the truth.'

The man frowned. 'Do not make me say anything against the commander, lad.'

'I won't take it that way, Tebrus. I need you to tell me the truth.'

Tebrus held his eye. 'Perhaps he is not himself, but he does not seem to care about such day-to-day matters any more. And why should he? He is a man of war, Jillan. When I have previously spoken to him about such things, he has told me to settle all as I see fit, with his backing.'

Jillan absorbed this. 'And Captain Gallen?'

'He is a Hero, Jillan. He looks after his men. Don't get me wrong, he is an honourable man, it's just that ... it's just ...'

Jillan sighed. 'Alright, Tebrus. I'll see what I can do.'

He half wished he'd stayed in his pallet, nightmares or not. Waving goodbye to Tebrus, he headed down towards the valley floor, where the main community of five hundred or so souls had settled around a lakelet. Hella lived with her father Jacob in several rooms off the back of a newly built warehouse, not far from the central Gathering Place. A good number of families had their homes arranged nearby, including a weaver, a farrier, some fisherfolk, planters and hunters, a metalworker, a stone mason, a carpenter, a wheelwright and a physicker. Further along the edge of the lakelet was a noisome tanner and candlemaker. Ash ran an inn in a sleepy hollow on the other side of the water, and just on from there was a makeshift barracks for the few remaining Heroes of Godsend and the several hundred Heroes who had elected to join them directly after the fall of the Great Temple. A punishment chamber had recently been constructed, at Samnir's insistence, and Duras the mason and Halson the carpenter had just started to put up a small school for Haven's dozen or so children.

Looking down upon their community now, Jillan felt a sense of satisfaction. This was the place Godsend had never managed to be. Here there were no battlements to confine the inhabitants. There were no bullying elders telling the People how they must live. There was no cruel Minister giving dire warnings, spreading fear and demanding the constant confession of the People's sins. There was no Saint to censor thought. This was how things were meant to be.

'Jillan! Down here!' called Captain Gallen from beneath the wooden roof that permitted meetings in the Gathering Place no matter the weather.

Jillan joined the soldier, who was paring an apple with a knife, and accepted the offer of a slice of fruit. 'Thank you.'

'You're welcome,' replied the captain with uncharacteristic cheeriness. His hair was unkempt and he hadn't yet shaven. 'I was out stretching my legs while it was still relatively quiet. I was half hoping to catch you too.'

'Really?'

'Yes. About Ash.'

'Ash?' Jillan repeated guardedly. 'What's he been up to now?'

'Well, given he's been in the punishment chamber for the last two days and nights, he hasn't been able to get up to anything at all. Surely you knew?'

'What happened, or shouldn't I ask?'

'Oh, it wasn't anything too bad. There was a bit of a to-do in the inn when one of my men raised a toast to the gods, harmless like, you know, just a turn of phrase. Ash took exception, apparently, saying the gods had never done anything for him and that he wouldn't have anyone drinking their health in his place, unless they wanted to be thrown out. It was his right, of course, being the owner of the place and all. And he has that kindly giant of his, Dor, to knock sense into people when they're not understanding things properly. Anyway, one thing leads to another, there are accusations of blasphemy, the Unclean side with Ash and start yelling that my Heroes think they own the place, that they want to build the Empire all over again, and so forth. Some pushing and shoving starts –'

Jillan covered his face with his hands.

'– and the commander is suddenly wading in among them and laying Ash out cold. Didn't think anyone could lay a finger on Ash, what with his sense of timing and all, but there you are. Everyone backs off, including Dor, for there's nothing more terrifying than the commander when he's decided on things. The commander picks Ash up by the scruff of his neck and carries him like that all the way to the punishment chamber. Locks him inside.'

'So where's the problem?'

Captain Gallen pulled a face and took a breath through his teeth. 'Well, it's tricky, you see. Ash has been screaming blue bloody murder that the commander has no right to come onto his premises and attack him like that, let alone imprison him. We have no idea how long the commander intends to keep Ash locked up either, but the longer he does the more people are going to side with Ash, especially now he's sobered up. Some are getting restless about the inn being closed, and my men are pressing me about their regular ration of grog. I've confined a few of the wilder ones to barracks, but they feel aggrieved, seeing as how little of the altercation in the inn was down to them.'

'And there's still this problem of the ongoing tension between Tebrus's people and your men, Captain. What of that? There are Heroes camping by the deep pool. Why are they not in barracks?'

The captain nodded tiredly. 'Yes, I heard about it. The barracks are full and they had to find shelter as best they could. Don't worry, I'm having new accommodation built as we speak. These newcomers are hard to deal with at first. Most have left General Thormodius's army, but a number are from even further afield.'

'They are deserters?'

'It's not entirely clear. Some, perhaps. Others say they have been given permission to leave. Most readily accept my commands, but a number are more … recalcitrant. I know, I know, it's messy, but I'm getting it under control. Beyond that, the trouble lies with the Unclean. Nothing we say or do will ever help them to like us.'

'Can you blame them? Especially when you still call them *Unclean*?'

The captain considered for a moment. 'I suppose not. Yet who is to say they have any more right to be here than us Heroes, some of whom also fought on behalf of Godsend, need I remind you?'

'No, you don't need to remind me. Alright, you make sure you've got these newcomers in hand and I'll talk to Tebrus about avoiding further antagonism.'

'And could you ... well ... er?'

'What?'

The captain was slightly shamefaced. 'Ask the commander about releasing Ash?'

'What? You're joking!'

'Jillan, he's more likely to listen to you. If I raise it, I'll effectively be questioning his orders. I'll be lucky if my jaw's left in enough pieces to ever ask him another question again.'

'He's not *that* bad!' *Is he?*

The captain scrubbed a hand over his face. 'No, you're probably right. I just haven't been able to get through to him lately. It's like I don't know him any more.'

'Perhaps you don't. Perhaps none of us do.'

'Will you try, though?'

'Of course. But first I have to see Hella. Otherwise she'll think I'm neglecting her, and that's the last thing I need.'

The captain smiled sympathetically. 'You're a lucky man, Jillan my friend.'

'So Hella keeps telling me.'

The soldier laughed and waved Jillan away. 'You deserve each other! Go with the gods, my friend.'

Jillan ran down through the community to Jacob's house. Hella was already waiting for him on the doorstep, arms folded in mock anger and her foot tapping impatiently. 'Oh, so there you are. I was beginning to think you were going to leave me to organise this wedding all on my own.'

'I overslept, dreaming of you!' he replied quickly, running up to her and half going to a beseeching knee.

'Get up and apologise properly,' she said, yanking him up and kissing him deeply. 'That's better!' she murmured. 'Did you really dream about me?' He whispered in her ear and she blushed fiercely. She slapped his chest. 'I don't think that's even possible ... is it?'

'It'll be fun finding out.'

'Once we're married, Jillan – *if* we're ever married, that is.'

His smiled slipped. 'What do you mean?'

'We haven't even begun to decorate the inn for the celebration. My father's finally managed to get material to dress the place, but Samnir's gone and locked Ash up. You'll have to sort it out, because I just don't have time. And it's men being stupid and fighting all the time!'

'I know.'

'No, I don't think you do! You seem to be avoiding anything to do with this wedding. You're hardly involved. I can never find you. You're always off hunting, dreaming or commu-u-u-ning with nature, or whatever it is you do when you disappear!' She stopped, worried she had spoken too harshly. She looked into his eyes with silent appeal, needing him to understand. 'Jillan, can't you see there won't even be a wedding feast at this rate? Every time father brings in a new wagonload of supplies, most of it gets taken by Captain Gallen and his men.'

'What? Surely they can hunt for their own food.'

She tilted her head and said quietly, 'You really don't know what is going on, do you? The captain says his men are too busy training, helping with the heavy building work and going out on patrol. Heroes have always been fed by the communities they protect. It's like a tax.'

'But we don't need protecting.'

'Jillan! Try not to be so dense. My father needs a lot of Heroes as guards when he goes out to trade on behalf of Haven. The desert isn't safe, you know that, with its tribes, giants and who knows what else. And if he ever ventures beyond the desert, there are thieves and bandits. If we stop feeding the captain's men, there will be no more guards and then there will be no trading at all. It'll all fall apart.' There were tears in her eyes now.

He felt helpless. 'Don't worry, we'll get married one way or another, I promise.'

'Don't tell me not to worry! *Do* something! Why won't you do something? It's like you don't even care. Don't you *want* to marry me?'

'How can you say that? Of course I do! It'll be alright.'

He reached for her, but she pushed him away, tears running freely down her cheeks now. 'Jillan, look around you! It's autumn already ... We were meant to be married at the end of summer. And I will *not* marry you in winter, when it's raining and the mud will ruin everyone's best clothes. If we don't get married soon, then ... then ...'

'No, don't say it. Hella, I'll make it alright. Trust me.'

'There are more Heroes arriving here every day. We haven't got room or food for them!'

He wanted to argue that they couldn't very well turn people away, that they couldn't send them back into the desert to die. But he dared not. 'I'll talk to Samnir and we'll work something out.'

'Promise?'

'Dearest Hella, together you and I have brought down an empire. We've seen the blessed Saviours themselves killed in the Great Temple. There are gods that are in our debt. If the heavens and the entire world must be moved so that we can be married, then move them I shall. If all of creation must wait until we have exchanged our vows to each other then, believe me, I will make it wait. *Nothing* can stop us from being married. If I must command winter and Akwar to hold off on the rain and snow – so that your dress is not ruined – then so be it.'

She gave him a small smile. 'That's very romantic.'

'With all that we have done, surely getting married is not an impossible challenge for us?'

She sniffed and moved into his arms so that he could hold her. 'It'll be alright, won't it?'

'Yes.'

'I'll see you tonight? You'll come to dinner as usual?'

'Yes.'

'You can bring Samnir if you like.'

'... I'll ask him. I'll talk to him about Ash and the new arrivals too.'

Hella reluctantly disentangled herself from his arms, kissing him on the cheek as she did so. 'You go, then. I need to open the shop, or the people will be complaining to Father about me. The carpenter's wife likes to bend the ear of anyone who will listen.'

'Can't you – you know – command her not to gossip?'

Hella's brow creased. 'Jillan, if I started commanding people about what they can and cannot say, or think, then I'd be no better than a Saint. You know I don't want this power I have. You shouldn't ...'

He put his hands up. 'It was just a joke – a bad one. I didn't mean anything by it. I didn't want to make you mad.'

'You shouldn't joke about such things.'

'I'm sorry.'

She sighed. 'No, I'm sorry. I'm being over-sensitive.'

'You're worried, that's all. It's okay.'

She gave him a sad little smile, said 'I'll see you later then,' and turned and went back into the house. Everything would be fine.

Something is wrong.

The Heroes and the Unclean would find a way to get along. There'd be no more trouble at the inn. Ash would be contrite and Samnir would set him free. Samnir would talk to General Thormodius and a limit on the numbers coming to Haven would be organised.

You should never have brought the People here.

The wedding would go ahead and he'd finally be able to spend his life with the woman he loved. Hella would be happy and Haven would thrive. He refused to listen to anything else.

Lost in a reverie, he was upon Ash's inn before he realised it. All was dark inside and the building appeared locked up tight. He left it behind him and marched on to the barracks that housed Captain Gallen's men. Whereas in the summer the accommodation had seemed functional but almost homely, now it looked badly used and slightly squalid. Damp had risen from the ground and got into the wooden planks of the quickly erected sheds. The walls were warped, buckled and sagging. Roofs were no longer level. The ground had been churned to mud, allowing water to collect in puddles and then to become stagnant and blurred with insects. There was a bad smell in the air from the latrines, and a brown cloud spread into the water where the barracks squatted next to the lakelet.

Jillan was grateful to turn away from the sight and disappear down the stone stairs to the underground punishment chamber. Yet the welcome awaiting him there was hardly any more pleasant.

'Where the hell have you been? Some friend you are!'

'They only just told me you were here. Ash, are you well?'

Jillan took a small lit lamp out of its niche in the wall and carried it over to the wall-to-floor bars and metal gate. A crazed face loomed out of the dark. 'What does it look like to you?'

Jillan gasped and took an involuntary step backwards. 'What happened to your face? I hardly recognise you.'

'That maniac Samnir attacked me in my own home, that's what. Almost blinded me in my left eye. He's the one who should be in here, not me!' The woodsman rattled the gate angrily. 'Get me out of here.'

'I-I haven't got the key.'

'Well go and get it.'

Jillan took a steadying breath and stepped towards the bars once more. Weak though the light from the lamp was, Ash retreated from it. 'I doubt it's going to be as simple as that. What did you do this time? You'd been drinking, right?'

'I may have had one. What of it? He assaulted me!'

'As you are so fond of telling me, Ash, one thing always leads to another. You must have had a fair few if even your famed sense of timing was too confused to save you.'

'I don't have to justify myself to you!'

Jillan was silent for a second. 'Do you even remember what happened?'

The voice that came out of the dark was suddenly more reasonable. 'Jillan, my friend, I haven't eaten for two days, nor has my slops bucket been emptied. It's so cold I haven't been able to sleep. I am probably still suffering shock. And no one has sent for the physicker to be sure that I don't lose my eye. How could I hope to have any sort of reliable memory after all that? I'm not even sure what day of the week it is. Beyond all that, though, by what right am I kept here? I came to Haven hoping to be free of unfair punishment and cruelty. I'd hoped to escape the senseless rules and laws of self-important men. Instead, I find I am persecuted here far more than I ever was under the Empire. I almost wish things were back as they were, for at least there was some order under the Empire.'

Jillan couldn't keep the shock from his voice. 'You can't mean that.'

'Can't I? Everyone knows I shouldn't be in here, but they're too scared of lord high and mighty to say anything. Where is he, anyway? He's sitting up there somewhere, with his head in the clouds, isn't he? Looking down on us and judging us all. Who is *he* to judge us? Who is *he* to judge anyone? He was known as the Sand Devil when he fought out here for the Empire, did you know that?'

'I've heard the stories,' Jillan said quietly.

'He was a killer. A monster. And now he gets to play holier-than-thou worse than the Saints ever did.'

'I'm going to talk to him, but –'

'No. Don't say anything on my account, Jillan, friend though I know you are. If you get on the wrong side of him, you'll be the next one to end up in here. I wouldn't want to see that happen to you. Hella would never forgive me, eh?'

'– but it would help if you were inclined to apologise.'

Aghast. 'You're kidding.'

'Not really.'

'I won't give him the satisfaction.'

'Ash, Samnir may have been a bit heavy-handed, but it sounds like he prevented a fight from starting. Surely you're aware of the tension between Tebrus's people and the Heroes. Your inn is where they inevitably rub up against each other.'

'And Samnir attacking me like that sets a good example to them, does it? I don't think so. It's out-and-out hypocrisy. Jillan, I know you want to be everyone's friend all of the time, but sometimes it just isn't possible. The test of a real man is making the tough decisions. You shouldn't be trying to side with Samnir on this one. Everyone knows he was out of order.'

They are imperfect beings. Their corrupt nature is already seeing them destroy themselves. There can be no saving them.

Jillan felt dizzy. He leaned against the wall and massaged his temples. The voice had not belonged to the taint. Was he going mad? It had almost sounded like Ba'zel, yet it had not been him.

There was the sound of a foot on the stairs. Nausea overtook him as he was assailed by the memory of Saint Azual finding him in a punishment chamber just like this one in Saviours' Paradise.

He is coming for you, warned the taint.

In a panic Jillan reached for the magic which he'd sacrificed in the confrontation at the Great Temple. There was the briefest flicker and then only emptiness.

'Jillan, are you alright? You look ill.'

Then the newcomer was upon him. A broken-nosed Hero carrying a plate and a cup. A nervous explanation: 'Come to bring the prisoner his breakfast. And a tot of rum to wash it down with, just as you requested, Mister Ash.'

Jillan looked to Ash in confusion. 'You said they weren't feeding you.'

'Not as I'd like, no.'

'Why are you doing this? Why lie to me?'

'How else am I going to impress the wrongness of my imprisonment upon you?'

The emptiness was dragging Jillan down, just as the blackness of Kathuula had drowned him in the shrine in the nether realm. He had to get out. His limbs were heavy and wouldn't obey him properly. He pushed past the Hero and staggered up the stairs, almost tripping. He reached the air outside, went to his knees and dry-heaved the apple and bread he'd eaten just that morning.

'Nice to see you too!' Ash called after him. 'Check on Dor for me at the inn. He'll forget to eat properly if he's not told. Say hi to Hella.'

With a trembling hand, Jillan wiped his mouth. What was wrong with him? He was acting like a young child afraid of the dark. Yet the sense of claustrophobia down in the chamber had felt so real. Escaping had been like climbing up out of his own grave.

'I need to see Samnir. Get a grip on yourself. You haven't woken up properly is all. Everything's fine. Come on, get up.'

The sound of his own voice somehow reassured him and he got to his feet unsteadily. As embarrassed as he was rattled, he moved away as quickly as his wobbly legs would allow. He made it to the sleepy hollow occupied by the inn, went to the veranda and gratefully sank down to collect himself. He slowly got his breathing under control. His head was a muddle. Was this how the Peculiar used to feel? Jillan imagined himself with a sword of sun-metal wrapped tightly around his head. It clamped down on his thoughts and stopped others from getting in. It seemed to work. Haven was the reality, not dreams of his parents' house or the visions down in the punishment chamber.

'Who's there?' boomed a voice from inside the inn. 'I can smell you. Jillan, yes? Do not try and take Ash's things. I will not let you. Go away, or I will be forced to squeeze you.'

'Dor,' Jillan croaked painfully. He cleared his throat and tried again. 'Ash sent me. He asked me to check you're eating properly.'

'I am not stupid. Ash has warned me not to listen to others. You will bring Ash here. I do not want you here without Ash. I will squeeze you if you do not go away.'

'Do you have enough food, Dor? Are you hungry?'

Dor's voice became suspicious. 'You are trying to find out how much food I have. You want to trick me and take from me. GO AWAY!'

There was proper rage in the giant's voice. Jillan pulled himself back up and prudently moved away. He had seen Dor *squeeze* people before. It had been a horrible sight. The giant's massive grip had tightened remorselessly on an unfortunate Hero who had thought to protest at the price Ash was charging for drinks. The man's collarbone had been crushed, and worse would have undoubtedly followed if Ash had not ordered Dor to stop. Dead customers were bad for business, the woodsman had patiently explained. As it was, no one had complained since, even when Ash had all but doubled the prices the following day.

Jillan reflected that Samnir might have been fortunate that his first punch had knocked Ash cold, as it had probably meant the woodsman had been unable to answer any dull question from Dor as to whether Ash needed any help. If Dor and Samnir had got into some sort of struggle, the inn probably wouldn't have been left standing. Would Samnir even be allowed into the inn in the future? What would that mean for the wedding? Jillan could not imagine getting married without the old soldier there. Would they have to change the venue for the celebration? Hella wouldn't be at all happy about that.

With new doubts and fears nagging at him, he started the long climb up out of the valley. It was a more difficult ascent than usual, for he was taking a different route from his normal one. Yet the physical exertion, and the need to concentrate on the immediate task at hand, did him some good. The further behind he left the community, the more his troubles seemed to recede. By the time he reached the upper slopes and the cleaner air he was panting and perspiring, but stronger in spirit and body than he had been for some while. He paused to catch his breath and looked down on the stirring community. Inevitably, he could enjoy a different perspective on things from up here. Then he was entering cloud level and the moisture in the air gently cooled his brow. He could see why Samnir liked it up here.

After a minute or so, he found the path up to the crag from which his friend liked to keep a watch. He followed the way up, came through the clouds and emerged into the overly bright world of the desert sun.

Squinting now, he scaled more steps. He was reminded of taking the stairs – what seemed a lifetime ago – to the top of the southern wall of Godsend to see the lone Hero who was stationed there in all weathers. The Hero would tell the boy wonderful and terrifying tales of the world beyond their small town, before the boy would have to run all the way to school to face the hateful Minister or risk being late and incurring the school teacher's wrath. The time with the Hero had always been a refuge of sorts from the day-to-day life of the community.

He smiled now as he clambered up to Samnir. 'Anything moving?'

Samnir continued to scan the desert, apparently already having heard and recognised Jillan's approach. After a second or two the commander replied gruffly, 'Thought I saw one of those large sand dunes move to the left earlier.'

'It did not!'

Scowling, Samnir turned his grey eyes towards Jillan. 'Know much about sand dunes, do you? Didn't think so. And who are you to challenge your elders and betters, eh?'

Jillan's smiled broadened. 'The creases in the corners of your eyes still deepen when you're not being serious. You can't hide it.'

'Damn this traitorous face of mine!' Samnir sighed. 'It knows me too well. It's no doubt why I never beat Captain Gallen at cards.'

Jillan looked out across the desert. There was a broken jumble of pink and orange rock ahead of them and all the way to the distant horizon, while there were drifting sands to the far left and right. There was a heat shimmer in the air, but no other sign of movement. 'Barren.'

'Yes and no.'

'Really?'

'A crow came out of the blue sky yesterday.'

'How is that possible?'

'It was clearly in distress, its flight was so erratic. It all but fell through the clouds and down into Haven. Dropped like a stone. Can't have survived.'

'What would it be doing out here?'

'An interesting question, one I have given some thought, but nothing obvious has occurred. And beyond the crow, there are scorpions, sand snakes and all manner of scurrying, burrowing and slithering things out there. There are desert giants, and no doubt rock creatures. The desert tribes too. And do not forget the lord of this land, Sinisar himself, King of the Court of Light. There are many beings and lieutenants at his command. So, you see, the last thing this place is is barren. Yet it has the *appearance* of being barren. It is almost a disguise. Much is hidden here. Much lurks just beyond what we see. And is that any surprise, when this land is ruled by the god of the light by which we see? If he wishes us blind, then blind we are. If he wishes us to see a mirage or some heated vision, then that is what we see. If he wishes us to wander without direction until we die of thirst, passing all unknowing on many an occasion within feet of a source of water, then it is a small matter for him to maze both eye and mind. I would wish this place *were* barren, for I fear it is far more dangerous than that.'

'You sound like you do not like it here.'

Samnir gave Jillan a grim little smile. 'Perhaps I do not like it anywhere, Jillan. I see the world through a soldier's eyes. When I look at Haven, I see a valley that is impossible to defend, a valley surrounded by more than human threats and enemies. How could I ever like it here?'

Jillan frowned. 'But Samnir, we've won. There are no enemies about to attack us. We don't need to worry about building defences any more.'

The soldier gave him an exasperated look. 'Do you really believe that?'

Jillan looked away, unsure how to answer.

'Are you like the rest then? You think I'm deluded and paranoid?'

'It's not like that.'

'Really? I was wondering how long it would take them to send you to me. How long it would be before they decided someone needed to help me see reason. Because the way I see it, it's the rest of you that are deluded.'

Now Jillan met his gaze without flinching. 'I told you, it's not like that. I'm not accusing you of anything, although that's what you seem to want.' He dropped his voice. 'Why must you fight everyone and everything all the time? I'm your *friend*.'

Fury flashed in Samnir's eye and his jaw tightened. For the briefest moment Jillan thought the man wanted to kill him, but then it was past. 'You ask me *why*? It's what I *am*. It's what I have always been. It is the nature of our bloody existence.'

Wide-eyed, Jillan shook his head and took a careful step back, suddenly very aware of the drop to either side of him. 'It doesn't have to be, Samnir.'

'Don't be a fool, Jillan. You've seen them down there. The constant squabbling and grabbing of resources. It's only a matter of time before they start fighting each other, before someone is accidentally killed.

They're all looking out for themselves, and the devil take the hindmost. You'll never change them.'

'No!' Jillan breathed, but feared his friend was right.

'More and more of them are pouring in to grab their share. Word has spread that you've discovered paradise, and they're all coming to claim it for themselves.'

'No. General Thormodius will stop it.'

Samnir threw back his head and laughed dreadfully. Tears were in his eyes. 'And there you have it. The way of the soldier. Fighting, walls and armies. Do you see it now? And you ask me *why*!'

Jillan turned and fled, in his haste coming perilously close to the edge. 'Jillan, come back!'

He didn't want to hear the words. He didn't want to be told things were even worse now than they had been under the Empire.

You know it's true. Will you at least listen to me now?

The guilt was too much. They were in Haven, home of the Geas. The People had their freedom at last.

You should never have brought them here. You should never have tried to find Haven in the first place. Now the elseworlders know where it is. They're coming for it. He's coming for you.

Everything would be fine. He'd promised Hella. The Saviours were gone. Saint Azual was dead. The gods would protect them.

Well, there's a first time for everything.

'Be quiet, damn you!' He hardly saw where he was going as he slithered down the steps and slope, didn't care any more.

Oh, you're talking to me now. That's some sort of progress, I guess.

'I destroyed you. You don't exist. You can never be trusted. You used me. You tried to kill us all.'

The taint sighed. *We used each other, Jillan, you know that. It is the way of things, is it not? You use Hella for comfort, and she uses you for the same. Such usage is often called love by the People, is it not?*

'You are the Chaos. Kathuula. The Dark Geas. The exact opposite of love.'

Perhaps. I am a part of you, though. I am the fierceness you see in Samnir's eye, that which keeps you all safe. I am the magic you wield to keep your enemies at bay.

Jillan stumbled into the desert and ran with slipping steps through the sand, no idea where he was heading. 'I don't want this magic!'

Come, do not be so disingenuous. You wanted it plenty when you had to face Saint Azual, Anupal, that idiot Akwar and Saint Praxis. It has saved you on countless occasions. In fact, your entire reason for coming to Haven that first time was to secure greater magic for yourself so that you could fight the elseworlders, was it not? You cannot deny it. This is all of your own making. It's a bit rich, not to mention ungrateful, to say you now do not want it.

'I don't want it *any more*! Why can't you just leave me alone?'

'Damn that boy!' Samnir growled to himself. He shouldn't have been so hard on him. It wasn't fair to take his frustrations out on Jillan. Yet he'd become more and more restless of late, and he was finding it harder to control his temper. Ash was lucky not to have suffered worse than a black eye.

What was wrong with him? Were they right? Was he really deluded? Did he see enemies where there weren't any? Did he *need* to have enemies and something to fight? After all, what use was an old soldier without enemies? None. He was just a tired old man who should sit quietly in the corner of the inn nursing an ale, only speaking when a youngster needed a story.

Was that it, then? Was he fighting against old age? Against himself? If he was fighting himself, he would only end up destroying himself... and perhaps those around him. Not for the first time, he wondered if he should leave Haven. They didn't need him here.

He watched Jillan disappearing into the desert. Should he go after him? No need. Jillan was more than capable of looking after himself. He wasn't a boy any more, after all. Jillan was a man now, soon to marry the woman he loved and set up home for himself. And the young couple wouldn't want Samnir hanging around, always in the way.

There was nothing for him in Haven. He should leave. But where would he go? He'd pretty much seen the world, and it was much of a muchness. He could go and hunt the gangs of thieves troubling the roads of the various regions, but once he'd disposed of all of them, what then? Perhaps he should go and climb a few mountains and see Torpeth. The holy man might give him some advice, although there was as much chance that the pagan would dance like a loon in answer to his questions and offer him a handful of pine nuts.

By all rights he should be asking the gods for their wisdom rather than a dirty naked holy man. Yet he could not bring himself to pray to the fickle gods of humanity. He did not trust them, blasphemous though the thought was. He had something of the devil in him, then. It must be why he was forever restless. The Sand Devil in him would not let him rest or know peace.

It was the Sand Devil that whispered to him that there were enemies out there, waiting for him to drop his guard. They watched Haven with an envious hatred. They lurked just beyond the ridges of the sand dunes, they crouched in the shadows of rocks, they tunnelled below them, they crept about in the corner of his vision.

It was only because of the Sand Devil that he had not already left Haven. It had told him something was coming. He felt it in the air, as if everything was stretched tight, as if everything buzzed and sang with it. He felt the pressure of it at his temples, like a niggling and constant headache. It was why he was so irritable and aggressive, even with his friends. His nerves and instincts screamed at him to *do* something. His fist tightened around the hilt of his sword until the knuckles cracked.

Something was coming for them. Something evil and terrible. He felt it in his gut, as if he'd been kicked or made to eat hot coals. There was a malevolence out there. Feeling sick, he realised he should not have let Jillan go into the desert on his own. Was it too late to follow him? There was no sign of him now.

He scanned the desert intently. There was something coming. Eyes locked with his own. The breath caught in his chest. He could not pull his gaze away and the distance between them suddenly became foreshortened. *Pull away!* She was right up to him now, the brightness of her blues eyes mesmerising in her dark and ravaged face. Her breath shared his own. She touched him, her body offering to share itself. Her thoughts began to join with his own. He would not have to be alone any more.

'My beloved Samnir! At last I have found you.' She smiled. 'You have watched the desert so intently, as if to bring me here by desire alone. How you must have yearned for me!'

He shook his head. *No!* 'I-I do not know you,' he heard himself saying thickly.

'Please do not send me away. I give myself to you and ask nothing in return. I will not even ask you to love me as you once did. I only ask that you allow me to remain. Will you take me in?'

'Why?' he struggled.

'It is too much to bear otherwise. Surely it is enough that we now have each other?' Her cracked lips touched his own. 'Take me in, I beg you.'

He'd been looking for something … for someone … in the desert. What had it been?

'You have found it, my gentle Hero. That for which you have always searched. That of which you have always dreamed. It is yours, if you will but take it. Will you take me in?'

Her thoughts shared his own. His eyelids drooped. She offered him comfort and companionship. She offered him rest. Rest at last. 'I will take you in, my beloved Izat.'

CHAPTER 2:

And the means

It was surely the most glorious place in all the world. The Court of Light was filled with only the most radiant of beings. They danced and sparkled, bewitching the eye, inspiring wonder and delighting the mind. Yet even they seemed dull in comparison to he who was at their centre. He eclipsed them all, even as they shared in his brightness and strove to add to it more than any other. All sought his attention, vied to come close to his shining power and begged the favour of his eye. For he was Sinisar. He was the sun god upon his throne, and without him there could be no life.

She knew this was no place for one born of an element as mundane and clumsy as rock. Where all the others here were ethereal and could move through the heights of the temple at will, she was left rooted to the ground, craning her neck just to catch a glimpse of them. Where they entranced any who beheld them, people had more often than not looked at Freda with pity. Children had thrown stones and called her names. Some had even made a sign against evil and hurried away lest she infect them with rock blight. She was ugly and heavy compared to the visifers, lumines and spectrals who surrounded Sinisar.

Yet he had invited her – Freda – to join his host! He had begged her to leave her own kind to be with him. She would be the greatest jewel in the temple's crown, he had promised her, for her skin had become diamond after suffering such extreme pressures to free his temple from the Empire. With his divine sight he could truly see the beauty of who she was, he said. His words had filled her mind just as his light had suffused her diamond body. He'd warmed her like no other ever had.

It had been a miracle of sorts for her. She still remembered the moment when he'd first asked her, although the memory felt like that of a dream. The memory of that moment sustained her, even when looking directly upon the court made her eyes burn terribly. She'd grown up in darkness, so inevitably it would be a while before her vision became accustomed to this place, and short periods of blindness were surely to be expected. And the memory of the moment sustained her when she was left companionless in the bottom of the temple for long stretches of time. As a god, Sinisar must always be busy, so she remembered to be grateful when he made time to see her and summoned her to the foot of his throne. Besides, whenever he summoned her he always gave her that smile of his and spoke kindly to her, before visiting the ecstacy of his will and desire upon her. He would gather the roiling fire and heat of the temple's upper vaults into himself – *the light of the world*, he called it – and then pour it into her, forcing the diamond matrix of her being to channel, focus and finally project images of parts of the world he chose to view. Any place that received the divine gift of his light should be his to know and watch. The court would share in the spectacle, singing Freda's praises and rejoicing at the blessing of their god. They loved her, they shouted.

Sinisar had been gentle with her at first, cajoling and almost playful. He'd only made modest demands upon her, asking her to show him how General Thormodius and their other human friends were doing in the Fortress of the Sun. He was particularly concerned for their welfare, just as he was for all those who were guests in his land. Yet his concern inevitably extended beyond the region of the east, for he was a god. He'd demanded – and the court had urged – that Freda make efforts to act as a lens to affairs much further afield. Wanting to please him who had given her so much, she'd cooperated as he'd forced violent amounts of energy into her and seared her to the core. Crying out in pain, she'd allowed them to spy on matters in Akwar's deepwater kingdom for some moments, but the distance and the foreign nature of Akwar's element had ultimately proved too much for her and she'd collapsed, her chest in such agony that she feared she'd fractured it. Sinisar had sighed in irritation and waved for Shezar – his haloed First Light – to take her from the divine presence.

'I have failed him!' she'd sobbed.

'Nonsense!' Shezar had beamed as he'd helped her along. 'All saw that you did your best. That is all you can do, is it not? We are all limited before his divinity. Try not to feel sorry for yourself. No one wants tears and wailing disrupting the court.'

'He is angry with me.'

'If he was truly displeased, do you think he would have me see you to a place of rest? No, he is only showing you concern. He wants to be sure you recover so that you can try again.'

'I will do better next time, I promise.'

'It would be wise that you did. Otherwise, you will only play into your enemies' hands.'

'Enemies?' She had blinked in confusion.

'Those who are jealous of your position at court. Some say you should not even be here.'

'Th-they do? But I thought they wanted me here.'

Shezar smiled pityingly. 'They tolerate you while you serve great Sinisar. As you amplify his majesty and please him, so you are indulged. When you can no longer do these things, there can be no place at this court for one such as you, one who is so ... so ... how to put it ... *earthy*?'

They reached the bottom of the temple, and she sank gratefully into the ground, letting the strength of the bedrock soothe her injury and heartache. She saw a measure of disgust on his face and blushed diamond-pink.

'I apologise,' he said. 'It is difficult for one of my kind to watch someone begrime and soil themselves so. To us beings of light, the children of the rock god are ... well ...'

'Dirty?'

'Yes. They wallow in muck and filth. It is anathema to us.'

'I understand,' she replied quietly, and after long moments of awkward silence he left her.

After that she found she was less enthusiastic about being called before the court. The next time Shezar had come to summon her, she'd claimed she was still recovering, but had assured him she was still faithful to Sinisar and would soon be well. The First Light had given her a disapproving look and then flown up into the heavens of the temple with the news. On the following occasion he'd been all smiles, polite and solicitous, but firmly insistent. With some reluctance she'd accompanied him to the audience chamber and placed herself before the bright-eyed god. Perhaps Sinisar had sensed something of her unwillingness, for there was a frustration about him. He'd used her with rough impatience and as a consequence she'd been unable to display much that was meaningful. He'd dismissed her without a word and turned his head away, apparently already seeking entertainment elsewhere.

His summons became far less frequent. It was only with slight guilt that she realised she was glad of it. She stayed in the shadows or in the ground as much as possible, so that the light would struggle to find her. She glanced up constantly, coming to dread the moment when she would see Shezar descending towards her. The glancing became a nervous tic.

Although she missed Jillan, Freom, her friends – and even Anupal sometimes – she didn't really mind being on her own. She had been on her own for much of her life, after all, and submerged in the ground she could commune with the infinitely slow rhythm of the wider earth. It brought her a sort of peace, which was only interrupted by the constant hammering of the sun-smith in his dungeon-like workshop deep below. She would often be about to drift away completely, as if on the verge of transcendence or some great revelation, when his clanging would bring her back to herself with unpleasant force. The problem was that he struck and worked sun-metal, the vibrations of which could not be denied. The ground did so little to dampen it that it was as if his blows were raining against her very temples.

When she'd first joined the court she'd gone to see how he was, but he'd only said confusing, disturbed or mean things to her, so she'd left him alone. Yet his relentless rhythm nagged at her, and now she decided to visit him once more, to see if she could convince him to take some respite.

His workshop was as bright as the heavens itself. Squinting, she made out newly forged blades and arrows neatly arranged in piles, and did her best to give them a wide berth. They were still alive with the smith's magic, such that just touching them would cause serious injury. The metal would dull in time, of course, and then it could be safely handled, until the point at which it came into contact with blood or some other magic, when it would flare with lethal power once more. Having been hurt by sun-metal on more than one occasion, she was extremely cautious around it, in the same way, she realised, as she was now wary of Sinisar. And sometimes she did fancy there was almost something *knowing* about sun-metal. She didn't like or trust it, but knew better than not to not show it a good measure of respect.

'My father sent you, did he?' the sun-smith panted between hammer strikes. 'His light cannot reach me properly down here, can it, especially with the glare of the sun-metal confusing everything? You are a spy. Well, you can report that I do not flinch from my punishment for one instant, just as my father suffered unendingly in the prison the elseworlders had me make to hold him.'

Freda now understood why he never stopped. He was punishing himself. She felt sorry for him, she realised. And he would kill himself if he did not stop soon. Blood ran from the corners of his eyes, eyes misted from having stared so long upon sun-metal. His hammer arm was so heavy with muscle that he leaned to the right – and that, combined with a constant swinging motion, had given him a horribly crooked spine. He seemed permanently bent double, as if his right hip had fused with his lower ribs. Looking at him, she wondered if perhaps he wanted to kill himself and if that was why he did not stop. 'I-I am not a spy. Sinisar does not know I am here.'

'It hardly matters.'

'It matters to me, but never mind.'

'All is of our own making.'

'I-I don't understand what you mean.'

His heavy breath was like the air from a pair of bellows. 'Why have you come here? What is it you want?'

'Why are you making all these weapons? The fighting is finished.'

'Is it? Maybe it's never finished.'

Clang, clang. The thought frightened her. 'You mean there will be more fighting? Who will it be against? Will Haven be safe?'

'I have already told you that all is of our own making.'

She wasn't sure that made any more sense than the last time he had said it. 'How do you know there will be more fighting? Are you sure?'

45

'Why else would I be making weapons? It is a punishment I do for my father.'

Clang. Like the door of a prison slamming shut. She couldn't think clearly. 'Is it Sinisar who has told you to make the weapons? Why would he want them?'

'Who knows? Perhaps he wants them in case the elseworlders should ever return. Perhaps he wants them for when one of the other gods turns against him. Perhaps he is just insecure. Perhaps he has a righteous and noble cause. Perhaps, perhaps. No matter the reason and the way, the fighting will come. It always does, and always will. It is the way of things. If there was no fight, all would be settled and there would be a type of omnipotence.'

She had heard friend Anupal say similar things. There was a rhythm to the sun-smith's words, an impetus that allowed her to sense something of his wider meaning even if she could not find any detail or specific answers in what he said. 'And omnipotence is bad because it ends free will. Existence will cease.'

He spoke as if in a trance. 'Existence will cease. That is why there is sun-metal, to prevent and defeat omnipotence. Without it, no realm can exist. That is why elseworlders always seek to remove it all. With the unstable element gone, there is nothing left to deny their will and prevent them from seizing the power of the Geas.'

Clang. 'Even if they destroy that realm in the process.'

'Even if they destroy that realm, yes. And that is why I am making these weapons.'

Freda smiled in understanding. He did not want to kill himself; quite the opposite. In a way he created all life here at his forge, with his magic and hammer. 'Thank you for all that you do, sun-smith.'

He took his eyes from his work for the briefest of moments and gave her a lopsided grin. 'You are welcome, friend Freda, you are welcome. The work itself is reward enough for me, but it is not entirely unpleasant to be thanked all the same. Now, you must hurry, for as ever the fighting is coming and it will all too soon be upon you.'

The ringing sound of the sun-metal was now somehow reassuring to her, despite the pain it caused. She never wanted it to stop. Let it ring forever. Her agitation of before now gone, she rose up out of the ground still smiling.

And came face to face with an incensed Shezar.

'Where have you been?'

'I was resting,' she said, trying not to sound guilty.

'With mud in your ears, no doubt,' he sneered. 'I have been calling and calling.'

'We will go now. I am summoned, yes?'

Her apparent willingness made him suspicious, however. 'You remain faithful to him, do you not? You have made a holy vow to serve him and no other. With his divine sight, he will see it in you if you are forsworn or lying.' He came close to her, burning with accusation and a cold fury she could not fully comprehend. 'In fact, as First Light, I will uncover any such treason and blasphemy myself. I will see into you.'

His umbra pushed against her, hurting her. She pushed him away violently. She spoke quickly, before he could come back at her. 'I am not for you! I serve *him*. Touch me like that again and I will tell him everything. You will be shamed in front of the court and ... and be thrown out!'

He glared at her, eyes blazing. A slow smile came to his thin lips. 'Very well then, rock woman, have your secrets. You dare to threaten me? Do not think I will protect you from your enemies or his displeasure any longer. You will have to stand up for yourself in court from now on. And I do not think you will last very long. In fact, I will take great satisfaction in watching you fall like the stone you are from your current place of grace. Come on, then. You have already kept him waiting far too long, and I will not accept any of the blame for your lumpen and sluggard nature.'

The First Light flashed upwards, disappearing from sight in the blink of an eye. In shock, she numbly followed him, travelling through walls and floors of crystal where she could. As she emerged into the audience chamber, she saw Shezar whispering in Sinisar's ear and then retreating to join the ranks of the heavenly host. The assembled thousands watched her expectantly. There was none of the usual adulation that greeted her arrival.

'Nice of you to join us, I'm sure,' Sinisar breathed. There was snickering in the court.

She fought against a blush of embarrassment. 'I was happy to receive your summons, my lord.'

His eyes glowed like coals. 'Well, we try to please, do we not, Freda?' Poorly suppressed laughter cascaded around her.

She shifted uncomfortably. 'Yes, my lord. I try to please you.'

'That is your only concern, surely. It must be your all-consuming passion, for you are sworn to me.'

'Yes, my lord.'

His brows lowered. 'Why then do you keep so to the bowels of this temple? What concerns you there? Surely your thoughts should be fixed on us always. You should want to be here in both body and mind. Do you shun this court, rock woman? Are we not to your liking? Do we not suit your lowly tastes? Are we not base enough for you?'

'I-I fear I am not worthy of you,' she pleaded, looking around in vain for a friendly or sympathetic face.

'So instead you would have us descend to your level?' the god demanded. 'Would you bring us down? You would have us attend on you!' The court muttered in discontent.

'No, my lord. It is not like that.'

'Would you contradict me, rock woman?' he asked heatedly. There was rising ire around her.

'No, my lord. I am still faithful to you.'

'Faithful, you say? And you will be happy to give us a demonstration of this faith, will you? You will obey entirely without complaint, demur or excuse, will you? You will give entirely of yourself, will you, so great is your faith? WELL, WILL YOU?'

'Yes, my lord,' she quailed. 'Just command me and I will do all I can.'

'Then receive my will, dearest Freda!' he commanded, unleashing power like the sun at her. The inferno hit her with such force that she was sure it would melt her. 'Show me my brother Wayfar. Obey me at once!'

Freda cried out as she struggled to channel the energy inside her, most of it spilling away and down into the temple. With an effort that brought her to her knees, she managed to cast an image of the god of winds sitting sighing on his throne. He was clearly bored and out of sorts.

Sinisar did not allow her any reprieve. 'And Akwar!'

Whimpering, she brought the underwater kingdom into some sort of focus. The image was blurred and fractured, but a gleeful Akwar could just be made out creating a giant wave to swamp a boat far above him.

'Now Gar.'

'I cannot,' she begged.

'Silence!' he snarled, ramming even more power into her. 'You *will* obey me. You are naught but the vessel of my will. You may have no voice of your own. Obey me.'

Some of her facets began to blacken, as if burned out. She cast a fitful mix of shadows and sickly coloured rays. Gar appeared to be in some sort of wrestling match with an oversized lava lizard. The rock god paused for a moment and looked up. 'Who dares trespass here?' Freda immediately scattered the image, praying it was now over.

'Haven!' Sinisar mercilessly pressed. 'This is the last test of your faith.'

Her diamond body ringing discordantly beneath his assault, she cast a final juddering image. Jillan, lost and alone in the desert. He was in some distress, looking up at the sun to try and navigate his way home. She gasped.

'Well, well. Now we see to whom your thoughts cannot help but turn. The mortal who thinks himself greater than the gods themselves!' Sinisar declared with fierce triumph. His face flamed wrathfully.

'He is my friend!'

'You are sworn to me. You will renounce him utterly or you will both be punished.'

'No!'

His power twisted into her cruelly and she was forced onto her front. Sinisar moved the sun in the sky, deliberately disorienting Jillan. The heat of the desert became white-hot and Jillan visibly wilted.

'No! It's not right. I won't allow it!' she screamed, cracking her diamond body, the sound shattering dozens of spectrals in the front rank of the host. Shezar only saved himself at the last by becoming invisible. Sinisar's power and fiery nature flickered for an instant, and he fell back in his throne with a groan. She threw him off, reflecting and deflecting devastation all around. Lustres were snuffed out. The court shrieked in horror and outrage. Sprites winked out of existence. With a wail Sinisar brought his sizzling and lashing power under control before it could undo his entire court and raze his temple to the ground.

Hugging herself closely, fearful that she would break apart, she sank into the floor of the audience chamber.

'Find her!' roared Sinisar, fully determined to bring an apocalypse to Freda and all her kind.

He'd fasted for fully three weeks now – surviving on just the rainwater that dripped from the roof of the rough shack – and still nothing. It seemed that the spirit of his father Slavin wanted no part of him. Without at least some acknowledgement from the ancestors of the mountain people, he did not feel he could ever accept the title of chief, no matter how much the living warriors of his tribe might demand it, and no matter how much they might already be using the title to address him in jest and hope. He wasn't ambitious for the title in and of itself – no, the issue was that without it Veena's parents would not agree to his being the sole suitor for their daughter's hand. It was only sensible that they look for the best match possible for Veena's hand. If the title of chief were to go to someone else, then … No, he would not think of such things, lest he tempt fate.

Perhaps his reason for wanting the title was the wrong one. His father, when alive, had wanted his son to find a life mate who would bring him stong allies and bear him many sons. Slavin would not approve, therefore, of Veena of the Waterfall Peak, whose parents were mere potters. It did not matter that her eyes were leaf-green and her hair night-spun. Among the clans and tribes of the mountain people the choice of a life mate was far too important a matter to be settled by the fickle preferences of a heart or that sickness youths called love. Perhaps this was why his father's shade had refused to appear to him.

He sighed, adjusted his meditation pose and tried to settle his mind once more. The uneven floor surface gave him a pain in his left buttock. He shifted a little to the right and nearly overbalanced. It was good there were none to watch his clumsiness, or he would have been teased by every warrior for months, perhaps longer. Worse, they might have given him the nickname of Aspin Wobblestep or some such – names were powerful things and could stay with you all through your life, and even into death. Now, there was a draught. He felt a chill. His nose tickled.

Settle. He released a slow breath, trying to empty his mind so that he would be receptive to any sign from the nether realm. He waited for he did not know how long. Still nothing.

'Come on,' he muttered. 'You hardly said anything when you were alive – the least you can do is make up for it now with a word or two. You don't have to go through a whole blessing or anything. Just a hello-and-bugger-off sort of thing. A clearing of the throat? A bit of wind?'

He almost giggled at that. He realised he was giddy and light-headed from lack of food. No wonder he couldn't concentrate. His thoughts were like a leaf blown hither and thither in one of Wayfar's storms.

Perhaps he should take another pinch of moon moss – the hallucinogenic plant the headwoman had given him to aid his vigil. When had he last taken some? Yesterday? This morning? She'd warned against taking too much, for it was highly addictive. Simon Softfoot had overdone it when young and had been having long conversations with rocks ever since. He opened one eye and looked down at the small pile of herb by his side. There was less than he remembered. Had a mouse got at it? If so, it was in for an unsettled night!

Laughter bubbled up inside him and spluttered out into the dead silence of the shack. It sounded joyless and flat. It unnerved him. Wasn't laughter usually full of life? The atmosphere in the shack felt wrong. And it seemed even colder now. Autumn was passing quickly, but surely it shouldn't be this cold. Goosebumps rose on his pale skin and he shivered.

Breath curled from his lips and drifted across his vision, turning all to mist. He could almost believe he was looking into the nether realm. Was he dying then, sat here in the freezing shack and not having eaten in ages? His teeth chattered words he did not know, words it was easy to believe were spells in ancient or forbidden languages. What horror might they conjure? He was suddenly more frightened than he remembered ever being before.

If this was the test of chiefhood, and winning Veena's hand depended on it, he must not fail. With a shaking hand he took up the last of the moon moss, put it in his mouth, fixed his thoughts on his father, closed his eyes and swallowed down the bitterness. He opened his eyes to stare straight into Slavin's livid gaze. He'd never seen the man so angry.

'You little fool!' the shade said severely. 'You should know better than to come here. I thought I'd raised you to be smarter than this.'

'F-father! I had to seek you out. It is the custom of our people to consult the ancestors when choosing a chief.'

Slavin smacked Aspin on the side of the head. The blow felt all too real. 'It is also the custom of our people not to force the issue when the spirits choose not to answer them.' Another smack. 'Three weeks I've had to endure your pleading and whining, with not a moment's rest. Do you know the toll that's taken on me?' Smack. 'You should know better than to disturb the dead. No good can ever come of it.'

Aspin wanted to cry. 'B-but why didn't you answer me?'

Slavin's sigh of exasperation was a death rattle. 'Have you not seen the signs? You are meant to be a reader. I fear for our people if they are now so closed to the world around them. I did not answer you because I did not want to lead *him* or those he commands towards the living. The land of the living and the land of the dead are already closer than they should be.'

'Lead who?' Aspin whispered.

Slavin beckoned his son closer and then clipped him round the ear. 'Idiot! Would you have me say his name and bring him here? Is it not enough that you have entered this place and I will have to expend the last of my strength to see you out of here? No, do not say anything, or you will make me regret ever having taught you that first word *father* when you were a child. It is wasteful to say more.'

Away through the mists a horn sounded. There came the clash of battle and screams of death. Eldritch energies arced and crackled. The mists swirled and a baleful red eye turned towards them. 'Come to me, little pagansss!'

'He has found us,' Slavin said grimly. 'You have already spent too long here. Your lips are blue. See the ends of your fingers. The nether realm draws the life out of you, my son. Quickly! He will be coming for you.'

Aspin rose stiffly, his limbs numb. 'Will our ancestors not hold him back?'

'Something has changed,' Slavin replied with a shake of his head, pulling Aspin after him and keeping a tight grip. 'He has found a way to drain us, just as he drained the People when he was alive. We are failing. Many are now under his thrall. We run and hide as best we can.'

'But how is that possible?' Aspin choked.

'I do not know, my son, but was it not ever thus? Have we not always known this fight with the others? It almost makes me feel alive again!'

'I will fight with you,' the warrior in Aspin averred.

'No!' Slavin turned wildly on his son, eyes staring and full of doom. 'That is precisely what he wants. If he were to capture you and drain one of the living, there would never be any stopping him. Think!'

Aspin saw it and was sick to his soul. 'He would rule the land of the dead absolutely. The spirits of our ancestors would be extinguished. There would be none left to guide and watch over those of us still living. And ... and ...'

Slavin nodded. 'Yes, there is more. He would have the necessary magic to enter the land of the living.'

Aspin gasped. He could barely speak. 'It is unthinkable.'

'The living will be unable to drive back his armies. The dead cannot be killed. The dead are fearless. They have nothing to lose and everything to gain. He will rule all, both the living and the dead. It will be the end.'

'Ye gods.'

Slavin's face was a death mask. He dragged Aspin away, moving faster and faster. Aspin gathered himself and ran for his life.

'I see you, little pagansss! There is nowhere you can go!' crooned the malevolent voice of the monster that came leaping from the battle.

The sight of it nearly overwhelmed Aspin. It was *him*. The evil Saint of the Empire who had tortured him in a punishment chamber. The Saint who stalked his dreams and turned them all to nightmares. The butcher who had put women, children and whole communities of his people to the sword when they had lived in the lowlands. The hunter who had driven them into the mountains and then forced them out. The destroyer who had then descended upon them as they made a last desperate stand in Godsend. The tormentor who had visited the tyranny of Praxis upon them. The executioner who had brought all humankind, the gods and the power of the Geas to its knees before the Great Temple. Aspin had thought his people had triumphed, but now he saw he was wrong. The executioner's blade had merely paused at the top of its swing, and it was that moment which had seemed a triumph or stay of execution. Now the blade was about to descend with the final killing stroke. He was death absolute and could not be defeated. It could only end with every last one of the mountain people dead. For he was Azual.

All but beside himself, Aspin sobbed, 'But what can we do, Father? What can we do? Tell me!'

The shade did not respond for a few seconds, except to pull his son onward with even more urgency. His voice was empty as he said, 'You ask something that is beyond me. Death cannot be held back forever, my son. But you must survive. And you must find a way for our people. Become chief and lead them. Find a way.'

They ran along a path of jagged black rocks made slick and wet by the mist. Even though they were sure-footed mountain men, the pace at which they travelled was dangerous. Aspin began to fear he would break his neck. Perhaps it would be safer to either side of the path ... or were there drops just through the mists that would see them fall forever?

Slavin seemed to become uncertain, looking off to left and right. He turned an appalling gaze on his son. 'Would you undo us here and now? You must control your thoughts better or all will be lost.'

Aspin cursed himself for a fool. Torpeth had warned him the last time they were here that every individual saw in the mist whatever they imagined the nether realm and death to be. Here imagination, will, body, life and death came together. If he could not discipline or master himself, then death surely would.

Azual's voice came panting hungrily behind them. 'I have you now, little pagansss! Look back and you will see the light of my power and vengeance.'

'Do not look back!' Slavin instructed him.

Aspin knew his father was right. He must not imagine death right behind them. He must not feel its cold breath on the back of his neck. Its cold hand was not reaching out to grab his shoulder.

'The entire air drips with my will,' Azual's voice insinuated. 'It's all around you. There is no escaping it.'

Aspin tried to block it from his mind. He had not heard the words. He desperately rejected the idea. 'We're nearly there, Father. Look, the path rises here. We are on our own mountain, where our people have always been safe. None can pursue us here!'

'Feel how cold it is,' Azual hissed. 'It is the life draining from you. You are slowing down, weakening.'

'It is the land of the living, Father! Right there. Look, I am bringing you home, Father!'

Azual laughed. 'You have made your last mistake, Aspin Longstep, for your father can *never* return to the land of the living. He can proceed no further.'

Slavin slowed. Aspin overtook him and tried to drag him on. 'Leave me,' the spirit of the snow-haired warrior said bleakly.

Tears in his eyes, Aspin fatally looked back. 'Please, Father. It's only a little further. We can go together. All will be well. Pleeease!'

Slavin shook his head mournfully. 'I cannot.'

A darkness was coming through the mist, looming up behind Slavin. A staring eye and burned face. Jaws slavering and drooling. Oversized, lithe and muscled. An animal stench of faeces and rot filled Aspin's nostrils and choked him. Could such a thing have ever been human?

Slavin let go of Aspin and turned away. Long spears came into his hands and he adopted the fighting stance of his people.

'Father! I'm begging you. Stay with me. Everything will be like it was before.'

'Get you gone or you are no son of mine,' came the stark response.

Slavin struck high, skewering Azual's shoulder, then dropped low and twisted his second spear in at Azual's inner thigh and groin. The Saint cunningly allowed the first spear to push him through three hundred and sixty degrees, however, meaning the second spear went wide. In extending with his second spear, Slavin now found himself within the monster's immediate reach. There was a sickening smack as Azual's elbow connected with the old warrior's temple. The blow would have felled almost any warrior still remembered among the mountain people, but not Slavin Longstep. His balance and poise were legendary. It was said that trying to strike him was like trying to push the wind. He was the greatest of the sky warriors. Even as the elbow hit him, he was moving with it to diminish its impact and harm. Although he staggered, he kept his feet under him and was able to block as Azual straightened his elbow to deliver a chopping hand. The sky warrior used the precision of an eagle strike then on the pressure point of the Saint's outer lower arm. Azual roared in agony as his arm was numbed to the point of paralysis.

Slavin came in with his other hand, to deliver an identical blow to Azual's exposed throat. The Saint pulled his chin down and turned his injured shoulder into Slavin at the last moment, so that the sky warrior's hand came into contact with the oily substance oozing out of the wound caused by the spear. Slavin immediately went rigid. He began to wither, his skin and substance becoming ashen. His blue eyes rapidly dulled as he turned them one last time upon his son. 'Go. Would you have me sacrifice myself in vain? I will end cursing your name. Go, damn you!'

Choking back the grief that threatened to overwhelm him, Aspin fled. The sound of Azual's jaws crunching through bone pursued him. Something splattering on rocks. A slurping lick of the lips.

'Stay with me. Everything will be like it was before!' the Saint's voice gurgled and mocked.

In a panic, Aspin scrabbled and jumped his way up. With short powerful legs and broad shoulders, he was one of fastest of his people over a rock field. Yet he moved as if through some thickness. As if in the slow motion of a dream. Nothing went as fast as it should. His mind raced, but the scaling climb went on and on. And the servant of the Empire was right behind him, there in his shadow.

'Nothing can be as it was before. He is dead. The thought overwhelms you.'

There. He was on the path up to the shack. Surely he would be safe if he could get there?

'But there's nobody here to save you. There is only you and me,' Azual whispered in his ear. 'Turn and face me, unless you are too scared. Are you a coward, Aspin Longstep?' *Coward!* echoed the writhing mists.

Was he a coward? How could he be brave running like this? But he dared not stop and face it. Look at what it had done to his father. It would surely do the same to him. He whimpered in fear.

'I am right on you now. I enter your footsteps even before you have left them. Look, I am reflected in the mists ahead of you. You are running straight towards me, about to enter my embrace. As, when young, you raced home and flung yourself into your father's arms.'

The last stretch. *Don't listen. Don't think. Don't feel. Don't weaken.*

'This is your new home, Aspin. Stay, and I will return your father to you. Come to me and he will be so proud.'

There was the shack. Azual was so close he could hear his dark heart beating and belching. Its thump sent a tremor through him, a tremor that wrongfooted him and sent him pitching forward into the shack's door. His forehead hit the wood and he fell sprawling inside. He kicked out behind him, not sure if he hit the door or the grasping Saint. Sitting right before him was his own ghostly outline. He dragged himself into the phantasm of the meditating mountain warrior and opened his eyes just as the door crashed open again ...

'There you are, silly ox! What are you doing snoring in here?' Torpeth chastised him. 'The headwoman has called us to her, and I do not want to be deprived of her presence a moment longer than is necessary. Come on, you should be well rested. All you've done is sit around for days on end. Up! Don't think I'm going to carry you. Oh, alright! We'll be here all day otherwise.'

The next thing he knew, Aspin had been hoisted over the holy man's hairy shoulder and was being manhandled down the mountain. His sore head was jounced around and he found himself far closer to Torpeth's naked behind than he ever wanted to be. 'Torpeth! You don't know what I've been through! Show some pity.'

'Pity for that which I do not know? Silly ox!'

He was too disoriented. It was too much. He gritted his teeth. 'You never wash, do you?' he complained.

'Silly ox! It is weakening to wash too often. Just look at the state of you! All for that Veena of the Waterfall Peak, I'll be bound. It lessens a person. Besides, my goats find it reassuring when they can properly smell me nearby. If I had a bath, they'd get all nervous and jumpy. They'd jump right off the mountain, I wouldn't be surprised.'

'Whereas you make the rest of us want to jump off the mountain.'

'Quiet, silly ox! You speak from behind. Would you want me to reply in similar fashion?'

'No, don't! Argh. Ye gods! It's fouler than the nether realm itself. I now see I have not escaped that place after all. Surely I have swallowed a thousand plagues.'

'It is a punishment for you, just as you are a pestilence and punishment for me. Of the two of us, I am sure it is me who suffers most!' Torpeth let rip. 'Albeit I am glad that I was not on the receiving end of that. A rotten pine nut, I think.'

'Ugh! You cannot be human. You are a demon sent to torture me. Put me down, damn it, before I pass out. I think I'm seeing double.'

'Do not struggle, or you will unbalance us and send us both tumbling down the rocks. Our injuries are sure to delay us. Then the headwoman will be angry with you.'

'Not if I'm dead, she won't. She'll be angry with *you*. She'll refuse to see you ever again.'

'Do not say so!' Torpeth gasped.

'Then put me down, because right now I'd prefer to die than be carried like this a moment longer.' He kicked his legs. 'Put me down, Torpeth, you maniac!'

The holy man reluctantly complied. 'Come on then, silly ox! Stop standing around like a pompous chief more worried about his dignity than saving his own people. There is not time.' Then the holy man was off, his bandy legs lifting and bending, his testes slapping against his thighs and his matted hair and beard getting in his eyes and mouth.

Muttering under his breath, Aspin followed him as quickly as his nausea and shaking legs would allow.

Freda tumbled down through the temple like an avalanche. She brought down crystalline walls and collapsed floors as she went, covering her trail with destruction, debris and dust. Maybe she would bury them all.

She fell into the shadowy space at the bottom of the temple. Just one more floor and she would be into the relative sanctuary of the sun-smith's workshop. The ground flared as she hit it. It was a hard barrier that threw her back. She lay stunned and exhausted.

Someone came to stand over her. A haloed face searing itself into her retinas. With a groan, she realised Shezar had moved at the speed of light to overtake her.

'What have you done?' he seethed, burning with righteous indignation.

'I never meant to—'

'Still you lie and seek to manipulate. All saw you defy his will. Now you will suffer for what you have done. You will be punished.' His power increased in intensity.

'Please, Shezar. I cannot take any more. I am ruined! Look at me.'

'Yes, you have always wanted us to look at you. You deliberately sparkled and twinkled to capture his attention, did you not? You bewitched him to win yourself a place of power within the court.'

'No, it isn't true.'

'You even distracted his eye from me, his First Light, after all I had done for you. You have brought this on yourself, you *whore*!'

He savagely drove his power into her.

'Noo!'

She tried to block him out and deflect him, but she was caught in the embrace of his umbra – it sent shocks into her and robbed her of all coordination.

'You have ruined yourself along with his temple. Shame and humiliation are all you deserve.'

'It was *him* who did this!' She wept and cried.

'You drove him to it. You made him so crazy that he was no longer himself. Did I not warn you that you were making enemies for yourself? Did I not tell you that you would bring about your own fall from grace? Well, that is what you have done. And now you force me to do this,' he snarled with satisfaction, becoming incendiary inside her.

He burned out the last of her shining facets and she became entirely a black diamond. She could no longer refract, focus or amplify light; rather, she absorbed and trapped it within her. Shezar began to lose himself in her.

'Release me!' he gasped in horror.

Her new being condensed and hardened. Her matrix snapped him off. His halo winked out and he was left a thin, grey and wretched creature. He tried to scream but was only capable of a pathetic mewl. He hardly seemed to have the strength to stand.

Freda was no longer the being she had once been. She was different, changed. She felt something she had never felt before. She examined the new emotion at her core and knew it as hatred. Smiling, she reached out, put her hand around Shezar's throat and casually crushed it. She watched the last light leave his eyes, tossed him aside and went into the ground.

She descended into the darkest places of the earth, where there was a complete absence of light. It was like returning to the time before she had met Norfred. Maybe she would have been better off never having met him, for it was he who had first brought her towards the evil of the Overlords. It was better here.

They would be coming for her, of course, but she hardly cared. Let them come. Let men dig or Sinisar come worming down through the cracks in the earth. If they failed to find her, then she would find them. *Yes*, whispered the hatred in her, *for you no longer fear them. Instead, you will make them fear you and your vengeance.* She liked the idea. Was this what friend Anupal had tried to explain to her for so long? Well, now she understood.

She moved purposefully back up towards the realm of the Overlords.

Torpeth helped the shivering Aspin to the threshold of the headwoman's stone cottage. 'Old Sal will soon see you restored, young warrior.' The holy man peered cautiously into the smoky interior.

'You hesitate and loiter like a devil who knows he cannot enter without invitation,' croaked the headwoman's voice. 'You are a devil, are you not, Torpeth the Great?'

'Beloved, I am whatever you would have me be. See, I have done as you commanded and brought the silly ox here.'

'Then be not a devil and enter, old goat. Sit him by the fire and furnish him with tea. Quickly, for he barely looks to be with us. No, do not speak, old goat, for I have heard all your words, every entreaty, every quip, every flattery, every claim and every excuse. All of them.'

Torpeth frowned unhappily but did as she bid, folding himself down next to Aspin. The mountain warrior sat stupidly with the bowl of tea in his lap. He couldn't quite remember what he was supposed to do with it. The holy man helped him lift it to his lips. He took several long sips, and warmth flooded his body, bringing him back to life. He blinked several times – when had he stopped doing so?

'Headwoman?' he rasped.

She leaned across the fire to look closely at his eyes, grunted in satisfaction and then moved back into the shadows. 'Nearly had you, didn't he?'

Torpeth's bushy eyebrows beetled up his forehead and then came all the way down. He knew better than to ask about whom she meant. He used a grubby finger to clean some wax out of his ears and then cocked his head over to the warrior to hear his answer.

Aspin nodded woodenly. Hoarsely, he replied, 'If it weren't for the spirit of my father ...' He swallowed painfully.

The headwoman sighed heavily. 'I am sorry, Aspin, truly. Yet know this – it is not just his spirit that is lost to us. Many of the ancestors came to me unbidden last night as I watched the fire. Never have I known such a thing. They begged me to help them, but I was powerless to do anything. Several destroyed themselves trying to enter the world of

60

the living! It is unheard of. One tried to steal my body from me, and I had to fight all through the night until he weakened and dissipated. The rest have fallen completely silent. Not in the normal way. I can usually sense them, but now there is nothing.'

For the first time in his life Aspin heard fear and uncertainty in the headwoman's voice. This scared him as much as anything he'd experienced in the nether realm. She'd always been as enduring, untroubled and somehow reassuring as the mountains. Something fundamental was wrong if she spoke like this. It felt as if his mind and perception were unravelling. It was only with a significant effort of will that he remained himself. Torpeth experienced a similar struggle. His eyes bulged. He'd bitten his lip so hard that it bled. He'd clamped each of his hands under the opposing arm to stop himself reaching for and holding on to her.

The headwoman nodded. 'Something terrible has happened.'

'Azual,' Aspin dared breathe. Everything fell silent, even the fire. 'He has found a way to drain and enthral the other spirits.'

The headwoman spoke as if being strangled. 'It cannot be. It *must not* be.'

Torpeth whined like an animal in pain.

'My father told me I must lead our people, but I do not know what to do. Headwoman, guide me. Please.'

Her face became furrowed with clefts, ravines and chasms as she pondered deeply. She stared into the fire for a long while, even adding herbs at one point. Eventually she gave up with a sorry shake of the head. 'Nothing is clear to me any more. I-I am lost.'

'Torpeth,' Aspin whispered. 'What say you?'

The small man looked at one of them, then the other, then back again, then at the other.

'You are making me dizzy. Speak, old goat!' the headwoman accepted.

'My words might mislead or wrongly influence,' he gabbled. 'Unless events have now become inevitable. Then my words are of no consequence. Yet if events are not set, how much influence might we really have? Precious little here in our mountains, eh? Should we attempt the Broken Path, enter the nether realm and join some great fight there?'

'I cannot think that wise,' the headwoman told them. 'Each time one of the living enters that place, they leave something of themselves there. Aspin, you hardly made it back this time. You certainly would not return if you ventured there again. And the living are *not meant* to be there. The longer and more often they go, the narrower becomes the divide between the land of the living and the land of the dead.'

'And that is what Azual wants.' Aspin nodded. 'Death seeks to claim us all.'

'How can one fight death? How is it held back?' Torpeth murmured. 'What are we? The living can never triumph in the nether realm. They can only triumph in the realm of the living. Yet triumph against whom and what? Where is the enemy in this realm?' He looked up at them. 'There must be an enemy in this realm, for surely the dynamic and consequence of one realm creates the dynamic and consequence of the other! Where is the enemy in this realm?'

'They are hidden from us. We must find them before it is too late,' the headwoman decided. 'You must go abroad in the world once more, Aspin, with whatever force you can lead, for this can be no small threat. It grieves me to ask it of you, but you must be a war chief to our people. You must lead our remaining warriors into the coming struggle.'

'Veena!' Aspin sorrowed.

'She will understand,' the headwoman said with some sympathy. 'She will be proud of you, as your father would also be. Make the most of your goodbye while the warriors gather. I will then proclaim you chief.'

'And you, old goat, will go with us, I take it?' Aspin sighed.

'Well, you will have great need of me, will you not, silly ox?'

'I fear so.'

'Of course you will, for I am a legendary warrior and there is none better to advise you in important matters of etiquette.'

The headwoman snorted derisively.

'Etiquette?'

'Indeed. How else will you know how to address that old windbag Wayfar?'

'Wayfar?'

'Of course, silly ox! We must seek him out in Hyvan's Cross and add his strength to our own. The gods have some power when it comes to death and the nether realm, do they not? Yes, he must be made to help us whether he likes it or not. And he may also know something of the elusive enemy.'

'Old fool! The last time you presumed to command the gods, you brought about their downfall and handed the world to the others. Have you learned nothing?' the headwoman reprimanded.

'It is true, beloved, that things could have gone better last time. But practice makes perfect, eh? If you would but let me practise making love to—'

'I will not hear it!' she yelled.

Aspin decided it was time to leave and got to his feet. Neither of them seemed to notice.

'Beloved, if you would but be a little more reasonable—'

'Reasonable?! You dare?'

Aspin ducked out of the cottage and went in search of his dearest Veena.

'I would dare anything for you, beloved, even your wrath.'

'You stink! You will not come near me. Go find a bath, old goat. Get out.'

'It is weakening to wash too often, beloved.'

'Yet if you do not wash often enough, it only strengthens my resolve to have nothing to do with you.'

'The ironies of existence are too cruel. Ours is a tragic relationship!'

'And make sure you wash behind your ears. Then offer up prayers of apology to holy Akwar for having so befouled his waters. Out!'

CHAPTER 3:

To see all undone

When he'd returned to the home-realm, collapsing the Gate to the Seventh behind him, Ba'zel had fully expected the warriors of the Declension to be there waiting in the chamber of the Gate. He'd expected to be pierced by their fangs, rent by their talons and crushed by the power of their combined presence. He'd expected it to be over in an instant. They would give him no chance to escape or trigger further destruction than he already had. He was an *unstable element* and could not be allowed to exist. He had fought against the Declension – a treason that was almost inconceivable. He had even destroyed one of the Virtues, and there could be no words for that.

What he had not expected was this. To emerge into the chamber to find just this one figure. His father, Faal. The uncanniness of it gripped Ba'zel and stopped him reacting immediately. It had been just like this when he had first left the chamber for the other realms. Now it felt like he had never left, as if none of it had ever happened. Suspicion – were the Declension deliberately seeking to create such an illusion so that they could use him? It made sense. If they were not going to kill him, then they wanted to use him for their own ends. It was in the nature of his kind. And had they not successfully used him in the other realms to do their bidding, despite all his efforts to the contrary? Had they not trapped him within the inevitable course of events decided by their will? The only exception had been in the seventh realm, where he'd helped see the Declension defeated ... hadn't he? The fact that he was still alive now made him fear otherwise.

Perhaps he'd somehow doomed the seventh, after all, just as he'd helped doom the other realms he'd visited. They'd made him the destroyer of worlds. He didn't want to blame himself for what they'd made him into – tried not to think of the millions upon millions to whom he'd brought death – but the truth was he had refused to undo his own being, and therefore he implicitly allowed their continued use of him. It was the truth at the centre of his being. Have him in some double-bind as they might, he was still complicit. He was as self-interested and intent upon the assertion of his own will as the Declension itself. Perhaps he was a true member of the Declension after all. Perhaps he was *the worst* of them. And now he had come home ... to be with his own kind?

The last time he'd seen his father, the patriarch had tried to kill him, had begged him to kill himself. His father had his powers raised and ready now, but they were also kept in check. Was he merely taking precautions in case he needed to defend himself? Surely he didn't fear Ba'zel, did he? There was no knowing, for the display of fear was a weakness and invited immediate attack from any present.

'So you have returned,' Faal said stiffly.

Ba'zel squared his frame. 'Perhaps it was inevitable.'

'Perhaps. It is certainly what would be expected of the Faction of Origin's offspring.'

His father had disowned him when they'd last spoken. Was he now reclaiming him? 'How fares your faction?'

'Our influence has increased significantly, now that we have claimed the Geas of several more realms and used their power to feed the Geas of our own realm. We have culled the beings of those realms, feeding most to the Geas and distributing the rest to be used and consumed by our own kind. We are stronger than we have ever been, and the home-realm is closer to being restored than at any other point during my own time. It has seen faith in our faction's cause grow far stronger. It is hoped that with the eventual fall of the seventh, the home-realm will become self-sustaining once more!' Faal's voice almost sang. 'It will be reborn, my son. The Declension will become transcendant!'

What have I done? Ba'zel thought shakily, the enormity, implications and horror of the Declension causing a crisis in his mind. 'What of the other factions? Surely the Faction of Departure describes the fall of these other realms as the inevitable reward for our progress on the Great Voyage through the cosmos. Do they not say the value of departure is now more proved?'

'You have grown in many ways, scion of my house.' Surely that wasn't approval in his father's voice? Where once it had been all he craved, now Ba'zel dreaded it. 'Yes, Starus's faction makes such claims. More than that, now the warriors of our kind are free to feed at will and in whatever amounts they desire, they are almost youthful. They chafe for new challenges, battles and conquests. They hunger for the fight and the Great Voyage more than ever before. Even the most ancient of them has rediscovered their ardour and urgency. They cannot wait to sweep into the seventh –'

'The way to the seventh is closed,' Ba'zel choked out.

His father seemed not to hear, energised by his own words as he apparently was: '– and on into the eighth, for the way has been found! *You* found the way on our behalf, my son. *She* saw it through your eyes. Nothing is hidden from *her*.'

I have done this. The fault is mine. I knew they used me. It is the truth at the centre of my detested being. 'The way to the seventh is closed,' he all but prayed aloud.

'Nothing is closed to or hidden from the Declension any more. Nothing is forbidden. Nothing is unattainable. The final secrets of the cosmos now reveal themselves to us. We will at last truly be able to follow in the footsteps of the ancient Chi'a. Where once they were lost to us and we struggled to find trace of them, now the path is all too clear.'

'What is it you say, Father?'

'A way to a nether realm has been found in the seventh. Surely the power of true disembodiment is soon to be ours! We will be free of these vessels that house but limit us. We will cast off these limbs and this carapace. No longer will they serve as barrier to our greatness. Our essence will become truly disembodied, just as our Geas will be reborn. Then nothing will be able to halt our progress through the cosmos. All will unfold before us. All will be ours. We will be the absolute origin and destination of the Great Voyage!'

Ba'zel now knew that dying instantly upon returning to the home-realm would have been a mercy. The piercing stone fangs of the warriors would have been cruel but kind. The rending talons would have been a killing caress. The crushing power of their combined presence would have brought him eternal rest and a peace of sorts. Yet mercy was not in the nature of his kind. No wonder they had not destroyed him. It gave them far more satisfaction to torture him with further use. It was a punishment far worse than death. And the truth at the centre of his loathsome being meant that there could be no escape from that punishment, from their will.

'And you will continue to lead us towards that transcendance, Ba'zel, just as you have already done so much as our instrument. The Council of the Factions will give you audience. Think of it, the first time any individual other than the Eldest herself has been heard! It is strange for me to form such words, but a Great Accord might at last be realised. Such a thing was unimaginable and unspeakable when I last saw you, my son. The council might be united for the first time in the Declension's existence. They can be persuaded to follow *you*, I am sure. You will be the Great Virtue who delivers the Declension its final salvation. You will lead us into the seventh and then through the entire cosmos.'

Jillan, I am so sorry. Forgive me, if that is at all possible.

Jillan blinked in confusion. There was as much light as he could want, but he only seemed to see less because of it. Hadn't the sun been at his left shoulder before? Now it was on his right. Had he been walking in circles without realising it? Or had more time passed than he'd thought? Was the sun still climbing higher in the sky or was it already past its zenith? He couldn't tell. If only he could think clearly, but the intense desert heat made it feel as if his brain itself was sweating uncontrollably, shrivelling up and reaching the point of extinction. He recognised absolutely nothing around him. He'd hoped to see the low clouds of Haven and to navigate his way back by them, but the horizon constantly shimmered and obscured anything that lay more than a few hundred feet away.

Covering any sort of distance was exhausting. Underfoot was either strength-sapping sand or else small rocks on compacted ground which tripped him, gave way beneath his weight or forced him to go around so that any sense of a straight line and bearing was lost to him. If only he'd brought some water.

You're lost, aren't you?

'Shut up,' Jillan croaked.

If you'd bothered to stop and listen to me in the first place, you wouldn't be in this mess now. You'd have realised I was trying to help you. Are you going to make the same mistake again? I'm not sure you'll survive if you do.

'Shut up.'

You don't need to talk out loud, you know. You're only wasting energy and moisture. The pain in your throat when you speak is meant to warn you of that. Or are you ignoring that too? If you must speak aloud, then keep a small pebble in your mouth.

'What are you talking about? I don't want to put a dry –' he coughed painfully '– and dusty …' He coughed again and gave up. He hesitated and then took up a small stone from the ground. He put it under his tongue and after a minute his throat eased. 'Amazing. Now get me out of this desert.'

Err …

'You can get me out of here, right?'

Perhaps. There is a possibility Sinisar is interfering somehow.

'What? Is he trying to kill me? I'm not sure how much longer I can last.'

And have you noticed you've stopped sweating?

'That's a bad sign, I take it.'

Very much so.

'Great. I don't feel good, that's for sure. My feet are really heavy. Maybe if I rested for just a minute …'

No. You'll find it even harder to get up – if you manage to get back up again, that is.

'It's so damned hot! Is that water over there?'

No, it isn't. A mirage. Heat haze.

'Because if it's an oasis, I could drink it dry. A nice swim. Imagine all that water.'

You're wandering. There are no trees, Jillan. Leave it.

'Why are you trying to keep me away from the oasis?' He suddenly became suspicious. '*You're* the one trying to kill me. I should have known not to trust you. It's you who forced me out here in the first place.' He broke into a run.

Jillan!

69

He threw himself down into sand. 'It's gone! There's nothing here. I could have sworn I almost tasted it. Cursed Akwar's playing tricks on me too. Why are they doing this to me?' he railed. 'I helped raise them back up. Why won't they help me?'

Jillan, calm down. You can't afford to waste your energies like this. Remove your tunic and cover your head.

'That'll only make my head hotter.'

It won't. It'll protect your head from the sun. That's it. Now, the gods are limited by necessity. If they were not, there'd be no free will or life for mortalkind. The gods are imperfect in nature. They are prone to whim, vagary and jealousy, just like any other being. There are any number of reasons for them to resent you. In helping to raise them up, you may have shown some sort of temerity, as if placing yourself above them. The gods cannot permit any to be above them.

'I never tried to place myself over them. It's ridiculous. Unfair.'

Yes and no. You had free will. It was your foolhardy choice to come into the desert like this. Without your armour too, I may add.

'It's still not wrong. What chance can I have if the gods are turned against me?'

Oh, come on. You've faced worse. Why don't you just give up then? Lie down and wait to die?

He hesitated. 'I can't.'

Why not?

'Hella would kill me. I've promised her we'll get married this year.'

There you are then. You're not completely hard done by. Think yourself lucky. Be grateful for what you have, rather than bewailing the lack of what you've never had, or have never worked hard enough to deserve. You humans generally complain too much, do you know that? That's probably why both the gods and the elseworlders have it in for you. They're just trying to shut you up once and for all. Can't blame them, really.

'Well, if you're so clever, how do I get out of this desert then? Whether this human complains too much or not will be a moot issue otherwise, because I'll be dead. And if I'm dead, woe betide you and me. Hella will be livid, and she'll come and find us in the nether realm. Then you'll really see what complaining's all about.'

Well, that's hardly fair.

Jillan faintly chuckled. 'You ancient gods generally complain too much, do you know that? Ooh. I'm feeling dizzy. What were we talking about?'

Hella.

'No, before that. Not about the complaining either. Oh. How do I get out of this desert? Come on, before it's too late.'

Seems like you're listening to me good and proper now.

'My undivided attention,' he mumbled. 'Get on with it.'

And what will you do for me in return?

'I should have known. Conniving to the last! I was right, wasn't I? You've deliberately been hounding me and spoiling my judgement. You wanted me out here and on my own so you would have some advantage. Are you in league with Sinisar or something? Or have the sleights of hand, misdirection and tricks been yours all along?'

So little faith, the taint tutted.

'What the hell do you want?' All the blood was in his head, thumping. He wanted to throw up, but knew it would fatally weaken him. He swallowed his gorge back down. More quietly: 'What do you want?'

I will not name it now. I will make some request of you in the future and you will do as I ask, without hesitation. You will be bound by this, the taint declared triumphantly.

'Absolutely not.'

The taint was disconcerted. How could it have misjudged? It knew the heart and mind of this mortal. *You will die if you do not agree. You will never see Hella again. She is everything to you.*

'Do you think I'm some sort of idiot? I've been tricked like this before, remember. Oh, that's right, you missed some stuff, didn't you? You were blocked and absent whenever the Peculiar was around, weren't you? Well, let me tell you that I was forced to make a similar bargain with him. If you think I'm about to do the same with you, Kathuula, you've got another think coming. It's too old. I've seen it all before. You gods need to freshen up your act. There's no way I'm going into the sort of open-ended agreement whereby I'm ultimately forced to betray all those I love, if not the whole of humanity. I'd rather die out here on my own.'

You're bluffing.

'Hardly. The stakes are too high.'

The taint wriggled uncomfortably in Jillan's mind. Damn this mortal.

Maybe Sinisar was right to see Jillan as a threat. *Very well. I will not ask anything of you that will generally harm humanity, in either the short or long term or in either a direct or indirect way. Will that suffice?*

'Nope.'

The taint muttered angrily to itself. Reluctantly, it added, *And specifically none that you love will be harmed.*

'Now you're getting the idea.' Jillan nodded drowsily. 'I will be bound by such terms. Come on, your turn. Let's have it.'

When the sun starts to set, Haven will send a search party for you. They will search during the morning of the next day also. You need to survive until then. You must make a line of rocks in the sand to indicate the direction of your travel. You will need to make a similar line every so often. The searchers will hopefully find one of these lines and know where to concentrate their attention. Your only other task will be to find some sort of shelter in which to wait and conserve your strength, be it in the shadow of a large rock or the hollow of some dune. A rock would be better, for it will retain some of the heat of the sun and help you through the freezing night.

'That's it? Not much of a plan, is it?' Jillan slurred.

More plan than you currently have.

'S'pose. No magic spell for this one?'

Sinisar could take direct acion against any attempt to change the region that is shaped by his will. I could attempt to bring you into the nether realm, but you have no holy or magical item to aid your progress. You are already weak, and I do not think you would survive it.

'A prayer to Gar or Wayfar for divine intervention?'

They will not answer you. They would not invade Sinisar's realm and risk provoking his ire simply for the life of a mortal.

'Of course not. Silly of me. With friends like these, eh, Kathuula?'

Indeed, Jillan, I cannot help but agree. These gods are no blessing to mortalkind.

'Almost makes me miss the Saviours,' he snorted tiredly as he finished his first line of stones and stumbled off in the direction that they pointed.

What he did not see or sense as he moved away was the slight breeze that blew sand against his line of rocks. All too soon any trace of a line would be gone.

Unaware, Jillan staggered on. The ground underfoot became firmer, which was a small mercy, but the sun continued to beat down relentlessly. His knees were sore and his chin was on his chest. He came to something of a ledge, a six-foot step down. The low escarpment ran a hundred feet in each direction and then curved around to make a wide apron of sorts. The wall to the right of the area offered shade from the sun! It was the reprieve he had been looking for.

He lowered himself down and headed for the shelter. It was then that he noticed the round holes and low caves all around the apron. Even better. And what if the caves went deep and there were aquifers? He almost sobbed with relief.

Stop. Can't you smell it?

The water? No, it was a musky sort of sulphur.

See the small bleached bones around a few of the entrances? Jillan, this is not a place you want to be. You must leave as quickly as you can. Before they sense you.

There was a chittering noise. Something moved in the darkness of the hole ahead of him. Long clawed limbs hooked onto the edge of the burrow and a spider six feet across eased itself out.

Summon your magic, the taint urged.

Jillan stood staring at the monstrosity. It had the hard chitinous exterior of a scorpion or crab. It was pale orange except for two blood-red eyes and a pair of glistening fangs as long as his forearm.

'S'alright. Probably a mirage.' Jillan frowned.

The spider skittered forward, stopped, then raised a finely spined forelimb, as if waiting for a shift in the air to indicate the sudden movement of any potential prey. It sprang to the right with a slight flex of its legs. Another leap and it would be on him. More spiders began to emerge onto the apron of ground. One drifted up into the air on a complex of long threads. It looked as if it was climbing across the sky and sun.

Release me! the taint shrieked, trying to fight its way free.

The last time I did that, you tried to destroy the world, Jillan thought back.

Idiot! You're going to die. And it won't be at all pleasant. Let me do this.

Your plan isn't going very well, is it? Or was this the plan all along? You probably wanted this to happen so you could get free. You're tricky like that. Besides, using magic drains me so much that it's likely to finish me off this time.

73

Ever so slowly Jillan took a small step back from the spider.

Don't! It can sense even that. Your magic! There's no more time.

Perhaps you're right. Jillan tried to call up his power, but his core was as empty as the desert.

The desert is not empty, you know that. Look harder.

A single drop of sweat ran down Jillan's forehead, tickling him. He had an insane urge to wipe it away, but knew the movement would betray him. It would be a silly way to die. The sweat ran into his eye. It stung ferociously and made him squint. The spider suddenly shifted round towards him and crouched low, ready to spring.

And there are so many of them, Jillan silently whined.

Don't panic. Don't even breathe. Concentrate on your magic. It must be there, else you would not hear me. Quickly.

Jillan's eyelid fluttered and the sand spider jumped straight at him, its legs spread wide like a weighted net and its fangs scissoring and shooting toxins. It fell towards him. Other spiders came scuttling in.

'Argh! Geas preserve me!' Jillan gibbered in terror, instinctively ducking and hiding behind his raised hands.

He was hit by the spider's weight and lacerated by the sharp edges of its scrabbling limbs. As it touched him, he was filled with such revulsion that he lost all reason. Red light flared from his hands. The spider squealed and was bowled backwards. The oncoming arachnids froze.

Power arced from Jillan to the first spider, splaying it out in the sand. Energy crackled at its joints and then speared out, catching the six closest spiders, and from them several dozen more. A magical web seared and cooked the predators beneath the desert sun. The stench of the green fluids and poisons that bubbled out of their seams and cracks was overpowering. Their bodies charred and smoked, filling the air with a dripping blackness. It coated Jillan's skin and then, as he chokingly took a breath, his insides.

He gagged, and his power winked out. He must have swooned for the next he knew he was in the sand, watching the scene side on. Drawn by the smell of burning meat, the entire nest of spiders was swarming out into the killing ground. There had to be hundreds of them. Was that a desert giant standing on top of the escarpment? It didn't somehow command these horrors, did it? He knew it was over. He had nothing left.

Taint? he feebly called, but there was no answer.

The sand spiders gorged on the fallen or dragged large pieces of them away into their burrows. One of the larger arachnids zigzagged towards Jillan, its movement stuttering, then too rapid to follow. It feinted once, twice, testing him, then plunged thick curved fangs deep into his thigh. Venom pumped into him. There was a second of two of excruciating pain, and then he felt nothing. He watched numbly as he was bundled and pulled across the ground into a tunnel and down into darkness.

Ba'zel accompanied his father back to their chambers and was shocked at what he found. The floor was an inch deep in the dust of their realm. When it had been Ba'zel's constant task to sweep these rooms, his father would not have tolerated even the thinnest layer of dirt. What had changed in Faal that he would allow this? What had happened? Ba'zel saw his old broom leaning in its usual corner and had to resist the urge to pick it up. But it was pointless to fight the dust. There was no holding it back. Had even his father come to see that?

To think of the realms that had been destroyed, the millions of beings that had been sacrificed, just to maintain begrimed chambers like these throughout the home-realm. Could it really be justified? The entire Declension thought so, of course. The maintenance of such chambers was the maintenance of the home-realm and the Declension itself. It was existence. To suggest anything else was a madness of sorts. These realms and beings *had* to be destroyed. And the successful destruction of those realms was proof that the Declension was more deserving and worthy of existence than any other. It was *right* that those realms and beings were destroyed. There was no doubt or ambiguity, for that would be death, that would be giving in to the dust, letting it fill their chambers and bury them for ever more.

No doubt or ambiguity. And yet Faal had allowed the dust to accumulate and deepen significantly. He was head of the Faction of Origin. He should be the last to allow such a thing to happen. If mere rumour of it were to get out, Faal's position would be severely undermined. Was his father's mind somehow compromised? Ba'zel suddenly feared he had infected his father with the insidious *instability* of his own nature. *I have done this. The fault is mine.*

How far had it spread? Was the entire Declension now infected? Was that why they welcomed rather than destroyed him? Was he leading the

Declension itself to its destruction? That couldn't be what he wanted, could it? Even though he'd fought against the Declension, the thought was still appalling to him. Would he destroy every realm and every other being in the cosmos, to leave himself alone for the rest of time?

Ba'zel went to the corner and picked up the broom. With practised strokes, he started to move dust towards the door. His father nodded in approval and watched as his son worked his way around the chamber. It was only when he reached the pair of cages in the far corner of the room that Ba'zel paused. As per his rank, his father had always had a lower being imprisoned in his chambers to serve as a private supply of blood and life energy. To have two such beings was a great luxury indeed, and clear sign of how the faction's power had increased.

'This one is a Selios,' Ba'zel said, gesturing towards the metal-sheathed being in front of him. The Selios watched him with devotion in its eyes.

'Yes, probably one of the last. There are few left, which is a shame in some ways.'

Was his father showing some sort of pity? 'How so?'

'Although its tough exterior makes it difficult to tap, its blood is strong. A shame I couldn't get another.'

No, of course he wasn't. 'A shame. The end of a species.'

'Necessary. A mere detail of the conquest of the fourth realm.'

'The fifth realm. The Selios occupied the fifth realm.'

'No matter.'

'And this one –' Ba'zel struggled to hide his shock as he took in the naked creature crouched in its own filth '– is human?' It was male and had red hair. In marked contrast to the Selios, its eyes were filled with hatred – not that Faal would be able to read or recognise the emotion in a human.

'Yes,' his father said with a certain pride. 'I am becoming something of a collector, no? It is an ugly creature, I know, but its blood is quite sweet, quite moreish. Some collectors are wary of human blood, because they fear it is addictive and can make us irrational with craving, but I have experienced no such thing myself. It is probably just an issue for the weaker or lower ranks of our kind. Indeed, a certain addiction among the warrior ranks might even be encouraged, because it will see them fight with a fierce frenzy when we sweep into the seventh in greater force. It is in large part thanks to you, Ba'zel, that we are now able to deploy much of the resources we had in the other realms to the seventh. The final conquest of the seventh is at hand.'

Ba'zel continued to regard the human. It could easily be Jillan in the cage. The thought was disturbing. 'Does it speak?'

'I do not allow it. I cannot have the meaningless chatter and grunts of lower beings interrupting my thoughts and contemplation of the cosmos. I know certain houses and members of my rank, members like Starus –' his father mentioned the head of the Faction of Departure with clear distaste '– allow their lower beings a certain freedom to perform menial tasks, but I think this gives the lower beings a false impression of their worth. It can only lead to trouble, interruption and waste.'

'Could it not be said that is also what we represent to the seventh?'

'What is it you say?'

He had overstepped. 'I was trapped in a box of sun-metal, Father. Do you know what that is like? You cannot. A human released me. I feel an obligation to them.'

'You should not. Just as it was no doubt the Declension's will that you were incarcerated, it was also the Declension's will that you be released. The human was our instrument, nothing more. It was simply our will becoming manifest and being played out in the seventh realm. As a consequence, the Geas of the seventh was revealed to us through you, the seventh will now fall to us and we will begin our conquest of the eighth. It was the Declension that released you, Ba'zel, not the human. Your entire obligation is to us and no other.'

Still I am trapped by the will and intention of the Declension. It is as if I am still in that box. It is as if I am in that cage with the human. His father's chambers were just another box. Was there no way out? Would he sweep these chambers all through eternity? The claustrophobia of his existence overwhelmed him. Even his physical form confined and trapped him. There had to be a way out. It could be that the disembodiment his father had spoken of before – the disembodiment suggested by the discovery of the seventh's nether realm – was his one true chance. It would only be for that possibility that he would agree to lead the Declension back into the seventh. If he could find that escape or release, then perhaps he could save his friend Jillan and the other humans, rather than destroy them. He had to be sure. Who would know more? 'Thank you, Father, I understand now. There is still much to learn if I am ever to be the Great Virtue. Have you seen Mentor Ho'zen at all? Does he still have chambers in the depths?'

'I have not seen him since your departure. He would have no cause to come to my chambers, and those of my rank avoid the depths and its lower ranks as far as possible.'

'You know that I fled the home-realm on the day that he did not come to give me a lesson, do you not? I assumed that you had told him not to attend. I feared that I would be fed to the blood pools because I had become too *unstable*. Was my assumption correct? Did you tell him not to attend that day?'

Faal stilled. 'Is this true?'

'Did you tell Mentor Ho'zen not to attend that day?'

'I did not!' the elder asserted, his nasal aperture flaring and his eyes glittering in anger. 'We were betrayed by him! Your departure suddenly makes more sense to me. At the time I simply took it as evidence of an increasing *instability* in you, an *instability* that was first suggested to me by Ho'zen himself. He will pay dearly for this. I will break open his skull and eat his quivering mind. He will expose those whom he served and then we will revenge ourselves on our enemies. My son, to think I once begged you to kill yourself! It was no fault of my own, but know that I regret it. You are the glory of my house and line.'

Ba'zel nodded his acceptance, not sure how else to react.

'Yet Ho'zen is unlikely still to be alive,' Faal continued intently as he pursued his line of thought. 'Those directing him would have devoured him. I would have done the same. Ba'zel, seek out Ho'zen's chambers in the depths to see if there is anything to be found there, anything that might indicate whom he served. Meanwhile, I will have a few trusted members of the faction ask discreet questions among Ho'zen's rank, line and community. If we could but find proof of guilt or evidence of certain knowledge, then the council will issue an official reprimand to our enemies. Our influence will increase accordingly and you will even more readily be proclaimed Great Virtue.'

Ba'zel nodded again, just relieved to have an excuse to leave Faal's increasingly close chambers.

'And Ba'zel?'

'Yes, Father?'

'Be careful in the depths. They are always dangerous to those who do not know them well.' He shook his head. 'Listen to me. I know you to have defeated the Virtue Obedience, and still I warn you like some overly protective wet nurse. You must think me weak to show so much fatherly concern.'

'Our enemies are powerful, Father.'

'Yes, they are. You are right to remember it. Go now, for I fear we have given our enemies too long to plan and prepare. We may already be too late. The Council of Factions will soon command our attendance. I will not have victory wrested from our grasp when we are so close and have sacrificed so much. We must find something regarding Ho'zen before the council meets, something that will shore up our position and allow us to clinch all. Go quickly, my son.'

Ba'zel gratefully put the broom aside, spared the human a last glance and hurried away.

His eyelids were gummed down. There was a stickiness over his mouth and nose which made it hard to breathe. His hands and feet were wrapped against him by some sort of clinging blanket.

Jillan blinked rapidly and got one eye open. He saw nothing. It was dark. Some sort of gossamer touched his eyeball. He realised it was webbing. A strangling cocoon had been spun around him. It was intended to be his death shroud, he knew.

He felt woozy. If he vomited while he was wrapped like this, he would be unable to clear his throat. He would probably choke to death. He fought against nausea and dizziness, steeling himself as best he could. *Don't panic*, he told himself. *You'll inhale this gunk and asphyxiate yourself if you don't keep your breathing shallow.*

It's the toxins in you, called the taint, as if from a great distance. *See inside yourself. Fight it.*

He concentrated. He saw himself secreted in a dark burrow beneath the baking desert. The sand spider that had captured him was waiting for him to die and start rotting. It would sup on his fluids and the running ichor of his flesh. It had injected some corrupting and corrosive essence into him to speed the process. Jillan saw the dark contaminant creeping through his every part. It had already reached the core of his being. It strangled the magic inside him. Only the slightest flicker of energy remained. He dared not use it.

You have no choice.

I'll die.

You'll die if you don't. Fight it.

He cried dry tears, terribly afraid. His death was here. He knew it in his soul, and grieved for the last of himself. They wouldn't find his body. He was to be devoured by an evil spider. Hella wouldn't have a body to mourn. She wouldn't even know what had happened to him. She might wonder if he had simply left her, fleeing the pressure and expectation of the wedding and the divided, failing community of Haven. It was as cruel on her as it was on himself. Would she ever find someone else or would she wait for him, watching the horizon every day for some sign? Would she die an old and lonely spinster? Would she die young and heartbroken? He hoped she could be happy. He half hoped she didn't love him as much as he loved her, as then she might move on and have some chance of a fulfilled life. But he knew she loved him more than that, loved him too much. It was why he had to fight.

He closed his eyes and gritted his teeth. His magic guttered, then flared against the poison within him. The darkness bubbled and boiled then ignited, burning with the power of his core. Fire swept through him and set the webbing around him smouldering. Although his body was now clear of the venom, his magic had nothing left to feed on and fizzled out.

Jillan struggled weakly to get free of the substance coating him, but his most vigorous movement only managed to stretch it, not snap it. He was becoming more tangled than ever, and the heat from the small fires around him was increasing.

'Come on!' he begged, knowing he only had moments before the exhaustion of having used his magic overwhelmed him.

A *scritchety-scratch* noise came hastily closer. It was the sand spider's armoured limbs levering and pulling it through the burrow.

'No. Please!' Jillan coughed, attempting one last wild effort. 'Argh!'

Spikes into his arm. Liquid death forced into him once more. Invaded. His core swamped. Lost. More webbing, this thicker and tighter than the last. No more breath. No more anything.

Ba'zel crept through the lower tunnels of the home-realm. There was no sun-metal to light the way, for it was far too valuable a commodity to be wasted on the needs of the lower ranks. While he could sense the way well enough regardless, the passage was narrow and he could not always avoid scraping joints and skull on the rock. If things became much tighter, he'd end up losing all the hard ridging on his head and seem little more than a newborn. He'd be easy prey for any elder that he suddenly encountered coming from the opposite direction. Maybe he'd be better off travelling in spectral form through the rock, but that had risks of its own, not the least of which was dangerously draining himself of life energy and strength while in his altered state. He'd then be completely incapable of defending himself when he emerged from the rock. He should have thought to bring a reserve of blood with him, even if its scent might attract the attention of the hungry or insatiable.

Fortunately the tunnel gradually opened up as he came to a wide intersection, with passages going off in all directions, including up and down. There were members of his kind prowling here, so he stilled warily.

Ba'zel caught the scent of a female, his nasal aperture quivering excitedly as he drew in a heady musk. Females could be extremely dangerous. He had to control himself, or he might end up being eaten alive while attempting the act of copulation. Some desperate or poorly bred females of lower rank were even known to work in predatory gangs.

He moved cautiously out of the female's proximity and found a hulking elder ahead of him. It was much scarred and missing a forelimb. Unbelievably, the way its other forelimb was raised, this once proud warrior seemed to be begging.

'What are you doing at this level?' Ba'zel challenged, knowing better than to betray anything but disgust. 'Do these tunnels not belong to the mentors of our kind?'

'And who are you to address the champion of the fighting pits, he who now offers his services as battle mentor?' the elder growled back, although he made no threatening move.

'I am not accustomed to giving my name to a mere cripple,' Ba'zel replied with the appropriate degree of scorn.

'Indeed? Then it is *you* who should not be at this level. This mere cripple could best you with just his one arm. What are you doing down here without your nursemaid, you pup?'

The elder was attempting to provoke the sort of proud retort that would tell him precisely whom he faced. This battle mentor was smart enough not to attack one who might well turn out to be from a powerful house or line. And that was no doubt why he had lived to such an age despite his injury – that, and the fact that he must indeed be formidable in combat.

'Do you know where Mentor Ho'zen had his chambers?'

This was not the response the gnarled warrior had expected. His head wove back and forth as if he mistrusted his senses. 'Ho'zen served the house of Faal, did he not?' There was a sharp intake of breath. 'You have travelled the realms, yes?'

Very smart. 'Your house or line?'

'None ... master.'

'Would you have one?'

'I do not know what you mean, master,' the battle mentor replied in honest confusion.

'Do you know the alien concept of *loyalty*?'

'No, master.'

'It means serving another without ever thinking to betray them. It means turning your back to another and being sure no attack will come from them. It is conspiring with another without any promise of individual advantage.'

'It is like belonging to a house or line, master?'

'Yes, but without the need for common blood.'

The elder was silent for a while, wrestling with the idea. 'It is more like belonging to a faction.'

'Yes, and no. It is a faction that has the closeness of house or line.'

'It is ... strange.'

'It is what I offer you.'

'In return for?'

'A loyalty that we both serve. You will be as a member of my house.'

'It is ... interesting, but there are terrible dangers. Other houses and factions will be turned against me.'

'There are also great rewards. The sort of rewards that have otherwise always been denied you, based on your rank, caste, poor birth and misfortune.'

More silence. 'This is a trick. It cannot be anything else.'

'There is nothing you have that I could not take if I wanted it. I could

82

force you into my service or, more obviously, buy your cooperation. I do neither of these things. Loyalty requires that you choose freely. If you make that choice, we are allies, not master and servitor. You are raised to the level of my house by it, and thus a stronger asset to me. I am therefore stronger. We both gain, but only as long as we both succeed. Should one of us fail, then so does the other.'

'Still it feels wrong.'

'And it will only feel more so, for it is not the way of our kind. Refuse it and it will be as if we never met. I will leave you begging for a continued existence, if that is the rightness of our kind that you so crave. I will leave you as the mere cripple who was once the champion of the fighting pits. I will leave you to your darkness and dusty memories. I will find another, for surely there are others like you.'

'Is this how you destroyed other realms? I fear you will also destroy us. It is too much difference. It is *instability*.'

'I will share a secret with you then. It is already the way of the other realms. It is the entire Declension that represents difference and *instability* to those other realms.'

The elder hardly dared whisper, 'Yet you would risk making us like those other realms? You would make us like the *lower beings*? It is as mad as it is senseless. It is treason against *her* will. They were right. You are *unstable*, scion of Faal.'

The elder had levelled the worst of insults at him. By rights, he should tear the ancient warrior limb from limb and suck out his insides. Instead, Ba'zel said, 'Then I will leave you here a mere cripple, rather than take you with me as a member of the house of Faal. You will mention nothing of this encounter to anyone. I will know it if you do and it will be your end. Step aside now, mentor.'

'Wait.'

'There is no more to be said and my time is too important to be wasted on a mere cripple.'

'I ... I will take you to the chambers of Mentor Ho'zen. You wish to enter, yes? I will capture a tunnel troll along the way and we will use it to trip the wards and snares protecting those chambers. One less tunnel troll to speak of our passing can only see us the safer.'

'I do not wish to keep you from your begging. Why would you do this? I must think it a deception.'

'It is no deception. I am not entirely sure why I do this, but I will have time to think more as we go.'

'What is your name?'

'Battle Mentor Dra'zen, master.'

'Very well. Then lead on, Battle Mentor Dra'zen, and let us go quickly.'

The chambers of Mentor Ho'zen were small indeed – little more than a resting place, desk and cupboard – and generally all that might be expected of a lowly mentor. What Ba'zel had not expected, however, was to find such a profusion and clutter of ancient scrolls. They filled the cupboard, covered the desk, had spilled onto the floor and even littered the mentor's bed.

Mentor Dra'zen cautiously lit a candle. 'I hardly dare move. I will either dislodge or trample these scrolls, or send them all up in flames.'

'Surely it is not usual for a mentor to have quite so many, is it? They are too valuable,' Ba'zel murmured.

'Indeed. And some of these are so ancient I would only expect them to be in the possession of one of the very highest rank.'

Ba'zel carefully unfurled one of the most yellowed scrolls. He winced at the slight cracking sound. 'It is in an antiquated style. Are you familiar with such, Mentor?'

Mentor Dra'zen peered closely at the scratches on the scroll. 'It is by one called Israine, of whom I have never heard. Hmm. It is neither *Interpretation*, *Inference*, *Implication* or *Iteration*. It appears to be a *Treatise*.' He abruptly turned his eyes away from it. 'If it is a *Treatise*, then it must represent an old line of thought that should have been expunged. We must destroy it. It is forbidden to read it.'

'What was it doing in Ho'zen's possession? It must have been given to him to read. If we can but ascertain the general nature of its contents, that might tell us from where it came and why it was likely given to him.'

'It would not be wise to read even for gist. Were we to take on but one word too many, then the line of thought might be reborn in us through implication, inference or speculation. We would be expected to end ourselves before the thought could be spread any further.'

Ba'zel, we are summoned by the council, came Faal's thought. *We are out of time. Have you found anything?* 'We must know. You must glance at it. Now.'

Mentor Dra'zen reluctantly obeyed. After a few moments his eyes widened. '*Instability!*'

'What?'

'It is a *Treatise* upon the nature of *instability*, upon whether it exists or not. Do we repeat ourselves over and over? Does the cosmos repeat itself for ever? Or does our existence actually represent an *instability* in the cosmos? Surely we are not all *unstable*, are we?'

Of course. *Yes, Father, I will have a scroll brought to your chambers. I will join you at the council when I can.* 'Enough. Battle Mentor Dra'zen, take it to my father's chambers as fast as you can. Set new wards around this place here. I have another matter to which I must attend.'

What do you mean when you can? *Except for word from her, the summons of the Council takes precedence over all. You must accompany me at once. Ba'zel! Do you hear me?*

He did not bother to reply. Instead he assumed his spectral form and rose through the rock as quickly as he could.

Storms of darkness. No direction. No reference point. Lost. Adrift. Black lightning piercing his soul. This then was death. It was everything he had prayed it would not be. Inevitably.

Ba'zel rushed into the tail end of the storm. He sensed something out there. There was no more time. Even through the dust he saw the sun pulsing like a heart. Waves of radiation battered him and cruelly pitted his hard exterior. He could not survive here long.

'I have returned as I promised! Where are you?'

We hear you, came the voice of the sifters, the storm-stalkers who were the only things that could survive on the surface of the home-realm.

'They ask that I lead them. What must I do?'

They will follow and hunt you, whether you will it or not. There is no escape.

'I know it. There has never been any escape, I now realise.'

In that the Declension are timeless. They must not be permitted to become entirely so, or the cosmos will be theirs to do with as they wish.

'In leading them, I will bring about the destruction of the seventh.'

Yes.

'There is no escape?'

There is no escape.

'When I think of the seventh's end, I feel ... I am not sure of the word for it.'

You feel grief and sadness. You feel as if you yourself are being destroyed.

'Yes, that is it.' He paused. 'I must go to the council now.'

And you will return to us again one day, after you have seen the Declension into the seventh.

He bowed his head. 'I will do so. All come to you eventually, do they not, even if only as dust?'

We sift the dust of the cosmos. Come eternity, all will have been sifted. From that too there is no escape. Remember it well, Ba'zel of the Declension.

'I will remember.'

He had defined his own death, he realised. The Saviours had won after all, then. There had never been any escaping them. He saw them there in the storms of darkness. He was circumscribed by their will. Six fearsome creatures stood in a circle around him, lancing and pinning him with their gazes.

'I have failed,' Jillan mourned.

No, it is I who have failed you, Ba'zel thought as he suffered the scrutiny of the six faction heads arrayed around him. Had Jillan just spoken to him? How was that possible? What connected them?

This is death and hell, is it not? Jillan asked. *Or is this the nether realm? The Saviours rule here now, do they not?*

We do not rule your nether realm yet, but will soon. Jillan, can you find no way to prevent it?

I do not know how. I am lost. I am dead, buried beneath the sands of the desert. Ba'zel, I am sorry, I have failed. To think of all those who sacrificed themselves — my parents, Haal, the Godsenders, Thomas, Slavin, so many mountain warriors — and still I have failed. Even in death there is no escaping the Saviours. I realise that now. We were foolish ever to have stood against them. What have I done? Ba'zel, what have I done? So many deaths my fault. So much blood, my soul has drowned in it. Minister Praxis was right all along. Sacrifice and duty safeguard the People against the

Chaos, *just as it is said in the Book of Saviours. He was right that I allowed the Chaos to rule my thoughts. My dark and sneaking thoughts! I connived with the Chaos, prostituted myself to it and became its creature. It was envy of the Empire, my own selfish desire, which drove me. And so many innocent people have paid for the corruption that I have spread. The safety of the Empire is gone, Haven is ruined and there are hardly any pagans left to speak of. The Geas itself will fall because of me, will it not? All will be destroyed. And now, finally, I will pay. I will suffer to the end of time with the terrible knowledge of what I have done. I am lost to the darkness of the Chaos. There will never be any to offer succour or surcease. Eternity alone with myself. I am my own punishment. It is of my own making. Being the consciousness or knowledge that was once called Jillan is the greatest of tortures. An* infinite *torture!*

Jillan described precisely the horror of being that Ba'zel also endured. There was no escape. What could he possibly say in reply to his friend? *Jillan, this is no nether realm. It is the home-realm of the Declension. We are somehow connected. Through me, a thread of your being or consciousness is here. In the same way I must be with you buried beneath the sands of the desert. Just as we share thoughts, so we can share strength, so we can share life. As I live, so must you, for I will not allow you to die, not yet.* He forced energy into his thoughts, making them shine brilliantly in the darkness of his mind, praying that the energy would be communicated to Jillan.

It hurts!

Then you live. But I must ask something of you in return. I fear to burden your soul more greatly than it is already burdened, but ask I must.

I will do whatever you ask, Jillan promised without hesitation.

It is a terrible thing.

Ask.

When we meet in person in your realm – as most assuredly we will – you must attempt to kill me, as I will seek to end you. Know this. When next we meet, Jillan of the seventh, it will only be as enemies. With that, Ba'zel of the Declension severed the connection and bowed to Elder Parsus, head of the Faction of Insistence, Convenor of the Council of Factions.

His eyes were open, but the dark was so absolute Jillan could not tell if he was blind or not. He could believe he was in the land of the dead, which might also explain why his limbs were now unencumbered. A drop of blessed moisture fell between his parted lips and he suddenly knew what it was to be alive and thirsty. So thirsty. Another drop and he was mimicking a suffocating fish. A trickle of water. He gulped it too quickly and coughed and spluttered. Something shifted. The water stopped.

'Who's there?' he croaked.

'I feared you were dead, friend Jillan,' came a relieved voice.

'Freda? Thank the gods! Where are we?'

'A place where the light cannot find us. Unlike you, friend Jillan, I have nothing for which to thank the gods. Quite the opposite. Indeed, if you are truly my friend, then you will help me bring darkness to them all.'

Through the rock of the subterranean hollow in which Freda and Jillan hid, holy Gar heard the rock woman's words. He sighed, his heart heavy with grief for his daughter.

Through the water, holy Akwar heard Freda's words. He was outraged by her blasphemy and immediately fell to conspiring with his brother Sinisar. Then he whispered to the shadows and his brother Anupal, the Lord of Mayhem, he who had magnanimously freed Akwar from the prison contrived by the cursed Izat beneath the city of Shangrin.

CHAPTER 4:

As happens to all things and plans

Chief Aspin and his fifty sky warriors flew down the mountain towards Godsend. Each made their descent in their own way, competing to be the first down. Where Altith was slight and hardly seemed to touch the ground, Lars used his weight to slide through slopes of shale no one else would brave. Aspin himself kept his knees bent the whole time and used a springing run, his steps becoming longer and longer until he outstripped all of them, all of them but Torpeth. The naked warrior stepped on the air and swirled down drops that would have killed anyone else. He rode the wind, easily avoiding all obstacles the ground sought to place in his path.

Aspin knew he did well even to keep the holy man in sight. Then a strangeness began. When Torpeth next touched the ground he struggled to lift off again, as if the weight of the mountain was pulling him back. At the same time Aspin felt strength come up through his legs, and he propelled himself onward with his most prodigious leap so far, fully twenty feet. He felt giddy as he reached the top of the jump and saw just how far he would fall. He struggled to stay upright in the air and frantically whirled his arms backwards to prevent himself pitching head first to his death. Yet how could he hope to land safely? His ankles would be crushed under him as he came hurtling down. Should he attempt to go into a roll? No, the momentum of his passage towards the lowlands would only increase that way, until he smashed into a boulder or tumbled over a lethal drop.

He came down hard and reflexively winced, expecting to jar every bone in his body. Instead, his joints held firm and the ground seemed to cushion him before lifting him into another giant leap. He was suddenly making up ground on Torpeth. Meantime the holy man had trouble lifting his head, let alone his leg. The naked warrior cried out to Wayfar, and a storm front came racing from out of the mountains to lift Torpeth bodily free of his predicament. As he was sent skirling on, winds battered Aspin back, so that he all but landed where he'd started.

The ground trembled and then slid out from under the chieftain of the mountain people. He cried out in terror as he rushed forward with the landslide, but he found he was not buried. Rather, it carried him on the most exhilarating ride of his life, as if he was rafting the roaring rapids of the spring melt. 'Look, he's just ahead. We'll catch him!'

Torpeth hung like a rag doll, as if his hands, head and feet were heavier than the rest of him. As strong as the currents of air that carried him were, his shape in the air was not properly dynamic. Apparently some competing force attempted to pluck him out of the sky and bring him back down to earth. The holy man would be pulled up one moment and back down the next. 'Stop! You will tear me in two. Stop,' he moaned.

The storm front darkened the sky, rumbled a warning and then struck the ground with lightning. The bolt landed worryingly close to Aspin, deafening him and causing every hair on his body to rise. The electricity had torn and scarred his vision. He no longer knew up from down or earth from sky. Did screaming and grinding teeth of stone now rear up to bite the heavens and bring them down? Or did the heavens smite at the earth to obliterate all that walked upon its surface? Either way, he was caught between them and powerless to do anything about his own survival. He was completely at the mercy of the devastating and careless forces of nature.

'Ye gods, preserve me!' he prayed, but could not even hear himself amid the war and clamour. 'Preserve us, for our task is too important to fail! Hear us. Saint Azual will come again!'

Torpeth was suddenly flung out of the sky down at Aspin. Their heads collided and Aspin saw glittering stars, spinning worlds, impossible reaches of the cosmos and a flea crawling out from between Torpeth's hairy buttocks. The landslide slowed, as if to take in the scenery, meandered through a stand of fir trees, took them to the bottom of the mountain and abruptly stopped, as if no longer wishing to travel with them. Even the storm front had apparently decided to have nothing further to do with them, for it had moved off towards Godsend.

Aspin and Torpeth lay unmoving for long moments. Then the holy man said, 'Now see what you've done, silly ox. In your vanity you thought you could best me, but instead you ended up bringing down half the mountain. It's only half the mountain it was. Serves you right if it gets angry with you and won't let you anywhere near it again. And mountains stay angry for a long time, you know, a *very* long time. All this for what, silly ox? Nothing. You did not best me, because none can. You should know that. Learn not to overreach. It is as important for a chief as a silly ox.'

'Old goat, you're sitting on my hand. Move your filthy behind before I catch your fleas. Now, trying to blame me for the mountain coming down is like me trying to blame you for the storm. It's just plain silly.'

'Omens are *not* silly. If you think them silly, it is only because you are a silly ox. No, omens are a matter of the gods. You need to read the world as well as you read a soul, Aspin Longstep. If you learn to read the world, then you will read the souls of the gods!'

'To do so would be a blasphemy. Their divine souls are sacrosanct.'

Torpeth shrugged. 'It's for their own good. Stops them getting too big for their boots. Besides, you can't always trust them. Look at what has just happened. They might have killed you.'

'You do not know that. Besides, the storm and landslide may have been natural occurrences and nothing to do with the gods.'

Torpeth glared at him. 'And you do not believe that. Since when have you been able to stride like a giant? Since when has any been able to match he who once commanded the gods? I would tell you to stop being a silly ox, but a silly ox is what you are. What, then, should I tell you, Chief Silly Ox? I used the power of Wayfar to aid my progress. I was hampered by the earth. There can be no doubt it was Gar. And Gar aided you. Wayfar and Gar used us. We tested ourselves against each other, as well as against the world and its gods. In the same way the world and its gods tested themselves against us and *through* us. It is as clear as the sky now seems.'

Aspin sighed and stood up. He looked down at the holy man, who remained sitting where he was but was now eyeing the sky suspiciously.

'Do you really think the gods would have killed me? Why did they not do it? Was it because I mentioned the Saint? Old goat, what do your omens tell you? I am listening, old goat.'

'Eh? What's that you say?'

'What do your omens tell you?'

Frowning furiously, Torpeth met his gaze. 'They tell me nothing good, Aspin Longstep. They tell me that the gods would happily use us mortals as playthings, or pawns with which to fight one another. They tell me that our lives are of no value to them. They tell me that the gods could very well be the enemy we seek.'

Hella poured herb tea into an earthenware cup and took it over to her father Jacob, who pored over a ledger at their kitchen table. He'd just meticulously entered the new supplies into the inventory, but continued to check over the numbers in search of a mistake. It was unheard of, however, for the trader to make any error with his record keeping. 'Here, Father. Refresh yourself after your journey. Leave off the numbers for now. They will still be there in the morning.'

Jacob leaned back in his chair with a defeated sigh. He closed his eyes for a second and squeezed the bridge of his nose between thumb and first finger. Hella placed a hand on his shoulder. He patted the hand affectionately and then squinted up at her with a tired smile. 'You're a good girl. Step into the light so that I can see you properly. Things are not so bad that we need to scrimp on the candles, you know.'

Hella frowned slightly. 'There are as many candles lit as always.'

Jacob harrumphed. 'Well then, the nights are getting darker. Or my eyes haven't yet adjusted from the brightness of the desert.'

'You need rest, Father,' Hella urged, pushing the tea into his hands.

As Jacob sipped the hot restorative, Hella looked more closely at him. With shock, she realised that what she had taken for mere weariness in her father were signs of old age. His hair was not dusty from the desert – it had turned grey. The lines on his face were not there because he was expressing care or joy – they were fixed wrinkles. His flesh did not sag simply because he sought to relax – he was losing his strength. When had it happened? How could she not have noticed before? It made her afraid. 'You've been overdoing it again. I told you to leave the loading and unloading to the guards Captain Gallen assigns you.'

'I do so. They happily do such work. I think they are otherwise bored.'

'Then you take too many trips without respite. It seems you are on the road more now than ever. It's not fair on yourself or the horses.'

Jacob glanced down at the numbers and shook his head. 'These supplies will hardly last two weeks. The valley does not feed us as well as it once did.'

'There are too many people here now. We seem to be supporting more Heroes here than we ever did in Godsend. And we shouldn't need any of them! We have to start limiting their numbers. Captain Gallen will have to start organising his own supply wagons.'

Jacob pulled a face. 'General Thormodius's army in the new Fortress of the Sun simply does not have more to trade or supply us with. True, Gallen's wagons could travel further afield, but the distances are very great and Gallen's own wagons would simply compete with the general's. Worse, Gallen's wagons might start competing with my own and then prices will go up. No, we must stay united as a community. I am already concerned that the barracks are beginning to operate as a separate community within Haven. It is not healthy, daughter.'

She nodded. 'There was trouble while you were away. The Unclean and Gallen's men. Samnir and Ash.'

Jacob groaned. 'You see? We must come together before the divides make themselves too great. I hate to say it, but we must have a council to decide things, as once we did in Godsend.'

Hella hesitated, uncomfortable with the idea. What would Jillan say?

Jacob sensed her unease. 'I know, daughter. Yet a council does not mean we have to be like we once were. We do not have to afford the families of council elders greater privilege than any other. We do not have to exclude the Unclean. We do not have to bow to the evil demands of a child-suborning Saint. As long as we remember ourselves, all will be well, you'll see.' He shut the ledger firmly and gave her his best grin. 'We will talk more of it later. Enough for now, though, lest we forget the greater joys of life. Come, tell me how the wedding preparations progress, and how you will make me the proudest father in the world. Tell me how even the gods will envy Jillan.'

She could not help her own grin and a creeping blush. 'Mistress

Halson has all but completed the dress with the material you brought. It is the most beautiful dress I've ever seen, Father!'

Jacob took Hella's hands in his own. 'You will make men forget their own names, my daughter. Your mother was the same, you know. General Thormodius has confirmed that he will come here in two weeks to conduct the ceremony.'

Hella yelped excitedly. 'Two weeks! But there is so much still to do. The Gathering Place needs to be decorated. The musicians for the dance need so much more practice if we are not to have dogs howling in accompaniment. Oh, and the inn! Samnir will simply have to let Ash out of the punishment chamber at once!'

Jacob laughed. 'Ash is in the punishment chamber? What's that rogue been up to now? Doesn't he know no one can save him if he ruins my daughter's wedding?'

Hella wrinkled her nose. 'The stew! It's burning!' She hurried over to the small hearth to swing the cooking pot off the coals. 'Here's me getting carried away with myself and meanwhile my road-weary father's dinner is being spoiled. This is Jillan's fault! He was meant to have been here in good time for the meal. What's keeping him so?'

'He's probably just lost track of time. You know what it's like when a man's about to get married. It's the duty of every other man to procure a bottle from somewhere to mark the occasion. Go and look for him, daughter. I'll content myself with some bread and a nap until you come back.'

'If he's drunk, I'll kill him. You promise not to start working on the ledger again?'

'Yes. Now give your father a kiss and off you go. Go save Jillan from himself.'

Hella planted a kiss on Jacob's cheek, donned her dark blue cape and went out into the night. Although there was precious little moonlight, the lights from the other houses were more than sufficient for her to navigate around the lapping lakelet and up to the silent Gathering Place. The light from Jillan's own home then guided her the rest of the way. It also promised there was someone home. She rapped on the door impatiently.

After a delay it opened, and Samnir was silhouetted against the interior. 'Who's there?' he asked dully.

'It's me. Hella. Jillan's meant to be coming to dinner. And he invited you as well, yes?'

'No.'

She waited, but the commander did not expand. 'Well, is he in?' She tried to look past him, but he narrowed the door.

'Jillan?'

'Yes, of course. Jillan.' What was the matter with him? Was he hiding something? 'Is he in?'

'No.'

'Then where is he?'

'He's not here.'

'You've already told me that.' She became suspicious. 'Samnir, tell me where he is.'

'I do not know where he is.' The answer was listless.

Was the soldier ill? 'When did you last see him?'

'I ... I have not seen him ... since he went into the desert,' he said vaguely.

'Desert? What do you mean he went into the desert? Where was he going? Hasn't he come back? When was this? Samnir!'

'I-I can't remember.'

'What?' She was exasperated, worried and angry all at once. 'What do you mean you can't remember? Samnir!'

Hella peered more closely at him to try and read his face in the dark, but he tilted it away as if listening to someone inside the dwelling. When he spoke, the uncertainty was gone from his voice, but his words were intoned as if they were not his own. 'I cannot be expected to know the comings and goings of every other person, let alone the reasons for what they do. I am not Jillan's keeper. He may have returned. He may be playing cards with Captain Gallen. Goodnight.'

He began to close the door, but she pushed back against it, saying frantically, 'Samnir, this is Jillan we're talking about! Don't you care? What if something's happened to him?'

He looked down at her with eyes as dark as the night. 'Jillan can look after himself.' The door was slammed shut.

Hella stood with her mouth hanging open, staring at the door in disbelief. Samnir had become someone she didn't know. Where had the soldier she'd fought shoulder to shoulder with gone? He'd spoken to her as if he didn't know her. Was it something she had done, or Jillan?

She backed away in confusion. What was going on? What about Jillan? Had Samnir argued with him? Was that why the old soldier acted so coldly and why Jillan had left? Was Jillan still out in the desert? If he was out there on his own, he might be in trouble … serious trouble. She didn't like to think about it. Maybe Jillan *was* playing cards with Captain Gallen after all. She turned for the path that would take her towards the barracks. Yes, if he was playing cards and had lost track of time, that would explain why he was late for dinner.

She was worrying needlessly. She was being silly. Everything was fine. She was just being silly. Samnir was probably tired and being his usual grumpy self. She was just being silly.

You know that's not true. You've never *been silly. You were never like Elder Litten's daughter Julia, who simpered so that the boys would carry her school books for her, or sobbed whenever she heard a sad story. You are* not *being silly.* Hella went over the scene with Samnir again. He hadn't just been grumpy. He'd been reticent and unsure of himself at first. That wasn't the man she knew, the decisive commander who had led battles as the Sand Devil and slain Saviours in front of the Great Temple. Something was wrong, very wrong.

She didn't believe Jillan was playing cards with Captain Gallen. The barracks were not the right place for such games, and the inn was closed because of Ash's incarceration. Jillan was capable of losing track of time, but he would not have missed night falling and would have known he was due for dinner. And why hadn't he passed on her invitation to Samnir? What had happened? Jillan was in trouble. She was sure of it now. She knew it in her heart and mind. She knew it from the pain in her gut and the ache in her bones.

He needed help. She would make sure Haven provided it, whether they liked it or not. All of them. Gallen, Ash, Tebrus, every last one of them. They would have to put their selfish differences aside for a while. Her father had been right about having a council to bring them all together and organise things. And if she could not persuade them, then she would *force* them to help. Without a qualm she would use her power of command to ensure that Jillan was safe and that this damned wedding went ahead as planned. It was the least they could do.

Samnir *had* been hiding something. She turned on her heel, marched back up to his door and hammered on the wood. 'Open this door!'

Torpeth insisted on presenting Aspin as the new chief to the small group of mountain people who now occupied Godsend. 'It will allow us to recruit a few more warriors, if we're lucky,' the holy man adjudged. 'And our people here will know better than us how matters stand among the lowlanders. We may learn something, eh, silly ox?'

As it was, ten extra warriors agreed to join them, although they seemed more enthusiastic about visiting Hyvan's Cross to explore new trading opportunities than serving the immediate interests of their new chief. Several of them even needed reminding that bringing their spears might be as important as carrying sample goods all the way to the central city of the region. When asked about the affairs of the lowlanders, the mountain people who now called themselves Godsenders explained that relations between themselves and the lowlanders were largely amicable, just as holy Wayfar had proclaimed things should be. However, they whispered, glancing around nervously, the priests were quite zealous when it came to collecting taxes for the rebuilding and further decoration of Wayfar's temple. It made it difficult for Godsend to build wealth or thrive, the new chief had to understand, so it was hoped he would show wisdom beyond his years and forgo any tribute or gift that might be owed to him by Godsend to mark his elevation.

'What are these things of which you speak, warrior?' Aspin asked the one called Bantith, although the Godsender had apparently adopted the appellation *Trader* Bantith.

'Chief Aspin,' the richly dressed man said earnestly, 'I have spoken truly. In trade one's word is as binding as a holy vow. They call it a *contract*. The mountain people of Godsend are known as honest traders. It is why the lowlanders are content to continue trading with us. I am not short-changing you, Chief Aspin, believe me. We simply do not have coin we can spare. That which we have is essential to us, for something called *cash flow*. Without it we will likely starve.'

There was snickering among Aspin's warriors, who were arrayed around Godsend's inn, the place chosen as the most appropriate for the receiving, hosting and sending off of the new chief. 'How can you starve?' Lars called. 'The surrounding woods are full of game. Or have you traded away all skill with a spear? We will send Blind Pol down the mountain to you, for even he could feed himself here.' There was open laughter.

Aspin tensed. His men and the Godsenders had insisted upon toasting his health with the inn's strong ale for the last several hours. A belligerent insult about Bantith's hunting and fighting prowess was sure to lead to a drunken brawl. No mountain warrior would let such an offence to his honour pass without challenge.

He therefore did not know whether to be grateful, outraged or horrified when Bantith gave an indifferent shrug that bordered on the contemptuous. *He thinks us savages. He does not need to justify himself to the likes of us.*

'He is weak!' Lars sneered. 'The soft robes and ways of the lowlanders have done this to him. He is no mountain warrior.'

Aspin looked quickly to his right, searching for Torpeth. The holy man was apparently busy exploring the inn's spitoon. He had dipped a finger into the sticky contents and was sucking on it experimentally.

Chief Aspin sighed. He was going to have to sort this one out himself. 'Your chief speaks!' Torpeth made a gagging noise, but Aspin ignored him. 'The reader of souls passes judgement!' Now there was proper silence. He let it last some moments, meeting the eyes of each of his warriors, then said quietly, 'Lars, you show your loyalty with more aggression than any other, but it will see too many heads broken, heads we cannot afford, few as we are. I thank you for your loyalty, therefore, Lars, but another word from you and I will tie a knot in that tongue of yours and make your big mouth swallow it.'

Lars grinned and bowed clumsily.

'As for you, *Trader* Bantith ...'

'Yes, Chief Aspin?' A precise well-practised bow.

'You should know better.'

'Chief Aspin?'

'If this had been a trade situation, do you think you would have just traded successfully with these people who had come down from the mountain?'

'I ...' Bantith hung his head. 'No, Chief.'

'No, Chief. You should know us better than any, and yet you go upsetting big Lars with talk of starvation. You talk to sky warriors of contracts and cash flow and blasphemously compare such things to our devotion to Wayfar. Have you forgotten who you are so quickly, Bantith? Have you renounced the way of the warrior entirely? Do you renounce your own people, those who helped make you what you are now? How can that be? You may as well renounce the sky, your left foot or holy Wayfar himself.'

'I ... I ...' Emotions warred across Bantith's face.

'If it is we who helped make you what you are now, however, then whatever we think to accuse you of, we are also guilty. *We* should know better. *We* forget ourselves. We should *all* be on our guard, therefore. We must remember ourselves, or I fear it will be our end. Look at how few we are. See how reduced we are. Yet still we are at each other's throats. Will we be forced to destroy ourselves? Must we? Surely this is not why we fought the Empire and the others for so long. Surely this is not why so many of our people sacrificed themselves. Bantith, when you fought not so long ago beside us at the Great Temple of the others, was it in the hope that you might one day stand here like this in your pretty robes, at odds with your own people?'

'No, it was not,' Bantith said quietly.

'No, it was not. In the same way, I never hoped to be a war chief leading the last of us in search of whatever enemy it is that seeks to raise Azual and claim us all. The enemy has not been idle, and has already begun to change the world around us, so that we seem out of step, crude, ridiculous and irrelevant. Do not be embarrassed to think us so, Bantith, for I know how we seem even to you. I have read it in you. The world has been changed around us and we did not properly notice until now. It makes us look dull and ignorant. It causes you to shrug at us with a mixture of indifference and contempt. I fear we are already too late to do anything about it. How can we fight the entire world? We cannot. How can we return the entire world to what is already past? We cannot. Our enemy is invisible to us. We do not know or understand the seat of the enemy's power. What then is left to us? Are we but nothing? Are we but the sigh of dying winds? Well? *Are we?*'

'No!' came a few scattered shouts.

'Answer me! *Are we?*'

'No!' his sky warriors shouted in fierce concert.

'No, we are *not* nothing. We must remember who we are in our hearts and as a people. We must remain proud. If we cannot wake each

99

day with memory of who and what we are, then we will not have any relation to the world around us, and that world will be lost to us. *We* will be lost. All will belong to cursed Azual. He will have drunk the essence from our bodies, minds and souls. We must *never* forget who we are, or all is lost.'

'I am ashamed of myself,' Bantith moaned.

'Be not so, good Bantith. This is not of your making. I believe you have suffered more than most, caught here between worlds. You have been near pulled apart by competing loyalties to your people in the mountains, the Godsenders, traders from other communities, the low-landers, holy Wayfar himself and his priesthood. You have done well just to remain faithful to yourself. In fact, I would have you – along with Lars – as my immediate advisers as we head to Hyvan's Cross. We will need strength and wit in equal measure, assertion and circumspection.'

Torpeth cleared his throat noisily.

'Old goat, you will no doubt give me advice whether I name you adviser or not.'

'That is true, silly ox. For, as you said, we would not want you forgetting yourself, now would we? You should therefore be grateful Torpeth the Great sees fit to share his wisdom with you.'

'We would be more grateful if you didn't also share your fleas with us and attract flies.'

The sky warriors laughed and nudged each other with elbows. Torpeth looked around with an excessive display of care and suspicion. 'Flies? Yes, I see them now. Why do they hover so close? Particularly that one. I have seen it before. Do you think it might be a spy? I remember there was a Saint who commanded the very insects of earth and air.'

The sky warriors exchanged glances, shook their heads and waggled their fingers to signal madness. Aspin smiled. 'Perhaps a bath would properly test it.'

'What? Do you run mad, Chief Silly Ox? We have no time for such things. The world stands in the balance! Save it, and I will have the rest of eternity for a bath. Until then we waste time even discussing it. Would you have us left entirely behind? Let us go then at once and see if we can outpace this fly! Come, silly ox, before you weigh yourself down too much with weighty matters.'

*

'Who's there?' Samnir asked dully.

'We will organise a search for Jillan.'

The commander was silent for a moment as if deliberating or struggling to process what he'd heard. 'We will organise a search?'

'Of the desert. We will send word to General Thormodius as well.' Hella put a measure of compulsion into her voice. 'You will help me, Samnir.'

'I ... I ...' He tilted his head back inside the dwelling.

'Who do you have in there with you? Tell me.'

'I cannot ... It is none of your concern.'

'And another thing! It's high time you let Ash out of the punishment chamber, don't you think? If you don't, you'll have a riot on your hands. And you'll be on your own with this one.'

'Ash?' he asked woodenly. 'How long has he been in the chamber?'

'Well, you should know, seeing as you're the one who put him in there. You're the only one who can let him out. You have the key.' Her voice thrummed with power. 'Go and get it. Now!'

Samnir turned away, letting go of the door. Hella seized her chance and pushed inside. Her eyes swept the room. There, in a shadowed corner, crouched a semi-naked woman with a hideously disfigured face.

'Who are you?' Hella asked, fighting the instinct to run.

The woman rose and attempted a smile, although it pulled her ruined face into a snarl more than anything. 'Do not be alarmed. I am an old friend of Samnir's. We are *close* –' the woman stepped into the light and rested a hand on the soldier's shoulder '– Samnir and I.' Her eyes were a mesmerising blue and held Hella where she was. 'You interrupted us during a private moment, my dear.'

Hella felt heat rising into her cheeks. This explained everything. This was why Samnir had wanted to get rid of her. This was what he'd been hiding. And she'd gone and embarrassed him terribly. She was mortified. She felt like such an idiot. 'I-I'm so sorry. I didn't realise that ... that ...' *Samnir might have a life of his own, that he might want to share his life with someone, no matter what she looked like.* Hella realised she had been so wrapped up in her own life and worries that she had not stopped to think about anyone else. Of course a grizzled old soldier could be lonely or in want of company. She'd simply been so used to seeing Samnir alone that no other possibility for him had ever occurred to her.

'Oh, that's alright, my dear. Now you're here, come in and we can get better acquainted.' The woman took a deliberate step towards Hella, beckoning with long fingers.

Jillan had no doubt absented himself so that the couple could be alone together. Hella backed towards the door. 'I should not have intruded. I-I will go and find Jillan. He's probably been playing cards with Captain Gallen all along.'

'Oh, but I insist. Hella, isn't it? Samnir and Jillan have told me so much about you. Stay. I hope that we can be friends, my dear.'

Hella found herself nodding. 'They have? Yes, of course. I'm sorry, I have to go. My father is waiting and the stew will now be getting cold. Goodnight.' She continued to edge backwards.

'Samnir, darling, make her stay.'

A bewitching smile. How could she have ever thought this woman was ugly? Such beautiful eyes. Hella's heel caught on a flagstone that was not completely flush with the others and she stumbled, her gaze breaking from the woman's own. Samnir's hands swept through the air over Hella's head as she lost her balance and turned in the same motion. Had he been trying to grab her or save her from the fall? She didn't know. She blinked hard and caught herself against the door, then fled into the darkness without a backward look.

She ran blindly, not slowing until she heard the lapping of water ahead of her over the sound of her panting and her thumping heart. She'd taken the path round towards the barracks, as far as she could judge. Yes, she could smell the latrines. The giant black hands smothering the stars had to be the thick oak trees of the inn's hollow. Her feet squelched in something unpleasant and water seeped into her shoes. She couldn't see where she was going. She tried to orient herself by the sound of the lake. Then another sound came to her. The soft slap of feet running towards her.

He'd followed her! *Oh, Samnir, no!* She dared not call out. How could this be happening? It didn't seem real. She bit her lip to prevent a whimper of fear escaping. Was he coming straight at her? Could he see her? She stepped into deeper shadows, towards the lake.

Samnir's sword of sun-metal suddenly flared into life and caught her in its harsh light. There was no hiding. He came at her with death in his eyes.

'No!' she shrieked.

Torpeth rolled forward, leaped high, somersaulted and collapsed to the floor. Aspin watched in bemusement. 'Finished?'

'I am truly exhausted,' the holy man panted. 'I cannot catch it. It has defeated me. I did not think it possible.'

'Perhaps it is just a fly. Leave it alone and it might not bother you any more.'

'This can be no ordinary fly. I am Torpeth *the Great*. It almost taunts me.'

'You are not all-powerful, Torpeth. Leave the poor thing be. Your reputation will not suffer for it.'

'This is not about my reputation, silly ox!'

Aspin rolled his eyes. 'It's another of your omens, then?'

'Foolish warrior! If the fly is a spy, it will see, hear and report all. The enemy will always be forewarned and will elude us for ever more. Worse, if the fly is our actual enemy, then we are powerless to ensnare or defeat it. It will likely wait till we sleep and then drink of our blood. We are doomed!'

'Then let us hope it is neither a spy nor the enemy. Torpeth, with all the energy you've wasted, I'm sure you could have taken a bath and then caught back up to us. Were you to bathe, the fly would be sure to lose interest in you.'

'That is precisely what the enemy would want. The enemy knows how bathing weakens me. Bathing would be a fatal mistake right now.'

Aspin sighed. 'Then it is fortunate we go to visit holy Wayfar. His warring winds will surely thwart this fly and keep it from us. That's if you can stay on Wayfar's right side, of course. You will try not to insult him, won't you? Are you sure your very appearance will not be an insult to him? Are you sure that a bath and a loincloth wouldn't—'

'Blasphemous dolt! It was the gods' own punishment that made me the naked warrior. Were I to don a loincloth, it would be in defiance of them. *That* would be insult.'

'Alright, but you won't say anything that will … well … you know?'

'What?' Torpeth prompted, watching the fly out of the corner of his eye.

'Well, upset him.'

'Me? Upset someone? Especially one whose patience should be divine?'

'Try not to test that patience, divine or not.'

'Would you have me say the sky is green?'

'Sometimes it is.'

'Would you have me say it's green when it's actually pink, silly ox?'

'You see, there's an example. It's potentially upsetting to call someone a silly ox.'

'Only a silly ox would be upset at being called a silly ox. Thus, the silly ox deserves to be told he is a silly ox, as how else would he come to know he is a silly ox to others?'

Aspin put his hands up. 'Old goat, I concede. You are right. I should not waste my breath and time on trying to make you behave like a civilised human being.'

'Only a silly ox would try to instruct an old goat.'

'Apparently so, Torpeth, apparently so. I think I now share your exhaustion.'

'Really? I feel much recovered, and it is just as well, for we must run all the harder for Hyvan's Cross to make up for the time you have wasted. And as we go we must pray all the harder to Wayfar that the wind will be at our backs. Come then, silly ox, and let us see if we cannot outdistance this cursed fly.'

'Stay back!' Hella desperately commanded the old soldier as he stalked closer.

Samnir paused mid-step. 'Hella, I simply come to light your way. Let us go together,' he intoned. He attempted a reassuring smile, but it was more of a ghoulish grin. His eyes were wide and staring.

She tried to calm herself, so that her voice would not quaver, so that it would have more power to keep the creature that had once been her friend at bay. 'Samnir, you do not want to do this. Remember who you are!' she commanded.

His foot came down. If he made a sudden leap for her, she knew she would be too slow to turn this time. 'Oh, but I do want to do this, believe me. I have wanted to do this ever since we first met. Remember who I am?' He gave a hollow laugh as he took another purposeful step forwards. 'I remember precisely who I am. I am the *Sand Devil*. I had forgotten it, but she has helped me see it again. For far too long I have fought against it, pretending to be someone I am not. And for what? To end up an exile in Godsend? Tragic. To end up a wet nurse to you and Jillan? Pathetic. To become a traitor to the Empire I'd sworn to serve? Unconscionable. To become a foul slayer of the blessed Saviours? Damned! Do you *hear* me?' he roared at her. 'Damned! *You* have damned me!'

His sword came up and his body tensed. Hella screamed. Yet as his foot came down, he slipped in the wet mud. Slender though the chance was, it was all she would have. She threw herself through clawing low-hanging branches and into the reeds at the edge of the lake. She floundered as the blade of sun-metal scythed after her. Its irresistible edge set even the wet plants burning. Water hissed and clouds of smoke and steam enveloped them.

'Where are you, witch? Do not resist. It will be over in a second. You won't even feel it. It will be better this way. Think of Jillan. You are his weakness. His enemies have always used you against him. You have only ever made unfair demands of him. Why do you think he went into the desert? To escape you and your power to command him. He does not want to marry you. He will not return to Haven as long as you are here. Haven needs his protection from enemies within and without, but you have driven him away. I will not let you put Haven and the Geas at such risk. None will. I have spoken to Gallen and Tebrus and both agree this is how it must be. Surely you can see that, Hella. If you truly love Jillan and any here in Haven, you will let me finish you. I will do it kindly. It will be quick. It is for the best. Come to me, Hella.'

She wanted to cry out a denial but knew he was trying to goad her into revealing her precise position. There were tears in her eyes as she dragged herself into the freezing water. She did not just fear for her life. She also feared the truth behind his words. Hadn't she herself accused Jillan of not wanting to marry her? Had she commanded Jillan unfairly? Hadn't she forced Jillan into a promise when they'd last spoken? She had. She'd threatened never to marry him if they weren't married before winter, hadn't she? How could she have been so selfish? It was her fault Jillan had fled into the desert. She saw it now. She had tried to command him, like some vain and heartless Saint. She was sickened by herself. He didn't deserve this, and she didn't deserve to have him. And now she would never see him again. Who knew what enemies were out there, enemies that would come for Haven now that Jillan was gone? What had she done to him, the one that she loved? What had she done to all of them?

The fight went out of her as she drifted away from the shore, away from the light of the sun-metal and into the cold darkness. Her feet and hands were already becoming numb. Samnir thrashed through the reeds for a while longer, and then the light of his sword receded, and the edge of the lake disappeared.

'Ye gods, what have I done? What have I brought myself to? They all want me dead,' she moaned through chattering teeth.

The water answered her with lull and lilt, silt and slap. Reflected stars came together to watch her.

'Holy Akwar, is that you?' she murmured, her eyelids heavy. She desperately wanted sleep. It would be so easy just to let go.

It is me, child, the water chuckled and gurgled.

'Will you drown me?'

If that is what you wish. You will drown in your own tears otherwise, it would seem.

'He is lost to me. Tell me that he is safe and happy.'

Who is ever completely safe, child? He lives. He has been happier. Much like you.

'Will he grieve my passing? My father will, I know. My poor father.'

All mortals know grief in their time. Their eyes fill with tears and spill the waters of life. Sometimes they drown in those tears, just as you do.

'I would not have them grieve so much.' Could she return to the near edge of the lake, or did Samnir crouch there with sword concealed? Should she attempt the far shore? It was quite a way and she had never been the strongest of swimmers. Once there, surely her father would protect her from the others, wouldn't he? If he could not, then they would flee Haven. Of course! Samnir's actions and words had played havoc with her thoughts. She hadn't been thinking clearly. There was no real need for them to kill her. They could just exile her instead. Samnir's lies unravelled in that instant. 'Jillan! Holy Akwar, I would not drown. I must find Jillan. I fear for both him and Haven.' She tried to strike out for the nearest shore, searching for the bottom with a stretched toe, swallowing filthy water, coughing and choking.

Very well, child. You would have me save you and him then?

'Yes!' she belched.

I can do so if that is what you want. I can return him to you.

'Yes. Please!'

I must have something in return. The gods must be served in their own way.

Something snagged her ankle and dragged her under. Her heavy dress weighed her down. She kicked for all she was worth, panicking. Her head broke the surface. 'Anything! Tell me what you want!'

Just as I return Jillan to you, so you must help return Freda to my brother Sinisar.

'Freda? What—'

You will be bound by this agreement and will not speak of it to anyone. Fail to agree and you will surely drown. Jillan, your father and all the mortals of Haven will then be drowned in their own grief. Agree or drown!

Muck filled her nose, throat and eyes. 'I agree, I agree.'

They heard Hyvan's Cross long before it came into sight. Unearthly music and the voices of an ethereal choir filled the air in praise of holy Wayfar of the Warring Winds.

'Wondrous is it not? The walls of the temple and city have been so moulded and hollowed that the winds sing a constant paean to the god,' Bantith explained. 'Traders had told me of it, but their words could never do it justice.'

'It is beautiful, and moving,' Aspin had to admit.

'How does anyone get any sleep with such a din going on?' Torpeth grunted.

'The music is a soothing lullaby, they say.'

'What about when there's a storm?'

'Wayfar deals with his holy city as he sees fit. The clash and discord of a storm betokens his ecstacy or displeasure. Sometimes he creates great magicks with his brother Akwar to bring water for the fields, and other times he must punish his people for their transgressions. Or so say his priests.'

'Therefore the people spend most of their time seeking to please the old windbag, eh?' Torpeth huffed. 'I bet they spend more time praying, keeping him entertained and lavishing all that they have on the priesthood than they do living their own lives.'

Bantith winced. 'We should be careful what we say, respected elder. It is said the wind can carry all that is spoken to his holy ears.' As if to emphasise the point, deep warning sounds entered the choir's hymn.

'Yes, *respected elder*,' Aspin echoed. 'It wouldn't hurt to show the care, tact and wisdom of your years for once.'

Torpeth sniffed, hawked and spat. 'Very well, Chief Wouldn't-Hurt-a-Fly. I shall not call him a tyrant. I shall not call his priests extortionists. I shall not say that the people of Hyvan's Cross are deserving of their own oppression. I shall not warn you that in the time before the others came among us—' The air whipped up and stole the words from his mouth, effectively rendering him voiceless. As much as he opened and closed his mouth and strained to shout, nothing could be heard. Torpeth became enraged, frothing at the mouth, stamping his feet and shaking his fist at the sky. It caused much merriment among the sky warriors. The ethereal choir became joyful.

'Well, we did warn him,' Aspin considered.

Bantith nodded, slower to share in the laughter than the others. 'If he remains mute, he will never be able to recant, beg forgiveness and then speak words of veneration for holy Wayfar. It is a terrible punishment.'

His eyes bulging, Torpeth bent over and slapped his behind. He probably produced wind of his own, but none could tell. Lars laughed so hard that his sides pained him. Altith had to wipe tears from his cheeks.

'At least no one will be able to hear him coming. Surely that is a great advantage for a warrior,' Aspin added.

'For an assassin maybe,' Bantith said dubiously.

Torpeth stilled and his eyes narrowed. He gave Bantith a slow nod.

Aspin and his sixty sky warriors came up the narrow valley to the walled and sculpted mount that was Hyvan's Cross, the holy city of Wayfar. When they came to the gates they found the way barred, and well over a hundred Heroes watching them from the ramparts, their helmets and buckles polished to a gleam.

'Who dares approach the holy city bearing arms in such number?'

wheezed the corpulent and balding captain of the gate, his voice carrying to them despite the distance.

Bantith gestured for Aspin and the others to stay where they were and went forward on his own. 'I bring the new chieftain of the mountain people, Chief Aspin Longstep, to you. He comes on a pilgrimage to the holy city to consult with holy Wayfar. These sky warriors you see are his honour guard. They bring their weapons above all so that they might be pledged to our beneficent god. They would have their spears blessed so that they may continue to fight in his holy name. They fought for that name when no other did. It was these weapons that saw holy Wayfar served even while the citizens of Hyvan's Cross were held captive by the cruel Saviours. It was these weapons that led the southern region at the Great Temple. These are the weapons of our god! We rejoice that they liberated our friends, the people of Hyvan's Cross. We rejoice that they saw us become one people beneath holy Wayfar. We are honoured you meet us as warriors, as brothers in arms. We come to celebrate with you and praise holy Wayfar!'

Aspin waved at his sky warriors and they all cheered. The harmonies of the wind around the city rose to meet them, and a good number of the Heroes were inspired to shout in adulation and raise their weapons in salute.

'Er ... alright,' the captain blustered. 'Alright! Open the gates!' There was more cheering. 'But no funny business. We'll march you up to the temple, but then the priests will deal with you.'

They entered the city and were immediately surrounded. The only things allowed to remain dull in the appearance of the Heroes were their blades of sun-metal. Awakened, the weapons were unpredictable and dangerous, as they immediately began to heat their metal hilts and char their leather bindings. Only those wearing thick gauntlets or those magicked to a particular weapon by a sun-metal smith could use a live weapon for any sort of extended period. Their swords aside, however, the Heroes were buffed and scrubbed within an inch of their lives. They made for an impressive sight, marching to either side of the shambling and begrimed sky warriors.

'Up this way Chief ... er ...' The captain nodded. 'Chief. Make way for the chief! Citizens, stand aside!'

As they made their way up into the city, the boots of the Heroes echoing and sounding like applause, the richly clad people of Hyvan's Cross became aware of them. They drifted to the sides of the thorough-fares to stare curiously and point at their progress. There were tentative waves and calls of welcome. Others nudged each other and seemed to titter. A few children marched smartly along with the Heroes or laughingly aped the sky warriors. Bejewelled parents pulled their own offspring away and ushered them back towards the stalls of traders, to continue with their shopping. Torpeth's nakedness elicited particular attention, with countless gasps, a fair few shrieks and the occasional shout of disgust.

'Hyvan's Cross thrives, it appears,' Aspin shouted to the labouring captain.

'Holy Wayfar be praised for his favour, and his priests for their care-ful administration! The people of Hyvan's Cross are blessed for their devotion and godliness.'

'Captain,' Bantith piped up. 'Is it true that those who cannot pay their tax are put out of the city by the priests?'

The captain kept his eyes straight ahead. 'Those who are unworthy or of bad faith are necessarily put out of the holy city. They cannot be permitted to dwell in the holy presence.'

Aspin frowned. 'What becomes of those who are put out?'

'What does it matter?'

'They are still holy Wayfar's people, are they not?'

'If they have not shown proper devotion, then they are adjudged to have forsaken him in some measure. They must join the sinners in Saviours' Paradise, Heroes' Brook or God ... some other town.'

'Where they must still pay tax, no?' Bantith supplied.

'Of course.' The captain was sweating now. 'It's not just about taxes, though, Godsender,' he said breathlessly. 'There are other ways of show-ing devotion. No, do not ask me any more questions. I am just a soldier. These issues of faith should be addressed to the good priests, and praise holy Wayfar we are now arrived at the temple! I will leave you here with them.'

They had reached the plaza before the towering and wind-tunnelled temple of Wayfar. A priest who was even larger than the captain saw them and came to confront them. His robes were grey and unadorned, but made of silk imported from far across the Bitter Sea. The edge of the material rippled hypnotically in the breezes ghosting around the plaza. 'What is this? Who disturbs the sanctity of the temple environs, where the humble and penitent wait upon the divinity's pleasure?'

The captain gave a measured bow. 'Holy Father, here is the new chief of the mountain people, come to consult with holy Wayfar. May I leave these visitors with you?'

The priest tilted his head back as if there was an unpleasant smell beneath his nose and looked the sky warriors up and down. Aspin could have sworn he heard the man mutter something under his breath about lice-ridden goat skins. The priest addressed himself to Bantith: 'You are this chief?'

Bantith smiled awkwardly. 'No, good priest. I am but a trader from Godsend. Here is Chief Aspin Longstep and ... and here is Torpeth the Great, long-living enemy of the Empire and those you called Saviours.'

Torpeth stuck his tongue out. The affronted priest beckoned his own precinct guards closer and absently waved the captain away. The soldier wasted no time turning on his heel. 'About face! At the double, march!'

'Welcome to the holy city, Chief Longstep,' the priest said curtly, all the while eyeing Torpeth with distaste. 'Please join the queue and wait to be called. Here is holy Wayfar's indulgence.'

The priest held out a flat piece of wood with the number *169* painted in gold on it. He dropped it into Aspin's hand and indicated the long line of supplicants waiting along one edge of the plaza.

Torpeth's bushy eyebows came down. Aspin stepped in front of the named warrior and smiled broadly at the priest. 'Good priest, how long are we likely to wait? The matter is urgent.'

'It always is. Someone in the line might be inclined to exchange numbers with you, in return for a consideration. Alternatively, you may wish to make a donation.' The priest cleared his throat meaningfully.

Torpeth's head peered around Aspin's elbow. The holy man snatched the piece of wood, stuffed it in his mouth and began to chew on it ferociously.

'He can't do that!' yelped the priest.

'Respected elder,' Bantith pleaded, 'please spit it out!'

Aspin tried to win back the priest's attention. 'Good priest! Hear me! The lives of everyone in the line, if not our entire world, may depend on us seeing holy Wayfar as soon as possible.'

'If you *savages* think your poor behaviour will get you seen—'

Lars came looming up behind Aspin. 'Do you want me to kill him, Chief? The fat priest insults both you and our people.'

'It's alright, Lars, I can handle this. Stay back.'

'Guards!' the priest barked.

'Good priest, there's no need—'

'Arrest them!'

'Look,' Aspin growled, struggling to keep his temper. 'We don't have time for this. Stand aside or—'

'He threatens holy Wayfar's priest!' The large man stood back and theatrically pointed his finger. The guards cautiously closed on the sky warriors.

'He has raised his hand to you, Chief,' Lars rumbled. 'I think these soldiers—'

Torpeth suddenly bounced past them, grabbed the priest's offending finger and snapped it in the middle. *Crack.*

'Aiee! Holy Wayfar protect me! Aiee!' The priest fell to his knees.

'Now you've done it,' Aspin muttered.

The guards were aghast. 'Surround them!' shouted their hard-eyed officer. 'Sun-metal to the fore. Keep them penned. Archers, ready your bows!'

'Chief, shall we charge them? We can take them!' Lars insisted, elbowing aside other warriors who were just as eager as he was to get forward. Every mountain man attempted to adopt the traditional fighting stance of his people, one spear held high and one low. There were curses and oaths as the sky warriors jostled for position, accidentally trod on each other's feet and unintentionally clouted a neighbour or two. Those on the outside of the group began to feint forward, to stop them being encircled and to give their comrades room. 'Chief, it needs to be now.'

The Heroes' officer raised his hand to signal the attack. 'Ready!'

'Wayfar, strike down your enemies!' the priest cried. The wind rose. The line of supplicants scattered, screaming.

'Chief!' Lars called, barely heard over the brave challenges and insults the other warriors threw at their opponents.

The two sides would massacre each other, Aspin saw. The sky warriors had a slight advantage in numbers, but they were hemmed in and would not have the freedom to use their full fighting prowess. The archers and the weapons of sun-metal would quickly take their toll. And even should the sky warriors prevail against these Heroes, how long before more came running from every direction? They could not hope to succeed. It would effectively be the end of his people.

'Hold!' Aspin yelled. 'Put up your spears!'

None seemed to hear him. A sky warrior's spear jabbed into the thigh of a Hero who ventured in too close. The priest shouted prayers to the heavens. The ethereal choir became louder. Aspin threw his spears onto the ground and waved for Bantith to follow suit. 'Torpeth, shut him up! Do *not* kill him, do you hear?'

The holy man grinned, reached out and carefully pinched the priest's throat, completely paralysing him. The choir dropped away.

Hands raised, Aspin stepped into the lull and bellowed, 'Enough!' for all he was worth. As the eyes of his men glanced towards him, he turned his back on the Heroes' officer – a deliberate insult and one that was of course near suicidal.

The officer's hand remained poised.

The sky warriors stilled. The Heroes froze.

Torpeth twitched violently, but his hand at the priest's neck remained steady.

The choir held its pause.

There was a complete hush.

In a normal voice Aspin repeated, 'Enough.' He turned slowly back to the officer. 'You know of our reputation, do you not?'

The officer nodded stiffly.

'You have faced us in battle before?'

Another nod.

'And I have seen the discipline and effectiveness of your Heroes. It seems to me at this moment that both will live or both will die. I would suggest that in return for the life of your strong-willed priest, you simply let us walk across the plaza. See! There is no queue to protest our progress. It seems all are inclined to exchange their position with ours. We would also not wish to deprive holy Wayfar of the issue we bring for him. We will return the priest, you will let us pass and it will be as if we were never even here. Things will continue as if we'd never come to Hyvan's Cross, as if we'd never even existed. Surely honour is served on both sides. If you find it is not, then no doubt we will meet at some place and time in the future so that we may die together. You need not say anything. Do not see us. We are mere ghosts of another place and time. Or less than that.'

Aspin reached down for his spears and straightened up. He made sure to carry his weapons upright as he silently drifted forward and past the officer. He did not look back to see if his men followed him. He knew they moved like shadows between the immobile Heroes. Leaves on a storm. Raindrops on the shoulder of a mountain. The last of the sky warriors. The last breath of a once proud people.

They entered the cold shadow of the temple and went through the portal.

Inside, the temple was a vast and impossible space. Its heights were lost in darkness except for an opening at an unguessable distance through which the winds of the world funnelled down and circled around the temple. There was the suggestion of other movement among the lofty shadows – large fluttering wings, swooping nightmares and the yawning jaws of unseen creatures of the air. Lower down the temple's walls there were short tunnels to the outside that allowed those at floor level to see, but also served as points of entry and exit for all manner of bird, insect, bat and flying reptile. More light was provided by a series of sun-metal discs set into the rock at head height at intervals of several dozen feet or so. A Hero stood to attention at the side of each disc. It seemed that the discs circled the entire temple, but the place was so large that many all but disappeared into the gloom.

The guards watched the gallery of supplicants waiting to be heard and judged, who stood or knelt with heads hung modestly or faces raised beseechingly. Priests moved among them to accept offerings and confer with them in hushed tones. Most of the supplicants were told to wait and a few were sent away. Those deemed particularly worthy were brought in turn towards the middle of the floor, the focus of the temple. There the tallest of the priests heard their plea or confession. Here was the high priest, whose robes – edged with runes of gold thread – floated around him like smoke. He had a hawk-like nose and a severe mouth. He was as close as most would come to the holy of holies. Beyond him, but dimly perceived, rose the mighty throne of holy Wayfar atop a wide dais. The god was present in his temple but largely defeated the eye.

Awareness of him came mainly through other senses, it seemed, senses that all might therefore believe were beyond the physical. For were not those touched by the will of holy Wayfar moved by an invisible spirit? Were not his divine winds everywhere? Did he not hear and know all? Surely there was no greater god than Wayfar of the Warring Winds!

A mother and father were called forward with their teenage son. The boy had come of age and must now prove his devotion to holy Wayfar. Only then might he and his family be judged worthy of the god's blessing. Such youths served as inspiration or warning to all the people of Hyvan's Cross, of course. The woman was sobbing, the father's face was grim and there was fear in the boy's eyes. The high priest was gratified to see such joy, strength of faith and awe in the three of them. He was about to give them instruction when a disturbance near the entrance had him bring his head up sharply. A large group of armed and rude-looking warriors was pushing its way inside. One of the ruffians appeared to be entirely naked! 'What is the meaning of this?'

'I am Chief Aspin Longstep of the mountain people. We would have words with holy Wayfar. We are his sky warriors. None faithful to him would prevent us, lest they risk his divine wrath!'

The high priest waved the guards back. 'I am High Priest Reeva. Tell me, Chief Longstep, where you come from, is it more usual to make *demands* of your god than it is to pray for guidance in how you might best serve him? If so, then maybe you think holy Wayfar should pray to you for guidance in serving your demands? Has the pride of your people grown so great? Would you place yourselves above him?'

There was a sighing and tutting from a number of the priests present. They gave the newcomers reproving and pitying looks. A number of Aspin's men shifted guiltily. Bantith looked to be in an agony of discomfort.

Aspin refused to be embarrassed. 'High Priest Reeva, you question our faith. We have proved it to holy Wayfar himself on more than one occasion, without the need for your own approval. Does your approval now supplant his own?'

Lars tittered, drawing glares from the priests. The shining Heroes around the temple tightened their grips on their weapons and glowered at the mountain men. Reeva drew himself up and looked down upon Aspin. 'Are you too proud to have your faith tested, *Chief* Longstep?'

Torpeth shook his head furiously at Aspin, setting free all manner of beetles and scurrying things. The holy man's eyes begged him not to say another word. Aspin bit his lip. What could he do? He was trapped. He should never have bandied words with the high priest. He'd shown himself up to be precisely the sort of oafish bumpkin he'd not wanted to appear. Reeva smiled sanctimoniously.

Aspin knew he had to make them listen somehow. But how to force the high priest to do so? The warrior in him urged that he hurl his spear. It would bury itself between the preening fop's eyes and burst out of the back of his head. Yet the reader in him said the high priest had magicks of the air that would turn the spear back. A bloodbath would ensue. Holy Wayfar would not look upon them kindly after that. 'I … am not too proud,' he said.

Torpeth rolled his eyes and put two fingers to the side of his head as horns. *Silly ox!*

Thunder rumbled in the distance, and then Aspin realised it was laughter issuing from the impossibly large chest of the god. The cloud and air that wreathed the deity rolled back and his awful divinity was revealed. Storms furrowed his brow, lightning forked within his eyes and his breath filled the entire temple. Inhaling, he could take all the air from their lungs if he chose. Or he could hurl them against the rocks with an angry exhalation. On the right corner of the throne perched a mighty golden eagle. It flared its wings and set its eye hungrily on the assembly. It was large enough to bite a fully grown man in two or carry him off in its beak to be eaten at leisure. To the left corner of the throne was a black wyvern, its neck snaking on the air and its flickering tongue tasting the human morsels that had come here.

'Then, Aspin Longstep,' Wayfar's voice gusted, 'you will first witness and understand the nature of true devotion before being tested yourself. It will also provide us with some much-needed entertainment, for we tire of the constant pleading and false promises of you mortals. Reeva, have the boy who would confirm his devotion to me ascend the spire of faith.'

Aspin watched as the high priest pulled a youth of no more than ten and five years from the hands of his mother. The father nodded encouragingly to the lad, although the man's face spoke only of anxiety and fear. Reeva took his trembling charge over to the base of a tall column of rock and pushed him up the first few stairs. 'Youth, you have nothing to fear. Rejoice, for you are in the presence of your god,' he enunciated clearly, as much for the benefit of the onlookers as the teenager himself. 'Ascend and be confirmed. Show him your devotion and receive his blessing. Ask for his help and he will catch you when you fall. Be not afraid!'

Taking slow and faltering steps, the youth climbed higher and higher. He pressed himself tight to the rock, terrified of the drop, finally crouching with his back to the central column and edging up the increasingly narrow steps that way. Winds tugged gently at him, seeming to help him along one moment and teasing the next. He reached the top and shakily rose into a standing position. His back remained bent and his balance was far from certain. 'Holy Wayfar!' he warbled, his voice breaking. 'I-I come to devote myself to you, heart, body and mind. My faith … my faith is true. I cast myself from this rock –'

Aspin realised what was about to happen. His eyes went to the floor at the base of the spire. Did poorly cleaned bloodstains discolour the stone there?

'– as sign of m-m-my desire to be accepted as worthy.' His toes crept to the very edge and he instinctively leaned back, almost tipping over, before coming forward and again nearly falling. His mother made a high-pitched noise in her throat and hid her tear-filled eyes against her husband's shoulder.

'All is well,' called the high priest. 'Holy Wayfar is ready to receive you. Complete the prayer of devotion.'

'If you judge me worthy, may your winds deliver me safely to the ground. If you sh-should find me wanting, th-then may your winds only speed my descent.'

Aspin looked to Wayfar. The god stared straight back at him, apparently ignoring the boy. Aspin *read* the god's mind …

… as the youth stepped from the platform into open space.

'Torpeth, quickly!' Aspin yelled.

The naked warrior was already moving, vaulting high and skimming over the crowd's heads. The winds mocked him and tried to down him, but he anticipated their every swirl and knot and used them to propel himself forward all the faster. The air howled in anger at being so cheated.

The youth plummeted, a despairing cry coming from his lips. The god's gaze remained fixed on Aspin. The chieftain of the mountain people stared into a maelstrom and was lost to it. There was only madness and destruction here. The god had no intention of saving the boy. Quite the opposite – the boy would die as a lesson to the sky warriors. Torpeth would be too late, for no mortal could thwart the will of a god.

At the last moment Torpeth took a prodigious leap, made his body spear-straight and shot down beneath the tumbling currents of air sent against him. He slid across the floor, arms outstretched, and powerfully pushed the youth sideways at the instant of impact. Young limbs hit the floor, bones shattering and breaking through skin. The youth's shriek of agony matched the wind itself. But he lived.

'Blasphemers! How dare you interfere!' the high priest raged.

Torpeth stood up and gave an extravagant bow.

'You have been tested and have failed!' Wayfar stormed, rising to his feet. The eagle and wyvern took to the air above him, their livid cries promising terrible retribution. 'On your knees, mortals! Such sacrilege cannot go unpunished. Torpeth the Great, you have gainsaid us for the last time!'

Every supplicant, priest and Hero prostrated themselves before the incensed deity. They were joined by a good few sky warriors.

Torpeth cleared his throat experimentally and at last found his voice. 'Well, pooh to you. What sort of tyrant would be so careless of an innocent youth's life? *Entertainment*, did you call it? You disgust me.' He spat on the floor of the sacred temple.

Wayfar took a threatening step foward, a hurricane forming in his wake. 'The youth lied. In his heart he was not truly devoted to me. I heard it in his every breath. None can breathe and not be known by me. I might still have chosen to save him, but foresaw you would intervene. It was not just the youth who was tested, it was also *you*. And you failed. We see now that you have learned nothing in all the time you have been allowed, naked warrior. You will no longer be tolerated. You will be cast out of this realm for ever more. You will be exiled from all those who dwell within the care of the Geas and the gods. You will be consigned to the nether realm for the rest of eternity.'

'Holy Wayfar,' Aspin dared. 'The fault was not Torpeth's, for it was I who directed him. We have become aware of an enemy stalking the world of the Geas. Through the evil spirit of Saint Azual, it seeks to raise up the nether realm. We still do not know the nature of this most subtle of enemies. We come to you for guidance and help, for the good of all. Do not condemn us, I beg you.'

'We will not suffer you either, Aspin Longstep,' Wayfar replied without hesitation. 'You who thinks to read a god! No mortal understanding can fully encompass the divine. In your arrogance you tried to read me, but instead merely read yourself, causing you to fail. Your arrogance is your failure. It is the failure of *all* mortals. In the same way you mortals think to read the world, and think you read an elusive enemy there, whereas all you are reading is yourselves. *You mortals* are the enemy of all. You are the enemy to yourselves, your base and selfish nature seeing you fight and lie to each other. You are the enemy to your own gods, as you have demonstrated, and you are the enemy to the very Geas itself. *That* is why the faith of mortals must be tested and they must be made to devote themselves to the gods. *That* is why the lives of the faithless are dangerous and not to be tolerated. *That* is why the gods exist above mankind and why mankind must be kept down. *You* are the enemy! The grasping, conniving and wheedling ways of mankind are what seek to raise up the likes of Azual, so that mankind can claim power and greatness over the Geas and the gods. Mankind has ever wanted to *rule* absolutely. All must be named, organised and directed by the will of mankind. You call it advancement, betterment or civilisation, but those are simple euphemisms for your selfish desire to be rulers of yourselves and all that you encounter. At root it is inadequacy and individual lack that drives you. You must continually compensate for it, and silence those who might speak of it to undermine you. Well, none can silence the divine winds of Wayfar! *You will not be tolerated!*'

'Goes on a bit, doesn't he?' Torpeth grimaced.

The god came forward, gathering his strength. The huge wingspans of the eagle and wyvern cast all the humans into shadow.

Aspin reeled. Was it true? Had he completely misread everything? Was he the enemy? He had sought out his dead father and tried to bring him back to the affairs and land of the living. In doing so, had he unwittingly allowed Azual a way to rise up? Every time one of the living crossed into the nether realm, the divide between the land of the dead and the land of the living narrowed further, didn't it? If so, it was entirely because of his selfishness that Slavin had been forced to sacrifice himself!

Yet his father had said that even before Aspin's visit to the nether realm Azual had found a way to drain other spirits. Also, the headwoman had been convinced they faced a wider threat. He must not forget himself. Wayfar was bearing down on them. Aspin flung out words: 'We have done nothing wrong, damn you! We saved a life that you had shown every intention of ending. In good faith we have come all this way to bring you a warning, *holy* Wayfar!'

'Save your breath, Chief Silly Ox, for I fear you will need it,' Torpeth advised.

Wayfar unleashed the full force of his fury against them. A brutal blast hit the last of those standing. Tornadoes spiralled out from Wayfar's hands, sweeping up bodies indiscriminately and dropping them from a great height back to the floor. Air lances punched forward, decapitating those who looked up, and throwing others back against the walls of the temple. Necks and backs broke. None of the supplicants avoided mortal injury, although nearly every priest of Wayfar found the necessary chant to have the assault pass harmlessly through or around them. Most of the Heroes were unscathed because they were armoured and already back against the walls. A dozen or so sky warriors were caught unawares, but the rest proved canny and hardy enough to ride the winds and land unharmed. But now the eagle and wyvern descended towards them.

'Spears ready!' Aspin shouted, adopting the fighting stance of his people.

'You dare defend yourself?' Wayfar bellowed. 'You would defy me and the punishment that is your due, even now? So be it. Every last sky warrior will be sent with you to the nether realm, Chief of Nothing! Reeva, your priests and guards will set upon these overreaching warriors at once. Kill them all!'

The eagle swooped straight at Aspin, beak stretched wide as if to swallow him whole. Aspin made a show of bracing and extending his spears, expecting the bird to flare its wings and pull up rather than impale itself. But the king of the birds was not about to pull up for such a small and detested creature waving nest twigs. Its head came down, its wings pulled in and it dived all the faster. Aspin realised his mistake. His stance was all wrong. He needed his weight forward – on the balls of his feet – to move and duck with any speed. He saw himself in the bird's eyes and realised just how much he was hated – the mountain people had invaded the high places of the world, places never meant for humankind. They had taken what they had no right to, just as the Saviours had when coming to this world, and now their transgression would be punished absolutely. Final judgement descended upon him. It could not be held back. It could not be avoided. Would he want to if he could? Part of him understood Wayfar's disbelief that he should think to resist.

His spears shattered and flew in all directions. The eagle's beak drove into the centre of his chest and swept him off the ground. He clung on for long moments before slipping and falling away.

The black wyvern came winding through the air, its sinuous neck mazing and mesmerising. It deceived and distracted, its dripping jaws high, low and weaving. Its obsidian eyes gave away nothing.

'I am not fooled, vituperous viper,' Torpeth challenged. 'You can slink and slide all you want, and still I will pin you. I will tie a knot in that neck of yours. I will wither your wiles and wilt your wings. That is warning enough, so no wailing and gnashing of teeth once it happens, or you will choke yourself.'

The wyvern spat a jet of clear liquid that burned the floor where Torpeth had been standing an instant before. 'Troll!' it railed.

'Oo! It speaks. You are a mimic, like a mynah bird, yes? You call in a voice familiar to the prey, to lure or confuse it.'

Without warning the neck lashed down and the jaws snapped closed on air. Torpeth finished his roll, calmly reached out his hand and laid it on the serpent's wide snout. 'The weight of being!'

The wyvern's head suddenly became too heavy for its neck to support and its bottom jaw crunched into the ground, dragging the rest of its body down with it. The holy man jumped nimbly onto the top of its huge head and walked down its back. 'And now you are pinned. The earth reclaims you from the sky, and here you will remain until Gar tires of you.' He cartwheeled down from the lizard, only to be clobbered by its tail and sent spinning through the air.

'So you are defeated, reviled Torpeth,' Wayfar boomed. 'None can command in this temple but me. No god can be invoked but me.'

Torpeth hit the floor, tumbling over and over. He lay still. He drew the shallowest of breaths and pushed it back out of his broken body. 'Owww!' His limbs were a dislocated jumble of impossible angles. He slowly pulled them straight, awkwardly got to his feet and twisted his head back round the right way. 'Oo, that smarts!'

The wyvern was still down, thrashing back and forth, but unable to pull its head up. The eagle, meanwhile, was coming back round for another pass.

'Up, silly ox!' Torpeth limped over to Aspin and set the dazed and battered warrior on his feet. 'This is no time for play. Your warriors are dying. You must lead by example. It is the least you can do, having brought them to this. You are in their debt. Tackle Wayfar's villainous high priest while I bring the old windbag himself back down to earth.'

Aspin was unceremoniously shoved towards the confrontation going on between his sky warriors and the priests and Heroes. Even as he watched, Reeva threw out green-tipped prayer darts that moved through the air as if alive and unerringly found the throats and eyeballs of three of the mountain men, one of them the slight and youthful Altith. Altith staggered, and before Aspin could find his voice to call a warning a Hero stepped up behind the youth and cut him in half. *No.* The other two sky warriors seemed to lose coordination and strength, the poison from the darts quickly bringing them down. *They're dying.* The sky warriors jabbed at priests with their long-reaching spears, but the wind slapped their weapons aside and more often than not pulled them out of the warriors' grasp. Now it was all the mountain men could do to avoid the slash and thrust of the enemy, all they could do just to stay alive. They tried to jump up high, out of the reach of the Heroes' blades, but time and again the wind collapsed beneath them and took them to a sudden death.

Aspin ran at the Hero nearest to him, reading and avoiding where the soldier would cut with his blade even before the stroke was begun. He drove his palm up under the man's chin, lifting him off his feet, and wrested the short blade of sun-metal from him. He spun to find Reeva already watching him.

The high priest raised his hands over his head, drew a deep breath and began a sonorous incantation. Aspin hurled the blade end over end straight at him. Reeva broke off and impatiently gestured for the wind to deflect the weapon aside. The sun-metal buried itself in his forehead and then opened up his skull. None could deny the bright element.

Priests and Heroes cried out in woe to see their temple leader felled, allowing the sky warriors precious moments to rally to their chief and retrieve weapons as they came. Nearly half their number had been cut down.

'Target the priests!' Aspin shouted, knowing precisely what would happen as a result. The wild-eyed grey robes insisted the Heroes protect the sacred persons of the priesthood and place their own bodies in the way of the enemy. The soldiers dutifully moved to obey, but now blocked the path of any air-based magicks the priests might conjure.

'Throwing spears!' Aspin called. 'None will miss! And throw!'

Thirty spears thudded into the ragged line of Heroes, nearly every soldier falling back into the priests and knocking them down. Men screamed in horror, gurgled as blood filled their throats or cried for the gods to spare them.

The chieftain of the mountain people was in no mood to see even one of them spared. 'On them! Quickly!' he commanded. 'Pierce the throats of the priests first. Move!'

'Wayfar!' came the panicking plea of one of the prone priests. 'Strengthen your servants. Let the creatures of the air aid us!'

Quietly at first, but with an increasing frenzy and rush, the air brought a terrible pressure to bear upon the membranes and faculties of the sky warriors. Dark clouds swirled up around the temple and raced in towards the mountain men, hiding all else from view. Their world became a buzzing, stinging, choking swarm of winged insects. They could not help but breathe them in and felt small haired legs and wriggling bodies against back of throat, eyeball and eardrum.

Torpeth waited, refusing to run. The eagle's talons extended. The holy man leaped and caught the edge of one huge wing. 'The weight of being!' The eagle tilted, spun in an unbalanced spiral and then crashed into the floor, crushing a number of priests and Heroes in the process. It lay squawking in fear and confusion, unable to right itself.

Torpeth landed lightly and glared at Wayfar. 'Now for you, tempestuous godling. Come, do not pout so. Is this not entertainment enough for you?'

The deity grew ghostly wings and rose from the ground. 'Hurry towards your doom then, Torpeth, as you have always sought to do.' With a clap of his divine hands and a puff of breath, a savage blast was released to smite the small man. The floor cracked. Invisible fists followed and battered him.

Torpeth's shoulders bowed for a moment. He gritted his teeth and took a leaden step forward. Then another. 'I am grounded. It seems the earth will have none of your petulance, Wayfar. You are a child thumping its fists in a tantrum. Now I am reminded why I was forced to take you in hand so long ago. Come closer and I will put you over my knee to paddle your behind as you deserve. Will you never leave off your churlishness and ill temper? Must the world be undone before you are satisfied? Come closer, Wayfar, I say!'

'Descend to your level, lowly wretch? Is that what you would have? For all your previous punishment, you are unrepentant and entirely unchanged. Admit it, despised miscreant, and damn yourself, just as you have always damned yourself!'

'*All* are damned when one such as you uses mortalkind for entertainment, self-satisfaction and validation. You must be brought down once more!'

'Then you would bring down everything, meaningless demon, including yourself. None will permit it. The Geas will not permit it. You are named *anathema* and excommunicate from the world! See what your stubborness causes. See how others suffer and are destroyed because of you and your insistence. See how they are ended because you brought them here and refused, in your selfishness, to be told *no more*. See how the creatures of the world turn on those sky warriors who were the last humans to allow you among them. Now that they die, there are none who will have you, betrayer. None. Not a single other member of your kind will have you draw another breath in this world, or exist here for a moment longer. You are banished!'

Another few steps and Wayfar would be within reach. Torpeth hesitated. He glanced back over his shoulder. He saw the sky warriors engulfed in a black roiling mass. Despairing, he flew back to his comrades and plunged in among them. 'The fire of being!' he coughed, and flame blossomed. With a *whoosh* and a screech so high-pitched it was felt more than heard the cloud became a pillar of flame shooting up, lighting even the furthest recesses of the vast temple.

As the inferno dissipated, shock waves went out across the temple, leaving the sky warriors on hands and knees vomiting up still-moving beetles, earwigs, locusts and flies or on their backs spasming and thrashing. Torpeth touched every one of them, muttering, 'The tears of being!' and their bodies flushed and expelled insectile filth and poisons onto the temple floor.

'Up, silly ox!' the holy man chastised the dazed Aspin, setting him back on his feet and putting a spear in his hand. 'This is no time to be resting.'

Giant flocks of birds were now forming and turning all to darkness once more. Their screeches drowning out all else, thousands upon thousands of feathered servants of Wayfar hurtled down with the wind to wipe out the sky warriors.

'The fiery tears of the earth thrown up to the sky! The heavens brought low!' Torpeth roared until his throat was gone.

Lava erupted up out of the earth, sheets of molten rock and metal arcing over the sky warriors in a defensive dome. Geysers of superheated water followed, combining with the dome and creating a violent reaction to incinerate anything that lived beyond. Pressurised gases jetted upwards and cascading explosions saw the entire temple buck.

The winds howled down, stronger in this sacred place than any other, and were the exact equal of the other three forces of nature. The fabric of existence was torn by the competing gods, and the sky warriors could no longer remain fixed in the world. The temple sheared, its colours bleeding and melting one into the other in the destruction. All burned away, leaving only ash and the greyness of the nether realm.

Jacob wiped his eyes and made a few more scratches with his quill in the ledger. The pen sounded strange to his ears. Perhaps it was splitting. He examined the end of it, but it appeared intact. He dipped it in the ink and tried again. The scratching it made on the stiff paper echoed strangely. Was his hearing playing up along with his eyesight now? Perhaps Hella was right that he'd been overdoing it. But what other choice was there? If Haven could not sort out sustainable supply lines, the community would fail. What then? A return to Godsend? Would that bring them into conflict with the pagans? Jillan had given the town to the mountain people, a generous gesture of reconciliation at the time but one they might all come to regret. The boy's heart had always been in the right place, but sometimes he simply didn't know what was for his own good, may the blessed Saviours ... no, may the *gods* preserve him.

Careful, you're getting tired, he told himself. *You don't know if the gods can hear your thoughts. Who's to say they'll be any more forgiving of a slip like that than Saint Azual himself?*

Tired in more ways than one. Tired of the road, tired of competing demands, tired of guarding word and thought, tired of this old body, tired of the constant struggle. If it were not for Hella ... Where had the girl got to? The stew would be congealed. He heard a faint scratching coming from the door. Belatedly he realised that it wasn't just his quill he'd heard before. He got up from the table with a smile. It was probably the feral cat that visited them every so often when it fancied warming itself by the fire or availing itself of any stew that might be going to waste.

'Alright, old tom, I'm coming.'

Jacob unlatched the door and it fell inward, some weight slumped against its bottom half. He caught the soaking body as it fell to the floor. 'Daughter!' There was no flicker of response. There seemed no breath in her. Her yellow hair was thick with filth and plastered across her bone-white face. For all the world, she seemed a newly disinterred corpse.

'Well, that went well,' Aspin fumed at Torpeth. 'What happened to your promise not to call him a tyrant? Couldn't help yourself, could you, eh?'

'It was you who argued with Reeva, and you almost got that boy killed, remember? Is it really my fault Wayfar wouldn't listen to you, silly ox? You need to work on your influencing and negotiating skills.'

'He didn't listen because you saw fit to insult him as soon as you got your voice back, you interfering old goat! If this is how we're going to get along with our friends and very own god, who needs another enemy like Azual, eh?'

Torpeth flinched at that. 'You should not speak his name, not here in this place.'

'Where's the temple gone, Chief?' Lars asked curiously.

'Are we dead?' Bantith wondered, looking round.

'Perhaps,' Aspin had to concede.

'Certainly feels as cold as the grave,' Lars grunted.

'That we feel the cold tells you we still live. We should hold one to the other,' Torpeth instructed the group of thirty or so mountain men. 'It will slow the drain of our life energy. Be of good hope, brave warriors, for your chief has travelled the Broken Path on more than one occasion in the past. We must be quick, however, before the dead awaken to our presence. They will seek to keep us here. Aspin, you must lead us, and all must fix their thoughts upon their chieftain.'

'Where do we go, Torpeth?'

'It is as you said, silly ox. Wayfar acts as if he were our enemy. There is something changed in him. Something corrupts the gods and the natural order of things. All is divided and about to be undone. The Geas itself is threatened. Here is the hungry ambition of our enemy. Was it not ever thus? We must make for Haven with all speed and pray we are not too late.'

Ah, but I cannot have you leaving so soon, my small pagan friend, came an all too familiar and eerie whisper to make Torpeth's hair stand on end. *You were sworn to be my man-servant, do you not recall? It was to be for your own improvement. Circumstance and a certain waywardness on your part saw us rudely separated, but now I am here to correct those things. Rejoice, Torpeth, for you are reunited with your master, and we will be together for all eternity.*

Torpeth's eyes bulged as a shade came out of the drifting mists. 'L-lowlander, is that you? P-Praxis!'

It is I, Saint Praxis. You were lost, Torpeth, but now you are found. All you pagans were lost to the blessed Saviours, but now you are found. Rejoice, for do you not see their divine will and purpose at work in all this, all that has happened and all that will come to pass? They allowed their holy representative to fall in the first battle at Godsend so long ago, precisely so that all this would come about, precisely so that you pagans would willingly come to place your souls in their hands here, and precisely so that the power of the Geas would willingly come to be placed in their hands in the future. And their holy representative only fell so that he could be raised up stronger than ever before. I should never have doubted them when I was tested and found wanting before their Great Temple. Now I see that all has happened as it was ordained by their divine wisdom and will. All is as they have ordained it. Come, we will take you to the holy representative and you will join his flock. Leave off your former waywardness, Torpeth, for you are bound to us both by your oath and the drop of consecrating blood I now take.

The shade of Saint Praxis grabbed something invisible out of the air and swallowed it.

'The cursed fly!' Torpeth gagged. 'That is how you knew we came here. It was of your realm and that was why it always slipped my grasp. Yet how could it exist in the land of the living to torment me and steal my blood?'

How? Why, by the will and blood of the blessed Saviours, of course. How else? They did not forget those faithful to them, even those faithful in the nether realm. They anointed and raised up their holy representative here, created the fly and took it into the land of the living.

'One of the Saviours came here,' Aspin realised. 'How is that possible? Who allowed it? Who has monstrously betrayed all humankind?'

Who? The shade grinned. *Who allowed themselves to be used by the Chaos, revealing before the Great Temple both the ancient name Kathuula and the existence of this realm? Who was this unholiest of avatars? Why, it was ever him—*

'Do not listen! None of you!' Torpeth urged.

—the foul bane of the Empire. Jillan, he whom you have always sought to help.

'Aspin Longstep, and you others, look at me!' Torpeth demanded. 'Do not look upon this livid ghoul. Do not let it fill your eyes and mind. Heed me. Shut it out of your thoughts and fix yourselves upon Haven. Leave me here, for I have ruined all and am finally caught. Flee while you can. Flee for all our sakes! Go, Aspin Longstep, and may the Geas protect you. Lift up your feet and your spirits. Raise yourselves, you men of the mountains! Put your faith in the gods of the living once more. For Wayfar! Shout it – Wayfar!'

The warriors took up the battle cry of their people, although it sounded lifeless in that shrouded place. 'Wayfar!'

Yet the watery gaze of Saint Praxis would allow them no escape. *See the mists draw back and your escort awaiting. The veil between the living and the dead is removed. Your lives are revealed as the dreams of the dead, just as your sleeping minds have always seen and known the spirits of this realm.*

The greyness surrounding them darkened and echoed with the ranks of the Empire's dead. They were without number or limit. They were led by the ghastly and pitiless wraiths who called themselves Saint Goza, Saint Virulus, Saint Dianon, Saint Zoriah and Saint Sylvan.

Take them! The holy potentate will feed upon their souls.

CHAPTER 5:

Save those who are timeless

'It's not the first time you've saved my life.'

'It's becoming a bit of a habit, friend Jillan, no?'

'How on earth did you find me?'

A pause. 'It is partly because of me that you ended up here. I focused the light of Sinisar so that he could see you alone in the desert. He moved the sun to disorientate you.'

'Ah. I thought it was my mind playing tricks on me. It's good to know I'm not going mad.'

'I knew the general part of the desert you were in, and when I came here sensed the vibration of your movement. Plus, I can still focus the light within me. I see things somehow. And then there was the desert giant, of course.'

'Desert giant? Yes, I thought I saw one. Did it call the sand spiders?'

'I don't think so. It beat the ground over and over, as if to show me where you were. It tried to communicate, I think.'

'And the spiders?'

'Oh, I killed them. I quite enjoyed it, really.'

'All of them?'

'Yes, even the big one in the cave where all the tunnels met. There won't be any more spiders to trouble people lost in the desert, friend Jillan. Friend Anupal once said it was never wise to leave an enemy alive behind you. I think he was right.'

A long pause. 'Are you alright, Freda?'

'What do you mean, friend Jillan?'

'You sound different somehow, that's all. Did something happen?'

The darkness chinked and chimed as Freda settled herself. 'I have had to leave Sinisar's court. He is angry because I damaged his temple and extinguished the First Light. It was foolish to think one of the rock people would ever fit in there or be properly accepted.'

'Did they hurt you?' Jillan asked gently, suddenly wishing he could see something, anything.

'Yes, but it was my fault for letting them do so. I was too n ... nai ... What is the word?'

'Naive?' he offered after a moment.

'Yes.'

'Freda, you should not blame yourself if you were the victim of another's cruelty or unfairness.'

'You are wrong, friend Jillan. *You* are being naive. The things that happen to people are because they put themselves in a place where bad things will happen. They do not resist when they should. They *let* these things happen to them. They only start saying they are a victim afterwards, when actually they are victims of themselves even before anything has happened. I *am* in large part responsible for what happened at the Court of Light. I must now expect holy Sinisar to seek revenge against me.'

'I can't accept that, Freda. It was not the fault of the People that they were claimed and controlled by the Empire. Neither was it my fault that sand spiders almost killed me out here in the desert.'

Oh yes it was. You didn't listen to me when I warned you about them. You were too busy feeling sorry for yourself.

'Friend Jillan, how can it not have been the fault of the People? Unlike you, Hella, Thomas, Ash, the pagans and friend Samnir, the majority chose not to resist. If there had been more like you, then the Empire probably wouldn't have come into existence. And the sand spiders? Forgive me, friend Jillan, but what were you doing wandering out here on your own, without any water? Did something happen in Haven?'

You know she's right.

Jillan ignored the taint. 'I-I came out here to clear my head.' Was that true? He wasn't even sure himself. Had he been running away? Where did he think he'd been going? 'I would have gone back, but Sinisar made sure I got everything turned around and upside down.'

'Yet surely you knew he might do such a thing. Surely you knew he might seek revenge against you for making the place of the Geas your own. Sinisar thinks it should belong to the gods far more than any mortal. In the same way, friend Jillan, when I used to work down in a mine, I always knew the world of the Overlords was a cruel and difficult place, but still I went there.'

Had he known such things? How could he not have known? Had he been in denial or too caught up in other things like the wedding?

Come on, you've known something was wrong for a good while now. Of course, you had your head buried in the sand, which didn't help matters. Buried in the sand. Get it?

'Freda, if a child is a victim of the adult world, that is no fault of the child.'

'We are not children, friend Jillan. We are not so innocent.'

He sighed. 'Perhaps you're right. Perhaps all those things are our fault and of our own making. Certainly that is what the community of Haven seems to be. I must try to put it right before it is too late. I'm not sure how, though. Freda, I feel bad for asking. You have already done so much, but do you think you might help me?'

The rock woman laughed softly. 'Be careful, friend Jillan, for I may bring more harm than help. As soon as I go above the ground, into the world of light, I will be seen by Sinisar or his followers. I am in no doubt that any who think to give me welcome or shelter will have a god as their enemy.'

'Then so be it, Freda. It seems that Sinisar already takes issue with the people of Haven anyway. Besides, what sort of friend would I be if I turned you away, after all you have done for me and the people? I will not give you up, Freda, and nothing will ever make me regret that.'

'I will help as I can, friend Jillan. How could I not? What would you have me do? What needs to be done?'

'Haven needs protecting, I think. Samnir tried to tell me the same, but I don't think I understood at the time. He spoke of walls and armies which would prevent too many new people coming to Haven, but I'm not sure they could ever hold back Sinisar or any of the other gods. Oh, if only Haven were still hidden!'

'Revealing it was the only way to be rid of the Saviours, was it not, friend Jillan?'

'Yes.'

'Have you thought of simply giving Haven up?'

The idea unsettled him, but he had to give it serious thought. 'I-I suppose we could. Some wouldn't want to leave, I imagine, and others would keep trying to enter unless permanent guards were put in place. The gods would still want the place for themselves and would have no trouble taking it.'

'I think that would be bad, friend Jillan. If Sinisar were to become even more powerful than he is now, it would not be at all good for mortalkind.'

'Just as it would not have been good if Miserath had claimed the power of the Geas. No, Haven must be protected, I see that. Yet what power can thwart the gods? Torpeth found a way, but in setting himself over them he brought about their fall and the fall of this world.'

'The Saviours had the power to keep them down, but I do not know what that power was, friend Jillan.'

'It was simply the power of another realm, Freda. Perhaps that is the key. They have already helped me once before. Freda, do you know where the desert giants dwell? Can you take us there?'

'I can, friend Jillan. Should we go now? Have you rested enough?'

He remembered Ba'zel had said the Declension would soon rule the nether realm. Or had that been the twisted dream and nonsense of one awash with spider venom, the last delusion of a dying mind? Either way, he knew the Declension was still out there and scheming a way back into the world. 'We should go at once.'

'Who presents themselves before the council?' asked the gnarly Parsus, head of the Faction of Insistence, Convenor of the Council of Factions.

'I am Ba'zel.'

A long silence. 'Of which house?' the convenor asked slowly, his lower jaw chewing the words as if he devoured an enemy.

'None.'

The silence stretched. The faction heads encircling him made their disapproval known. They increased the power of their presence, although the tremors therein made it clear that the manner in which his answer broke with ritual and the requirements of hierarchy caused no little consternation and intrigue. 'Explain.'

Although it was his own father standing behind him, or perhaps *because* of it, Ba'zel had never felt his back so exposed. 'I was disavowed.'

'Do you wish to join some new house?' came the husky female tones of Ga Shelle, head of the Faction of Expedience. She had replied quickly and risked the censure of the convenor, but clearly judged the risk worth taking.

The convenor and the other heads seemed too intent upon his answer to raise any objection to her blatant play. After all, they had expected nothing else of the head of such a faction.

'I am a house unto myself. Already I have a retainer.'

'His house is entirely allied to the House of Faal,' his father interjected, to pre-empt the others and end any chance of their finding advantage through this uncomfortable line of enquiry.

The heads of the factions ceased exerting the power of their presence unduly and deferred to the convenor once more. 'Why do you bring yourself before us?'

'Did you not summon us? What would you have of me?'

The convenor lowered his head, presenting crest and horns as if about to attack. 'You dare make demand of this council?' he rattled.

'He is young,' the insatiable Graven, head of the Faction of Consumption, drooled.

'But he has an experience at odds with his youth,' droned Hyun, head of the Faction of Contemplation.

Starus, his father's principal opponent, chose not to speak. He watched all, unmoving.

'Speak,' the convenor directed Ba'zel.

'I was disavowed and outcast. Now I am summoned. I abide and am ready.'

'You abide?' the convenor replied, with a certain archness. 'Do you say you are no longer *unstable*? Do you say you should not be destroyed?'

This was the moment Faal had been waiting for. 'Convenor,' he dared interrupt, 'if Ba'zel were truly *unstable*, his answer could not be trusted in any event. I wish for the council to know that a scroll describing an expunged line of thought was found in the chambers of Mentor Ho'zen, who taught my son and was the reason for his flight. The *treatise* is attributed to one Israine and concerns itself with the nature of *instability* and how it may be appearance only.'

The enormity of Faal's assertion caused the longest silence yet, as the council members furiously wondered at the implications. Hyun even swayed where he stood, as if physically assaulted.

'You read the scroll?' Graven finally asked, and not without hungry cunning.

Yet Faal was prepared. 'No, of course not. It is forbidden. A member of my faction was persuaded to read it, to reveal its gist. Then the individual was torn apart and his substance reduced to ash. Do any of you have knowledge of the name Israine?'

There. The accusation was made. One of the factions had procured the scroll and passed it on to Mentor Ho'zen, all so that Ba'zel could be taught to seem *unstable* and the Faction of Origin harmed.

'The council is now sealed,' the convenor proclaimed. 'None may withdraw or make excuse. Any attempt to do so will be taken as admission of misdeed. One of the factions has overstepped. One of them has attacked the wider order of the Declension. It has jeopardised our progress on the Great Voyage itself. It has committed treason againt the Eldest herself!'

She had been named and invoked. *Her* attention had been drawn to the council and now the judgement would be *hers*.

Did Ga Shelle's breathing suddenly come more quickly? Was that a sign of guilt? Ba'zel realised that his own had also quickened. It was fear. Still Starus did not move or speak.

'Do any of you have knowledge of the name Israine?' Faal repeated.

'Mentor Ho'zen would have been of the Faction of Contemplation, no?' Graven gulped with a certain relish, tasting opportunity.

'Where is Ho'zen? He has disappeared?' Ga Shelle asked Hyun pointedly.

'Like many other mentors, Mentor Ho'zen was a member of my faction,' Hyun conceded, 'but his bloodline was not related to any of the major houses identified with my faction. As a result, he was not well placed within the faction. He had little privilege or access to our rarer lines of thought, extant, expunged or otherwise. I do not recall even having met Mentor Ho'zen. His rank would have been far too lowly for me to associate with him. Similarly, I have no knowledge of what has become of him.'

'His bloodline was through House Tresis, a minor house allied to my own,' Parsus the convenor admitted.

'Strange that you should use such an individual to mentor the scion of your house, Faal,' Graven leered. 'Some would say you created a conflict of interest within Mentor Ho'zen, one that now sees this council suffer internal conflict. Your carelessness – or was it wilfulness? – might also be an attack on the wider order of the Declension. Perhaps the treason is yours. Perhaps you gave the scroll to Mentor Ho'zen. Perhaps you have now disposed of him.'

Ba'zel was alarmed by this turn in the argument. It could see all of his father's ambitions undone. Yet part of him had to wonder just why his father had chosen such a mentor for him.

'Graven, I admire your faction's commitment to bettering itself and finding advantage whenever it may, but surely you can do better than that. Your argument lacks sense. I would have no reason ever to commit such treason, particularly when it saw my only offspring named as *unstable* and pursued by a Virtue. Besides, my choice of Mentor Ho'zen was anything but careless. The few mentors related to my own bloodline already had charges. Those within my faction would have likely taught what is already known within my faction, and would have used the position too much to elevate themselves within the faction. No, better to use a mentor of lowly rank but considerable ability and breadth of knowledge, a mentor who had been used by a number of major houses of different factions, a mentor who had come recommended as expedient by Ga Shelle's house itself.'

Ga Shelle inclined her head to confirm Faal's assertion. 'Your faction, Graven, would have had the means also to know of Mentor Ho'zen, would it not?'

'What do you mean?' The largest of the council members swallowed.

'Mentor Ho'zen was of lowly rank. He would not have had regular access to the blood pools and would have needed to find sustenance elsewhere. All know that the Faction of Consumption largely controls the collection and distribution of life energy from the other realms. Mentor Ho'zen no doubt visited the distributor assigned to his level.

Who knows what the mentor may have agreed to in return for greater sustenance? Is that not possible, Graven?'

Graven precisely mimicked the way in which Ga Shelle had inclined her head. 'It is possible, although I have no knowledge of this lowly mentor or the name Israine.'

'Then it appears,' the convenor directed, 'that Mentor Ho'zen was connected to each of the factions save the Faction of Departure.'

All eyes turned to Starus. His faction was now conspicuous by its lack of a connection to Mentor Ho'zen. No faction with a traceable link to the mentor would have dared the misdeed. At the same time, the enmity existing between the factions of Origin and Departure was no secret. Mentor Ho'zen would have been precisely the sort of weapon the Faction of Departure would have chosen to develop and use.

Ba'zel felt hope surge. He should never have doubted his father.

Elder Starus's gaze bored into Ba'zel. Softly, the head of the Faction of Departure spoke: 'I would have no reason ever to commit such treason, particularly when it saw my only offspring named as *unstable* and pursued by a Virtue. Those were the words of the council member. No reason except it saw realms fall, the offspring presented as a potential Great Virtue to lead us on the Great Voyage, and the other factions accused of misdeed. No reason except it delivers *all* to the Faction of Origin. Surely that is the *only* reason to commit such treason. Surely that is the *only* reason to risk your only offspring. It would have seen your faction's reason to exist made manifest and your faction's entire ambition realised. How could you *not* have thought to commit this treason? The words of the head of the faction are revealed as both disingenuous and concealing, but there is as much traceable evidence to connect that faction to the misdeed as there is to connect my own, which is to say there is none.'

All was poised. Hyun and Ga Shelle looked to Faal in support, while Parsus and Graven looked to Starus.

A sense of dread crept over Ba'zel. The play was still with Starus, the momentum was his.

'The entire misdeed is embodied in this creature before us,' Starus pronounced. 'It is the creation of competing ambitions. Is it a Great Virtue or corrupting *instability*? Should it be allowed to lead us? Will it be our salvation or doom? We can only know by materially contesting the issue. By ancient precedent, the Faction of Departure challenges the Faction of Origin to Right of Ascension.'

'No!' his father said faintly.

Hyun moaned and Ga Shelle gasped. Parsus made no sound, but Graven laughed and openly salivated.

Her mind came among them and they all stilled. *Challenge is made and recognised. Do the other factions protest?*

'No, most holy!' Hyun, Ga Shelle, Parsus and Graven replied in concert.

Faal, do you accept the challenge? Refusal is admission of guilt.

'Y-yes, most holy,' Faal stuttered.

Then so be it. In one cycle from now Ba'zel will fight the champion of council member Starus's choosing. And then *She* was gone.

Ba'zel did not fully understand what had just been agreed. He knew nothing of this Right of Ascension, save that it had caused his father to display a shameful degree of fear. Starus's glittering gaze was still fixed on Ba'zel. Where before there had been vengeful hatred in the elder's eyes, now there was only triumph.

As at every dawn, Samnir used his sword to singe away the worst of his stubble and strapped the weapon to his side. The routine of it reassured him somehow. The world was the same as the day before. Surely no disaster had occurred. The acrid smell of the burned hair also helped clear his head somewhat. All was well. He was well.

Had he slept? He could not remember. The dark hollows around his eyes in the reflection of the water bowl suggested he had not, or had suffered troubled dreams. It was not surprising, given how concerned he was for Jillan and Hella.

'What trouble has that boy got himself into now? Hella's right – we should organise a search.'

He felt a hand on his shoulder. With a mere touch she calmed his agitation. She made him whole.

'You must first see that she made it home safely last night. She was all but frantic about Jillan when she left here. When you went after her, to light her way, she hardly seemed to recognise you. She was irrational and distracted, apparently seeing and hearing things. She fled from you and you let her go. You have since become worried that – given the state she was in – something unfortunate has befallen her.'

Yes, that was how it had happened. As he'd approached her, she'd said something like *You don't want to do this*, as if he wanted to do her harm. Inevitably images of such harm had flashed through his mind, and then she'd become even more terrified, almost as if she could read his thoughts and they only confirmed her accusation. Her Geas-given power must have got the better of her and amplified her fear and confusion beyond all control. If she now read dark and stray fancy and feeling, then the gods pity the poor girl. Her life would not be worth living.

'I will go and see that she made it home safely last night. Something unfortunate may have befallen her.'

'Something unfortunate. Go quickly, before any others have risen.'

Samnir stepped out into the grey light and strode down towards the lake and the path around to Jacob's house. It was good to have the weight of his sword at his side. It reassured him. All was well. He was well. He was not losing his mind. She made him whole. The gods pity the poor girl. The harm he had imagined doing to her was a mere image she had suggested to him. She'd terrified herself.

He rapped on the door of Jacob's house. There was the sound of movement within. Some moments later the trader's wan face looked out.

'Samnir, the gods be praised!'

'I came to see if Hella made it home safely last night. She was all but frantic about Jillan when she left.'

Jacob pulled the door wider. 'Come in, come in.'

Samnir stepped over the threshold, dark shadows accompanying him. 'Where is she?'

'I've made her as comfortable as I can. She was soaked through when she returned –'

Samnir looked around, hardly listening. His hand went to the hilt of his sword. All was well. He was well.

'– yet it did not rain last night. Can she have been in the lake? What happened? I got her out of her clothes, into blankets and laid by the fire. She was soon shuddering so much I thought she would injure herself.'

'Where is she?'

'I wanted to go for the physicker, but dared not leave Hella alone. Now you're here, one of us can go.'

'You go. I will stay.'

'Of course.' Jacob nodded, reaching for his cloak. 'But what happened? Something with Jillan?' The small trader touched the commander's arm. 'Samnir? You do not look well yourself, my friend. Is something amiss?'

Samnir blinked, seeming to realise where he was for a few seconds, and then shrugged off Jacob's hand. A few inches of his blade now showed above its scabbard. 'Where is she?'

Jacob paused. He slowly moved between Samnir and a doorway leading to one of the bedchambers. 'She is resting more comfortably now. Best if we do not disturb her, eh?' He tried to coax the larger man. 'Why don't you tell me what happened?'

'I went after her, to light her way,' the soldier replied without inflection. 'She hardly seemed to recognise me. She was irrational and disturbed. She fled from me.'

All was well. He shoved Jacob violently aside. Crying out, the old trader fell, cracked his head on the hearth and went to the floor. Blood trickled from an ugly wound at his temple. His eyes rolled back in his head and he stopped moving. All was well.

Samnir brought his sword all the way free, its light driving the gloom and shadows in the main room back into the bedchamber where he knew he would find the girl. He stepped to the doorway. The harm he did her was a mere image she herself suggested. She put it in his mind, but he knew it wasn't real. She terrified herself. He came to light her way, the poor girl. She was lost in the dark and he would bring her the sword, no matter her complaint.

Close as he came, however, the pitch-black of the bedchamber would not recede. It breathed. A carrion stench assailed him. He felt the hot panting of its maw against his face.

He could not bear it being so close. Why did the sword not drive it back? Its glowing orange eyes looked into his soul.

He cowered before it. The black wolf took in his scent, growled angrily and showed its teeth. Saliva dripped onto Samnir's neck and made him flinch.

She made him whole. She offered his spirit comfort. The wolf sank its teeth into his soul and savagely tore at her influence, rending it until it fell away.

Rabid one, release the pack member you call Ash. Fear not, I will watch him as closely as I must now watch you. Bring the physicker for the old one and the female belonging to the pack member you call Jillan. Rabid one, you have always fought fiercely, but you are not always wise. That weakness has threatened the life of our pack. Allow such a thing to happen again and I will tear out your throat. Go, before I decide to put you out of your misery.

Tail between his legs, Samnir ran for all he was worth. He coursed around the lake, intent upon obeying his pack leader.

'Who have the Faction of Departure named?'

'Luhka Sha, first champion of the fighting pits and Lead Warrior of the Declension,' the battle mentor replied evenly.

'I see. He is large?'

'Easily twice your size. Size isn't his main strength, however. His is brimful of life energy from the hundreds of opponents he had devoured over the centuries. He has absorbed the tactical knowledge and fighting styles of generations of warriors.'

'Ah. Do I have any chance at all?' Ba'zel struggled not to show his apprehension, lest it be construed as fear.

Dra'zen considered for a moment and then demurred: 'You have defeated a Virtue, have you not?'

'Answer me more directly.'

'Let me tell you this then, young master. Whether it makes me coward or not, I am glad I lost this limb and was allowed to retire from the pits before it was my turn to face him. My life for a limb was a good exchange, to my way of thinking.'

'What is this object?' Ba'zel asked dubiously of the thick twelve-foot pole Dra'zen had given him. It had a metal ball the size of his head on one end and a flat chopping blade on the other.

'It is a weapon, young master.'

'Truly? The broom with which I sweep my father's chambers is less cumbersome. It is ceremonial, yes?'

'In the right hands this weapon is devastating. The balled end can crack and crush an opponent's exterior plating, the other end can cleave and prise. It is more than ceremonial. It is the means by which the majority of challenges are ended.'

'How so? Surely challenges are ended by the presence and powers of the opponents long before the use of such a primitive implement is necessary.'

'No. Opponents more often than not either exhaust their powers against each other or do not use them at all. Invariably a challenge ends in physical combat.'

'And he is twice my size.'

'Perhaps more than twice your strength. Certainly he will be faster and more accomplished with this weapon than you.'

'I cannot prevail.'

'You cannot. I would say it was unlikely, but Luhka Sha is a master of excluding chance and the random from all proceedings. It is one of the arts he has learned over the centuries. Few others of our kind have ever been known to achieve it. All lines of fate appear to end with him. In the same way, he has such life energy the entire cosmos seems to turn on him. Next to him you will feel as thin as a shadow. He almost occupies a world more actual and substantial than our own. You will begin to fade when you are in his presence.'

'He sounds to have the power of a null dragon, or its opposite.'

'As you say, young master. Come, ready your weapon, and let us see if you can best this one-armed cripple. Or would you prefer your broom?'

Ba'zel took a number of long steps back from the battle mentor and held his polearm out in front of him, parallel to the floor, hands shoulder width apart. He adjudged this the best posture to defend against any blow, be it from right, left, above or below.

Dra'zen shook his head. 'Your mother was less than a tunnel troll, I've heard.' He swept the heavy ball of his weapon round in a slow arc from a long way back.

For a split second Ba'zel stood agog at the unexpected insult. Then he realised there was an attack coming and braced himself to deflect it away. It was only at the last he realised the oncoming ball had a wicked momentum that he would be unable to block. He tried to jump back out of its reach, but was far too late. The ball knocked his weapon aside and took his legs out from under him.

He landed in an unceremonious heap, his weapon beyond immediate reach. Instinctively, he rolled to one side. Dra'zen's blade struck sparks against the floor where Ba'zel had been the exact moment before. He rolled again, but – discarding his own weapon – Dra'zen used his only hand to catch one of Ba'zel's legs and drag him across the floor on his front. Dra'zen's stone jaws lowered around the join between Ba'zel's spine and skull and gripped it tightly. The battle mentor lifted the youth in his fangs. One shake of his head and it would be over.

Ba'zel had immediately gone limp, the nerves at the scruff of his neck pinched and paralysed. He felt the elder shudder with hunger and excitement. Digestive acids trickled out of the sides of Dra'zen's maw and down Ba'zel's back, etching his hide with marks of shame.

Ba'zel saw that his retainer relived the brutal battles of the fighting pits in his mind's eye. The thrill of victory and feasting on a defeated opponent's insides. It was intoxicating, impossible to resist. It had lured many to their deaths. It had seen warriors accept challenges where good sense and permanent injury had advised hiding as deep as the home-realm would allow. Even those who were mere spectators found themselves drawn back again and again, becoming caught up in the battle lust and feeding frenzy, and all too soon in a fight to the death with their closest neighbour.

Dra'zen dropped Ba'zel. 'This loyalty you have asked of me is a difficult thing, young pup. It leaves one with a very empty feeling,' he said in disgust.

'It is no more enjoyable for me, I assure you, Battle Mentor,' Ba'zel panted.

'How is it that you still survive? You are weak, and yet they speak of you as a Great Virtue. How is that?'

'I do not truly know. It might be something the lesser beings call a *winning personality*.'

'A winning personality?' Dra'zen chewed. 'Well, let us hope it proves more effective in your challenge against Luhka Sha than it has so far in this contest between us. Again. Retrieve your weapon. Your father's blood is unworthy even to be returned to the feeding pools, I've heard.'

'And your blood is so lacking that all consider you a lesser being.'

'I will see to it that those words are the last thing you ever eat, you pup!'

Freda carried Jillan through the earth and into a subterranean space. She pulled him up a sloping tunnel that she said would bring them above ground not far from the oasis of the desert giants. The light gradually increased as they went and Jillan took a closer look at his large friend to see if there was sign of any harm done to her by Sinisar's court.

Yet darkness clung to Freda so that, no matter which way Jillan turned his head, he could make nothing out. Even as they stepped into the direct light coming from the tunnel's exit, she remained an absence in the air. At her centre she was pitch-black, as if a void that swallowed all light. Or was she now of a substance that totally defied the light? It was like looking into the sun and being blinded, but in reverse. A black sun that drank in all colour and vision rather than enabling it.

Jillan feared what she might represent, what her appearance – or lack of it – might mean. What had happened to her? She seemed to be a walking, talking negation of the world. And it scared him. *She* scared him.

Even her edges were indistinct, as if the fabric of the world bled into her or she drew in all its energy, vibrancy and life. Wherever she passed, the rocks and sand were left dull and faded, and shadows were intensified.

'By the gods, Freda,' he could not help but exclaim as he shielded his eyes from her, 'how have you become like this?'

'It is precisely *by the gods* that I am like this,' she clanged and chimed. 'Do not be concerned, for I do not experience any discomfort. And it pleases me to know that I may well bring discomfort to them. Besides, I am now with my friend and helping him and all those I know in Haven. I am happy – certainly happier than I have been since I went to the Court of Light, anyway. Surely that must make you happy too, friend Jillan.'

Yes, Jillan, live a little. That's what life's for, after all.

He tried, for his friend's sake. Despite the queasiness in his stomach – not to mention the way his hair stood on end and how his skin crawled – whenever he glanced towards her, he tried to be happy for Freda. Only to fail. The sense of fundamental *wrongness* he'd experienced in Haven, he also experienced here.

She was still Freda, though. Beneath it all, his brave friend was still there. When she'd carried him through the ground, she'd had the same hard edges and strength he'd always known. She'd always been judged unfairly on how she looked – perhaps this was no different. He must not judge her, especially when her current condition was no fault of her own, even if she did perversely wish to blame herself.

If there was something *wrong*, then he would do his damnedest to fix it. He would not give up on Freda or Haven. How could he, after all they had been through? It was clear now that they were beset by enemies just as they had always been. He realised that he'd been deluding himself in thinking the fighting was over just because the Great Temple had fallen. He'd been so desperate for it to be true, so desperate for that quiet life with Hella, that he'd made himself deaf and blind to all sign that their enemies were only becoming stronger.

The fighting was far from over. Perhaps it was never over, as Samnir had suggested. There was no use running from it, for it was in the nature of things, it seemed. It could not be escaped. He saw that now. He would face it. He *had* to face it, for the alternative was the loss of everything.

He would bring Haven to the fight, and that would hopefully see the divisions within the community forgotten or overcome. Yes, hopefully it would see common purpose asserted among them once more. In not understanding they would have to fight sooner, perhaps he'd been responsible in some ways for the divisions developing in the first place. Who knew what inroads the enemy had already made into Haven by exploiting those divisions? Who knew if the situation in Haven had already deteriorated so far that it was beyond saving? He had to return before it was too late.

'Freda, you're right. I'm delighted to be helping our friends in Haven. Let's see what these desert giants can offer us and get home as quickly as we can. You will have sanctuary there and be welcomed as a friend,' Jillan said with a new sense of determination.

That's the spirit.

They stepped into the glare of the desert. The heat physically assaulted Jillan and he grimaced. Instinctively, he stepped into Freda's dark umbra and found things more tolerable there. Fifty yards ahead of them was a wide group of red and fleshy trees the like of which Jillan had never seen before. While they had bulbous bodies and offshoots, they were also festooned with clusters of vicious spines that spiked the sky and prevented anything getting close to them. Although there was no wind to speak of, the trees seemed to sway one way and then another. The ground trembled with the movement. An odour of death filled the air.

'I do not like this place, friend Jillan. Are you sure we should have come here?'

A rhythmic thudding like a heartbeat came up through the rock and sand beneath their feet. 'I think they know we are here. It would be rude to leave now, don't you think?'

'Maybe the vibration is a warning. Maybe they are telling us to stay away.'

Jillan slowed his pace as they came closer. He could now see veins through the semi-translucent skins of the trees. A dark liquid moved sluggishly through them and wept from the glistening ends of the upper spines. 'Er ... maybe. They do not mean to attack us, though, I would guess. They lose the element of surprise by this noise.'

'Unless it is a war drum of sorts, summoning giants from all across the area. They may be converging from all directions even now.'

'Ah. There is that.' Jillan glanced over his shoulder to see if there was any sign of their being surrounded, but the desert remained mercifully empty. 'Right. Let's not panic.'

'I am not panicking, friend Jillan,' Freda informed him evenly.

'Good. That's good.' The taint snickered.

Shadows moved among the trees and a dozen giants burst towards them, hungrily sniffing the air. They were all larger than Freda and reeked foully. Their faces were distorted by capacious foreheads, bone-crushing jaws and protruding teeth. The yellow orbs of their eyes showed red veins and a violent insanity of sorts.

Jillan raised his power with an effort but could not take his eyes from one of the skins in which the nearest giant was loosely clothed. Was that a stretched human face there? Those were the eye holes. A missing nose. Mouth stretched wide in an unending scream.

'Jillan! What are you doing? They are no longer a threat,' Freda interrupted.

He blinked. His magic had continued to build without his realising it. There was a terrible pressure in the air that set hair standing on end and membranes buzzing. The giants had thrown themselves to the ground with yelps and whines of submission. With an immense effort, Jillan reined in the gathering storm and forced it down into his core, where it raged and battered against its confinement. It had him dizzy for some moments.

'Sorry about that.' He grinned awkwardly at the giants. 'We were just passing by and thought we'd ... well, you know, drop by to pay our respects. Only if it's convenient, of course.'

Refusing to look at them and keeping its head low, the largest of the giants came to its feet and gestured for them to follow. It moved to a narrow gap between two of the thorny succulents, waited until they had started to follow, and disappeared from view. It was then a tortuous journey back and forth through a deadly maze of needles, and under and over the impossibly sticky loops and tangles of the plants' roots. Even their guide took extreme care not to come too close to the unwholesome vegetation. Freda nudged Jillan several times to point out the desiccated bodies of desert rats that had apparently got caught in the thick and putrid resin secreted by the roots and been skewered and drained of their vital fluids by the dipping lances of low branches. After that they came to what was unmistakably a human skull showing from beneath the overgrowing roots of one of the fetid trees.

Jillan shuddered. 'Poor devil. I hope it was a quick death.'

'I doubt it was, friend Jillan,' Freda replied blandly. 'The plant probably injects something to paralyse the victim rather than kill it outright. That way, the plant has as long as it needs to extract as much of the victim's essence as possible while it is still fresh. Maybe they were alive like this for up to a week.'

'Alright, we don't need *all* the detail, Freda, thank you. They must have been desperate to come in here, that's all I know.'

Desperate like you?

'Maybe it was one of the people of the desert tribes looking for water. Or a Hero looking to spy on the giants, friend Jillan.'

'Maybe.'

'Or the giants sacrificed someone to this tree. If the giants gave the victim water and small amounts to eat every so often, then the victim may have taken months to die –'

Ooh. Creative. A woman after my own heart.

'– if not longer. A year, maybe? All the while, the tree would have had a ready supply of fresh blood.'

'Enough! Honestly, Freda, I don't think it's healthy to dwell overmuch on it.'

'Really? I find it quite instructive, friend Jillan, but I can see you're a bit squeamish and sensitive about such things, so shall not speak further of them.'

'I'd appreciate that, Freda, thank you. All this is making me feel quite claustrophobic, that's all.'

'You're welcome, friend Jillan. I understand, especially after the sand spiders and all. Don't worry, though, because you're safe with me here. The trees wouldn't be strong enough to hold me, and the long thorns wouldn't be able to penetrate my diamond skin.'

'That's reassuring to know,' Jillan said faintly. 'Just so long as these carnivorous trees aren't somehow magically imbued, what with all the blood they drink.'

Freda fell silent at that – much to Jillan's relief – and navigated the trees more cautiously from there on in. The ground sloped down now, and they moved among the larger and older dripping trees of the oasis. There was a good deal of shade and an unpleasant darkness to the gory soil.

Then they came to the bloody pool at the heart of the giants' home. Around its edge were a dozen of the monstrous plants, their fat roots sunk directly into the mire, feeding bloated trunks and swollen limbs. They constantly rained red tears, ensuring that the source of their nourishment did not dry up. Jillan spied rotting carcasses in the filth and sensed a miasma of power hanging over the place. The blood was kept animated, alive somehow. And it was aware. He felt it watching them.

'Ye gods!' Jillan gagged, covering mouth and nose and backing away.

The giant leading them moved back towards Jillan and impatiently gestured him on. They went round the pool and came to a den built of bones – both familiar and unfamiliar – and ragged skins stretched between trees like trophies. Here, an even larger giant awaited them. There were a dozen or so other giants nearby, but they hung back or hunkered down so that they were never in full view.

Apart from his size, the first among the giants looked much like the others to Jillan. The only other things that set him apart were a necklace of many different skull types, and rattling bones worn around ankles and wrists. The bones clacked now as he filled an upturned human skull with blood from the pool and offered it to them with a grunt of command. His movements were measured and timed so that the bones played a music of sorts. Sound and movement seemed as one for this being.

Jillan shook his head in disgust and refused the grisly offering. *Careful not to offend him.*

The giant's heavy brows came down. He pulled a begrimed piece of flesh from a small bag at his waist and thrust it towards Jillan with an angry clack.

Again Jillan refused. 'Can you understand our language?'

The giant stamped in a circle, throwing skull and meat into the pool to create a gulping counterpoint. As he finished, he spat the words, 'I am Speaker.'

'I see. Thank you for guiding Freda to me before. I am Jillan.'

'You are Jillan. You bring Ba'zel. We hate people of Jillan. You die forever.'

With a clash of alarm, Freda roughly pushed Jillan aside and came at the giant. The giant moved with her sound, spinning with it and drawing it out so that it became a harmonious chord. Somehow he had moved behind her.

'Freda, wait!' Jillan called frantically and got himself back between the two of them. 'Speaker, I am sorry about Ba'zel. We need your help. The god of this region will attack us in Haven. Can you help us? You are from another realm, yes? Do you have a power we can use against the sun god? Will you help us?'

Again the giant stamped in a circle. 'You bring Ba'zel. Your people die forever.' The giant looked to be grinning or leering.

'Are you saying the Saviours will come against us too? If we die, they will come for you next. If we stand together, we might be able to drive them back. Don't you see?'

Three times the Speaker went onto his toes and then back down onto his heels, his bones rattling in time to the raining and pattering of the blood from the trees. His words drizzled down. 'Speaker say what Seer see. Jillan bring Ba'zel and Saviours. Your people die forever and ever.'

'No!' he shouted. 'You *must* help us. Don't you care? Why did you help Freda save me from the sand spiders if you're not going to help us, damn you? We will help you in return. Please!'

Tears falling. 'Speaker say no definition for realm of Jillan. Speaker say definition for realm of Speaker.'

Sounds like a no to me. Oh well.

Jillan was crestfallen. He stared at the Speaker.

'Do not worry, friend Jillan,' Freda said gently. 'You will find a way. You always have before. Let us go to Haven. You said we must be quick, yes? I cannot go through the ground here. It resists me. We will first walk out of this horrible oasis, and then we will travel swiftly. I look forward to seeing Hella, Samnir and Ash again. I have missed them. Come, friend Jillan.'

The dark pall that was Freda took hold of Jillan and pulled him away through the loathsome forest. They did not look back.

Izat remained hidden in the dwelling she shared with Samnir. If all had gone well, the witch Hella would be dead by now. When Jillan learned of it he would be devastated and highly unlikely ever to recover. He'd turn on Samnir, perhaps even kill him, but ultimately blame himself for not being there to prevent the death of the woman who was his sacred heart. Once Hella was dead, Jillan would have nothing. His life and Haven would become all but meaningless to him. The Unclean, the Heroes and the People would continue to argue among themselves and inevitably turn on each other, but Jillan would no longer care enough to stop them and keep them together. Quite the opposite, for he'd be disgusted with them and would simply walk away. Haven would tear itself apart and be ready for the taking.

It was the very least the bane of the Empire deserved. Izat had lost everything because of him. Everything. Her Sainthood, her kingdom, the love of her people and, worst of all, her beauty. If it weren't for him, the Disciple would never have come to Shangrin and forced her to mutilate herself. This was the first moment of satisfaction she'd had since that terrible day.

The revenge was delicious. She delighted in it, felt almost restored. Amazing that serving the desires of the Peculiar also saw her own desires fulfilled. He was the god of such things, after all. Resitus, the Righteous Revenger, wasn't that one of his names? He would be pleased with her, she hoped. Perhaps he would allow her to rule in his name here in

Haven. Yes, she would be as she once had been. She would reclaim her rightful place as queen.

She'd learned much from the Peculiar. He'd explained how simple and self-deluding mortals were. He'd shown her precisely how their thoughts and emotions might be decided for them, precisely what made certain beings gods and others their servants. And, to her wonder, he'd been completely correct. It had been childishly easy to walk into Haven and start making it her own. For all their weapons and powers, its inhabitants were clueless and inconsequential.

To think that they presumed a right to Haven! Such facile and tawdry beings could not be allowed anywhere near the power of the Geas. No, it would be hers to rule instead. And that power would surely see her divine beauty returned to her. Indeed, it was inevitable, for she was so much more than these mere mortals. She had lived for millennia, and now she decided the thoughts and emotions of these mortals for them. She would be both their Saviour and goddess. Her will would define their lives.

'At last! I am divine,' she crooned to herself. 'Geas, come to me. I will it.'

The shadows in the dwelling thickened and she felt a powerful presence. A predatory gaze. The burning eyes of the wolf!

Izat, you were warned before, among the ruins of Godsend. You have no claim on the member of my pack you call Jillan. The one called Ash made it clear you were not holy. Yet still you come here to steal.

She drew in a sharp breath and pressed herself back against the wall. If she could have passed through the bricks, she would have done so.

'Mercy! I have lost so much.'

You ask mercy of a wolf? Ash showed you mercy before and now you come here to steal from us. You have lost so much only because you first stole so much. You will feed us with your own flesh.

'You dare not taste my blood.'

The wolf stalked towards her. *I am a wolf. Of course I will taste your blood.*

'Look into my eyes, wolf. See yourself and your thoughts reflected there. See that you do not wish to hurt me in any way. See that you will do all that I command of you. Come closer and see.'

Tongue lolling out, the wolf obediently padded forward. It lunged and ripped out her throat.

'Are you ready?' the battle mentor asked as he passed Ba'zel the weapon he would soon be using against Lukha Sha.

'No.'

'Good. It stops you becoming complacent.'

'Dra'zen, it is hard to be complacent about one's death.'

'You'd be surprised, young master. When one of our kind has lived a long time, they consider themselves as having a great deal to lose or as having very little to lose. A few delude themselves that they are immortal or invulnerable. Their death comes, needless to say, as a considerable surprise to them.'

'Into which group does Lukha Sha fall?'

'I am not sure, master. You do not appear formidable, so perhaps he will consider himself invulnerable. He might become complacent, more so if you behave fearfully, shameful though it may be.'

'That will require little pretence on my part.'

'Good. You will be all the more convincing.'

Ba'zel nodded. 'It might be best not to fight well?'

'Fight well and you risk winning his respect. He will not toy with you. He will see you dead with speed and efficiency.'

'I see. Fight badly and I may live longer.'

'Perhaps, though it heaps yet more shame on you.'

'Dra'zen, I have already known more shame than any of our kind. I was named *unstable*. I was disowned by my father and faction. A Virtue was sent to bring me a punishment worse than death. I was named an enemy of our kind even as I was used to bring genocide to enemies of the Declension. The one thing I have learned in all this, Battle Mentor, is that it is better to be alive and shamed than it is to be dead and shame-free. I will fight badly.'

'It is difficult to fight deliberately badly. Your every instinct will have you do otherwise, just to survive, which of course will see you fail all the sooner.'

'Then perhaps I cannot win.'

'It ... saddens me.'

'Thank you, Dra'zen. Thank you for your loyalty also.'

'I'm still not sure I understand what this *loyalty* is. It seems like an idea from a line of thought that should have been expunged long ago. Yet ...'

Drums began in the depths of the home-realm. They were like a slow heartbeat at first, pushing a full-blooded sound up through the levels, bringing the members of the Declension up towards the central battle chamber. Soon the tempo of the massive instruments would increase, like the quickening pulse, breath and excitement of a warrior preparing for the fight.

'I must go,' Ba'zel said.

Dra'zen held him back with his forelimb. 'Yet this *loyalty* would have me share with you one thing more. Lukha Sha has never been able to produce offspring. It is a subject of which none dare breathe, for fear of the killing frenzy it produces in him. If the fight becomes a prolonged torture, master, that is how you can have him end it instantly.'

'Thank you – I think.'

Ba'zel and his battle mentor stepped from their chamber into a crowded tunnel. Elders, mentors, warriors, watchers, distributors, infants and tunnel trolls alike made their way forward. Any moving too slowly or trying to travel in the opposite direction were quickly trampled. With his cumbersome weapon constantly buffeted and snagging, Ba'zel nearly tripped several times – if it had not been for Dra'zen supporting and protecting him, he would have been unable to make it to the central battle chamber at all. As it was, he kept his feet and used his weapon to bring down any who threatened himself or Dra'zen too greatly. They made it into the chamber and, where all others scaled stairs to find the tiered seats allowed their rank, they skirted around the floor of the wide chamber to where Faal and the highest ranks of his faction were seated.

Faal stood as they approached and gave Ba'zel a short bow, those around him bowing more deeply. 'Welcome, Ba'zel of House Ba'zel, and Battle Mentor Dra'zen of the same house. Ba'zel, you are privileged to fight in the name of the Faction of Origin, and we are privileged to have you fight in our name. Yet you do not do this simply in our name. You do this in the name of all our kind. Succeed in this Right of Ascension and you will be invested as the Great Virtue. All factions will follow you and progress will be made on the Great Voyage as never before, all for the Geas of the home-realm, the heart of the Declension. You will be the Saviour of our kind!'

Should I let Lukha Sha win then, simply to prevent the Declension's progress? No, that would only slow the progress, not prevent it. Another Great Virtue would eventually rise. *Should I attempt to win? As Great Virtue, I might seek to doom our kind rather than save it, but always the Declension has succeeded in using me to realise its own will.* Trapped. There was no winning either way, damn them. He felt sick. 'Goodbye, Father.'

Faal hesitated. 'Goodbye, my son, for surely you have the right to ascend, to become so much more than my son, to become the Great Virtue of the Declension.'

How can any have such a right over others? It is too terrible. I want no part of it. Would I have a cosmos in which there are no rights? No. His head hurting, Ba'zel bent to the ranks of the Faction of Origin, and to Dra'zen, and then turned away.

He stepped onto the floor of the arena, moving from the top of one short stone pillar to another, making for the centre. The pillars were about four feet high, the floor beneath covered in a thin sheet of sun-metal to prevent any combatant from assuming their spectral form in order to escape below.

From across the arena came the colossal being that was Lukha Sha. His long powerful limbs levered him across three or four pillars at a time. His carapace was a mass of ridged scars, scars that had only seen his hide grow thicker over time. His front was covered in heavy plates that seemed to have a near-magical strength, judging by their iridescent gleam. His mighty crown of horns was stained black with the blood of all those who had fallen to him.

Ba'zel found he could not have taken his gaze from his opponent even if he'd wanted to. The first champion of the fighting pits and the Lead Warrior of the Declension filled the eyes and mind of any in his presence. He was more substantial and incipient than anything in the foreground or background. He was so vivid, all else looked an unreal shadow. Ba'zel felt his sense of self diminish. If Lukha Sha told him to kill himself there and then, he was not sure he would have the wherewithal to resist the other's will.

'This timid infant would present itself as the Great Virtue?' came the guttural rumble of Lukha Sha. 'No, this cannot be my opponent. This must be some retainer come to take my effluent to the feeding pits.' The Lead Warrior jetted stinking urine over Ba'zel, then defecated and cast it at his opponent's maw. 'Now bring me the representative of the Faction of Origin!'

The teeming thousands called out in approbation. Let the weak among them be put down and reused so that the rest might become ever stronger, so that nothing might stand in the way of the Declension. Let all who were lesser be driven out from the body like a disease. Even some of the Faction of Origin were caught up in the great cry of the Declension's will.

'I refuse to believe we are even of the same species!' The Lead Warrior spat acid. Ba'zel's skin burned and blistered.

The Declension shared Lukha Sha's contempt and Ba'zel wilted before it. He fell backwards off his pillar, smacked his head on the top of the pillar behind him and fell to the floor of sun-metal below. Fluid leaked from his skull and ignited the area all around. *Whoosh.*

Lukha Sha took long precautionary steps back from the inferno. Ba'zel crawled across the searing surface in the opposite direction, used his weapon for a crutch and hauled himself up onto another pillar.

Shameworthy though the tumble had been, it had freed Ba'zel of the Lead Warrior's mesmerising and blood-filled gaze. The world came rushing back in and he heard the entire Declension howling its derision. The pain of his injuries now became all too real and he wondered if his head wound would ultimately prove fatal.

Keeping his eyes down, as if in deference, he took a step back towards the centre, his weapon held out in front of him to face the challenge. His vision swam and he struggled for balance.

Lukha Sha leaped forward and swung the balled end of his weapon around in a deadly arc. Here was precisely the move with which Dra'zen had toppled him in their first practice match. Ba'zel knew he should try to jump back out of range, but his lower limbs would not coordinate properly. An unstoppable weight was about to crush him. Panicking, he assumed his spectral form and the ball went straight through him. It caught the lowered end of his own weapon and tore it out of his ethereal grasp, flinging it far beyond reach.

Ba'zel retreated as he returned to his material form once more. He stepped backwards. And again. What else could he do now he was weaponless?

Luhka Sha leaped again, easily closing the distance between them, sweeping his weapon round once more. Ba'zel took on his spectral form for the instant of the ball's passage through him, then became solid in order to push his enemy's weapon round ever more quickly. He darted in towards the Lead Warrior, pushing along the entire length of the weapon as it turned. The extra momentum twisted Luhka Sha round, so that his back was partially exposed to Ba'zel.

Here was his chance! Ba'zel sank shadowy claws through Luhka Sha's exterior, made his hands real inside the warrior's flesh and prepared to tear him open. Suddenly realising his mistake, Luhka Sha released his weapon with a snort of disgust and became a shadow himself. Quick as a flash he pivoted, caught Ba'zel's wrists and wrenched Ba'zel's claws out before they could do any serious damage.

The huge Lead Warrior stretched Ba'zel wide and hoisted him on high. He turned in a slow circle, displaying his victim to the baying ranks of the Declension. 'Is this your Great Virtue?' he roared. 'Well? I can't hear you, you wretches. Answer me! What say you?'

Ba'zel saw Faal's head drop in defeat. Battle Mentor Dra'zen's nasal aperture flared in anticipation of blood and gore.

Ba'zel felt the joints separating where his upper limbs were connected to his torso. The top part of his spine tore out through his back. Unbidden, acid bubbled up into the back of his stretched maw, eating away at his throat even as he struggled to spit it free. His vision blurred.

'You whine like infants!' Luhka Sha bellowed, whipping the assembly into a frenzy. 'Answer me! Is this your Great Virtue?'

'NO!' they cried in an ecstasy of hatred.

Ba'zel's mind swam free, rising above the scene. He saw his father's shame, knew that his abject failure would see the Faction of Origin tear apart its own leader and remove all record of his name and bloodline. There was the battle mentor, regretting ever having spoken to Ba'zel in the dark of the lower corridors, wishing that he had killed Ba'zel himself before it had ever come to this, knowing that he had been tricked by the other's lies and would now be hunted and executed as a member of the mad House of Ba'zel. He saw the terrifying Luhka Sha and knew this was the shape that the Declension's rule of the cosmos would now take.

All life and every Geas would be taken up by the Declension and torn asunder. Ba'zel's friend Jillan, Samnir, Hella, Ash and the entire seventh realm would be picked up, pulled apart and discarded.

See what will happen if you refuse to serve me.

There was another with him. An immense and oppressive intellect. *She* was there, and could not be escaped. 'Why do you need me? I do not want to serve. I do not want to be the destroyer of all things.'

You are the unstable element *made flesh. The* unstable element *must be made to serve if the Great Voyage is ever to be complete. You* will *serve me! Refuse, and all that has ever had meaning to you will be undone.*

He wanted to commit suicide at that moment. His father prepared to do the same. So did the crippled Dra'zen. The bloodline and loyalty with which they were joined to him trapped them and would bring them death. He was responsible. And his friend Jillan would be ended in the same way. The things in which he'd placed his hope and faith were perverted by his end and turned into weapons more deadly and inevitable than the Declension had ever commanded before. He could not allow it! Yet if he agreed to be bound in *Her* service as the *unstable element*, she would at last have the means by which to conquer the entire cosmos. How could he? Trapped. The Declension had made his existence his snare.

Fail and you have seen the consequences. Fight on and you agree to serve me.

He couldn't see a way. He saw everything and nothing.

Suicide? He was shrivelling. His face was pressed against sun-metal. His skin had burned away, and now his soft interior and eyeballs were cooking. He had slipped from Luhka Sha's grasp by changing form, but the Lead Warrior had followed him down and pinned him where there was no chance of escape.

'Smells good,' Luhka Sha drooled in Ba'zel's ear, broadcasting the thought to the avid assembly so that they could share in the moment. The smell of charred flesh spread through the chamber and saw a number of the nearest spectators unable to resist chewing on their own limbs.

Sun-metal. He had been here before. The horrendous box. He became incredibly dense and crystalline, as he had in the seventh realm.

'I prefer my meat as fresh as possible, however,' the Lead Warrior was saying, lifting Ba'zel's hindquarters at that moment and putting them between his massive jaws. He opened his gullet and began to swallow Ba'zel whole.

Ba'zel sawed with his lower limbs, their edges sharp and penetrating blades. He kicked back, and his talons punched out through the back of Luhka Sha's neck. Protective magicks dissipated from the Lead Warrior's carapace.

The mighty warrior made a 'Gak!' noise of frustration, yanked Ba'zel free and hurled him fully halfway across the arena. 'That will be your last craven defence, whore to your father's faction! You do not have the strength to maintain such a form for more than a handful of seconds.' Luhka Sha took an angled leap over to his weapon, scooped it up and came spiralling back towards Ba'zel. 'By which time I will have shattered, pounded, smeared and powdered you into a dust so fine not even the sifters will find trace of you.'

Ba'zel shook. Luhka Sha was right. He could not last much longer. He returned to his broken natural state to conserve what little he had. If only he could win a moment's respite. 'Your words and actions are as *impotent* as your blood!' he blurted.

'WHAT?' Luhka Sha thundered so loudly it echoed around the chamber and all but silenced the crowd.

'Impotent!' Ba'zel flung at the Lead Warrior.

'Impotent!' shouted Dra'zen.

Luhka Sha's head snapped round and marked the battle mentor. Dra'zen thrust suggestively with the nub of his lost limb and made the begging noise of a male looking to arouse the appetite of a female.

'Silence, you mutilated troll! If you were a real warrior, you would have ended yourself long ago. You are a disgrace to all warriorkind. Your existence is an offence. None sees or hears you.'

The warrior ranks of the Declension – most of whom sat with the Faction of Departure – seethed at Dra'zen's cowardly insult of the Lead Warrior. Terrible challenges and dire promises were made. Faal himself had to drag Dra'zen away, and Elder Starus ordered that guards restrain the more outspoken before violence erupted and engulfed the entire chamber.

Luhka Sha brought his head back round, just in time for it to meet a devastating blow from the weapon Ba'zel had wasted no time collecting while the other was distracted. It obliterated Luhka Sha's face, nearly tearing away his lower jaw, caving in his nasal aperture, cracking his forehead wide and making a ruin of his crown of horns. The Lead Warrior's brain glistened wetly through the crack.

'Finish him!' Dra'zen demanded over the cacophony of the crowd. 'Strike now!'

Ba'zel turned with his weapon, bringing its bladed end whistling round. Yet Luhka Sha was not to be bested so easily. Generations of training and combat were not about to be undone by one cunning blow. The Lead Warrior's balance and poise did not fail him for an instant. His weapon had begun to describe a shimmering defensive shield even before the battle mentor's shout. It covered his retreat now, easily holding off every effort and attempt by the increasingly exhausted Ba'zel.

Luhka Sha deliberately put distance between them. He crunched his jaw back into place. Then he squeezed his skull together, allowing the crack a few moments to knit. 'Thank you for reminding me not to kill you too quickly,' came a near-unintelligible slur.

'Sorry?' Ba'zel panted.

You have annoyed me greatly, Luhka Sha's mind replied.

'We just got off on the wrong foot.'

I feel ashamed to have been touched by the weapon of one so weak.

'Maybe the shame is too great for you to bear, Luhka Sha? Perhaps you should kill yourself here and now.'

How is it you have not already died, when you are clearly so weak?

'I guess I just never learned how.'

Your utterings are senseless and crazed. It is a further symptom of your weakness. None like you can be permitted existence by the Declension. You must die!

So saying, the Lead Warrior put his weapon back into motion, this time to create a shining web of death around him. He twirled ball and blade faster and faster, until they made the air sing. It was a haunting sound, as if it already mourned Ba'zel's passing.

Ba'zel's eyes widened in fear. He dared not try any sort of flailing attack. He did not doubt that to come within reach of the Lead Warrior now would be fatal. Instead, he hopped back onto another narrow pillar, and then another. He had no choice but to hesitate each time as he glanced over his shoulder to avoid any misstep. A slip now would surely end it.

Meanwhile, Luhka Sha came on without pause. His long measured strides steadily closed the gap between them. The Lead Warrior would not rush. He avoided any mistake of his own. Ba'zel's death came relentlessly closer, inevitably closer. No escape would be permitted. The trap inexorably closed. The Declension willed it.

Luhka Sha enjoyed and relished the coming moment. The Declension roared in anticipation. The cosmos turned on it. Ba'zel turned to flee. Blood pounded at his temples, deafening him. He watched his feet and hands and wondered at them in this final moment of his life. This was all he was. He tried to feel the moment to its maximum, to make as much of it as he could, to cram whole lifetimes of experience into that briefest of instants. If only he could find eternity there.

The hungry breath of death on the back of his neck. Stone fangs at the joint between skull and body. A blink.

And everything stopped. Members of the Declension froze mid-scream. Faal stood agog and unmoving. Luhka Sha's teeth touched the skin of Ba'zel's neck but went no further.

Ba'zel tottered forward in the stone silence, only his ragged breathing to be heard in the chamber. He moved away from the motionless Lead Warrior.

The world came rushing back louder than ever before. Luhka Sha's jaws snapped viciously and he started in consternation. Where was his prize? The crowd's triumphant crescendo fell into confusion.

Ba'zel's lower limbs collapsed under him, robbed of all strength. He'd used all he had to hold death back for an infinitely preciously second. The power of his presence had stilled Luhka Sha just long enough to get beyond reach.

Yet the reprieve would not last longer than it took Luhka Sha to reorient himself and leap upon his helpless victim. Luhka Sha turned.

Interesting. But just another of your tricks. And it was your last trick, crazed one.

With ferocious force, the Lead Warrior exerted the power of his own presence. The air in the arena twisted and warped, such was the magnitude of the assault.

Every inch of Ba'zel's hard exterior buckled. Then, with a scream beyond hearing, his exoskeleton shattered. Every elder in the chamber flinched in appalled horror. Never had they seen such a fearsome display from any individual of their kind. Every elder except Elder Starus. Stone-like he sat, staring at Ba'zel, his focus and action clear to all.

Outraged, Faal and the ranks of the Faction of Origin came to their feet as one. 'You have overstepped. All saw it!' his father accused the head of the opposing faction. Ga Shelle of the Faction of Expedience and Hyun of the Faction of Contemplation also came to their feet.

'There was nothing to see,' Starus replied evenly. 'You simply protest because your representative and the crazed ambitions of your faction are at an end. The Declension will at last embrace a proper Departure from this exhausted and empty realm. Unfettered, we will now truly progress on our Great Voyage and realise our destiny. We are freed, brethren, freed! We will finally transcend what we were and come to rule the cosmos, as it was always meant to be!'

Even before Starus had finished his prepared speech, Faal had turned to pour his gaze on the oozing and barely twitching wreckage in the middle of the arena. He directed every vestige of his strength towards his son. Dra'zen was the first to follow suit. Then every rank of the Faction of Origin.

Slowly they restored and raised him back up. With a snarl Luhka Sha sought to intervene, but the power emanating from Ba'zel forced the representative of the Faction of Departure back. He fought against it, strained with his every sinew, but could not come close enough to attack.

Ba'zel's eyes drank in the warrior, stripping him of his power. Yet Luhka Sha was suddenly bolstered as well. He grew, fed by command of the Faction of Departure. He matched Ba'zel and exceeded him once more. The factions of Expedience and Contemplation imbued Ba'zel with yet more power. Insistence and Consumption came in to swell Luhka Sha. The entire chamber teetered. The realm shook as the Declension wielded titanic forces of will and destruction.

Ba'zel stared up at the monstrous Lead Warrior, commanding that he break, imagining it, tricking him, tripping circumstance, twisting fate. Luhka Sha loomed over him, hammering at him, battering, unbalancing, feinting, undermining. The Lead Warrior conjured the ghosts of the generations of warriors he'd consumed, and drew on their ancient lore to find ways through and around the enemy factions. He strangled the flow of their power to Ba'zel. Ba'zel felt himself slipping.

'No!' he begged.

And here your struggle pivots. On your decision to serve or not. Is your ego beyond all compass? Will you allow it to destroy you? Or will you recognise it cannot triumph over all else? Will you see your limits, accept their definition and serve me? Or not? She simpered in his ear. *It would be nothing for me to tip all in your favour. Nothing at all. Simply bind yourself to my service. For now you must decide. It is the way of things. Refuse and you fail. Existence always comes down to this. It is the nature of will. Without it, there is nothing. Now, Ba'zel, now.*

He had lost. 'I bind myself to your service.'

And I accept you, Ba'zel of House Ba'zel. This moment is a further delight for me, for it will reveal, one way or another, whether the troublesome Israine was right. Oh, I am sorry, are you familiar with the concept of delight?

'I learned much from the beings of the seventh realm, most holy.'

Indeed. Come, then, and let us see if you are the unstable element *made flesh or not. Be the* unstable element *for me, Ba'zel, and undo Luhka Sha. Let us see if I have successfully brought about the living incarnation of that element to serve as the instrument of my will, a will that must therefore become absolute throughout the cosmos. You will be our greatest triumph. For you are my son and I saw you raised and put through the sorts of trials that would force the hand of the cosmos. At last the one principle and element to resist me will be mine to command.*

It had been *Her* all along. Of course it had. *She* had conceived all this before *She* had given him his birth. From the beginning, he had been defined and given existence by *Her* will and self. It was *She* who had seen to it that he was schooled so that he would be *unstable*. It was *She* who had seen him flee his father and become the opposition to the Declension. It was *She* who had made him into something so inimical to the Declension that he could undo a Virtue and entirely destabilise the Declension's will in the seventh realm. And it was *She* to whom he had bound himself. It was *She* whom he served.

The stronger Luhka Sha became, the more clearly Ba'zel could see the flows of power and magic maintaining the Lead Warrior. It was a simple matter to destabilise and disrupt those flows. Ba'zel drew the power to himself instead. Luhka Sha immediately began to fail.

Ba'zel drained the greater part of Luhka Sha's life energy from him, reducing him to a dull and listless creature. The once mighty champion groaned and fell to his knees, barely able to keep himself atop the pillars. His head lowered until he had fully abased himself.

The Lead Warrior is the first to acknowledge and submit to the Great Virtue, he who is Ba'zel, the Eldest spoke to every mind. *All will follow him.*

As one the Declension bowed to their Great Virtue, he who would now deliver them the cosmos.

CHAPTER 6:

Or those that were never created

'So, Praxis, old friend, how have you been since, you know, you died?' Torpeth asked delicately, bringing his face up close.

'Silence, impecunious imp!' the Minister retorted, slapping him away.

The holy man ducked easily and came back, blocking the spectre's gaze, distracting him. 'Come now, lowlander, you do not mean that. The dead crave anything they can get from the living. You want my words and attention, for they help sustain your spirit. Don't be shy. You know you are as happy as I am that we are reunited. You have missed your lively servant, yes?'

Saint Praxis softened his expression and came even closer to the mountain man. He wrapped long arms around him and clasped him tightly. He inhaled Torpeth's breath and smiled malignly as the small man shuddered. 'Still you do not see,' came the sibilant whisper. 'It is your own sin that has brought you here, pagan. You now number among the dead, and will do so for ever more. There is nothing I want from you, for where you are dead I am now *un*dead. I am the master and you are the servant. It was always thus, was it not? You are the sinner who begs my forgiveness. It is *you* who begs *my* word and attention. It is *you* who pesters *me*. It is you who comes close, though you know you only deserve my punishment for your past waywardness. Your soul is conflicted, is it not? Yes, see how you flinch at my touch, even though it is you who has come to me. You are torn. You fear the punishment but desire it so that you might then be forgiven and saved from your

165

deadly sin. What is it you always used to say when you were alive, dear Torpeth? What was it about payment? Come, whisper it in your friend and master's ear.'

Unable to break free, unable to meet the secret knowledge in the Saint's eyes, Torpeth mumbled miserably, 'Payment is ever due.'

'Yes, that's it,' the Saint sighed, his lips touching Torpeth's ear. 'Payment is ever due. That is why you have come to join the dead, is it not? Your debt has become too great even for you to bear, poor Torpeth. You see? It is not I who wants anything from you. Instead, it is you who wants something from me. Understanding. Compassion. Strict guidance. The cruelty that is kindness. Peace. That's it, isn't it? You have never had true peace, have you, my beloved Torpeth? Always restless, always fighting. Always capering. Always defiant. Never with any peace. Nothing but torment for years beyond counting and even beyond your own memory. No peace. Is that what you would have of me then? Peace?'

Tears like diamonds fell from the holy man's cheeks. 'Yes,' he confessed.

'Would you have me lay you down here so that you might rest in peace for ever more?'

Torpeth nodded forlornly. His lips replied in the positive, but his breath had given out.

'I cannot hear you,' Saint Praxis said gently to the ancient being who was no more than a child. 'Say it more loudly, sweet Torpeth. Say it as a prayer to those who want nothing more than to hear the truth of your sacred heart. Say it as praise and thanks for their love. Say it as you rejoice in their mercy. Say it for your final absolution and salvation. Say it so that the torment can finally end and you can rest in peace.'

His heart and mind close to breaking, Aspin watched as Saint Praxis lowered Torpeth the Great to the misty ground of the nether realm. The small man was stiff, his lower jaw slack and his eyes empty of life. He was dead. How could it be? How was it possible that the mountain man who was as annoying as he was energetic was deceased? The naked warrior who was as wise as he was foolish, as brave as he was repulsive, was no more. How? This was the land of the dead. Where then was his soul? Was it trapped within the mortified flesh or had it been drunk by the despised lyche that was Saint Praxis?

166

'Damn you!' Aspin choked, abandoning the protective huddle of his men in a bid to strike down the hated apparition.

'Chief, no!' Bantith of Godsend begged. 'We must stay together.'

'With him!' Lars demanded of his comrades, lumbering forward.

Phantoms raced in among them, snarling, mocking and mimicking. Saint Sylvan was suddenly between Aspin and Saint Praxis, moving so fast that he mazed the eye and deceived the mountain chieftain's spear. Aspin's thrusts and strikes were wasted effort, and energy that only fed his tormentors. Now he'd lost contact with his men, he lost body heat at an alarming rate. He could see his breath. It escaped his trembling lips and took on the shape of new phantasms. Was his own ghost about to leave his body? Becoming fearful he retreated again, and that encouraged the dead even more. They came at him now as if invigorated.

Just as he'd gorged himself in life, Saint Goza was the hungriest of the dead. The massive shadow of his stomach was a void that could never be filled. He spread his arms wide as if he intended to gather all the mountain men up in one go. His prodigious lower jaw hung in anticipation, making his eyes and head seem too small. He had the square teeth of an ogre, which were used for the chomping, grinding and tearing of bone, flesh and hide. He was a nightmarish cannibal, larger and more terrifying than life itself. 'Just a nibble!' he avidly confided to all those he came near. 'Nothing more than a taste. Give me a morsel of yourself and then I'll move on to another person. I promise. A tender crunch, chew and swallow. Spare it to spare yourself. If all give a small bit willingly, none need have everything taken from them. No need or room for selfishness here. All must share. You *must*!'

'Here is all you'll have of me, you beast!' Lars braved, plunging his spear fully half its length into Saint Goza's gut.

The giant Saint shuddered and fell foward so that Lars's left arm up to the elbow was engulfed. The warrior cried out – the limb he pulled free was cruelly withered, a lifeless and torpid thing. 'Oh, sweet gods!'

Shadowy tendrils reached round and past Saint Goza, winding like serpents tasting the air in search of prey. The hair of Saint Zoriah the weather witch floated and curled around the mountain men. Black lightning flickered between the strands, permanently tearing apart the mist of the nether realm and immolating any shade unfortunate enough to be in its path. Bantith took cautious steps back, fearing the touch of death, but that only seemed to attract Saint Zoriah's power and bring it twisting towards him all the faster. It was all around his head, the strands about to ensnare and strangle him. He froze, not daring to breathe or even call out for help.

The majority of the mountain men were dismayed by what befell their leaders, and were caught between going to their aid, holding their position and falling back so that their numbers and their own lives would be preserved. There was a chaos of shouted warnings, instructions and pleas. Men collided with each other and several were tripped. One tried to run but fled into the cold embrace of the serried ranks of the dead, lost all strength and disappeared from sight. The grey of the mist became speckled with buzzing motes of darkness. It was the madness of the overwrought and terrified. Incoherence made manifest, as when the vision of an exhausted person becomes spotted and unreal. Saint Dianon brought his stinging, crawling, writhing power to bear.

'They are not for you!' Saint Virulus whined jealously. 'Goza, you presume too much. Their life energy is not for you. You will obey good Saint Praxis, for he is the voice of he who sits the throne.'

Saint Goza had been about to bury the distraught Lars under his massive bulk, but hesitated. He glanced towards Saint Praxis, flinched as if struck and then took careful steps back from the warrior.

'Know this,' came the dripping voice of Saint Praxis. 'All that exists in the nether realm belongs to him alone. None may take anything for themselves unless he commands it. Where is the doubt in this? Answer me, Goza.'

Saint Goza's jowls wobbled as he tried to get a grip on himself and find his voice. 'There is none.'

'Will you make excuse?' Saint Praxis's gaze was ravening.

Saint Goza looked as if he shrivelled. 'There is none. I know that. There is only punishment, service and penance.'

'Yes. Now lift Torpeth's body. We will bring it with these others to the foot of his throne. We head for the dread temple at the heart of this land.'

This could not be happening. The dead should have no control of the living. 'Come together!' Aspin commanded, his voice breaking despite his best efforts.

'Oh, it is far too late for that, pagan,' Saint Praxis informed him

168

smugly. 'You have already betrayed yourselves. You are allowed a last vestige of life for now only because he wishes to take it from you himself. I should tell you that the spirits of all your pagan ancestors are imprisoned in the temple, including the last traces of your father, Chief Aspin. Resist now and they will be ended. Come willingly and you will at least be with them for a while.'

'My father!' Aspin moaned.

'Slavin, yes. And your grandfather. And you, you are Bantith, yes? Your mother has such a gentle soul. I know. I have tasted it. She misses you greatly, but mourns that you have not spoken with her in such a long time.'

'I-I meant to say a prayer. Life in Godsend is just so …' the trader replied hopelessly.

'This way, pagans. Your good intentions have paved your way to the hell of the dread temple, where you will beg his punishment. You were never really alive, you pagans. You were always *un*alive at best. Bring them.'

Freda brought Jillan up through the ground and into his home in Haven. The place was dark and empty. The hearth was cold and unswept. The air was dank – the small dwelling had not been aired. And beneath the dankness there was another faint odour, an odour similar to those they'd encountered at the blood oasis.

Jillan shivered. *Someone walk across your grave?* 'Can you feel it?'

Freda gave the impression of turning and shrugging. 'I feel nothing, friend Jillan. What is it?'

Maybe something you ate?

'The atmosphere in here … it's *wrong* … as if something terrible had happened.'

'There are traces of blood between some of the stones.'

'A lot of blood?'

'How much is a lot, friend Jillan?'

After all, if someone's guts are hauled out, it's surprising how far they stretch.

'Did someone die?' Where was Samnir? And Hella? Ye gods, Hella!

'I do not know.'

'I thought you could see things, or something like that.'

'Only if there is enough light to focus. We have been in the earth, friend Jillan. And I do not think I can look back in time.'

Interesting idea. But she'd need to find light that was around at the time, old light if you like. The event would need to have left an impression on the light too. Not sure that's possible, even with a violent event. Besides, Freda tends to avoid the light, haven't you noticed? She probably won't even want to try it, for fear Sinisar will find her. He already knows where you are, though. You know that, right? He'll have heard you speak of coming here even while you were at the oasis. Bit careless of you, speaking like that in broad daylight, eh?

Jillan took a calming breath. The panic and paranoia inside him receded reluctantly. He looked more deliberately around his stone house and spied his armour in the shadows of one corner. He went to it and buckled it on. He felt better for having done so. Its runes shone and winked at him.

'Jillan, there is someone else here!' Freda warned, moving quickly to confront the deeper shadows within one of the bedchambers. Smouldering eyes watched her.

'It is the wolf, Freda. Ash's friend. It's alright.'

'Wolf?' the rock woman asked uncertainly, backing away. 'I-I don't remember any wolf.'

'Of course you do. It's always around.'

'I do not sense its movement upon the stones as I do with others.'

Wolves are stealthy, came the cunning lupine thought, as if it was their own. *Invisible if we choose.*

'Wolf,' Jillan asked as he came forward, 'what has happened here? Is all well in Haven?'

Your lack of vigilance and your absence have allowed hangers-on of the elseworlders to come among us. They came stealing in to cause havoc, like a wolf entering an unguarded chicken run or a field of sheep. Once I became aware of them, I chased them back, but the damage is done and remains with us like a sickness. Our pack turns on itself, its members affrighted and crazed. I would put down those who are the most distressed and diseased, for they are a danger to the rest, but the numbers are too great. Our pack would be left too small to defend itself in the future.

'We humans cannot put down the distressed and the diseased, wolf. It is not our way.'

The wolf huffed. *It is not your* way, *one who calls himself Jillan.*

'It is not the way of *any* of the humans in Haven!' The wolf let its tongue loll free and showed its teeth. It seemed to be mocking him. 'Anyway, you can't put them down, so what would a wolf do instead?'

A wolf would leave the pack, to ensure its survival. The pack leader would abandon the others, save perhaps the strongest of the females. The pack would separate. A panted breath.

'If I were to do that, we could be hunted down individually. There is strength in numbers, no?'

There is weakness also. Too many mouths to feed. Too many to hide effectively. Too great a scent to mask. Constant challenge of the pack leader. Yet it is the way of you humans. You have all manner of words for it, do you not? Community, society, tradition, tribe, race, kingdom, empire... useless and confusing words, all. It simply means you will not abandon the pack even as it becomes rabid and threatens all.

'I cannot leave Haven to Sinisar!'

Why not? If his pack is the stronger, then it would be wise to give up this territory. Let his pack compete with the hangers-on of the elseworlders while our pack reforms and recovers.

'Wolf, may I speak?' Freda chimed. 'Sinisar does not simply want this territory. He wants to destroy me, Jillan and probably our entire pack. If we run, he will hunt us. He may allow our weaker members to join his own following, but all others he will ultimately seek to kill ... Hella, Samnir, probably Ash. He is a wolf that seeks to devour all other wolves.'

That is not the behaviour of a wolf. It is not our way, even for one that is rabid.

'No,' Jillan said sorrowfully. 'It is the way of men and gods, men and gods who call themselves sane. Wolf, we must fight here with what numbers we can.'

I will mourn your passing, one who calls himself Jillan. You know I cannot remain.

'You are a wolf.'

I am a wolf.

'I will explain to Ash, if I can find him when he's sober enough to take it in.'

You must act quickly then, for Hella, Samnir and Ash are already caught up in the frenzy of our pack. Keep them alive as you may. Do not hesitate to put down any who are so crazed that they would seek to prevent it. Farewell, rock woman.

'I will not hesitate, friend to Ash.'

He gave me hedgehogs and squirrels to eat. They tasted good. The hedgehogs were too prickly for me to open and the squirrels too quick to catch. Ash has his uses. It may serve you and him well to remember that. Farewell.

The shadows in the bedchamber became less substantial and the wolf was gone. Jillan went back to the corner of the room and lifted his bow and quiver from where they lay. Now to find his beloved Hella amid the frenzy.

Houses like dead dreams stood to either side of the road to the dread temple. They cast gravestone shadows down upon the Saints, Aspin's warriors and the silent army of spectres guarding them. The must and decay of death permeated everything, and haunted the mountain men with visions of being buried deep in the ground, trapped. Claustrophobia and grief held them in a waking rigor mortis. Aspin saw the faces of his brave warriors turn ashen and fall slack, almost torpid. Their eyes became desolate and their heads dropped. Their movements became slow, stilted and shuffling, until they were strung out along the road rather than bunched together. Soon they were indistinguishable from the shades around them.

Only quick Bantith seemed able to hold on to any of his vigour, and he kept so close to his chieftain that they frequently bumped or touched. Aspin could have kissed him for it. Were it not for that closeness and companionship – that *connection* to life – Aspin was sure he would have failed along with the others. The eyes of the Godsender moved with constant terror, making him look like he was having a fit, as he glanced at every shadow and flinched at every unexpected movement. It was as if he sensed a killer right on top of them, but could not pinpoint from where the final moment would come. His low whine and the failing breath of his comrades were all that could be heard.

The houses gave way to shattered palaces and ruined castles. Vast slabs of black basalt lay broken, as if giants had warred there. The works of man were as nothing before the power of the nether realm and the terrible force that ended all things. What hope could there be for the realm of the living? Its fall to the nether realm was inevitable.

Then came sculptures and contrivances stretching beyond sight. Feet and limbs of impossible size made clear the insignificance and impermanence of those that travelled below. The curve and sweep of colossal forms, an unimaginable expanse of midnight substance and nightmare hue, painted the lost gods of ages past who were now at eternal rest. There was the suggestion of wing, horn and predatory fang, but there was also warp, twist and monstrosity to defeat human understanding, terrorise the imagination and humble any claim of intellect and philosophy. There was exquisite poignancy and then there was loss beyond description. Beauty and ugliness were meaningless. The only definition was the passing animation known as *life* and the eternal petrification that was *death* and the nether realm.

Aspin's wits fled he knew not where. He was limp flesh twitching a few last times, as if in its final throes or already submitting to mortification. He was in life's funeral procession, seeing it taken to its final resting place at the dread temple. Saint Goza carried the body before them, the body that had once been called Torpeth the Great, he who had known and seen more life than any of mortalkind. He had revelled and exulted in it like no other, even rising above the gods themselves for a while. Yet it could never have lasted, for he was ultimately mortal and limited by his own nature. Indeed, it was the inevitable and self-fulfilling actions of his very self and nature that had ensured he could not last. Ultimately, his very attempt to overreach and be *more* had exposed him fatally. In rising above the gods he had seen them fall, and near undone the world that allowed him life and existence. To save himself he had raised them back up, but they had been left with no choice but to punish him and put him down for ever, lest his understanding of existence cause him to rise once more.

The body was not just Torpeth, it was all mortalkind. All mortals sought to better themselves or improve their situation. The fight to survive required it, nay demanded it. It saw them reach and overreach. Fight and strive. Win and lose. Live and die. It saw all of them live, all of them die. Every last one of them. And now that moment approached. All ended at the dread temple.

The sense of loss was all-encompassing. Devastated plains stretched away to both sides of the road now. Life-sucking winds scattered and obliterated hundreds and then thousands of the Heroes at the periphery of the ghastly army. The huge number remaining hardly noticed and did not care.

'Keep to the road and you will not be harmed,' Saint Praxis intoned. 'Only those who step off the path are lost.'

Lost, Aspin thought to himself, and looked out across the wasted vista. Grey swirling columns chased back and forth, scouring all in their path. One raced towards Aspin, spinning so fast it rent the air around it as if with long claws. It shredded everything – light, substance and spirit. It was a demonic dervish come to take his soul.

Aspin cried out in fear and dragged Bantith with him to the other side of the road. A taloned and emaciated devil leaped at them. It had black holes where its eyes should have been, a porcine snout and needle-like teeth. It was need incarnate. Saint Sylvan was suddenly there, preventing the two of them from stepping off the road.

'Pay it no mind.'

'What is it?'

'It is a malacant, the spirit of one who is no longer remembered by any of the living. It wanders these plains for eternity, always searching for, but never finding, what it once was. It will not even know the name it once had when alive. It is an empty and mindless thing, knowing only anger and hunger. Treat it as if it is not there and it will have no power over you. Focus on it, cower from it, step from the road, and it will have you.'

Saint Praxis turned his head to give Aspin a lifeless grin. 'It will not directly attack any who travel on the road in the direction of the dread temple, for such travellers belong to he who sits on the throne. But should any prisoners stray from the road, then the malacant will not hesitate, for it is the guards who will have failed *his* will.'

'It's almost worth dying for,' Aspin replied without any trace of humour. 'What about those travelling on the road *away* from the dread temple?'

'The malacants are free to attack them, and do so in overwhelming numbers. There is no return from the dread temple for the likes of you. None whatsoever.'

'Abandon all hope?' Bantith groaned.

'Attempt to take but one step back along the road now and malacants from all around will come to pull the soul out of you, stretch it from one end of the nether realm to the other, and then use that as their endless plain,' Saint Praxis taunted. 'They will scour, dig and delve into it, scrabbling, churning and trammelling it. The torment will be without end. You have betrayed yourselves. You are committed to this path and there can never be escape. As is his will, for ever more.'

Bantith sobbed in despair.

'Yet you will return from the dread temple,' Aspin said.

'If that is his will. If he wills it, we will carry forth his will. The Saints are his servants, no more than that. As he wills it, we are given the strength necessary to travel the realm unchallenged. In his name, any can be made to sustain us.'

'How?'

Saint Praxis hesitated. It was clear a part of him knew it might be best to demur, but he had become more avid the longer he had spoken, the longer he had enjoyed their attention, the more he had been able to instil fear in Bantith. He was more animated now than he had been at any time since they'd entered the nether realm. 'I was the first to be allowed holy communion by he who sits the throne, he who commands both life and death. I was anointed and blessed with his eternal blood. I then went forth to raise up these good Saints, and spread the glory of his word and will throughout the nether realm. It has seen a wondrous transformation come about, such that we will soon bring his glory back into the realm of the living, as it was always meant to be. As is his will!'

Blood. Somehow Azual had become imbued with the magic of the elseworlders once more. One or more of the elseworlders had to have survived the fall of the Great Temple and found a way into the nether realm! The Empire had been reborn in the nether realm. And now the entire nether realm was on the verge of rising up to claim the land of the living as its own. Azual's army would be immense, beyond imagining. It would comprise the dead of the countless generations of human existence. Surely there could be no hope for Haven or the Geas. The Empire of the Saviours would be absolute. 'Ye gods. What have we done? Damn you, Torpeth!'

Jillan and Freda stepped out of the small dwelling. As if on cue, Ash and Tebrus came up the slope towards them.

'Freda, can you see where Hella is and if she's alright?'

'I will try, friend Jillan,' the rock woman murmured. She drew in light, so much that it was as if the sun dimmed. She was a rent through the fabric of the day. 'I see her! A woman cares for her. Jacob is there. He is hurt.'

'And Hella?'

'It is not clear.'

'What happened? Freda, tell me!'

'I-I do not know. There is no way to—'

Ash reached them. 'I'll tell you what happened. They were attacked by that maniac, that's what happened! I tried to warn you, but you wouldn't listen. Now see what's happened. Hella's damned lucky to be alive. And Jacob ...'

Tebrus hung back a step, eyes on Freda. He made the sign against evil. 'What apparition is this? Does death stand at your shoulder, Jillan?'

Jillan looked from one to the other. 'Stop. Where is Hella?'

Ash dropped his accusatory tone. 'We'll take you to her, won't we, Tebrus?'

The broad leader of the Unclean closed his eyes for a second so that he could avert his gaze from Freda, and then was careful not to look in her direction. 'We've set guards around Hella's home so that they can't get to her. Don't worry, she's well protected.'

'So that *who* can't get to her?' Jillan asked impatiently as he pushed past them.

'Gallen and his men, of course,' Ash replied. 'They came with weapons, demanding to talk to her, but no one trusts them not to pick up from where Samnir left off.'

'It was Samnir?' Jillan could not help asking. 'Samnir?'

'We must hurry, friend Jillan,' Freda said behind them. 'There is some trouble. Many people are shouting. Pushing and shoving.'

'Treachery!' Ash breathed. 'I knew they couldn't be trusted.'

They ran down the slope at full tilt, Jillan's heart pounding. He could not believe what was happening. Samnir had attacked Hella? Were the Heroes now intent upon harming her? It made no sense. All she'd ever done was help the Godsenders, the People of the Empire. How could they now be turning on her? Had the Saints returned? Did they control the minds of their army once more? Was the nightmare beginning again? His head spun. Or had the nightmare never gone away?

His vision jolted and jarred. He hardly recognised Haven any more. It was nothing like the first time he had run down this slope, when he'd raced the Peculiar to the Geas. Then he'd had wings at his feet. Now he moved as if through mud, slow and laboured. The perfect Haven of his memory was now the dream, a dream that faded and disappeared in the harsh light of day. It was all wrong, all upside down. What had he brought them to? What had he done? Hella.

His power rose up. It did not snarl or rail. Its will and his own were one. Its determination was absolute. Implacable. If he had to unmake all to save her, then unmake all he would. If he must undo himself in the process, then that was the price that he would pay. But it might still all be for naught. 'Freda, you are faster. Go stop them. Do whatever must be done. Quickly!'

The ground trembled as the rock woman surged below and past them. Jillan remained sure-footed and Ash's perfect timing saw him untroubled, but Tebrus lost his balance and fell back behind them.

They must all be stopped. He would stop the world if he could. How dare they threaten his beloved? How dare they! 'How could you let this happen?' His voice was the sound of mountains breaking and forests falling.

Ash sprang from outcrop to flat stone, to tree stump, to packed earth. His features moved as adroitly as the rest of him. 'How? You ask me how, you who left me languishing in a punishment chamber? You should be asking the question of yourself, Jillan Hunterson, not me.'

'You will never accept responsibility, will you? For anything. Are you still that coward, then, Ash? *My friend?*'

'*Friend*, now, is it? Now you remember the term. Now, when I am free of that prison you made for me, now when you are most in need of my help.' His words danced with the rest of him, never missing a beat or a step. 'Responsibility? How can I exercise it when you keep me imprisoned? I cannot. Yet still you will demand it of me. If I am a coward, Jillan Hunterson, then you are still that petulant boy who knows nothing of the world. Who is it helping you now? Who was it saved you from Izat at Godsend? Who was it ended the Saviours besetting Samnir at the Great Temple? And what have you *ever* given me in return? *Ever!* A prison. And nothing more.'

Jillan glared at the woodsman, seeing only the shifting face of the

Peculiar, hearing only the Peculiar's taunting words. He didn't even know his friends any more. 'You have only ever imprisoned yourself, Ash. Your hut in the forest. Your inn. The punishment chamber. All prisons of your own making, or ones that you sought out. Would you blame the Empire? Would you blame me? Then do so.'

'And who would you blame for what has befallen Hella and Jacob? Would you blame me? Would you blame Samnir? Then do so.'

There could be no winning this argument. It was the way of men and gods, even when it threatened all.

Jillan gritted his teeth and bent his head, concentrating on his running. They were past the Gathering Place already. They veered left and in among the houses.

'Ash, tell me this. What did Samnir do to them?' Jillan panted.

'What do you think? He attacked them without provocation, just as he'd previously attacked me. Tried to kill them.'

'But why?'

'Because you don't know him as well as you like to think. Because you wouldn't listen to me in the first place. Because you like to think ill of me just because I enjoy a drink too many sometimes. He's the Sand Devil! Yes, he's helped us in a few fights, but only in the way of an ill-fed dog of war. Send him against the enemy and he will serve you well and take his fill. But once the fighting is over, beware, for he will have a taste for blood and take his next meal wherever he can. You should not lie down to sleep before you have destroyed that dog, no matter how well he has served.'

'Where is he?'

Ash spat on the ground. 'He threw me out of the punishment chamber and took my place. It is the most easily defended place in Haven, after all. Once we found out what he'd done, we came for him, but Gallen and his men turned us back. The Heroes look after their own. They're as thick as thieves. And now they've come for Hella.'

He didn't want to believe it. He could not. Samnir was the old soldier who'd stood a quiet vigil over his childhood and freed him from the clutches of Minister Praxis.

He was a disgraced soldier who knew nothing of loyalty to the Empire and army that clothed and fed him. He was the corrupt sentry who took a hefty bribe from your father to let you out of Godsend all those years ago.

178

Bribe? There had never been a bribe, had there?

Don't be naive. Of course there was a bribe, paid once you were safely out of town.

Samnir was his friend. Samnir had offered him a kind word and told him stories when all Jillan had been getting at school was Haal's bullying and insults. Samnir was almost a father to him now Jed was gone.

He was an ambitious man looking to find advantage and influence within Godsend. You were precisely what he needed, and he's kept a close and possessive watch on you ever since.

It couldn't be true, and yet it was happening before his very eyes. How could he have misjudged so badly?

Do not be angry with yourself. You have betrayed no one, his magic remonstrated.

No, it was Samnir who was the betrayer. The rage built even higher in Jillan. The sky above Haven deepened, traces of lightning flickering among the looming clouds. The wind shouted and moaned. There were the jostling crowds a hundred feet ahead of him, a silhouette like Kathuula one moment and starkly lit anger the next. He smelt ozone, human sweat and fear. He didn't recognise any of the stretched glaring faces. He tasted blood in the back of his throat. How *dare* they do this? The storm began to whine.

Freda exploded up out of the ground in the midst of the fray, earth, rocks and people flying in all directions. The front rank of Heroes toppled with no line of inhabitants left to push against. Screaming soldiers pitched into her light-absorbing umbra and were swallowed by it. Their cries for help were hideous to hear. Some were dragged free and others crawled out, but every one of them was badly affected – whether with hair turned to white, skin turned ashen, a shaking like palsy, or eyes staring and haunted.

'Ye gods, protect us!'

'It is the gods that punish us for Haven.'

'No, it is a trick of the Unclean. Hold your ground!'

'Lies!' hurled back a tough wielding a cudgel, clearly one of Tebrus's men. 'The Heroes are in league with some demon. Kill it!'

'Stand back, people of Haven! It is me, Freda. Clear the way for Jillan. Stop!'

Heroes jabbed their spears at her. The inhabitants struck with staves and whatever tools they had brought with them. Freda swatted at them, crushing armour and sending people howling to the ground. Both sides fell back for a second, until sun-metal flared and rallied them once more. Light slashed through Freda's shadow and sank into her hard body. She roared with the force and agony of a volcano. Her assailant was killed with a single skull-breaking blow of her fist.

'Together!' Captain Gallen called. 'As one! Ready!'

'NO!' Jillan yelled, his voice a thunderclap, but none turned to heed him.

Freda smote the ground and broke it apart beneath the feet of any within a dozen yards of her. Men, women and Heroes alike were brought down, dragging others with them. Those beyond them at last began to retreat. All except the giant Dor, who had been positioned on the doorstep of Jacob's house, apparently to guard it against all entry, and had been watching carefully for his chance. Now he leaped forward with a shouted challenge to tackle the threat. He matched Freda for size and – catching her off guard – managed to get his arms around her and bring her down.

'Dor, no!' Ash called, but the giant didn't hear him.

'Sun-metal!' Captain Gallen called, crawling forward on hands and knees. 'Quickly, before the monster rises. For Haven!'

The wolf had told him not to hesitate. As Freda dragged Dor into the ground, Jillan cast aside his quiver and bow and unleashed raw force along the street, to throw back all that were still standing. Inhabitants were lifted off their feet and flung against walls or sent rolling and tumbling. A wooden spar holding up a roof creaked ominously, then gave way and became a missile that just missed several heads. The roof leaned precariously, shedding tiles that went spinning with deadly force. One punched like a blade into a helpless Hero's breastplate, but fortunately failed to pass all the way through. The sky came down on Haven, pressing everything low. Jillan's runes blazed redly through the murk, writing murder on the pitiful buildings and people before him.

Ash put out a hand to restrain him, but Jillan shrugged him off savagely as he marched forward to the home of his beloved Hella. None would prevent him, not while he breathed.

'What has possessed you, Jillan? Do you attack the People now?'

Ignore him. He is the Peculiar seeking to bend your mind.

'Must all obey you as if you were now Saint? Will you destroy all, as Azual did at New Sanctuary?'

He nearly hesitated then. *If you were such, he would not dare offer such dissent. He would fawn instead. Do not let him distract you or find purchase upon you. He is just one more who would manipulate you. Do not hesitate. Your father told you that when you first left Godsend. Do you remember?*

Yes, he remembered. He should have struck at his enemies all the sooner and with more conviction. Then he might not have lost so many that he held dear. Why had he delayed? Why had he hesitated? He wasn't sure any more. Perhaps he should never have left Godsend in the first place. It was all muddled but in some ways clearer than it had ever been before. He would strike them all down so that none would take Hella from him in the way they had taken his parents. None.

'Jillan, you are crazed! Do you have Samnir's illness? What is it you intend? I cannot let you harm Hella.'

Ash was suddenly in front of him. Jillan went to push him, but Ash turned his torso at the precise moment, grabbed his wrists and yanked him forward so that their faces were close.

'You *will* answer me!' the woodsman vowed, the whiskers of his unkempt beard tickling Jillan's cheek and the sourness of ale unmistakable on his breath.

Jillan fiercely met his eye. 'Why would you prevent me seeing Hella, Ash? What are you hiding? All this has played to your advantage, has it not? Samnir is out of your way, and the people and the Unclean are up in arms, a match for Captain Gallen and entirely at your bidding. Your cowardice causes you to seek power wherever you can, does it not? Controlling people makes you feel safe. If I see Hella, what will I learn that will see your schemes all unravel, eh?'

Ash's eyes flickered and Jillan saw the truth of his words confirmed there. The woodsman opened his mouth to make a denial and counter-accusation, but Jillan was not about to allow it.

'No! You listen to me. I know what fear is and I know what it does to people. I know it makes them drink more than they usually would. I know it makes them say and do things at odds with their nature. I know it makes strange and twisted creatures of them. I do not blame you for it, Ash. I do not blame you. Step aside now and all will be well. None will be hurt further than they already have been. You will be my friend as you ever were, as will Samnir. You have my word on that. But fail to stand aside, fail to unhand me, and I will wither you where you stand. You have caught hold of something more terrible than you know. You grip the very thing that will torture you beyond endurance. Your perfect timing cannot save you now you have grabbed a power for yourself that will harrow your very soul. Let go of it, Ash, *my friend*. Or rue the day that we first met. Seek to keep me from Hella, the woman I will marry, and you will destroy yourself. This moment is where you decide who you are and what the rest of your life will be. It is all yours, Ash, all yours. Choose.'

Ash dropped his eyes, looking down at the white-knuckled and dirty hands with which he manacled Jillan's wrists. His fingers were bony and had cracked and blackened nails. His mouth quirked. 'Well, if you put it like that, I don't have much choice, do I?' He still didn't look up. He frowned and his hands shook as if they fought him. He grimaced and finally uncurled one finger. 'I do rue that first day we met, you know. I had a nice hut in the woods with plenty of game and homebrew, and the wolf to keep me safe.'

'The wolf has left.'

Ash sighed. Another finger loosened. Then he let go.

Jillan went past him and strode for Jacob's house. The woodsman followed. The ever-doughty Captain Gallen was just coming to his feet again. Freda rose once more, and crouched, waiting. There was no sign of Dor anywhere. The group came closer together, watching each other warily.

'Captain Gallen, Ash, you will help the injured as you can,' Jillan ordered them. 'There will be *no* further confrontation. If I hear but one raised voice, then woe betide the pair of you. We can no longer afford this infighting. Our enemies gather. If it's strife, conflict and grief you want, then do not worry, for there will be more than enough to go round. Far more. Pull yourselves together. I'm going inside now. Freda, watch these two, will you, because I trust them about as far as I can throw them. Freda, you're in charge, understand?'

'Yes, friend Jillan,' the rock woman replied as Jillan moved away.

Captain Gallen straightened up and saluted.

'It's good to have you back, Jillan,' Ash called. 'I've said all along you should be doing more. Now, Freda, about Dor. He can come across as a bit oafish and heavy-handed when you first meet him, but he's really not that bad. Quite sensitive, really. You know, he has a kitten he feeds every day? I think the two of you could come to be quite good friends. Like what you're doing with the new look, by the way. You haven't hurt him too badly, have you? He's single, you know, and … Ow!'

'Stop speaking, friend Ash. I'm in charge,' Freda rumbled and clanged.

'Alright, alright! Put me down. Gallen, get her off me.'

'He's still speaking, Freda. Maybe if you shake him? Harder? Just a suggestion. Pull his tongue out?'

They travelled the road to the dread temple, across blasted plains, past sucking bogs and through hills yawning like hellmouths. They passed through storms of ire and anguish, several mountain men disappearing in despair. They cried in vain for mercy or relief, but their words meant nothing. There was only the dread temple, the pilgrimage of death and the sacrifice of life. It awaited them, inevitable. They realised it had always been there in the middle of their sight, invisible at first but still the focal point, the most real thing in the entire landscape. The knowledge of it had been with them since birth, even if it had been forgotten or wreathed round with dreams and misty memories. Always there. Right before them. The spot in the eye. The place just before the forehead that all struggled to focus on with just their two eyes but that could sometimes be seen with the mind's eye. The monster hiding in plain sight. The oft-visiting nightmare crouched and waiting in the back of the brain. The thing that searched for a glimpse of the soul. The tarmigant that stalked, leaped and wrestled the struggling soul to the edge of the pit.

The dread temple. The Eternal Keep. The throne of the King of the Dead. The anvil of the soul. The mouth of Time's ogre.

Aspin looked up at the midnight walls. They stretched skyward, only pointing and defecating gargoyles breaking the monotony. The wailing from within was overwhelming, a plague to all rational thought. Did they sing insanely or scream in pleasure? The sound pierced and penetrated, stroked and sucked. It made Aspin want to slough off his skin and flesh. Tear his genitalia away, pluck out his eyes. The stench of offal and filth made his stomach clench then writhe, as if it would climb up out of his mouth or force its way out of his behind.

His elbow was an agony of fire. He looked down. Bantith gripped him so hard there that his nails had drawn beads of blood. The nostrils of the accompanying Saints quivered and their eyes were brought to the red jewels. Saint Zoriah's tongue curled and flicked. Saint Sylvan shimmered in agitation. Saint Goza drooled, and his stomach groaned. Saint Virulus measured all jealously. Saint Dianon buzzed with such a pitch and intensity that the realm around him seemed to dissolve. But Saint Praxis judged them all.

'Here is reminder to you all of your sin and failure. Once-proud but ultimately pathetic beggars and hangers-on. You come crawling to his door to beg of him, for you have and are nothing yourselves. You will do and say anything in the hope of alms or to be taken in, when your only due should be contempt and a beating from the door. Do you want that contempt and beating?'

'Yes, anything!' the Saints pleaded.

'Even if he should then decide he has no use for you?'

'Oh yes!'

'Just let us abide here in the shadow of his walls, good Praxis!'

'Why should he allow this? Are you worthy even of that?'

'No!' they mourned.

'No. Not even worthy of that. And still you dare to covet what is his. You will not look upon the pagan chief again or your shade will not be suffered to exist a moment longer. Just one glance and you will be Saint, name or shade no more. Goza, bring Torpeth. You others gather up the mountain men. We enter the gate. You know how perilous the journey will now be. Even a Saint walks in fear here.'

Saint Praxis hammered on a pair of doors many times his height. They boomed and their surface shifted beneath his touch. A million eyes looked down on them.

'Open in his name!'

The door became a thousand mouths, gnashing and whispering. They babbled nonsense, but somehow their voices wove together to form a mighty tone: 'Why do you come here?'

'To see his will done,' Saint Praxis answered without hesitation.

'You presume to know his will?'

'I always *beg* to know his will better,' Saint Praxis answered just as readily.

'What tithe will you pay him that is not already his?'

Saint Praxis hesitated, took a half-step back from the door and exchanged a glance with Saint Virulus. The latter's face showed only terror.

'The lowlander will kiss the devil's arse for him and polish it to a shine!' Aspin managed to shout before breaking into a coughing fit.

Saint Praxis rounded on him. 'Silence!' he spat venomously. 'Silence for the sake of your father's spirit! Your blasphemy will see us all undone.'

'If there is so little hope to be had, it makes no difference, lowlander. You will have no satisfaction of me. Nor will that misbegotten and masturbating usurper Azual. Take me and my men to him and we'll see him brought low, just as he was at Godsend. We have seen your blessed Saviours brought down by mere men, remember. There was nothing righteous in them and how they persecuted the People. They named their manipulation faith, they named their persecution of mortalkind salvation. Mere tricks. The tricks of conniving and evil-minded creatures! I piss on both them and their Saints.'

Saint Praxis gave Aspin a chilling smile. 'So be it. The last vestige of your father's spirit is forfeit. You will see it consumed. Will that not see you suffer, and by that will we not have satisfaction of you? Very well. Then you will share in our entertainment and enjoyment of his soul. You will partake of it yourself. Have you ever tasted of a man's soul? Ah, but it is quite something, quite delectable. Particularly a pagan's. So different, so satisfying. We will then move on to your men. What a feast that will be, with Torpeth as the main course and centrepiece. You will be the guest of honour, my sweet chieftain ... and of course the dessert. So, you see, he will have his satisfaction of you, either way. His will and desire are all-defining in this place. I told you. Your defiance is utterly meaningless.'

The shade of Godsend's Minister addressed the door once more. 'These pagans are the tithe we pay. They are the last warriors of the mountain people. Allow them and us entry to the dread temple, and there will be none left to defend the few pagans that live. Soon the land of the living must bow to his will and also pay him tribute.'

The two doors cracked open and it was like the world breaking apart. It was the lid being thrown off a coffin and its dead occupant rising up. It was feet leaving the very edge of the bottomless pit and falling for ever. It was vertigo, a rising stomach, the mind losing its place, the end of all reference point, and being swallowed by the beast.

'The gods forgive and preserve us!' Bantith squeaked, but the words died on his lips.

'Forward,' Saint Praxis commanded, flanking the mountain men with Saint Goza and Saint Sylvan on one side, while Saint Zoriah, Saint Virulus and Saint Dianon lined up on the other. 'Keep your eyes ahead. Not a glance or step out of place.'

'I will not go another step!' Aspin vowed, digging his heels in, but the gaping interior of the Eternal Keep pulled him forward and his men bumped him from behind. 'Stop! You don't understand. Please!' He was tipped across the threshold and pushed on, the doors closing behind them with a boom of finality.

Aspin's breathing became high-pitched, sawing and tearing. He couldn't slow his heart. 'Praxis. What is this place? Can't … can't …'

Saint Praxis did not look back. 'You know what this place is.'

Bantith held up his chief. 'Slow down. Concentrate on each breath. Innn aaand ooout! Innn aaand ooout! That's it. Innn aaand ooout. Easy now.'

Men went past them, oblivious.

'You cannot afford to linger,' Saint Praxis's voice echoed back to them. 'The things that roam these corridors will find you all too quickly. Malacants more terrible than you can imagine, each the sole survivor of a cage of millions. They fight and consume, collaborate and betray, dominate and violate, until there is but one left. Those individuals are the vilest of entities, and as potent as they are vile. They are let into the corridors to catch the unwary and reach into other cages to snatch at the weak. Move with us or be lost. Here we are sealed within his will, held in his mind like thoughts. You must remain with this progress and train or risk being abandoned and forgotten for ever.'

Aspin clung to Bantith. 'I-I'm alright. Th-thank you.' He held the Godsender with one crooked arm and, as Lars went past, snagged hold of the large warrior's tunic so that they were all pulled along together.

They were hauled down corridors lined with vast cages disappearing beyond sight. The lost souls within preyed and warred on each other. Horrific deeds played out unceasingly before them. Aspin looked away, only for his mind to replay what he had seen over and over. He knew he would soon go mad or turn on himself.

For a long time Lars showed no awareness whatsoever, but finally he blinked as if waking from the longest sleep. The tragedy of his expression made it clear he would prefer never to have awakened. 'Ch-chief? Is that really you? I have been bad, haven't I?' he moaned. 'That is why I am here. I will be punished and tortured for what I have done.'

'Lars!' Aspin said as if in prayer. 'Lars, good Lars. It is me, Chief Aspin. You have done nothing wrong. You are returned to us. Be brave. We must help the others.'

'I am no longer strong enough, Chief. Look at my arm.' The warrior mourned his withered limb. 'Do you think I will ever have it back?'

'You'd still beat me in an arm-wrestle, I'm sure. It'll grow back again, you'll see. The headwoman would tell you to stop being such a baby. She'd ask if your manhood was similarly withered, and then she'd cackle. Wouldn't she? Can you imagine it? You can see and hear it, yes, Lars? The women of the village will line up to test your claims, just as they always have. You'll have a whole tribe of sons.'

Lars frowned, trying to picture it. 'Th-the headwoman? It's difficult to remember, Chief. I'm scared.'

'You've never been scared of anything, Lars. You fought and defeated holy Wayfar. Remember how angry he was?'

'W-Wayfar? Our god. I should never have defied him. Chief, what have I done? I am damned. We're all damned. That is why we have ended up here! Our sins have brought us here.'

'No,' Aspin begged him, shaking his head. 'We'll get out of here. I'll get you home, I promise. Lars, you mustn't give up.'

Lars's eyes became desolate. 'Home? I don't remember it.'

'Yes, you do. You're a mountain man. You're a part of the mountains. Bantith, tell him!'

'Mountains?' the Godsender asked vaguely. 'I left them behind, I think. I went somewhere else. Where did I go? I was lost. That must be why we are here.'

'Bantith, no! Not you too. Hold on. Just a little longer.'

Nihilistic laughter came from ahead of them, surrounding them, becoming louder, drowning out the mountain chief's words, playing havoc with rational thought. Aspin clapped his hands over his ears, losing his hold on his two warriors. Listlessly they moved away from him. He was losing everything. Perhaps even his mind. 'No!'

Oh, but yesss, my little pagan, came the voice of the dread Saint, he who was the nemesis of Aspin's people and all the living. *And so you have chosen to return to me as penitent sssinner. Chief now, is it, little pagan? I have killed many pagan chiefs jussst like you. I have drunk their sssouls. Of your own choosing, action, volition and will, you have brought yourself before me, brought yoursssself before the King of the Dead, to bend your knee at the foot of the throne and offer up your sssoul. It is fitting and the divine jusstice of my all-defining will.*

'Azual!' Aspin whimpered and whined, taking a few final steps after Bantith and Lars, entering the scene that was the abject horror of Azual's throne room.

The space disappeared into a murk of pestilence and filth in all directions. Chains hung down in pairs with vicious hooks at their ends. Countless groaning souls were thus suspended, their feeble movements seeing them slowly twist and swing. An empty pair of hooks waited prominently to one side of the throne. Saint Goza took Torpeth's body over to them and pushed first one and then the other into the holy man's back. He did it so that the hooks came up under Torpeth's shoulder blades to hold his weight. Then the Saint went to stand at the nearest foot of the throne, while Saint Praxis guarded the other foot. The two of them silently directed the other Saints in the disposal of the twenty or so mountain men who had brought themselves to the terrible heart of the dread temple.

Saint Zoriah, Saint Sylvan, Saint Dianon and Saint Virulus brought the unresisting mountain men forward one by one. The warriors were crammed into individual cages the sides of which were just three feet in length. Each cage would then be lifted and added to an immense pile on one side of Azual's raised throne. There the cages and their wretched occupants remained until the king casually reached out with an enormous taloned hand to pluck one up. With a two-pronged tool, Azual would gouge out the imprisoned soul piece by piece and guzzle it down. The empty cage was then discarded like the shell of a mussel or snail over his other shoulder, where there was a vast pile of empties.

Aspin stood alone, all six Saints watching him while their king dined leisurely. The mountain chief could neither speak nor swallow.

Care to join me, little pagan? Never tried one? You really should. They're very moreish once you get ssstarted. Look at you, you're all ssskin and bones, hardly enough to clothe a sssoul. Come, I insssist!

He did not move. Could not.

Do not try my patience, pagan. I command you.

He stared unendingly.

Join me willingly or watch me feast first upon the pitiful thing that was your father, and then your men. Or climb into a cage of your own for all it matters. Go ahead. Into a cage with you. What's the matter with you? Are you as feeble-minded as these others? Below with him, until he is ready to join usss.

'Wh-where are you taking me?'

Why, where you have always been, my corrupt and sssnivelling little pagan. In the punishment chamber beneath Saviours' Paradise. You have been chained there sssince I first captured you.

'W-what?' Saint Goza was taking him down a short set of stairs, leading him into a small cell and manacling him to a wall. The smell, the look, the damp air, the feeling of the stone, all were the same. He was back in Saviours' Paradise.

You have hung there for years. That has been your entire life. Buried beneath Saviours' Paradise.

'I-I escaped.'

In your mind you escaped. I encouraged sssuch dreams, for I could sssee them the entire time. And do you know what, little pagan? In those dreams you betrayed the whereabouts of your people. You showed me all I needed to know to see them finally exterminated. You are the lassst of them. While you were lost in your world of fancy, all fell to me and the rule of the blessed Saviours became absolute. They transcended this world and I, as their most loyal ssservant, was chosen to command in their stead.

'We toppled the ... the Great Temple.'

Did you? How is it that I rule then, pagan? How is it that you are chained beneath Saviours' Paradise? All was dreaming, dreams that I gave you. There was never any essscape, never any battle at Godsend. I am not even dead. I am the eternal resurrection.

'Please!' Aspin sobbed.

To whom do you plead, little pagan? You abandoned your god, did you not? And he abandoned you, long ago. The gods have long since passed from

189

this world, their tyranny and jealousy ssswept away by the divine majesty and mercy of the blessed Saviours for the People. Ah, but I sssee. It is to me that you plead, then. Do you beg for my punishment or mercy? Or is it both? For are they not the sssame?

It was true. He had abandoned his god, fought against him even. He, a mortal, had thought to fight the divine. How could he have ever imagined he might succeed? Mortality could only fail in such conflict, in such self-conflict. All he had achieved was his own loss and damnation. The gods had turned away from him and his people for ever. He had sacrificed himself and his world. They were no more. He could no longer see or remember his beloved mountains. He was no longer a part of them. He didn't even understand the word *mountains* any more.

'Yes,' he wept. 'Yes, damn you!'

The door to Jacob's house opened as Jillan approached, and the physicker looked out and ushered him inside. The air was close in the main room. A bundle of herbs had been set to warm and smoulder on the hearth, releasing a soothing scent and sleep-filled smoke. There was a figure bundled up in blankets in front of the source of heat.

''Bout time summat was done about that ruckus,' Old Sheela the physicker groused. 'Like they was goin' outta their way to disturb my patients, it were. I'd been about to go out there to cast a curse or three on them. You spared me the bother, young 'un, and they should be thanking you for that. Now quit talking so much. They need rest.'

Jillan – about to ask at least a dozen obvious questions – closed his mouth and followed the crone to a pair of chairs off to one side. He helped her into her seat and then sat on the edge of his own. He was impatient for answers, but the wise woman was not about to let him make loud demands and get himself and her charges all worked up.

Old Sheela watched with small old eyes, her wrinkled face unreadable. 'Ah, that's better,' she said in a low voice. 'You'll want to know Jacob has a broken head bone. He should survive it, providing he gets several weeks of peace and quiet. He'll sleep a lot, but that's as it should be. I'm hoping he'll be himself after that, but that'll be for the gods to decide. He might be a fair bit slower than he used to be. He probably won't be able to be our trader no more.'

'The wedding,' Jillan breathed. 'We'll have to wait till … till …'

Old Sheela made a tutting noise. 'Could be a long time, young 'un. Such hurts and harms take a greater toll on those of Jacob's age. Best not to wait unnecessarily. Life can't wait on one so old.'

This was the moment he should ask. She'd suggested the wedding would be able to go ahead. She'd implied Hella was … Yet, he was too terrified to ask. He made a mute appeal.

She gave him a gapped and brown-toothed smile. 'Your lady will recover without any ill effects. And the child growing inside her has not been harmed neither.'

What did she just say? the taint asked in shock and palpable envy. *When did this happen?*

His jaw had dropped so far that it near dislocated. 'Bu … Wha … How did she become … How did it happen?'

Old Sheela snorted. 'In the usual way, I imagine. You needn't go looking all innocent and surprised neither. Haven quickens the sap and seed like no other place, eh, young 'un?' She winked at him.

He felt his face colouring. 'C-can I see her?'

'I doubt there is much I could do to stop you, is there? Just don't go shaking her awake.'

He was immediately up and to the threshold of the small bedchamber. He was halted by the sight of her. She filled his mind. He breathed her scent deeply, taking it down into his lungs and to his heart. He felt her heart, her blood and strength, and was made more complete and more powerful by it than he'd ever known. Gone were the uncertainties, doubts and fears of his youth. At last he knew who he was. It was as if her voice of command spoke secretly to him and told him to be the man, husband and leader they both needed him to be. She was his goddess. He was utterly humbled by her.

She watched him now with eyes of magical blue and silently commanded him closer. He went to her, knelt and took her hands in his own.

'Are you really here?' she breathed.

'I am here, Hella. I'll not leave you again.'

'Promise?'

'I do. I swear it on my life. On my soul.'

'You still have one, then? You haven't lost it somewhere?'

'I've only lost it to you, Hella.'

She smiled gently, her eyes drooping. 'That's nice.'

'Hella, can you tell me what happened?'

She frowned slightly. 'What happened? Dark. Samnir was there. Trying…' Her hand tightened in his. 'Trying to kill me!'

'They *said* it was him,' Jillan muttered.

'Wait. There's someone else. A scarred woman with beautiful eyes… Samnir, it's *me*, Hella!'

He'd pushed her too far. 'It's alright, it's alright. You're safe. Hella, look at me, you're safe!'

Suddenly the physicker was there, shooing him out. 'Drink this, girl. Another sip. There, that's it. You rest now.'

Old Sheela turned to reprimand him, but Jillan was already halfway to the front door. It was time to see his friend, his friend who would have killed the woman he was to marry – and an unborn child as well – and get some answers. If he did not get proper answers to his questions, then he could not afford that friend to live, as much as he loved him.

As she watched him leave, Old Sheela gave another of her gapped and brown-toothed smiles.

Holding a torch, Jillan came down the stairs of the punishment chamber. He'd insisted the guard and Captain Gallen remain above. The figure behind the bars of the cell did not look up as Jillan descended.

Jillan watched the commander in silence for a few seconds before speaking. 'Well? What have you got to say for yourself?'

'I have nothing to say for myself,' Samnir replied, head down.

Another pause, longer than the first. 'I have little to say for myself either, Samnir. I was stupid to go out into the desert alone. If it hadn't been for Freda, I wouldn't be here now. Ever seen the spider things that live out there?'

Samnir nodded. 'When I fought for the Empire out here, we lost a few men every month to them.'

'They say you locked yourself in here and threw the keys out through the bars.'

Samnir released a breath. 'I'm a danger to all those around me. I shouldn't be allowed any sort of freedom.'

'Ash said you were a dog of war with a taste for blood. He said you should be put down.'

'He's right.'

'And Hella is pregnant.'

This brought Samnir's head up at last. He met Jillan's eyes. The commander clearly did not know whether to laugh or cry. His delight at the news only increased his torture and misery. Tears of self-recrimination came to his eyes. 'I cannot even ask your forgiveness, Jillan, because I do not deserve it.'

'You are happy for me, though, yes? There is no one else I care to tell, you see.'

'Of course I am happy for you, Jillan. Hella is ... is well? And Jacob?'

Jillan nodded. 'The physicker says Jacob will mend. Hella is awake.'

'Thank the gods.'

'The scar-faced woman with beautiful eyes, Samnir. It was her, wasn't it? Izat?'

'It was my fault!' the old soldier confessed. 'I should have denied her. Jillan, I was too weak. I allowed her into Haven. I put everyone at risk. Everyone! I could not even defend myself against a creature such as her. Jillan, look at me! There is nothing left to me. I have done terrible things, betrayed every principle I thought to have, brought down the Empire I'd pledged to serve, led friends to their deaths, so many friends, slain our blessed Saviours ... and now tried to murder those people who are the closest thing I've ever had to a family. I've destroyed everything I had, and destroyed who I was at the same time. For a moment I fooled myself into believing we'd done it all to build a better place, but look at us. This place is no better than Godsend.' There was only defeat in his voice. 'There is nothing left to me. Empty. When you strip everything away, Jillan, there is nothing. Nothing.'

Jillan spoke carefully. 'Izat is no ordinary woman, you know that. She was your Saint, was she not? She controlled you, body and mind.'

Samnir did not reply.

'And she knew you better than anyone, Samnir, knew how to make and unmake you. She made you the Sand Devil, the wasting force of the desert and Empire. She always manipulated you. It is a terrible thing, the sort of invasion that makes you despise yourself just for existing. And she has continued to manipulate you. She knows your weakness and has used it to break you.' Jillan remembered the traces of blood that Freda had detected in his home. The wolf had been there too. 'But I think she is gone. Do you sense her presence anywhere in Haven? I do not.'

Samnir gave a slight shake of his head.

'You are free of her at last.'

'I am a monster. I will never be free.'

'If we give in to it, none of us will ever be free, Samnir. As you told me before, we will always have to fight. I did not want to hear it when you told me – I ignored it – and that ended up putting Haven at risk just as surely as your actions against Hella and Jacob did. The signs were all there, but I refused to see them, allowing our enemies to creep ever closer, work their way in among us and undermine us.'

'No, Jillan. It's not true.'

'Yes, it is, damn you!' he replied vehemently. 'Sinisar moves against us. He tried to kill me in the desert.'

'What? Why?' Samnir asked quietly.

'And ... and ...' He swallowed. It was so hard to say it out loud. It became real when he said it out loud. He didn't want to say it. He spoke the horrified words: 'The Saviours were not destroyed. They are coming back, Samnir. I have seen things—'

'Ye gods, no!'

'Dreams too, Samnir. *Real* dreams. The spirits of my parents in the nether realm. I think they have been taken by *him* again. He is stronger than ever. It's all falling apart, Samnir!'

'It cannot be. It must not!'

'The Saviours have manipulated us throughout, so that we would help them find the Geas. And now they are coming to claim their prize. I don't know how to fight them, Samnir! The giants say we will all die! But you know how to fight better than anyone I know. You will help us. You must!'

Samnir was shaking his head wildly. 'I don't. I'm not that person any more.'

'You *are*! You *have* to be!' He breathed hard, fighting for composure and control. 'Samnir, they cunningly sought to create division among those who would defend the Geas. They have sought to break you and me. They have sought to murder Hella. Why would they do this unless they knew we might otherwise have some chance of successfully throwing them back? If we can hold together, if we refuse to break, if we keep fighting, then surely not all is lost. I cannot believe there is no hope. I *will* not believe it. Get on your feet, soldier, or are you turned *coward*?'

Samnir laughed bleakly, the sound echoing eerily. 'You can call me many things, almost anything under Sinisar's cursed sun, but not that. Better that I were, perhaps.'

'Are you more cowardly than Ash, then? I did not see him mope like this when he was in here. He screamed for his freedom.'

'You will *not* compare me to that urine-soaked reprobate!' Samnir bit back.

'Should I not, Samnir? Will you hide in here while our enemies march upon Haven? Will you leave Hella's defence to Ash? Then surely it would have been kinder if you had been successful in killing her before.'

'I told you not to mention his name to me,' the soldier growled in warning.

'Why? Do you fear that name, Samnir? Do you fear that the two of you are actually alike? Or is his name more fearsome than that of the Sand Devil? Surely it is, if it sees you cower in here.'

Samnir's face was at the bars now. 'I do not cower from that sly-tongued tripping jack-a-ninny!'

'He says it was only his tripping that allowed you to defeat any of the Saviours before the Great Temple. He says you are a witless thug without any appreciation of artistry.'

I don't remember him saying that.

'Artistry? It is only piss-artistry that he knows. Let me out of here, give me my blade and I will carve him with more artistry than he has ever experienced!'

'Yet, Samnir, our enemies could well stand in your way before you get that chance.'

'Then they will rue the day, believe me.'

There was a kerfuffle at the top of the stairs and Captain Gallen came leaping down. His eyes were wide and he juggled the keys to the cell. They jangled and clattered at the lock, nearly as loud as his panicky words. 'An army messenger comes! He all but killed his horse getting here. General Thormodius and Captain Skathis have quick-marched the entire Fortress of the Sun through the night, to arrive before the divine host that follows in their wake. Holy Sinisar and his Court of

Light have taken to the skies fully arrayed for battle. Commander, they are heading for Haven!'

Samnir stepped out of his cell, rolled his shoulders a few times and let his neck crack. 'Then let it begin.'

CHAPTER 7:

In their maker's image

Captain Skathis grimaced and ran his hand back through his sparse hair, feeling the map of old scars covering his scalp. They smarted and itched beneath the rising anger of the desert sun, ghostly blades pushing into his skull. He would have screamed at his men, but he had no moisture in his throat. He hated this place. He hated the sight of it, for the constant glare from weapons and armour that gave him a permanent squint. He hated the dust that got into his nostrils, ears and mouth, that got beneath his clothes to cause friction and sores, that got into his rations and down into his gut. He even shitted the stuff, which was far from comfortable and made him irritable beyond endurance, not that he was known for being particularly pleasant in the first place.

He hated the place so much that there was nowhere he would have rather been. And the same went for the lean and kinless men beneath his command. For here there were none interested in taking their barren bit of desert from them. Captain Skathis's men all knew that if it weren't for the army, many of them would have had to turn to banditry somewhere just to survive and would eventually have been hunted down or betrayed. A knife in the back, a blade across the throat, a public hanging before a jeering crowd or a slow death upon a gibbet – that was all that awaited them back in civilised society. It made their difficult life in the desert a blessing by comparison, for all its dangers. And when death eventually came out here – be it by sand spider, desert giant, wild tribesman, burrowing sand mite, unseen snake or silent scorpion, although probably not old age – then at least there would be comrades to provide you a decent enough burial and say a short prayer to the gods on behalf of your departed spirit.

It was more life than he'd ever thought to have. Far more. He still shuddered to remember his existence under Saint Azual's thrall. The things he'd done. The constant horror of a dispossessed mind. Too terrified and guilty to have a thought of his own. All sense of self so sinful that it had to be locked away and forgotten. How could he not then revel in the life he had here in the desert, as hateful as the place was? He enjoyed being a brute to his men, because he *chose* to be a brute to them. He was *free* to be a brute to them. And they enjoyed his brutality too. They almost seemed to encourage it in him. They would sometimes *choose* to be slack in some duty or in carrying out some order precisely because they got to choose to be so. He was sure he'd spotted several of them smiling secretly to themselves when they'd caused him to become particularly irate and to mete out unusually harsh punishment. They seemed to delight in it, in the discomfort and pain of *living*. The discomfort and pain made them feel alive in a way they never had under the Empire. In fact, the reason they delighted so much in it was what made them soldiers – they were prepared to fight and even die for it. They *chose* to fight, even if that ultimately meant choosing death. It was a choice freely made.

So when the lookouts General Thormodius kept posted near holy Sinisar's temple reported the collapse of its crystal dome and towers, the roar of the enraged god and armed beings of light taking to the air, the men of the Fortress of the Sun had responded with ready purpose and in some cases barely suppressed excitement. All knew the fight was at last here. General Thormodius had dispatched messengers to the temple to enquire politely if the fortress might render any aid and to ask what holy Sinisar intended. At the same time, he'd roared at the rest of his men to get their battle gear together and to form up at the double in order of battle. Two very singed messengers had returned to inform the general that holy Sinisar had been outraged mere mortals would presume to demand answers of a god. How dare the general offer him *aid*. The only things mortals could offer were worship and obedience. It was time the mortals of Sinisar's region learned their place. It was time they were brought to their knees to worship in awe and fear. They must be humbled for all time. They must never again dare to overreach, as they had when taking Haven for themselves. Everything would be taken from the mortals so that they understood they only had that which was allowed them by the gods, even their lives. The mortals were to be put out of Haven and then Sinisar would pass judgement on all those within his sun-drenched lands. The general's messengers had only been permitted to leave the temple with their lives so that they might carry the word and will of their god to all.

General Thormodius had wasted no time organising his army of five thousand men into marching order and setting out for Haven. His timing was good, for the sun was already close to setting, meaning that his army would complete most of its march during the cooler hours of the night. Added to that, the current phase of the moon meant it would be little more than a sliver, so the Court of Light would be unable to travel too far until the sun was again ascendant.

'General, if I may?' Captain Skathis had asked as they'd navigated their way through the dark. The officers all rode horses and carried burning torches, but they had to pick their way carefully, and the men had no trouble keeping up on foot.

'Of course, my old friend. What is it?' the large leader asked, wielding his torch in his good hand while controlling his steed with the reins looped around the stump of his other wrist.

Captain Skathis lowered his voice so they were less likely to be over-heard. 'Do we side with Haven? A number of our men are known to make obeisance to the sun each dawn.'

The general's eyes were hidden in the shadows beneath his heavy brow. 'We simply go to attend the wedding of Jillan and Hella. I have agreed to oversee the making of vows.'

'And we come in full panoply as a sign of respect. It is the closest we have to our Holy Day best, as it were.'

'Quite so, good Captain, quite so. We hurry ahead of the Court of Light to be sure of getting the best seats, yes? Let that be how the officers respond should any of the men challenge them.'

'Yes, General.'

'After all, it is unthinkable that we would stand against any of the gods, is it not? No man would do so and hope to survive.'

'No, General. The officers will also say as much, making no mention of the exploits of Torpeth the Great. And none will need mention that the blessed Saviours were resisted and brought down, though no sane man would have attempted it.'

'Then we understand each other, good Captain. We will simply arrive at Haven and place ourselves between that place and any guests who arrive after us. We will array ourselves so that none may take our place. Should any attempt to force the issue, then we will be forced to defend ourselves like any sane man. Our men are well trained and used to following our orders. Surrounded by their unflinching comrades, all acting in concert, I'm sure that not a one will think to do otherwise, no matter whether the sun rises, falls, completely blinds them or turns its face away. If you have concerns about any particular individuals, then be sure they have stout men to every side.'

'Of course, General.'

'Like you, I pray that there will be no unpleasantness. It would be a shame to see Jillan and Hella's special day marred. Yet over the years I have developed a keen sense for when trouble approaches. It makes my bones ache and my stump itch. I can smell it on the wind, feel it beneath my feet, taste it in my morning ration of water and see it in the passage of the sun and stars. Let me tell you, good Captain, that sense has allowed me no rest for a good many days now. It was with me even before the pretty roof of Sinisar's temple fell in on his pretty head.'

'I have felt something of it too, General.'

'You have?'

'Yes.' Normally, he would never have spoken of such things to anyone. Yet here in the empty night, with the only person he'd ever come close to trusting, he found himself whispering of his dreams. 'I see him more and more often. It was unclear at first, but now Saint Azual's bloody eye is as vivid in my mind as it was when he ruled the southern region. He is becoming more real. It is like he is reaching out to me from the land of the dead. He speaks to me. I try not to listen, but I know he wishes to command me once more. I fear he sees all through my eyes again. General, what is happening? Is it connected with what happened at the temple and what we will face at Haven? What is this trouble that comes upon us?'

'You are haunted by a restless spirit, and not just any spirit either,' the general rumbled. 'You must resist it, just as we resisted the Empire before the Great Temple. You will not weaken, good Captain. You *must* not.'

'Yes, General.'

'I dread to think what it might betoken. Is it connected? The pagans would say all things are connected, Captain. Just how they might be now is beyond my knowledge and wisdom. We still have not learned precisely what caused the destruction at holy Sinisar's temple. I have questioned our messengers a second time, but they are none the wiser. I do not think it was the god's own anger that brought his house down, for his Court of Light poured forth as if searching for the culprit and intent upon some sort of vengeance. It seems that the inhabitants of Haven have offended the shining deity somehow, but I cannot fathom how they can be blamed for the temple.'

'When a hive is threatened, General, its angered bees will attack anything and everything.'

'Then we must prepare ourselves, for surely we will be stung, whether we side with Haven or not. It seems the trouble that comes upon us cannot be avoided.'

Skathis's throat tightened. 'So we must defend ourselves against a god. May he forgive us our blasphemy! Yet it is holy Sinisar himself who forces us to commit that blasphemy. Is it not fundamentally wrong, General, against all sense of natural order? There can be no winning such a battle, for god or mortal. Is this how the Empire will find opportunity once more?'

'You ask of things beyond my understanding, Captain. All I know is that none thought the battle against the blessed Saviours could be won, and still it was. We should perhaps have faith in ourselves, Captain. We are soldiers and will always be so.'

Captain Skathis saluted his grey-haired superior. 'Yes, General, and proud to be so.'

General Thormodius nodded. 'Captain, the initial attack will be from the air. Our first line of defence will need to be archers, then javelins. We have five hundred archers and a similar number of throwers, yes? All are equipped with quarrels or javelins tipped with sun-metal?'

'Yes, General, but there will only be a dozen such arrows per archer. We have enough bows to equip another five hundred men, but they have had little recent practice, and each of the thousand archers would then have just six of the sun-metal arrows.'

'Do it. I doubt any archer would have time to release a dozen shots anyway, given the speed at which beings of light will come upon us. The archers and throwers will need to be spread throughout our number, and each must be closely guarded by men with blades of sun-metal, and sun-metal shields if we have any. Will we have sufficient?'

'Perhaps. I do not have an exact count on the blades, but I know many looted sun-metal from the fallen when they fought at the Great Temple.'

'It is well that they did.' The general sighed. 'I cannot think it a crime when it may see us survive rather than die. Surely every man has a right to compete for his own life and it not be called a crime? Yet what are the gods doing to us when they force us to such acts? It makes a mockery of all sense and morality.'

Captain Skathis looked around to be sure there were none using cover of darkness to listen in. 'I do not know, General. It makes me fear it is *we* that err, in not submitting to the will of holy Sinisar. Should we be turning our weapons on the inhabitants of Haven rather than against him? Maybe Haven was never meant for us mortals. Should it be left to the gods alone? My every instinct, feeling and thought say no, General, but I must be sure we do not make a terrible mistake.'

'Should we turn on the innocent people of Haven for refusing to leave that place? Should they be driven out just as the Heroes of the Empire long ago drove the pagans from their lands? Should we now become an enemy to Jillan, Samnir and Hella, those who sacrificed so much to see us freed of the blessed Saviours? Should we make Jillan regret ever having shown us mercy when by rights he could have had us executed for all the things that we had done?'

'No,' the captain whispered intently, and then more fiercely, 'Never!'

The general raised the stump of his wrist towards Captain Skathis. 'Every day this reminds me that I was a coward to serve the might of the Empire and commit atrocities in its name.'

Captain Skathis hung his head in shared shame.

'Every day it reminds me I was a coward to raise my hand against the innocent people of Godsend. Every day I rejoice that Samnir cut it from me, for it meant I could commit no further ills with it. Good Captain, the Sand Devil shamed me further at that moment, for he also allowed me to live when I would never have allowed him to do so. Should I ever turn on the innocent People again, upon my own kind, then may he take my other hand and then my head!'

'Yes, General! I know now there is no mistaking it. I would rather die facing holy Sinisar, and suffer his divine inferno for the rest of eternity, than betray our people. Damn this god that would build his religion over us and raise up a holy empire! He will not have Haven while I breathe. He will not be allowed the power of the Geas, to create and destroy as he wills it. He will not be allowed to resurrect the spirit of cursed Azual!'

And so they marched through the night, racing the dawn to Haven. Messengers were sent in advance to bring warning to the inhabitants. Exhausted but determined, the army arrived above the hidden valley of Haven and deployed itself as commanded by the general and his officers. The men were told to get what rest they could but to sleep with one eye open. Captain Skathis waited now, feeling the map of old scars covering his scalp smart and itch beneath the rising anger of the desert sun. How he hated this dusty place, but he was sure there was no place he would have rather been. He *chose* to fight, even if that ultimately meant choosing death. It was a choice freely made.

He watched the people of Haven come up from their home. There was Samnir, with the ever-trusty Captain Gallen at his side, leading five hundred apparently well-fed Heroes. The commander still had a hardness of gaze about him that left none in any doubt that he had only become more lethal with age. The Heroes of Haven did not move with quite the same discipline as the general's own men, but they had a certain vibrancy about them that now seemed to ripple through the army. He felt the tiredness of their journey through the night disappearing.

Next came a motley group of a hundred or so men and women holding weapons in a way that said they knew well how to use them. Their gazes were both circumspect and defiant, and gave Captain Skathis a twisting feeling in his gut. There was a queasy and unpredictable magic of sorts about these individuals, the sort that would have seen them shunned, hunted and often put down in the Empire. They could only be the Unclean. Yes, there was the rakish woodsman Ash to the fore, with a broken-faced giant at his side. And the broad man in the red tunic was likely to be Tebrus, leader of the renegade band originally out of Heroes' Brook.

Finally came Jillan, with several dozen villagers clutching household tools and farming implements too tightly filing behind him. Captain Skathis experienced a flashback to the first battle at Godsend, when this youth had brought down Saint Azual and seen himself named bane of the Empire. Jillan had grown a good few inches since then and filled out some, to be sure, but still had the same open sense of reality that the Empire had considered so dangerous. There was a power to it that drew every eye. Yet, where Jillan seemed more substantial than any other in the field, the runes of his armour winking conspiratorially, at his shoulder was a threatening absence that had to be his very opposite. Captain Skathis refused its pull, for he feared it was death's shadow trying to draw him in.

General Thormodius, Captain Skathis, the army officers and the leaders of Haven came together.

Samnir stepped forward. 'Well met, General! Captain Skathis.' He nodded. 'I take it you do not come to test us as you did at Godsend?'

'Indeed not. We come to make what amends we can. See the heat and fury that now rises into the sky above us. It would seem your very existence has once more angered the powers that be, Sand Devil, but we will stand with you this time.'

Samnir gave a tight smile. 'I never could stay out of trouble, no matter how hard I tried, eh, General? It's not just me, though. I blame that Jillan. He's caused no end of grief, antagonising hard-working and holy Ministers, upsetting one holy Saint after another, getting an entire empire into a lather and then putting the noses of the gods out of joint for having raised them up and making them beholden to him. Quite inconsiderate really.'

'Hey!' Jillan shouted so that they all turned to him. 'I was still young back then. It was Ash who encouraged me and caused all sorts of havoc in Saviours' Paradise, not to mention tripping up our most blessed Saviours. He clearly consorted with the Chaos.'

'Oh, picking on the Unclean again, are we?' the woodsman responded tragically. 'Look, I was on my own in the middle of the woods, minding my own business, when Jillan turns up with his tales of woe. Out of the goodness of my heart, I decided to help him out – and he helped

204

himself to a good deal of my homebrew, did I mention? – and when we get to Saviours' Paradise, he decides to rescue that pagan Aspin, who'd been mistaken for Jillan. But here's the rub – it was *Captain Skathis* who mistook Aspin for Jillan! It was his incompetence that has brought us all here today.'

They all looked at him. He shifted uncomfortably. 'Well, it's a nice day for it, no?'

Ash threw up his hands in despair. 'A nice day, he says! We're all about to die and he says it's a nice day.'

Samnir and Captain Gallen nodded in agreement.

General Thormodius clapped his captain on the back. 'Aye, it's a nice day, good Captain. Rarely have I seen a better day for it. It gladdens the heart and soul. Come then, and let's to it before we waste this day.'

As one, the leaders of Haven and the Fortress of the Sun turned to face the majesty of the heavens and the divine wrath of Sinisar of the Shining Path.

Ba'zel moved silently through the lowest level of the home-realm. The dust here was so thick that his abdomen dragged a path through it for long stretches. He was the only one to have passed this way in aeons, but this place was far from a tomb. He felt the Virtues watching him. It was all but a physical assault. They made forays against the edges of his mind, only to hesitate because his apparent weakness had to be a ruse. He was the Great Virtue. He had defeated Luhka Sha, the Lead Warrior of the Declension, the greatest champion ever to come from the fighting pits. This uncertainty that the Great Virtue projected must be intended to encourage the appetite of the Virtues so that they would rush in without proper caution and become ensnared. How could it be otherwise? They reluctantly allowed him to come closer, even though their main purpose of being was to prevent any from coming near the entrance to *Her* lair. It was possible for a member of the Declension to pass through rock, of course, but doing so would invariably leave them so weakened that they would not be able to pose any real threat to the Eldest. All others must approach through these tunnels and face the terrible Virtues of the Declension.

'Welcome, Brother,' they whispered as Ba'zel stepped into an ante-chamber lined with sun-metal on floor, walls and ceiling.

He twitched as he remembered the box of sun-metal in which *She*'d chosen to trap him in the seventh realm. He resisted the urge to look back over his shoulder, suppressing the irrational fear that a door would be closing behind him to seal him into a place of infinite torture once again. He faced the three grotesque beings positioned before him. Their eyes were white with blindness – a consequence of prolonged exposure to the glare of sun-metal – but that only seemed to have given their other senses a more awful acuity. Their minds literally *ate* his thoughts, and the thoughts of all those above. There was a preternatural stillness here of a sort he had never thought to experience, of a sort at odds with existence. It was a stillness worse than death, for it was *voracious* and would never have its fill, not till the entire cosmos had been consumed. It pre-empted the continuation of life. It sought to make a stillbirth of all that was to come.

Here were the Virtues of the Declension. Their stone fangs and largest horns had been replaced with shining sun-metal – cruel insertions that made their owners all the more formidable but surely caused the sort of agony only the insane could endure.

Ba'zel cautiously bowed to them, making sure not to expose the nape of his neck. They returned the motion in equal measure.

'What would you have of us, Brother? It cannot be Obedience, for he was our brother and the Virtue you destroyed. There is therefore no Obedience to be had of us.'

'I am the Great Virtue. I will not command you, but you will follow or pay the same price as our brother.' Ba'zel kept perfectly still. Any mistake now and they would be sure of their own power against him.

The Virtues matched him once more, refusing to be drawn. They waited, testing him further.

'As the Great Virtue, I name myself to you as DESTRUCTION. I am the *instability*. You erred too greatly when you attempted to force the Virtue of Obedience upon me, and in that greatness of erring made me the Great Virtue over you. I am of *your* making. I am of the Declension's making. I am of *Her* making. Name yourselves to me, as I have named myself to you. Follow where I have led ... or would you insist Destruction comes to you? For I *am* Destruction, as the Eldest is my witness!'

And in that invocation he had them. They could not hide their agitation. They betrayed themsevles to him.

'I am SACRIFICE,' shuddered the smallest but most insidious of them.

'I am DUTY,' complained the most fixed but most heavily armoured.

'And I am REVELATION,' the largest but most ghostly spat violently. 'Where would you have us follow?'

'The fall of the seventh is at hand. The way to the eighth is revealed, but we will be resisted by its guardians, guardians who have found a place in the seventh and may therefore interfere. At the same time the seventh has a defining nether realm. Its dead will rise and be offered up come the true Revelation of its Saviours. Our kingdom must come, our will must be done, on earth as it is in spirit. That will be the true apocalypse of the seventh.'

Revelation hissed in aggravation. 'So be it. I will go with you and bring the lesser beings of the seventh the final judgement of the Saviours. Yet beware, Brother. Do not think to stand in my way, for that judgement will be irrevocable and none will escape it.'

Ba'zel carefully backed out of the antechamber. He had managed to remove one of the Virtues from its place outside the Eldest's lair. He prayed it would be enough.

The vault of the heavens was a sea of fire and light. Sinisar's court sparkled and bewitched the eye as much as it dazzled and blinded. Visifers, lumines, spectrals, scintillations and fire elementals created an entrancing kaleidoscope of colour and mazing pattern. Their shining weapons and magical skeins made them as dreadful as they were beautiful to behold. The divine vision they presented entirely filled the sight of any who looked upon them, mesmerising the viewer, paralysing all thought except for the majesty of Sinisar, he who resided at their heart and was the source of all light, power and life. Without him existence could not be. Without him there was only night, cold death and the void. Without him there was no verdant valley called Haven, no home to mortalkind, no individuals called Jillan, Samnir, Ash or General Thormodius. Without out his beneficent illumination there was no immediate or infinite, no near or far, no distance or depth. He was the close companion at their shoulder and the god of eternity. His frown was the enemy right there who would strike you down in the blink of an eye; his displeasure was the damnation that would see your soul tortured.

Overwhelmed, Jillan knew there could only be humility, inadequacy and supplication before this entity. He must give everything in the hope that his existence might be tolerated. He was about to join all the other defenders of Haven on their knees when a shadow intruded at the corner of his eye, interrupting his devotion. Freda had come to stand with him.

Next came an angry voice, a voice of command and power that disrupted the defenders' display of worship. 'What is the meaning of this? Get up, all of you.'

'Hella?' Jillan asked in shock and wonder. 'Is that you?'

She stood in red leather armour, one hand on the round of her hip and the other flourishing the runic blade Thomas had forged for her before the last battle at Godsend. The weapon's symbols glinted and dissipated Sinisar's influence. Her face was pale but determined. 'Well of course it's me. Who else would it be? I have come to see how our wedding preparations proceed. Do tell me they are complete for I'm not inclined to patience any longer.' She panted to catch her breath, obviously weak.

'Beloved, should you be out of bed in your … well, your condition?'

Hella did not answer him, for Samnir was approaching.

The old warrior went to one knee before her and bared the back of his neck. 'Hella, I …'

'You were not yourself. I know that. You need not say more. That which sought me in the dark merely had your form, but no other part of you. It was not that true soldier and friend who saved me upon the walls of Godsend. So be yourself now and lead these others. Stand.' She turned to face Sinisar. 'As for you!' The sky was filled with the power of her words. 'You should know better! What precisely do you think you're doing? You'd better have come to bring me a wedding present. Even so, you're too early. Things are nowhere near ready yet. You'll just have to come back later.'

'Mock me at your peril, wretched mortal! The only gift I bring is your doom!' Sinisar crackled, his eyes blazing and igniting a number of the beings around him.

'I think that's a no,' Aspin breathed.

'Then you're no longer invited,' Hella shouted, matching the deity's own rage. 'For the last time, I will not have anyone, I repeat *anyone*, getting in the way of my wedding. I *will* marry Jillan, whether you like it or not, no matter if you're a drunken innkeep, a homicidal commander or a churlish god. Do I make myself *clear*?'

'Yes, Hella,' Jillan dutifully answered.

'Yes, Hella. Sorry, Hella,' Samnir answered guiltily.

'Yes, Hella. Sorry, Hella.' Ash grinned, giving Sinisar a sidelong look. 'If I were you, I'd just nod and agree. You're already in enough trouble as it is.'

'Prattling fools! The gods need no invitation to enter Haven. Stand aside or all will be turned to ash.'

'You think you don't need an invitation?' Hella asked dangerously. 'You think the gods are entitled to this place, do you? Then why was Haven hidden from you along with everyone else? Why did Miserath need Jillan and Freda's help to find it? Why, even then, was the power of the Geas denied Miserath and permitted to Jillan instead? I think it's because the gods are the *last* beings who should be allowed Haven. I think they can't be trusted with it. I think they'd try to rule absolutely and make a hell of existence, if not destroy it altogether. Now, for the last time, get you gone! Haven is not yours and never will be.'

The sky became molten and its angry heat drove the defenders back. Sand began to melt, forming puddles of glass. A host of vengeful fiery angels now threatened and accused the defenders of Haven. 'On your knees, mortals, or be undone! Beg forgiveness for your crimes. None can deny a god what is his by divine right. I do not require the invitation of vain and meaningless beings when I come to claim what is mine. Hand over the rock woman at once, and pray that I will show you mercy, for you harbour a fugitive from holy justice. While a member of my court Freda did murder my First Light. See how her dark deed has permanently marked and stained her. She blackens Haven itself, defying its light and life. She impinges upon and transgresses against the Geas itself. Do not tolerate her among you or I must think your minds shadowed by her. Give her up and seek to redeem yourselves, or you must all be driven out of Haven. On your knees, mortals, or be complicit in her sin and blasphemy against the heavenly Court of Light!'

Jillan looked to Freda, eyes questioning.

The people of Haven whispered to one another.

A scattering of men from the Fortress of the Sun went to their knees, abandoning weapons so that they could clasp their hands together and raise them in appeal.

'We will follow your lead, but decide quickly, Jillan,' Samnir advised with quiet urgency, General Thormodius also nodding his support.

'Jillan, if Sinisar will leave if we simply let him take …' Hella suggested without any conviction and not quite meeting his gaze.

Jillan frowned, and his head went to the side. Yet he knew better than to hesitate now. Not now. Not at this moment, when everything teetered on the edge. He gathered himself before the situation could get entirely beyond his control. He gathered all of them. 'No. Freda has saved my life on at least two occasions. She has saved all of us. If it wasn't for her, Saint Azual would never have been brought down. If it wasn't for her, Saint Izat and the Disciples would never have been thwarted. If it wasn't for Freda, Haven would not have been found, the Saviours would never have been defeated and the gods would never have been raised up. *You*, Sinisar, who was freed by her from the prison beneath the Great Temple, owe her an eternal debt. Yet what do you offer her instead? Threats and condemnation. We allowed Freda to join the Court of Light. You had a responsibility of care towards her. How is it that this most innocent of beings has been made to suffer? What abuse was heaped upon her to bring her to such a state? You talk of justice, Sinisar, but then threaten to destroy us if you do not get your way. Where is the justice in that? It is *you* who are accused. It is *you* who must answer *our* questions about what your Court of Light has wrought. It is *you* who will be held to account!'

Sinisar rose from the throne of the sky, a searing apparition to lance every eye and mind. It was like falling into the centre of the sun. 'I am your *god*!' Fire rained from the heavens and the defenders had to raise their shields to save themselves. The shield strap of one unfortunate snapped, he was exposed and suddenly engulfed in screaming flames. 'The divine will always be but a mystery to the mortal. It cannot be explained to lesser beings, for it is beyond their compass. My will and actions *are* a holy justice that will always be beyond your limited understanding. They are all the answer you will have, proud and self-damning mortal. The rock woman is ours. You will give her to us!' The sun poured down on them, running over the edges of shields and splashing deadly drops onto flesh. The cries of the beset Heroes were hideous.

The firmament trembled under the assault and then sloping pillars of rock rose out of the desert to provide the army of mortals with a semblance of protection. Rock people hauled themselves up out of the sand and used their bodies to shield the most threatened.

'Freom! My brother!'

'Sister, what have they done to you?'

A sculpted giant reared up upon the tops of the pillars, bestriding them like a colossus. His body was of gold-veined white marble, his eyes were glittering sapphires and his brow was crowned with every conceivable gem. He raised his head fearlessly, daring the powers above not to halt their tyranny. Here was holy Gar of the Unmoving Stone, come to the aid of his daughter! 'What is the meaning of this?' he cracked and rumbled, landslide, volcano and cataclysm all promised.

'Your daughter freely joined the Court of Light. She is mine to command!' Sinisar answered, tempering his display of power.

'But you will never own her body, mind or adamantine spirit. Surely you know that, Brother,' Gar remonstrated with his fellow deity. 'In the same manner, I could never catch the light of the sky and keep it for my own. It is impossible and against nature.'

'She vowed herself to me,' Sinisar insisted hotly.

'He really does whine, doesn't he?' Ash called from where he sheltered.

'Will you NEVER be silent?' Sinisar seethed. 'Woodsman, I will shrivel that tongue of yours.'

Ash yelped and crouched in the darkest shadow he could find.

'You promised her love and gave her only hurt. It is *you* who broke the vows and compact!' Jillan shouted, his magic at last filling the desert. There was no division within him. No division to lessen him. No doubt, hesitation or apology. 'I will *not* let you take my friend, just as I will not let you take Haven.'

'Jillan,' Hella ventured. 'In all conscience, should we really risk so many people just for one—'

'Enough, Hella. I will not hear this from you. I know it is not you speaking, for your power deserts you in this. Some evil has extracted a promise from you, I know it. Peace, beloved.'

Hella nodded gratefully, wiping away a tear with a trembling hand and smiling as she could.

'Sinisar, my brother,' Gar ground. 'What is my daughter to you? Why this continued obsession with her when you call her marred and stained? How can it be worth all this? The lives of mortals are not meaningless and not entirely ours to do with as we wish. I beg you as brother, and demand as god, that you leave off this vengeance and allow Freda to see out her days here in Haven.'

A cunning look of triumph transformed the god of light's features. 'Would you stand with the mortals in this, then, *Brother*? Would you stand with them against me? Would you make this a contest of the gods? Then so be it.'

The haze of the horizon thickened, and storm clouds raced across the lands of the east. Holy Wayfar of the Warring Winds and his flights of followers came to the aid of his brother of the air. The earth cracked and steam forced its way up through fissures and vents. Superheated geysers exploded all around, scalding the Heroes of Haven and forcing them to flee the temporary refuge the rock god had afforded them. Holy Akwar of the Wandering Waters now joined the fray, billowing and deadly.

'What madness is this?' Gar ground. 'What possesses you, Brothers? Would you destroy all?'

'The mortals have undone my temple in Hyvan's Cross!' Wayfar thundered. 'No punishment or reprisal is too great. The mortals must be put down so that they know their place for ever more.'

'Akwar, my brother, you share the bosom of the earth with me. You cannot turn against me. Stand with me and the balance will be preserved. Sinisar is your opposite. He is fire to your water.'

Akwar returned a pitying look. 'Poor Gar, always so slow and ponderous—'

'Where Akwar was always too slippery,' Ash couldn't help saying, his observation carried to the gods by the swirling power of Wayfar.

'I will drown him,' Akwar swore. 'I will rapidly freeze and thaw his body so that his own blood shatters and explodes his eyeballs, heart and brain.'

Ash whimpered and bit down hard on the knuckles of one hand.

'See what trouble you get yourself in with that timing of yours?' Samnir chastised him. 'Bet you wish you were safely locked up in the punishment chamber now.'

Ash nodded in abject terror.

'Too slow and ponderous to notice the greater scheme of the gods unfolding around you. Forgive us, Brother. You could not be included at first because you would have weighed us down. In being as obvious as you are honest, you might have betrayed us to these conniving and overreaching mortals. Join us now and all will be well. Haven will be ours, with none to prevent us. We will have such power that we will never suffer challenge again, including from the elseworlders. Indeed, we will have the power to strike at the elseworlders in their own realms should we need to. Our world will at last be safe. There will be a proper order to things. No more will these tawdry lesser beings dare to question us and supplant our will. Ultimately they seek to drag us down and take our place. It is an outrage and crime against all creation, Brother! They are parasites upon our sacred body. They are vermin that nibble away at and befoul all we are. Well, no more!'

This will not go well, the taint spoke for Jillan's own mind. *Perhaps it was never going to. The only words of consequence now will be actions.* 'Be ready!' Jillan instructed Samnir and the general. The two commanders passed on orders to Captain Gallen, Captain Skathis and Tebrus. The defenders began to pull themselves into some sort of shape, although a good number of them babbled terrified prayers to any god that would listen.

'Brothers, you know that Haven was never meant for us,' Gar was saying heavily. 'You know that my children have always served as guardians to the sacred valley. We have always believed that something of this place is within each of us. Do you not still have that sense? It is the power of the Geas. How can we not continue to serve and protect it? It would surely be our undoing otherwise.'

Hella came to stand with Jillan. 'Let us do this then, beloved. You are the husband to my heart. I need no silly wedding day and dress to know that. The times we have had together are all I have ever needed to know my life both complete and fulfilled.'

Jillan gave her the world in his gentle smile. He gave her his soul. He touched her cheek. The taint was right. There were no more words. Something had Sinisar, Wayfar and Akwar in its grip, and he would have to undo it or die trying.

'Our time of servitude is past,' Akwar sneered. 'You are no guardian, Gar, for you have failed to protect Haven from the mortals, the basest of creatures. Surely you know how they have already despoiled it. Would you protect them while they perpetrate such a crime? Would you *serve* them? It is both sickening and offensive. Yet you are obdurate, are you not? An unmoving stone? A brick. A dull and stubborn thing. Very well, we will force you to see the truth of things.'

Jillan called upon the magic with which he had filled the desert, a force more frightening and immense than he had ever wielded before. His power seemed to have grown as the *wrongness* had increased, as the sense of doom had come ever closer. He would eclipse the sun god and snuff him out. He would bring a sudden and awful stillness to Wayfar. He would wring the divinity out of Akwar and watch it suffocate like a fish flopping on a riverbank. If it was an apocalypse they wanted, then it was an apocalypse he would bring them.

He would not hesitate. His father had told him all that time ago never to hesitate. He had never understood why, not until now. At last he understood. He would do everything, all this, to protect Haven, the woman he loved and their unborn child, a child innocent of all offence – save existing – to god and nature.

The blood-filled flea hopped and crawled into the mouth of the dead body. In the perfectly still room this slightest of movements was enough to tip the head of the suspended body down and forward. The chin hit the body's chest, and its teeth were brought together, crunching down on the flea. The life force left the flea and passed into its host, feeding its sullen spirit and dragging it back to wakefulness.

Torpeth convinced his lower jaw to drop open again, and then cajoled all the other fleas about his person to climb into his waiting mouth. The parasites had fed on his blood while he lived and had therefore kept his magic animated beyond death. Now they reinvested him with that magic and animated him once more. He gratefully bit down on them and accepted the vital sustenance.

I will not forget this sacrifice, you mighty fleas. You humble me, for life and death turn upon you. Nay, the heavens and hell turn upon you. The rise and fall of empires and gods. No life is meaningless, no matter how small. I aspire to be as mighty as a flea one day. I will devote myself to it, for you are my makers, and therefore my gods. I will follow your example for the rest of my days. I will write songs and great poems to the first among you, that first flea who bravely had me bow my head and accept the sacrament of its

essence. I will offer up praise and worship to that flea and its pantheon. I,
Torpeth the Humble, do so swear it.

Torpeth worked his jaw. 'See, silly ox, if I had taken a bath as you'd suggested, what then, eh? There would have been no fleas to save us. Do you see just how silly and short-sighted you are now, silly ox? Silly ox? Are you there? Where are you, silly ox? What, got no fleas of your own? That'll teach you, eh? That's what comes of having too many baths. Baths will be the death of you. I did warn you they were weakening, no? Did you not listen? No? A shame. Even more silly of you, really. Where are we, silly ox? Why does my back hurt so? Feels like hooks beneath my shoulder blades. Not a pleasant feeling. I do not recommend it, although – to be sure – if it were a choice of hooks or a bath I now know to take the hooks every time. It's a useful rule. I must remember it or pass it on to someone, in case it should ever prove useful again.

'Silly ox, if you're not answering me, it must mean you have gone and got yourself into some sort of silliness that requires Torpeth the Humble to come and help you. I should stop hanging about here, waiting for you to come and help me, eh? I would be waiting a long time otherwise, perhaps the longest time. Who knows just how much silliness would happen in the meantime? Perhaps so much silliness that it became the norm, making the serious seem silly by comparison. There would be little place for Torpeth the Humble in such a world. I must follow the holy example of the flea, therefore, and hop and crawl my way to a place of proper sacrifice. Fear not, brave fleas, I will see your sacrifice avenged, and see to it your enemies know themselves less than fleas.'

He slowly raised his legs, up past his waist and higher still. Up, bending double, feeling like his spine was being pulled out through his back. He inched and contorted until his feet were past his head, where he wrapped his ankles around the chains. He hauled with his legs and painstakingly levered himself off the hooks. His legs could not hold him and he slithered and fell to the stone floor, hitting his head.

'Ouch.'

Torpeth the Humble got to his feet in the throne room of the Eternal Keep and regarded the vacant seat of power upon its dais. 'Hmm. An empty throne, silly ox. Very symbolic. Also very tempting. It seems my fleas are to be revenged almost immediately.'

He climbed up onto the throne, crouched and defecated.

There were cages piled up to his right. Their occupants moaned gently. 'What is this now, silly ox? A curious pastime. Are you somewhere in there? Is this the silliness you've got yourself into? Are those not the skins of mountain goats I spy there at the end?'

The holy man came down from the throne and picked his way over to the cages most recently added to the pile. 'Bantith, is that you? What are you doing? Do you hear me, Godsender? Where are your wits? Do you sleep? Will you snore?' He gently slapped at the cheek of Bantith's face, which was pushed up against the bars of his cage. The mountain man's eyes came open with the human contact. 'Bantith, what have you done to yourself? You're all in knots. It is a strange way to deport yourself, and really of little use to your people, eh? We really don't have time for you to be indulging yourself like this. I am sure there are other places we need to be if our people are to have any hope of survival.'

'T-T...'

'Eh?'

'T-T...'

'Yes, I heard it the first time. I just don't know what you mean.'

'T-T...'

'It's no use, you're making no sense. It's not surprising really, when you insist on having yourself all squashed like that. Hard to breathe, I imagine. I really don't know why you do it.'

'Help.'

'Help? Help who?'

'Me.'

'You?'

'Free me.'

'Free you? Well why didn't you say so before? At last you're making some sense. There's hope for you after all, and therefore hope for our people. Alright, let me see. Ah, here we are, pull this, push that and wiggle so. There you are. Free. Well, come on, out you get. What do you want? Further invitation? A round of applause? We need to hurry, before the owner of that throne comes back and goes getting all upset. You need to want to get out more. That's how it works here, you see. We're trapped by our own beliefs, desires and fears. We're victims of ourselves. We're our own worst enemies. That is what hell is – having to face and deal with yourself. You can't escape yourself, you see. I understand

216

that now. That's why there is never any escape, but it doesn't mean you should give up wanting to get out and trying to be free. It's the wanting and the trying, the constant fight and battle, that gradually changes us, you know. So, although we can never be entirely free of the confines of our reality, we can at least change our prison in changing ourselves. There you go. Now you're getting it. You're nearly there.'

Bantith stood crookedly before the holy man of his people and sobbed like a newborn. 'Thank you.'

Torpeth shrugged. 'You had to do it yourself, as hard as it was. No one can do it for you. It's the nature of being. Sorry about that. Now, go and see if any of the others want to wake up and be free. You'll need to give them a prod or slap first. Meanwhile I need to find out where that silly ox has got to. We really don't have time for all this hide-and-seek, but that's the young for you. Everything's new and exciting to them, even when it's dangerous. They get quite giddy with it. That's why they're all silly oxen. It makes me miss my goats something terrible. You don't have any fleas, do you?'

'Fleas? No, holy one.'

'Shame. You must stop bathing so often.'

'Yes, holy one.'

'Good. Oh, and always choose hooks in the back in preference to a bath. Remember that.'

'Yes, holy one.'

'Fine. Now. Silly ox! Where are you?'

Jillan's magic rose up and dragged the sky and its invaders down. Holy Gar clapped the flats of his hands together and the ground buckled. Suddenly the defenders were thrust skywards, soaring uplands taking them up towards the enemy.

'Spread your feet! Keep your balance!' Samnir roared across the army.

'Weapons ready!' Captain Skathis bellowed.

'Annihilate them!' holy Sinisar demanded of his Court of Light as the sky sagged below them.

'Archers, release!' General Thormodius yelled as their enemy came into range. His officers echoed his command across the field, and over five hundred arrows tipped with sun-metal tore through the sky. A dozen spectrals did not see the missiles coming, and described beautiful rainbows of death before fading from existence, but the rest of Sinisar's host could not be hit, for they moved with the speed of light. They shimmered out of harm's way, only for the arrows to continue tracing upwards, where they found secondary targets among holy Wayfar's followers. Several hundred rocs and drakes fell screaming and tumbling, tearing holes through Sinisar's ranks.

'Archers, ready!' the general called again. 'Release!'

'My children,' holy Gar rumbled. 'Fling your rocks now to devastate my foolhardy brothers.'

Freom and several hundred stone titans lumbered forward and hurled boulders as large as houses at those who threatened Haven. Again the majority of the beings of light easily avoided the assault, leaving Wayfar's winged warriors to suffer the brunt of it instead. The god of the world's winds roared like a hurricane and blew the rocks back, sending them crashing down through unsuspecting lines of lumines and careless constellations of visifers. The angry god's breath did not stop at the rocks either; it swept whole swathes of scintillations into the deadly path of the next flight of arrows searing through the air; it buffeted fire imps so badly that a number were entirely extinguished; it even rocked Sinisar upon his throne.

'Brother! Are you my ally or enemy?' Sinisar demanded.

Jillan yanked hard on the centre of the sky, trying to bring the sun god low. Freda saw what he did and pulled all the light she could out from below the divinity. It was as if the sky was about to drain away down a black hole.

'You dare?' Sinisar roared, lifting his glorious majesty up out of his throne. He wobbled slightly and his blazing crown slipped to one side.

'Archers!' the canny General Thormodius called. 'Target him! Make a cage of your arrows so that there can be no escape. Release!'

Sun-metal flew at holy Sinisar. The god's eyes widened in alarm as he realised the very real threat to himself. He sprang up, trying to climb the sky, clawing higher, only to be brought back down by Jillan and Freda's determination.

'Whore!' holy Sinisar spat, suddenly turning and spewing the furnace of his being down on all below him. He was diminished by it, but it burned away the wooden shafts of every arrow spearing towards him so that the sun-metal fell away and rained death down on the cursed mortal who had dared claim the power of the Geas for himself.

'No!' Freda clanged and spread herself over Jillan and Hella so that they could not be harmed.

The rock people attempted to shelter as many of the mortals as they could, but hundreds upon hundreds of Heroes were incinerated by the god's wrath. Ash somehow found one of the few places to avoid the rolling inferno and saved most of the Unclean. Holy Gar saw to it himself that most of the commanding officers were spared. Yet all the villagers who had followed Jillan up out of Haven were lost, completely burned away. Captain Gallen lost all of his men but a few dozen. No trace was left of them, as if they had never existed, as if their lives had been nothing. Well over half the defenders were lost in that terrible moment.

'See what you have wrought,' Sinisar coughed.

'Archers!' General Thormodius cried, holding the stump he had for an arm aloft. 'He is weakened. Ready!' Fifty bows came up, even if the hands holding them were no longer steady. 'For Haven and our fallen comrades. Release!'

'No!' Sinisar raged. 'You are mere mortals!'

Now, the taint whispered with a deep satisfaction.

Jillan did not hesitate. He reached with both the power of the Dark Geas, Kathuula and the Geas of Haven. Vast unseen hands grabbed the god by his limbs and spreadeagled him across the sky. The deity struggled mightily but could do nothing to break free.

'Release me! This is an outrage beyond words. None can hold me. You do not know what you do.'

'It cannot be!' holy Wayfar wailed. 'It must not be.'

The tears of Akwar blurred all.

Even holy Gar was horrified.

The vengeance of the mortals of Haven came home into the body of holy Sinisar. The sun-metal sank into his flesh and a bloody light poured out of him. The sun-metal went deeper, going through him and piercing his very essence. The Court of Light screamed in anguish and denial, not believing what they saw, though it was by their very substance that they saw, knew and even experienced it. The swirling dust, rain, wind and light of the conflict spread the red sun across the sky as if it ran with gore. The sky bled, its sacred life running out and soaking into the ground. Sinisar's body went limp and he fell through the air. There was a sickening thud and he lay at his brother's feet, unmoving.

'Now you've done it,' Ash breathed.

'None will live!' boomed Wayfar, his roiling clouds darkening to a funereal black and lightning sheeting violently from one horizon to the other. Much of the Court of Light had failed with their god, but now holy Akwar joined his power to that of his tempestuous brother in order to bring the storm that would see the world of mortalkind end.

Aspin hung in the punishment chamber beneath Saviours' Paradise. There'd never been any escape from here. There'd been no Jillan to lead them against their enemies. Azual had never fallen. Saint Azual ruled all. The pagans were lost, gone. There was no ability even to resist. It was meaningless before the absolute reign of the Empire. Meaningless.

Had his dreams been meaningless also? Had … what was her name? … Veena … been nothing but a creation of his own imagination? Of all his dreams, it was her face that he still saw. How could that be? How was it that he could see her raven hair, leaf-green eyes and snowy skin? How could she be so real to him when all else was gone? How was it that he could despair of himself and all else, and yet still hope for her? It was love, of course, yet was the feeling just another fiction? Why did it not leave him when all else did? It should leave, but it was stubborn. How could it persist when the rule and definition of the Empire was meant to be absolute? How could it linger and loiter around the punishment chamber as if it intended to creep down and rescue him?

It must be another dream, but unlike the others it refused to be banished. Veena was there at his ear, whispering solace and promise. He felt her breath tickling his ear. 'Wake up,' she asked of him. She had bad breath. 'Wake up, silly ox!' She smelt of goats, as if she never bathed. He felt nauseous as he woke to look into the eyes of his beloved Torpeth.

'There you are, silly ox. I was thinking I was going to have to give you the kiss of life.' The holy man's face was dangerously close. 'I'm glad I no longer have to. Who knows where your lips have been?'

Aspin gagged. 'I thought you were dead.'

'Ordinarily I would have been, but with the chief constantly getting himself and our people into trouble, I find I can't rest peacefully. Besides, the ancestors of our people really aren't much company to speak of. All

220

they do is drone on about the glorious deeds they completed in life. Don't get me wrong, some of them are all very worthy, but they don't seem to know when enough's enough.'

'That's rich. Old goat, are you going to get me down from here, or what?'

Torpeth pursed his lips. 'That would depend.'

'No, it wouldn't. Now get me down.'

The small man cocked his head as he pondered that. 'Perhaps you're right. First time for everything, eh? Alright then. Pull this, push that and wiggle so. There you are.'

Aspin's manacles came undone and he fell to the floor. He landed on his knees with a crack. 'Oww! Careful, would you?'

'Stop complaining. *Thank you* is what you're looking for.'

'Well, help me up then.'

Torpeth shook his head in pity. 'You have to get off your knees your-self, silly ox. It's symbolic.'

'Bugger symbolic. Help me up.'

'No.'

Cursing roundly, Aspin levered himself up. 'You can be really annoy-ing, you know that?'

'It is one of my numerous talents, not that I ever get thanks or ap-preciation for it. Do you think it's any fun for me, having to annoy my people to keep them on their toes, silly ox? No, it isn't. All I get is self-pitying complaint and ill-founded accusation. It was just one more reason why I couldn't stay dead, silly ox. I soon realised that none of the living was going to offer up prayers of thanks for all the suffering and sacrifice I endured on their behalf. No one was going to sing a sad song, build a shrine of remembrance or think wistfully of me. It's just plain ungrateful, do you hear? So I've had to come back to teach you, the silliest of oxen, the meaning of decent ancestor worship.'

'Your goats would have missed you, though.'

'I have no doubt they would, for they are loyal and unswerving, unlike some I could mention. However, with only them to mark my death, I would probably end up in some sort of goaty nether realm, which would be a cantankerous and uppity place, I'm sure. Besides, the admirable qualities of my goats do *not* excuse you, *Chief* Aspin, who should behave as a good example to our people, so that every respect is shown to their holy man.'

'Alright, you win. Get us out of here and I shall give you as much gratitude as you could ever want, even though it was *your* fault that we ended up here in the first place. I will even put in a good word for you with the headwoman.'

Torpeth's eyes became young again. 'You would do that? Then I am no longer aggrieved. Let us go at once. At last I have hope. I am fortified anew. Aha! I almost pity our enemies. Pick up those clumsy feet of yours, silly ox. This way!'

They climbed up out of the punishment chamber and into the throne room of the King of the Dead. Bantith waited with twenty disorientated mountain men, most of whom had been furnished with spears and bits of hide armour from the litter behind the vacant throne.

'Chief? Is that you?' big Lars asked. 'What do we do now?'

'We get the hell out of here, that's what we do.'

'But, Chief, how can we leave without first trying to free the spirits of our ancestors?' Bantith dared ask. Most of the men nodded.

'Our ancestors will always live in our hearts and minds,' Aspin insisted. 'That is all they have ever required, I now realise. My own father's spirit would not want me chasing shadows here for ever. Indeed, the last time I was in the nether realm he called me a fool and cuffed me round the head just for coming here. The living should never become too preoccupied with the dead. We have already been here too long, I fear.'

'That is so,' Torpeth said. 'Those devils Praxis and Azual held the spirits of our dead over us as a ruse, to find a hold on our hearts and minds. Shrug off all concern and fear, therefore, for this entire prison is a ruse comprised of our own misgiving, mistaking and misapprehension. We must navigate its maze back to the land of the living, for it is that land where all our thoughts should be. We must not be late in bringing aid to our allies, or all may fall. Do not let us be negligent in our duty to the living, our friends and people.'

Bantith assented. 'The spirit of my mother would understand, I know it. How do we go from this place? They said there was no escape or hope. That too was a ruse, yes?'

'Quite so, good Bantith.' Torpeth smiled. 'See, there is hope for you yet. We will go as we came – by our own volition. Just as we made this prison for ourselves, of ourselves, so we must unmake it. Just as we allowed spirit guides to bring us here, so we must summon those who can take us hence. Indeed, now that we all share this understanding, our new guides should be arriving presently. Ah, there you are, Thomas. What kept you?'

The shade of the giant blacksmith came from behind Azual's throne. His hammer dripped gore and his eyes glowed with the heat of his soul's forge. His black hair was plastered to his forehead with sweat, his lungs worked like bellows and his bulging muscles looked to have been strained beyond their tolerance, but there was a savage grin fixed upon his face. 'Well met, little man!' he managed. 'Apologies ... I got carried away back there for a while ... And I had a devil of a time dragging these harpies away from the malacants. Brave men of the mountains, may I introduce my three daughters, Ausa, Betha and the youngest – and fiercest – Stara.'

'Friend Thomas!' Aspin declared in delight. 'How is it you come here?'

'The Empire could never defeat me in life. Do you really think I would let it defeat me in death? It was little matter to break into this place, in truth, for the walls are not as formidable as they appear. The guards were of little consequence – I imagine they get precious few people trying to break in. I come to help my friends, of course, but also Betha has been quite determined to see you again. There's been no end of *Aspin-this* and *Aspin-that*.'

'Father, don't! You'll embarrass me,' Thomas's auburn daughter cried. She dimpled. 'Hello, Aspin.'

The mountain men covered their smiles as their chieftain became flushed and flustered. 'I ... er ... Hello, Betha. It is good to see you.' Then he blurted, 'I'm sorry. I'm now pledged to another.'

Betha pouted for a moment. 'No matter, I prefer that one anyway.' She pointed at Lars, who yelped in surprise and alarm, and caused his comrades no end of merriment.

'He's almost as tall as Father,' her elder sister Ausa giggled.

'What's wrong with his arm?' Stara asked loudly. 'Besides, he's not as handsome as Jillan.'

'Hush now, girls,' their father chided them. 'We must not forget our manners. We should also be introducing our companions, should we not?'

Two other shades approached. One was a hefty youth wearing assorted bits of armour, while the other was a ragamuffin girl whose face was hidden by straggly hair, and from whom exuded an unhealthy intensity. When Aspin looked upon the latter his scalp prickled, his chest tightened and he thought he saw things moving in the corner of his eye. The soul reader in him advised extreme caution with this creature.

'Haal!' Torpeth welcomed the first shade, clapping him on the shoulder.

'You remember me,' the shade said with obvious gratification.

'But of course. You are Haal Corinson, hero of Godsend, defender of Hella's honour and true friend to Jillan. We shared many a toast with you once we'd brought down that calumnix Azual. Your name is still spoken with reverence among our people.'

'It is?' the shade asked, standing taller. 'I am honoured. Thank you, holy one.'

Torpeth moved to the second shade and gave a funny sort of bow, clearly to see more of the face beneath the hair. Shakily he straightened up. 'You were once of Thorndell?'

'I am Anara,' came the surprisingly gentle voice.

'Follower of Miserath!' Torpeth accused. 'What would you have of us, witch?'

All of the mountain men made warding signs against evil and retreated. Thomas's three daughters came to stand with the witch-urchin and glowered at the men.

'I am a follower of the Dewar Lord, yes.' The witch-urchin nodded. 'I remained faithful where others did not. I gave my life to free him from Saint Izat's prison, when *you* had turned your back on him, traitorous Torpeth. Were it not for the Dewar Lord, Haven would never have been found and the Empire defeated. I am not here for *you*, holy man, that is certain, so what is it *you* would have of *me*?'

'You twist and turn like your master, I see. The Dewar Lord helped defeat the Empire, did he? Or did he instead attempt to take the power of the Geas for himself, to realise his own selfish ends?'

The daughters of Thomas bared small pointed teeth. Their dark gazes promised Torpeth punishments of which he had not even begun to dream.

'The Dewar Lord made the ultimate sacrifice so that the Empire could be defeated. More sacrifice than *you* have ever made, Torpeth-the-never-satisfied. The Dewar Lord is one of the gods, and you would all do well to remember that and offer up thanks. Were it not for the holy lord, the pantheon would not have survived to rise another day. Your pitiful Wayfar would have been left whining and wailing for all time, were it not for the Dewar Lord first aiding Jillan against Azual. Yet I do not come here now in service or defence of my god. Neither do I come here to waste my words and spirit on the likes of you, godsforsaken Torpeth. No, I come to aid those who would help Jillan of Godsend, he to whom I owe a debt.'

'Or so you say,' Torpeth bit back. 'Miserath's intent was to defeat the Empire, was it? Funny that. Does the Empire really look defeated to you? Is Azual really cast down for ever more? Why, then, is he not here? Is he perhaps instead marshalling his limitless army of the dead out on the plains and preparing them to march on the land of the living? Why have we mountain men been forced into this realm? Is it perhaps that we offer too much challenge to gods who are being corrupted by their own dark brother? Has Miserath really made the ultimate sacrifice or is he actually about to make both the nether realm and Haven his to rule? Is the truth not that he has played you for a fool all along, silly girl?'

Stara raised clawed hands and prepared to leap. Betha spoke the opening words of a cantrip. Ausa scribed the air with gestures. Anara blew a kiss towards Torpeth, and the holy man was forced to perform impossible katas to defend himself. His movement was so fluid and continuous that it was only perceived after the fact. The mountain men took up fighting formation.

'Enough!' Aspin and Thomas boomed together, stepping with Haal into the middle of the confrontation and forcing their respective sides to back down.

'Stop this, daughters! You *will* behave. These people are our friends. They are guests in this realm.'

'Torpeth! What's the matter with you? I hear the truth in Anara's words. She is here to help us. How is it you cannot control yourself? Do you not see where this confrontation will lead? Would you have us fighting among ourselves? Would you do the job for our enemies? Would you betray Jillan, Haven, the gods and all? *Stop* this. As both chief and soul reader of our tribe I command you. Your instinct and stubbornness could see us trapped as easily as any of our fears and fantasies.'

Torpeth hunched his shoulders and folded his arms as if to trap his hands and prevent them getting up to any mischief. 'They started it,' he grumped.

'They are *children*. How old are you?'

'That's not the point.'

'It *is* the point. Your age and knowledge bring as much help as they do hindrance, further means to trap and divide us. You said this place was of our own making, did you not? Surely you can read enough of souls and know yourself sufficiently to hear the truth in my words.'

'Maybe your words are also a trap, silly ox.'

'Keep this up and I will need to tell the headwoman of it. Last chance, old goat. Refuse to repent and we must leave you here while we depart.'

'There will be none to guide you, Torpeth,' Thomas admonished the small man. 'We are the last.'

Aspin grinned. 'Think of it as symbolic.'

'Bugger symbolic,' the holy man said uncomfortably. His face fell further. 'Perhaps it is the final test of Torpeth the Humble. It is *so* difficult, silly ox.'

'I know, old goat. To think that all can be won and lost on something so silly, eh? Something so slight. Something so trivial. Something so subtle. Something so cunning!'

'Yes,' Torpeth whispered, his eyes widening. 'I almost missed it. Oh, but what a ruse this was, almost beneath any notice. Is there no end to Azual's subterfuge and subversion? Or was it my dear friend Praxis, he who knows me better than any other, who brought all manner of sophistry into this place to complement the usual tortures and depravations? Or forces beyond them, even? Are they still agents of their omnipresent Saviours? Do the schemes of the others now snare this place along with the land of the living? Anara, forgive this old goat, for suddenly I am overtaken by even greater fears. Lead us from here, I beg you.'

The head of the witch-urchin dipped in acknowledgement. With the other spirit guides, she led the mountain men past Azual's throne and into the harrowing corridors of the Eternal Keep.

Thomas held back slightly to speak with Aspin. 'See what this realm has done to my beloved daughters, friend Aspin? It breaks my heart to see it. As their loving father, I do my best with them, but they are less and less themselves. I am losing them! There are too few in the land of the living who remember them, you see. More and more I do not recognise them. It takes all my strength to keep loving them, friend Aspin, and I am ashamed to admit there have been a few moments when I feared them. Even their dear mother has all but given up on them! Can't you help me?'

The agony in Thomas's appeal was such that Aspin suffered it himself. 'Friend Thomas, ask whatever help you would have of my people and it will be provided.'

'Perhaps what I ask is wrong, but is there not some way you can return them to the land of the living? I can do nothing for them here. Can you not take them with you? It is a small favour to ask in return for leading a friend and comrade-in-arms out of the dread temple, is it not? No, do not look at me so. I must ask it of you, as I dote on them and am nothing without them. It is my weakness, I know, but pity me for it rather than hate me, I beg you. Love of one's children should never be a weakness, but this place perverts and corrupts all that is good. I have never asked anything else of you, mountain man, as the gods are my witness. But this I ask, for the care you once showed my poor sweet Betha – free them from this hell they call the nether realm. Free all the innocent children who are made malacants by this place. None deserve to be so twisted and tormented.'

How could he refuse such a request? Was it another trap or ruse? Nothing of what he read in Thomas suggested so. Yet was it not said the road to damnation was paved with good intentions? Torpeth loitered nearby, conspicuously eavesdropping. The naked warrior's eyebrows beetled down in warning to Aspin.

'We will … we will do what we can, friend Thomas.'

Torpeth sighed and shook his head disapprovingly, then shrugged and went to listen in on the muttered conversations of Bantith and the others. Thomas seemed satisfied and strode on to catch up with his wayward daughters, Anara and Haal. Aspin was left to march on in his own space for a while, worrying how soon it would be before he was forced to go back on his word.

They followed a trail of ichor and entrails down long screaming corridors. The evidence of the path Thomas and the others had cut to come and find the mountain men was horrific enough, but the cages of the damned to each side seemed even worse to Aspin. The captives of the dread temple wailed and pleaded for a merciful end, constantly looking over shoulders or up into the air for unanticipated threats.

'You can do anything you like to me!' a curvaceous woman begged of Bantith. 'Just strangle me as you do it.'

'One-arm, fight me if you are man enough!' a wild-eyed warrior challenged Lars.

'Take my child!' a mother called to Aspin. 'Consume it as you will. Pity, kind lord.'

'Old man, we are ready!' a pair of youths who looked to be brothers shouted lasciviously to Torpeth, one bending over while the other thrust suggestively.

'Masters, I repent. Let me serve you. I will punish your enemies for you.'

It went on and on. The spirit guides appeared oblivious to it all, but Aspin's warriors kept close together in the very centre of each corridor, well beyond the reach of grasping hands and spittle.

They turned into another corridor, and then another, left, right, right and left. They went down where the air was insufferably hot, and up high where it was too frigid and thin. The occupants of the cages began to look and sound the same to Aspin, and he did not know whether to be relieved or afraid for his soul that he was now inured to them. His men no longer seemed so harrowed either, and a few thought to mock the damned, make rude gestures or feint with their spears.

Aspin was about to demand of Thomas how long it would be before they were free of the madness when he noticed the ichor on the floor of the latest corridor had already been passed through by several dozen pairs of footprints. 'We are going in circles. Stop! We have been this way before. You men, halt when your chief commands it. Torpeth, these are our own footprints, are they not?'

The holy man crouched low to the floor and sniffed. 'Yup. There's no mistake.'

Thomas came back to them; his daughters, Haal and Anara, stayed further down the corridor. 'We should not stop, friend Aspin,' the blacksmith warned.

'No, Thomas? Explain to me how it is we have already come through here.'

'Corridors will often look the same, friend Aspin. It is just one of the tricks of this place. Just as a mind repeats the same thoughts over and over, so the same corridors have to be travelled over and over before something new occurs or is encountered.'

'Might that not see us trapped here for ever?' Bantith fretted.

'It sees the dead trapped here for ever,' Thomas conceded, 'for they are always the same. They can only repeat what they were in life. But the living constantly grow and change, always experiencing and becoming something new. And the living also change whatever they encounter. See! The footprints of your passing have changed the look of this corridor and all like it. By contrast, my steps leave hardly a trace. Trust me, you mountain men, it cannot be long now. Soon we must reach the limits of the dread temple. The King of the Dead cannot keep the living confined against their will, or there would be no sense to existence whatsoever.'

'Aye, that is the threat,' Torpeth agreed. 'Quickly then, blacksmith. Enough speechifying and repeating corridors. Come, silly ox. No more stopping.'

Aspin came close to the naked warrior and whispered, 'I read only truth in Thomas. It cannot be a ruse, can it?'

'If it is a ruse, silly ox, then life and death are but ruses. The gods are but a jest. The Saviours are charlatans. Our own thoughts are designed to deceive us. That way, all meaning ends. So, enough of ruses, I say. We must now have belief and assert ourselves and our thoughts, else we cannot escape the maze and quandary. Enough now. Know yourself a silly ox and be that silly ox, just as I will know myself a naked warrior and be that naked warrior. A deal between us, silly ox?'

'Yes, a deal between us, old goat.'

'See, only a silly ox would agree to such a deal.'

They came then to a wide and open crossroads. The cages had receded, to be replaced by a silent tension. Smoking torches cast flickering shadows, which danced around each of four sacrificial altars set on the corners. The stone blocks were much stained and glistened, evidence that they were used regularly.

'We are nearly there,' Thomas said.

'And you have never been further away!' buzzed the voice of Saint Dianon as he emerged from the route ahead of them. Saint Goza lumbered in from the way to the left, Saint Zoriah drifted from the right and Saint Sylvan was suddenly close behind them.

'Are we betrayed?' Thomas growled as the mountain men formed a defensive circle in the middle of the crossroads.

'Indeed you are.' Saint Dianon nodded.

'Oh, goody. I was hoping we would be.' Torpeth capered. 'Things are always much more fun that way, don't you think? Intrigue, mystery and excitement as we wonder who it was among us who whispered to the enemy.'

'The Saint lies,' Aspin countered. 'I can read it in him. He merely seeks to create division among us. Stand firm, you men. Make ready to revenge yourselves on these soulless creatures of the Empire.'

'Can we play with the Saints, Papa?' Stara begged. 'Can we, pleeease?'

'It's dangerous, dear heart,' her father replied.

'Oh, you never let us have any fun, Papa. Just this once?' Ausa asked softly, Betha nodding in support.

Thomas threw up his hands in mock despair. 'I'm outnumbered, I see. Just don't go ruining your dresses. You know what your mother is like. I'll never hear the end of it.'

'Oh, thank you, Papa!' Betha beamed, coming to stand on tiptoe and kiss him prettily on the cheek.

Thomas gave Aspin a helpless look over his daughter's shoulder. 'I spoil them, I know, but I can't help myself.'

Shaking his head, Aspin rallied his men. 'Are you ready, you men?'

'Yes, Chief!' they shouted.

'The fat one is mine,' Lars warned his comrades, levelling his spear at the all-devouring Goza.

'Then fight for the living, brave men of the mountains! For Wayfar and Haven! For the living!'

'For the living!'

The fury of the heavens broke upon Haven and its defenders. Holy Wayfar brought hurricanes of such force they threatened to tear the very earth from its roots. Holy Akwar brought down a deluge to wash every living thing from the desert. His driving rain was so thick that those caught in it struggled to breathe and felt themselves drowning. The ground became slick beneath feet and then a sinking bog. The god of the earth, for all his strength and size, could not stand before the combined might of his vengeful brothers. Mudslides at the edges of the uplands swept away dozens and then hundreds of soldiers.

Captain Skathis, at the centre of the tumult, was sunk up to his knees in mud. That was all that kept him in place before the devastating winds and merciless torrent that had carried so many away. He held his short sword of sun-metal before him, and it seemed to cleave through the assault just enough to allow him breath and life. General Thormodius lay stricken not far away, barely managing to keep armoured chest and head free of the muck. Captain Skathis wanted to go to his leader but dared not shift his position.

Wind and rain seemed to slacken for a moment, and Captain Skathis raised his head. The immediate clamour from the sky announced that the manner of attack had now changed. Rocs and winged serpents descended upon them, talons outstretched and jaws wide. The largest of them, a black-eyed golden roc, came straight for the captain and the general.

Captain Skathis waved his sword. 'Here, you stupid bird!'

The roc brought its wicked beak down, pulled its wings in slightly and arrowed towards the foolhardy human. Captain Skathis realised his attacker had no intention of slowing, so leaned forward with head down, gripped the hilt of his blade with both hands and extended it as far as it would go. The huge roc barrelled into him, burying him beneath its immense chest and sliding them both along fully thirty feet. Skathis was pressed deep into the slurry. He swallowed the clogging filth and choked. He could not move. The last of his air left him as his body was forced down into a grave.

Tearing calluses and skin from his palms, Ash hauled his chest up onto the rocky area that stood free of the turbulent waters cascading across the uplands. The stones were slick and rain sluiced down, threatening to dislodge him. The wind rose and ripped at him. He felt his grip slipping, and then Tebrus had his wrist and was pulling him up. The storm howled in frustration. They slithered across the rocks and lay flat in hollows with the rest of the Unclean. Wayfar tried to scoop Ash out, but the woodsman braced hands and feet against the rock and managed to stay anchored.

You are right to grovel before me, annoying mortal, but it will not save you, Akwar hissed.

Ash stifled a sob. How had it come to this? This was not fighting. It was barely surviving. It was utterly futile to fight gods. Why hadn't they let him do the talking, the idiots? His lips were almost too numb to form words now, and Wayfar's displeasure so deafening it was unlikely they would hear his plea anyway. 'It would be too late to apologise, I take it?'

I am glad you have not yet drowned, for that would be too quick. I will instead take your blood from you, drop by agonising drop.

The temperature plunged and the rain turned to slashing hail. Hard, sharp ice lacerated the Unclean with a million blades. Ash cried out as myriad nicks and slices appeared on the backs of his hands. His cheeks were slashed to ribbons. He had his eyes squeezed shut, but Akwar set to flaying the lids.

Scream your mocking words, woodsman, or offer up a prayer. Open your mouth again and I will cleave your tongue from its root. Very well then, I will peel your lips back for you and carve into your gums, to remove your teeth so that they are no longer in the way.

He could not bear it. This hiding he attempted was beyond endurance. It was not a life. He wasn't even sure it was survival. It was merely waiting for death, experiencing it cut by cut, drop by drop. And whether he liked it or not, he was somehow responsible for having led the Unclean to this as well. He had used them when it suited him to secure his position in Haven, but now they lived and died with him. Their blood was on his hands, their blood was his blood, and that blood was running out onto the rocks.

'Are you going to just lie there like a coward?' he exhorted himself. 'Are you just going to let it happen? Tell yourself it will be just like going to sleep, go on. Except sleep never hurt this much, and you can be sure that any dreams you might have in the sleep of death are going to be highly unpleasant. You've seen the godforsaken nether realm. You know what's in store. Call yourself a coward? What self-respecting coward would just carry on lying there? If you were a real coward, you'd get up and beg for your life.'

He lowered his head. Akwar flayed the woodsman's scalp. Blood trickled down Ash's forehead and into his eyes.

I will shear your skin and bone, to expose the mind within. I will saw into it and make you gibber and foam. Tears and urine. Snot and bloody excrement. Your bodily fluids will boil and freeze. Your bladder will shrink and swell, collapse and burst.

Ash came up, bent and tortured. 'Take me then. Stop wittering on. I got the idea pretty much straight away. Honestly, anyone would think you don't have anyone to talk to. What's the matter? No real friends or followers? Are you surprised when all you do is obsess about different ways to punish mortals for your own inadequacy? So go ahead. Take me and let these others go. They're innocent, after all.'

I care not. None here is innocent. All will die. I have spoken, and so it shall be.

A savage blast hit Ash, ice blades and spears darting towards him. Holy Wayfar shrieked with glee.

'Murat! Girl, protect him!' Tebrus yelled, the power of his determination making him felt and heard, even though the maelstrom deprived them of all other senses.

The only other member of the Unclean who dared show herself above the hollows where they were spread was a plain gaunt-eyed girl in her late teens. Despite the chaos around them, her hair hung lank and unmoving. There was a calm and stillness about her. She reached out with it and touched Ash. The shards and icicles holy Akwar had hurled at him simply fell out of the air and shattered on the rocks a few feet from the man of the woods.

Unclean! Akwar and Wayfar snarled together. *Haven must be cleansed of you once and for all.*

Out of the swirling grey came towering ice giants, wielding spikes longer than Ash was tall. First a dozen, then fifty, then hundreds.

'Tebrus,' Ash shouted in panic. 'What now? Run?'

'There is nowhere to go!'

'Damn it. Where's Dor when you need him?'

As the flood had started Samnir had rid himself of his armour with a curse. 'Armour off, or you'll all drown!' he'd commanded the fifty or so remaining Heroes of Haven. 'Up onto those pillars if you still have strength. Others onto the lee side to hold on as best you can!'

The water had risen alarmingly quickly, lifting men onto stone columns that would otherwise have been impossible to scale. The raging waters increased in force and one column was toppled over, half a dozen men carried off in the process.

Captain Gallen thrashed around. 'Can't swim!' he gulped. His head went under.

Samnir dived in and pulled him back up. The captain grabbed and clawed at him in panic, nearly dragging them both under. Samnir punched him in the face, hard. The captain went limp. Samnir got a grip under his chin and towed him to a pillar, where two Heroes reached down for Gallen, but the wind took the chance to overbalance them, and all came crashing down on Samnir.

Samnir dived again to get free of the flailing limbs, only to be caught by a stronger current. He kicked strongly and held his position. He gave his all and regained a few precious feet. Something slithered around one of his ankles and gripped him tightly. Then he shot forward and sideways at frightening speed. He twisted sharply and narrowly avoided having his head crushed as he passed between two of the pillars. The suddenness of his passage and the pressure of the water kept him otherwise helpless – his arms without sufficient strength to force their way down to the sword at his waist.

Up, smashing into unseen flotsam, and into angry air that was just as impossible to breathe as the water. He dangled from a huge curling tentacle. He was lashed violently against the surface of the water and lost all feeling in one arm and shoulder. *Probably for the best*, he thought, struggling for consciousness. The leg held by his attacker felt like it was about to be torn off at the hip. His kneecap had already slipped, so torn were the muscles around it. 'Now you're making me really mad, you arse-dwelling demon! Swum out of Akwar's suppurating behind, did you, you backward and cowardly leech? Enough with the hide-and-seek, I tell you.'

Upside down, he saw Captain Gallen and several of the others pointing past him in horror. 'A monster from the deep! The first among holy Wayfar's servants. The kraken! The Geas preserve us!'

Samnir was dangled on high above the vast gilled head of the sea creature. Its eyes were the black of the bottomless oceans, it had the rending beak of a giant squid, its skin was armoured with barnacled scales, and spined fins went from its crown to the distant tips of its tail. 'So there you are. You reek almost as bad as you look. Put me down. Alright, don't say I didn't warn you. This is going to hurt you as much as it does me.'

With his good arm he pulled his sword of sun-metal from its sheath and with a perfunctory swipe lopped through the thick tentacle. The kraken screeched and reared back. 'Stop whining,' Samnir grunted as he fell onto the top of its head. He landed on his dead arm, so felt little of the impact, although he was sure it was being scraped raw by barnacles and razor-sharp scales.

Samnir planted the tip of his sword to steady himself and lever himself up, then brought his full weight down on the blade, sinking it all the way to the hilt in the leviathan. He got his knees under him and dragged the blade forward and back, opening up the beast. He plunged the blade deeper, working quickly, and then wormed himself down into the cleft.

The kraken bucked and arched, toppling over backwards and rolling over and over. Massive waves hit Captain Gallen and the Heroes on the pillars, robbing them of all purchase.

Samnir had wedged himself deep and would not be budged. The kraken righted itself beneath the water and tilted downwards, preparing to find depths where no mortal could survive. Samnir immediately went to work, sawing, hacking and stabbing with all he had. Black ichor and poisons curled around him, but his blade burned it away, even underwater. Flashes like lightning lit up the surrounding murk and he felt the kraken shudder beneath him. Was it shocked or did it now know fear?

'Don't worry. It'll be over soon,' Samnir said grimly, pushing his arm as far as it would go. His sword hit something tough and passed through it, as it did everything else.

The kraken listed forward, its head going down and down. Its movements were nothing now.

Samnir's lungs burned fiercely. He emptied them entirely, trying to equalise the pressure. His ears burst and his vision went.

Over soon for both of us, he thought.

The surface was too far away now. He had become disorientated, was not sure which direction it was anyway. *At least I won't have to put up with Ash's inane self-pity any more. I'll miss him in a way, but won't miss being the Sand Devil. It's good at last to put him to rest. A fitting end.*

Holy Gar lifted Jillan and Hella above the flood and took them up the sheer face of a crag. His rock people were little troubled by the tumbling waters, and clambered up to join them. Holy Wayfar's winds hit them with tornadoes of sand and stone, but the golems remained anchored to the ground and shielded the two humans. The darkness that was Freda came up through the crag and deposited the huge Dor near them.

'Fank you, Freda,' Ash's over-large lackey coughed and spluttered. 'Dor like Freda. Dor will help Freda.'

'Seems you've got yourself a new friend, Freda,' Jillan observed.

The shadow did not reply.

'Look out!' Hella cried.

Out of the suffocating sandstorm came a fearful drone. Black swarms of winged beetles and other insects swirled down on them.

Dozens landed on Hella's head. A giant millipede sought to climb into her ear. Scarabs on her face bit and stung her. Weevils burrowed into her hair and delved into her scalp. Her screams were terrible to hear.

Jillan tried to help her, but she couldn't keep still. An emperor scorpion reared up at the nape of her neck. Not stopping to think, Jillan snatched it up and squashed it in his palm before it could strike.

Things clawed at him, at his eyes, trying to wriggle into his mouth. Flies crawled up inside his nose and worked their way towards his eyes. He snorted hard, feeling his tracts burn and then tasting his own blood at the back of his throat. He wiped his eyes again and again against the inside of his elbow, crushing and smearing creatures and their poisons across forehead and cheeks. He felt light-headed as he was pricked with toxins. Desperate for air, he had to open his mouth to breathe. Fluttering and worming things were immediately in his throat. He bit down on them and felt their juices trickling across his palate. He tried to close his gullet, but something was still alive and forcing its way down into him. It caught for a moment, choking him. Small spiked limbs and feet hooked onto his insides as it dragged itself down towards his centre.

His stomach spasmed in revulsion and he vomited painfully, but the thing was still there! It would not be dislodged.

Help me, he screamed in silent terror. *Oh, Geas, no.*

He was writhing on the ground, Hella rolling next to him. He tried to raise his gorge again, but he was empty. Dor was on his knees.

'Friend Jillan, what must I do?' Freda moaned. 'Tell me what to do!'

He tried to draw up his magic but it was fitful and disorientated, contaminated by the agents invading his blood. Even if it had been whole, he did not know exactly how he might have used it *inside* his own self or to remove the creatures plaguing Hella without hurting her.

Your magic alone cannot stand against the gods of this world, the taint observed. *You cannot escape your own physical nature or their command of the physical nature of your world. They have almost reached the heart of you. They will eat you from the inside out, taking the magic at your core first. Once that is gone, you and I will lose our connection and bond. I will be unable to help you. Hella will die with you, along with your unborn. Such a waste. Such a waste.*

You can save me.

If you give yourself to me. I must be free to do what I must, without hesitation or compromise. Your mind will only second-guess our actions otherwise, despite your best efforts, and that hesitation will end us. It is the only way.

You cannot ask me to trust you, taint. You are the Chaos. You are Kathuula.

I do not ask you to trust me. I simply ask if you would have me save you and your loved ones. The alternative? You die. Hella and the child follow. Samnir, Ash, Gallen and Tebrus, Skathis and Thormodius. None will be able to stand against the gods without you. You have led them to this. Their spirits will be broken when you are lost. Wayfar and Akwar will break the earth. Gar will be shattered and Freda shackled to be their plaything. Haven will be their throne and an age of suffering will befall mortalkind that will make them yearn for the days of the Empire like never before. In secret the People will pray to their blessed Saviours and curse your name for having betrayed them. They will call their Saviours to the second coming, even though it sees the People finally judged and this world ended. Look into her eyes, Jillan, if you can, and watch her die.

He turned his head towards his beloved Hella, whose movements had begun to fail. His heart broke to see her ravaged face. She looked longingly at him, shedding bloody tears. There was such understanding and forgiveness there that it tortured him more than he already suffered at the hands of the gods. He saw her knowledge of the life they would never have together. Her hand ruffling his hair. A son dandled on his knee. Lying together in a warm and fragrant meadow. Giving her a small posy of wild flowers, and then apologising because they could never match the beauty he saw in her. Seeing her delighted with them anyway, simply because it was he who had given them to her. Becoming older and sharing so many joys and fears together. Becoming tired, then one day finding the posy he had given her so long before, pressed, dried and put away for safe-keeping. Yet none of that would happen. All was lost. All was ashes and grief. How could he deny her?

He gave himself to the taint, allowing Kathuula to enter the world of the living through him. The way from the nether realm was now open. Its power was as terrifying as it was awesome. It filled him, swallowing and destroying the servant of the gods that sought to undo him. And still the power grew. It spilled from his eyes and mouth, taking in Hella and cleansing her of the crawling filth that covered and undermined her. They rose together, Jillan and Hella, he a terrible force that none of this world could withstand, and she the will that would command all to their knees before them.

'Come, beloved.' She smiled gently at him. 'We will bring these gods low and have them sanctify our marriage amid the colour and noise they have chosen to bring us. We will be husband and wife at last, and then go to our home of Haven.'

Torpeth vaulted up onto one of the sacrificial altars and sprang onto the back of Saint Zoriah's shoulders, wrapping his naked thighs around her neck. He proceeded to yank out handfuls of hair from her scalp.

'Aiee! Torpeth, no. Mercy, I beg you. Without my hair I am nothing.'

'Oh, don't be so vain, Zoriah.' The holy man looped the hair he'd ripped from her head under her chin and started to garotte her.

Stara went to her knees, wailing and sobbing. 'Holy Saint Sylvan, where are you? Please free me from these devils. I want to be your follower. I can tell you the pagans' secrets if you will let me serve you.'

The fleet-footed Saint was suddenly before her. 'Why would you wish to serve me, witch?' he asked suspiciously, his eyes never quite still.

'You are so handsome.' Stara blushed. 'I will follow you even if my father does not approve.'

'Handsome? You think so?' he preened.

'Of course. Besides, you have a bloody power that I want.' Stara leaped at him, hands clawed.

Saint Sylvan tried to dart away, but Ausa and Betha had laced his shoes together and he crashed into the stone floor. They were on him in a trice, sinking teeth into his neck. The witch-urchin crept close and, with a simple touch, froze him. 'Drain all that he has and he will never rise again.'

Thomas watched for a moment and then joined Haal, Lars and Bantith against the mighty Goza. The giant Saint was slow in his movements, but his strength meant that any blow with which he caught them was likely to be devastating. They therefore kept a careful distance.

'He's mine, blacksmith,' Lars warned.

'Surely there's more than enough of him to go round.' Thomas smiled.

'Saint Goza, would you mind waiting for a second while these two sort out their differences?' Bantith politely enquired. 'Such things are quite important to the mountain people, you see. Is that not so, Haal Corinson?'

Haal nodded. 'It's some sort of honour thing, I think. Precisely who you fight in battle, the names of those you defeat and the names of those who ultimately defeat you are the measure of a warrior. They need to establish who has the greater claim to your name, Saint Goza, or there is a risk some will not be remembered for their true worth, including yourself, holy one. It is a constant cause of argument among the mountain people, I hear, and even starts feuds between families.'

There was a mixture of confusion and annoyance in Saint Goza's small eyes. 'I do not care about—'

Bantith's expression became pained and he waved his hands to stop the Saint saying anything too unfortunate. He beckoned the giant forward to share his council. 'Holy one, if I may?' he said softly. The giant leaned towards him. 'Surely even you wish to be remembered, no?'

'I ...'

The Saint stopped. At the precise moment he had opened his mouth to speak, Lars had taken a step and thrust with his spear to full extension, its tip entering the huge gourmand's mouth and piercing the back of his throat.

'There is something for you to chew on,' Lars said.

'His eyes!' Bantith urged. 'He must not be able to feast those on anything. Quickly!'

Haal flicked out a small dagger, closely followed by a second. They caught Saint Goza perfectly. The Saint bellowed in agony and lashed blindly around him.

'Now each may have his share,' Lars agreed.

'Don't mind if I do.' Thomas nodded and launched his massive hammer.

Aspin and his remaining men faced Saint Dianon. They cast a flight of spears at the nondescript figure, but the servant of Azual made the air vibrate and shake with such intensity that every weapon was taken from its course, all going wide of their mark.

Reading him carefully, Aspin ran forward, apparently to engage him hand to hand. The mountain chief's membranes buzzed fiercely. An eardrum ruptured and his balance went. He felt warm blood drip onto his lip from his nose. He kept his eyes locked on the Saint and pushed on through the pain. He saw the twisted creature's confidence wobble and then fail completely. It turned to flee, as Aspin had known it would. The chieftain of the mountain people cast his spear, knowing exactly where it would hit. It thudded into the top of the Saint's back and, having come down at an angle, went down into his heart, stopping it for ever.

Horns blared and drums of war shook the nether realm. It was a command so awful it was heard and felt by every soul. It was the will and punishment of the King of the Dead. None could escape it or refuse its call. His armies had been marshalled and were now on the march. *As it pleased me, and as I prophesied, so the way to the land of the living is open. The Empire will become absolute through me. The final reckoning is at hand. All are resurrected and all are cast down by my judgement.*

As is your will, holy one, spoke the nether realm.

The faces of the mountain men turned ghastly as if they too numbered among the dead. They looked around in terror and loss, not seeming to know where they should go or what they should do.

'I am a fool.' Torpeth swallowed, no longer interested in bludgeoning Saint Zoriah against an altar. 'These four could never pose any real threat to us. We should not have allowed them to waylay us. The sole reason for their being sent here was to distract us from returning to our world in time to prevent the way opening. I should have seen it before. Oh woe!'

'Can't the way be closed again?' Aspin demanded.

'I do not know.'

'We have to try.'

'Well of course we do, silly ox. Come then, you mountain warriors. Put off your trivial Saints and let us fly with holy Wayfar at our backs like never before. May he grant us his mercy and the divine rush of his winds, for all life now depends on it. Fly!'

'This way.' Thomas showed them, scooping Stara up and placing her under one arm. 'The breach in the Eternal Keep is here.'

'See Jillan, Hella, Samnir and Ash, you men of the mountains. Hold them in your eyes, hearts and minds, for that will bring us from this place to those we know and love. Put your entire will and being into it. Let the mountains be your strength and holy Wayfar your breath. See them there. Do you not see them as I do? How beautiful is the world of life. We know nothing of this lost place here any more.'

Hella bade Freom and his rock people to go to the aid of the Unclean battling holy Akwar's ice giants. Holy Gar nodded his assent, and Freda asked Dor to go with Freom.

'Friend Ash needs you, now, Dor,' Freda asked. 'Do this because I ask it.'

'Yes, Freda,' the giant answered dutifully and lumbered away across a causeway of stepping stones holy Gar raised up for him.

'Enough of your tempestuousness, holy Wayfar!' Hella commanded the sky. 'Cease your torrid display, holy Akwar. Nothing is achieved in this save the death of powerless mortals who would perhaps have worshipped you better if you did not so punish their existence. Come forth to face us!' Her only answer was the raving wind and biting blizzard.

'Brothers!' holy Gar implored. 'One of us has already fallen. Is that not enough? Surely that is lesson to us all.'

When there was no change in answer, Hella nodded to Jillan and he swept the blinding and occluding elements of the intemperate deities aside. He parted the dark curtains of the sky, revealing the scoured and scarred landscape beyond. There stood holy Akwar and Wayfar, towering to the heavens. They had raised holy Sinisar once more.

The sun god was severely injured, but there was still a splendour to him. In pushing back the winding murk and concealing mists that had wreathed the desert, Jillan seemed to have helped Sinisar shine again. The only thing holding back the god now was the fact that holy Gar's earth had encased and trapped his feet. Yet even as they watched, holy Sinisar burned the ground away and stepped free.

'It is time we settled this,' Freda chimed, and moved to confront her enemy. The dark umbra around her grew to match the light coming from the holy lord she had sworn to serve.

Jillan went to help the rock woman, but holy Gar held him back. 'Allow them this, Jillan. There must be a reckoning between them, as much as I fear the outcome.'

'Her own presumption will now see her ended, Brother.' Holy Akwar laughed. 'Is it not meet? Is it not a rich delight? Is the inevitable logic of it not delicious?'

'Destroy her and have done, Brother,' surly Wayfar counselled. 'We have spent too much of ourselves on this already. I tire of it.'

'There is no remorse in you, then, over-proud Freda?' holy Sinisar sneered.

'Remorse?' she replied with a gentle sadness. 'Remorse that I would no longer allow you to abuse me and would not let you further harm those I love? No. Remorse that your First Light attacked me and I was forced to defend myself? How can there be? Remorse that your rage against me destroyed your own temple? Not really. Remorse that I could not make you love me better? Perhaps, my lord, I feel remorse for that. Yet, as hard as I try otherwise, I am still Freda, daughter of the holy rock god. And, as hard as I try, I cannot find any remorse in myself for that.'

Holy Gar stood tall and proud as he watched his daughter and listened to her words. Diamond and ruby tears trickled from the corner of one of his divine eyes.

Akwar spat in disgust. Restless Wayfar sighed discontentedly.

'You will not be permitted to stand against one of the gods like this. You may as well defy your own father. You will bow to accept your punishment. Repent and the reprisal may not be fatal!' Sinisar's words became increasingly heated as he spoke. His power built and his gaze became fiery.

She stoked his rage even higher. 'I have already received enough punishment at your cruel hands. I will never submit to you again, my precious lord.'

He was incandescent now. 'Then I will turn you into molten slag!' He poured white heat on her, and all were forced to turn away or lose their sight.

Freda stood unflinching, absorbing all his fury. He increased its intensity, trying to vaporise the shadows enshrouding her. Yet they took in and nullified his power. Incredibly they then reached out as if to embrace him. 'Let me take you to me, my lord,' she sighed.

His face ran like wax. Any semblance of skin and hair disappeared. He was faceless now, pure heat and light which withered and blasted all around it.

Still she sought to gather him to her. 'Come to me, my lord. I will hold you for ever. Surely that was the vow you first had of me. Surely this is what you have always wanted.'

Tendrils came for him and he suddenly backed away. Seeming to panic, he turned to climb the sky, but the shadows caught him and yanked him back down.

'No!' the divine inferno roared. 'This cannot be. It is wrong.' The shadows moved to engulf him. 'Brothers, aid me!'

'None may intervene!' holy Gar rumbled in warning to the two watching brothers. 'This is of his own making. It makes its own judgement of him. To interfere would bring that judgement down on you also. It is the way of things. You know that as you know yourselves.'

Freda came to holy Sinisar and took him in her arms. She made comforting noises as she squeezed him down and into herself. She drank him all in, allowing him to fill her. There were glaring flashes and dazzling sparks. Suddenly he was gone.

Freda stood alone. The darkness that had surrounded her had been cancelled out by Sinisar's power. She was a perfect balance of light and dark now. She was herself, simple rock.

'Freda, you are you again!' Hella said with joy. 'You were always yourself, of course, but now you look ... well, as you were before. Healed?'

Freda smiled shyly. 'Yes, friend Hella. I am back as I once was, as I should always have been.'

'Welcome back, daughter,' Gar rumbled with deep affection.

'What have you done to our brother?' holy Akwar demanded. 'Return him at once.'

'He no longer has a place in this world,' the rock woman replied. Only she could hear Sinisar's screams, trapped as he was within the matrix of her being.

'You do not know what you have done, daughter of the rock god,' a troubled Wayfar blew. 'Without our brother, we are all lessened. 'You must return him or all will bear terrible consequence.'

'He is gone. I have no way of returning him,' Freda said truthfully.

'Then we are all doomed.'

Torpeth saw holy Sinisar disappear into the woman of rock and knew he was too late. 'Too late!'

The mountain men ran through the murk, the legions of the dead all too close behind them. The wail of the horns, the cries for blood and the soul-pounding drums were a harrowing cacophony like no other – the sound of the approaching apocalypse.

'Do not slacken your pace, Torpeth,' Aspin urged. 'We are there. Look, do you not see them?'

The holy man's face had lost all its life. 'He stands there in the armour I once wore. He oversees the fall of the gods, just as I once did. Just as I failed mortalkind then, so I have failed them now. I only see myself there. All is one. We are too late, Chief Aspin Longstep. The dead follow in our wake and we now will see the end of days.'

'No. Not after all we have been through.'

'I am sorry, silly ox,' the naked warrior said fondly. 'Truly I am. Here is the punishment for which I have waited so long, to suffer and witness the full horror of my transgression. Payment will now be made.'

*

244

Watching from his vantage point in the desert, the radiant youth that was the Peculiar smiled. 'And all came to pass as he had promised his beloved Thraal it would. Sinisar is fallen. There is no unity left to the gods, no harmony to the power of their Geas. The definitions of mortal life and death collide and undo each other. Now is the moment, elseworlder. This world is yours for the taking. Call to the others of your kind and let them know my end of the bargain is fulfilled. Are you not pleased, dearest Thraal? Is it not marvellous? Am I not a wonder? Thousands of years of planning and effort, and at last my wiles and ways are manifest as essential and supreme to all.'

Elder Thraal tilted his head to give the slightest of acknowledgements. 'When D'Shaa first asked that you be unleashed on the world, I foresaw such an Armageddon might follow. You will claim it is in your nature, but why would you betray your own brothers? Why would you betray your own world? It is senseless.'

'Senseless, sweet Thraal? Surely you protest too much. You elseworlders are as familiar with betrayal as any other beings. Come, do not deny it. What else was the Empire you created for the mortals other than a vast betrayal and falseness? What were your promises of blessed salvation other than lies and illusion? You are not so innocent, I think. Need I ask what happened to the Great Saviour of this realm, hmm, my disingenuous friend? You are naughty, Thraal, but I love you for it. We could not have had such a perfect relationship otherwise.'

Elder Thraal shifted his stance, but otherwise would not submit to the Peculiar's insinuating interrogation. 'Why give us this world? What greater deception is behind it?'

'The why is as per our bargain, a bargain that binds you. You elseworlders will build me a seventh and final chamber of sun-metal. You will allow me to use your Gate to leave this world and finally be returned to the cosmos. I *will* be free of this most underwhelming and pitiful of prisons. I will come and go as I please, without any yea or nay from your kind. None can hold me forever, do you hear, my most caring Thraal? Not even you.'

'You are the *unstable* element of this world, Peculiar. That is why it could not hold you. Yet I must have your pledge not to act against the interests of the Declension if we allow you to use the Gates.'

'Now it is your words that are meaningless, darling Thraal. Do you not appreciate the irony?' the Lord of Mayhem simpered. 'No? You never did have much sense of humour, did you? That is your failing, you know.' He shifted into the form of a jowled and well-girthed man, and shook with uproarous mirth.

'You rave. I will have your pledge.'

The Peculiar laughed all the harder. 'Don't! It hurts! Here, at the end of the world, you ask for meaningful words and good sense.' He howled and cried with merriment. Wild glee became giddy hysteria, became winding madness, became the cataclysm.

The being that was Elder Thraal reared back from the quixotic god in consternation, as a precaution in case the insanity was infectious. 'Eldest, hear me,' he bespoke the cosmos. 'My eyes are yours, my thoughts are yours. Let them be the Gate to your will and desire, to all that is the Declension. Let them come. None can gainsay you.'

The taint within Jillan howled in delight, wreaking havoc with Jillan's thoughts. He no longer had the power to supress the terrible force that was Kathuula. *Wild glee became giddy hysteria, became winding madness, became the cataclysm.* The gates of the nether realm had been opened, and all the dead, horrors and nightmares therein now rose into the land of the living.

Did he see right? Torpeth, Aspin and a group of mountain warriors sprinted towards him, but following them out of the filth of the struggle and storm came the unending and sightless armies of the dead. The merciless wraiths would fill the entire world, he knew.

'Is that Thomas?' Hella asked in horrified confusion. 'And Haal too? What does it mean? Jillan, I'm so scared. Jillan!'

'We must flee,' Akwar gurgled in terror. 'Gar, hide us!'

'There is nowhere that they will not find us,' the rock god replied with a tomb-like voice. 'There is nowhere that we can go, Brother. Nowhere.'

'Will the Geas not save us?' holy Wayfar begged breathlessly of Jillan. 'Jillan, you *must* save us.'

Jillan opened his mouth and all that was heard was the unearthly laughter of Kathuula.

Out of the murk came the most frightful and dreadful of beings. Wherever it looked, its bloody eye flayed and tortured the souls of the living. At its left hand was the unbending and unforgiving Praxis, come to administer to this world of the damned. The King of the Dead came among them, he who was Saint Azual, herald and servant of the eternal Empire of the Saviours.

CHAPTER 8:

But in the clumsy mould and forge

*A*re *you ready, my son?*
I am ready as you command it, Ba'zel replied carefully to the mind of the Eldest.

Lead our warriors into the seventh and make it ours. Take the nether realm, then open the way to the eighth. We make progress on the Great Voyage that none have made since the Chi'a themselves. It pleases us.

As is your will, most holy.

Here is the seventh as our servant Thraal sees it. The Eldest furnished Ba'zel with the necessary waking dream. *It will guide your passage through the Gate.*

I understand, eternal one.

The Eldest paused. *You will be rewarded for what you do, Ba'zel. Name what you would have of the Declension.*

Ba'zel became wary, knowing that now more than ever *She* was likely to be testing him. Indeed, every moment as a member of the Declension was a test of sorts. *This opportunity to serve both you and my kind is reward itself, and all I require.*

Do not try my patience. Great Virtue you may be, but I could make your next breath your last, your next word your epitaph. My allowance of that breath and word is an act of generosity in itself. I could halt all thought in your mind instantly. Every member of the Declension knows individual aspiration and ambition. Without it, we would not have the wherewithal or impetus for our Great Voyage. It is blasphemy and offence to us that you would claim to have none. By your former actions and behaviours, we also know you speak an untruth. You dare offer up such untruth to us, my son? Most disappointing. And clumsy. Did we err in making you Great Virtue, perhaps?

Her wisdom was so vast he could never prevail. *She* saw and knew all. *She* had him every way. *It was individual aspiration and ambition that saw me hope to gain advantage through the untruth, all-knowing one,* he confessed. *Forgive me. I am unused to exposing myself. It is ... uncomfortable for me.*

Indeed, Her mind mumured with voyeuristic satisfaction. *Name what you would have of the Declension.*

Certain lesser beings of the seventh are known well to me. I claim them as my own. When I go to seek the way to the eighth, ownership is to pass to House Faal. My father's house will oversee the disposal of those lesser beings here in the home-realm. He suddenly stilled, fearful that he had revealed too much.

The Eldest was silent for the longest time. *She* must be suspicious. Would *She* err on the side of caution, simply deciding there was too much risk in having him live? The pressure of the moment and *Her* scrutiny made every bit of him hurt. He couldn't bear it. He was about to break, but then *She* spoke. *Is that all? There is precious little value in these lesser beings. Why do you not make request for greater rank and power, as others do? Why not ask I punish the Faction of Departure and your other enemies?*

My father has become a collector of lesser beings. He has an appetite for them, and I have a ... a certain attachment for some of them. They use the term friend, *most divine. They talk of concepts of which I had been previously unaware. Strange concepts that may bear further investigation and create particular advantage. Indeed, as an example, I have bound my battle mentor to my house more surely than most could.*

The concepts of which you speak are the aberration and weakness of lesser beings. They are compromise and confusion. If you turn them into weapons to use against any who resist us, however, I will allow it. After all, it was in a similar way that we first established ourselves as Saviours in the seventh, and saw the People become willing members of our Empire and their own undoing. Very well, claim these lesser beings as you see fit. Go.

*

250

Ba'zel looked to his right. 'Battle Mentor, all is ready?'

'Yes, Great Virtue. All understand what you have commanded,' Dra'zen replied.

Ba'zel looked to his left. 'Lead Warrior, you know your role?'

'Yes, mighty one,' Lukha Sha replied, abasing himself to an unnecessary degree.

Ba'zel had chosen to spare the champion's life, restore him in the home-realm's blood pools and swear him into House Ba'zel. Both Faal and Dra'zen had been outraged, protesting that Ba'zel could only be perceived as attempting to shore up his own strength, that he therefore betrayed his own weakness. Yet Ba'zel had refused to change course. 'These perceptions would be a concern were I to remain in the home-realm. Yet I do not. I go into battle with the nape of my neck on display to the assembled warriors of the Declension, the majority of them belonging to the Faction of Departure. Who better to guard my back then than Lukha Sha, he who knows the warriors of that faction better than any other and he who has mastered every fighting style known to our kind? I am the Great Virtue, and I have spoken. Peace, or you will be named wet nurses. Father, I take my leave now. I assume you will not seek to kill me, as you did the last time I departed this place?'

'I am glad I did not kill you. Who else would I have to sweep the dust from my chambers? You will return one day, perhaps, as you did before.'

'Perhaps, Father. Or I will see you at the end of the cosmos. Father, there is something I must say. You know I am named Destruction, do you not? I am sorry that I cannot think of the Geas of our realm as permanent. I therefore fear there will be difficulty for us at some point in the future. I ask now that you forgive me for whatever happens, as I must act by way of my own nature.'

Faal lowered his head in understanding. 'I know this, my son. You must act in the manner that the Declension has made you. There is nothing to forgive. Leave now and bring destruction to all that would stand in the way of our progress on the Great Voyage.'

And so Ba'zel, he who was the Great Virtue of the Declension, returned to the seventh realm with the blessed Saviours of the People, and then came the final and terrible moment that was their judgement.

*

'Ah, Jillan, there you are. We have unfinished business, you and I,' Saint Azual drooled. 'Bring me the bane of the Empire on his knees!'

More and more of the dead appeared, coming out of light, wind, rain and earth, drawing on the world of the living to give themselves substance, taking the gods' own elements for their own. Lines of gruesome Heroes filled the desert to the horizon and beyond. The warmth of the world drained away and the cold fear that was the power of Saint Praxis rose to take its place.

'They should not be here,' Aspin cried. 'Something must be able to hold them back. Holy Wayfar, help us! Akwar and Gar, how do we seal the way to the nether realm? There must be a way. There must be.'

'See what you have done, you pathetic mortals!' holy Akwar sobbed. 'In refusing to bow to your rightful gods, you have destroyed all balance and order.'

'Chief Aspin Longstep,' holy Wayfar moaned, 'do you not see that it was you who led them here? You should have died in my temple. You should have been consigned to the nether realm for ever more. Why did you not stay there? Why?'

'And you, Jillan, saw to it that Sinisar was brought low, with the help of my daughter, to my regret and shame. Yet we gods were also culpable in some degree,' holy Gar mourned. 'How was it we allowed ourselves to become so divided?'

Jillan's eyes took in the witch-urchin Anara. He felt sick. Of course. 'Miserath.'

Torpeth sprang over to him and peered into his eyes. 'Are you in there, hmm? Miserath, you say? I wouldn't be surprised. Now what are we going to do about it? Concentrate. A bit of magic wouldn't go amiss now, don't you think? After all, these gods here were never up to much, were they? Hella, speak to him and bring him back to his proper self.'

Taint, why will you not help us? Jillan demanded and pleaded.

The taint laughed all the harder. *My true power is at last free of the nether realm. I will never let you return it there.*

Jillan tried to draw on his own magic, but the taint blocked it. Jillan appealed to the Geas, but Kathuula neutralised that power also.

'We must be quick, friend Hella,' Freda counselled. 'They are coming, and I do not think I can hold off so many, not even with friend Thomas and my people, Dor and the Unclean over there.'

'Jillan, come back to us,' Hella said fiercely, both love and her power to command gripping him.

He managed to speak over the taint's own thoughts. 'I-I am powerless. It is Kathuula. His death magic here has grown too great. It ... it's my fault,' he said inadequately.

Yes, it is, the taint sang.

'Jillan, it is not your fault, believe me,' Aspin averred. 'I now believe one of the Saviours survived the fall of the Great Temple. Somehow they entered the nether realm, probably with the help of cursed Miserath. It was they who invested Azual with the blood and power first to rule the nether realm and finally to enter the land of the living when the chance came. And I suspect that chance was contrived by Miserath also, with the help of several of his suborned brothers. Jillan, we have been used and betrayed, and have always been so.' He turned his gaze upon holy Akwar and Wayfar, who shifted guiltily. 'See the truth of it there.'

That's it. Waste what little time you have on pointless recrimination.

'I had no choice,' Akwar whined. 'It was the price of being freed from my prison beneath Shangrin. You don't know what it was like. None of you can know what it was like.'

So Miserath had not been undone by the lava and molten armour of sun-metal, Jillan now realised. Because of some binding agreement, holy Akwar had gone to the aid of his brother. It was typical of the god of infinite wiles and guiles to have taken such a precaution. He always had an escape, it seemed. He always found a way. There was always a trick, distraction, twist, sleight of hand or double bluff to ensure he got what he wanted. And what he had always craved was the power of the Geas.

'We must go to Haven!' Jillan declared. 'Surely it will provide some refuge, and the Geas must help us.'

'The dead are upon us!' Akwar squealed. 'Run!' He poured and trickled away as fast as the ground would take him.

A miasma of mould and decay rose up to surround them, frigid and clammy hands reaching for them. Those commanded by Saint Azual pressed in, their sheer numbers the only thing to inhibit them. Holy Gar tried to bring them down and bury them, but he could not hold so many, and phantoms sought to devour even him.

'Stay back!' Hella commanded shrilly, using her sword to give her a second of space.

'Your Geas can no longer command me,' Saint Azual exhaled from a thousand thousand gaping mouths and torn throats.

Freda battered down those coming close to her, but for each one that went down, two took its place. She became wild then went into the earth, to emerge right next to Jillan and Hella. She grabbed them and took them underground with her.

'My children,' holy Gar rumbled to the battling Freom and his golems. 'Take the Unclean below and on to Haven. Go.'

Aspin's warriors thrust, stepped, blocked and twirled, but the souls marching on them did not pause. The dead could not be hurt. They embraced every blow and strike against them, as if taking a lover to them one last time. They came ever closer, limbs severed, trodden on, mangled, tangled, mashed, crushed, face on face, hands pushing into chests seizing and squeezing, fighting for every drop and trace of life that was to be found. To them there was only life. The need for it was all-consuming. They would not hesitate to do anything to have it, even though they murdered it in the process. They throttled and choked it. Clawed and ripped at it. Bit and tried to cram it down.

Aspin knew it was hopeless. 'Torpeth, I see no escape.'

Torpeth rolled his eyes and began an ululation. 'W-A-A-A-Y-F-A-A-A–'

'Alright, alright!' the air complained.

'– A-A-A-R-R-R!'

'Come ride upon my back then, sky warriors,' holy Wayfar blew, appearing among them. 'Step high, you mountain men.'

Aspin and his men leaped up and skimmed over the heads of the dead. They were lifted higher and swirled across the sky towards Haven.

'This is the way to travel, eh, silly ox?' Torpeth called.

'Don't think this is going to become a habit,' holy Wayfar warned, rushing them down into the valley at alarming speed and then dropping them from a difficult height into the Gathering Place, just as Freda and the rest of the rock people were emerging.

'Ow! Careful!' Ash shouted. 'Torpeth, get your filthy behind out of my face. I'd prefer to be dealing with those unholy ghouls above than your posterior. No one deserves such punishment. Dor, grab him.'

The naked warrior fell back from the approaching giant, planting his rear even more firmly in the woodsman's face. 'I am trapped!'

'Ack! Dop! I can'd bread boperly!' came Ash's muffled voice.

'Forgive me, lowlander, but I am caught. Your nose is wedged so deep I cannot get free.' Dor growled and made a swipe for the lithe mountain man, who bent at the middle to duck. 'Careful! You open me even wider. His head will disappear entirely up my arse. He might never get it back.'

'Old goat, enough of your madness!' Aspin demanded, reaching for him, reading how he would try to dodge, getting a hand into his beard and then yanking him fiercely away from the unfortunate innkeeper.

Torpeth staggered, went into a forward roll and came back to his feet. There was no sign of merriment in his face. 'Do you not see, silly ox? The woodsman's perfect timing has deserted him. There is no time left, perfect or otherwise. It has run out for all of us.'

The heads of holy Wayfar and Gar dropped.

'No, don't say it,' Hella begged. 'Where is Samnir? Where is the general? And Captain Skathis and Gallen? This is our home. We can still fight for it. Look, Thomas and Haal are here. The Unclean. The rock people. The mountain warriors. Holy Gar and holy Wayfar. All are here. We can fight. There must be hope! We still live! The Geas will help us. Jillan, tell them!'

Sounds a bit hysterical to me. Can't blame her, really.

'Samnir still lives. I would know if he did not,' Jillan insisted. 'Hella's right. The Geas will help us.'

The rock people and the Unclean stood in misery. Freda and Dor stood together awkwardly. Aspin gave his friend a half-hearted nod of encouragement. Torpeth sighed gently. The eyes of Thomas and his daughters, Haal and Anara, spoke only sympathy and loss. The shadow crept across Haven. They all looked up to see the dead lined along the length and breadth of the valley's rim.

'We stand in the midst of death, even we gods,' holy Gar rumbled.

'Yes, Brother. Never did I think it. It is all around. It is all I see now,' holy Wayfar whispered sadly.

'What are they waiting for?' Tebrus wondered.

'Perhaps they are unable to enter Haven. Perhaps here is our hope,' Hella said.

'Damn, I need a drink. Maybe there is time for that at least,' Ash sighed.

Then, to the head of the valley, behind Saint Azual and Saint Praxis, came a hideous nightmare, crawling and picking its way into the world, spiking and sucking on all that dared look upon it, climbing into minds and draining away all thought and spirit.

Aspin shook with horror and vomited upon the ground, his guts heaving and heaving even after he was empty. He spat blood and bile, the reader in him trying to help him towards suicide. Torpeth yanked hair out of his own scalp, gnashing and wailing. The gods were beside themselves, grief and panic divesting them of all coherence. The rock people and the mountain men threw themselves down. Freda hunkered low and whined, torturing the helpless Dor. Nearly all of the Unclean went to their knees to scream prayers and confessions. Those that did not opened their veins and moved to cut the throats of friends. Thomas, his daughters, Haal and Anara, reeled.

The Saviours had come. They were entering Haven.

Ash wiped his mouth with a shaking hand. 'I'll be in my inn if anyone wants me.' He coughed weakly. 'Come, Tebrus. Let's go drink to the end of the world.'

'Jillan!' Hella wept, inconsolable but wanting only him.

'I must get to the Geas,' Jillan pleaded. 'At the end of the valley.' He grabbed her hand and pulled her after him. 'Come on, Hella. Please! You can't give up. You mustn't.'

They ran down into the small community. People called out to them, asking what was happening, although they surely already knew. A couple of young women clutching keepsakes asked anyone who would stop for them if the Heroes of Haven had yet returned. Other inhabitants were intent on nailing the shutters of their homes closed, deluding themselves that makeshift barricades might yet keep them safe.

Hella pulled him sideways. 'My father! He's all alone. I can't leave him.'

'Jacob will understand!'

'No. Go on without me. I'll wait for you here, Jillan. Go.'

He wanted to implore her. He wanted to shake sense into her. He wanted to rant. He wanted to tell her so many things. But there could be no hesitating. There was no fond farewell. No lingering and meaningful look. No promise or exchange of vows. No last-minute reprieve.

He raced down through the chaos, narrowly avoiding collisions, only just keeping his footing. He stretched and strained every sense and sinew. He felt them behind him, bearing down on him. They focused their will and intent upon him and his armour flared more brightly than it ever had, although some of its golden runes became so hot the surrounding leather was charred and one of the securing straps was burned through.

That's it. Run, Jillan. A race to the Geas, just like the last time you and I were here. There's a quite satisfying symmetry to all this, wouldn't you say? A telling irony. A suitable closure. An exquisite and poignant design. Exciting, tragic, hilarious, intriguing, all things to all actors and all audiences. Ah, it is a delight. It is the past, present and future all at once, it is life and death, it is the divine and the mortal, the beginning and the end. It is my moment of triumph. Struggle for me, please, so that my moment lasts, so that it is not over so quickly that the effect is anticlimactic. Come, have hope. Imagine that even as your strength fades, you will still manage to reach the Geas and single-handedly defeat the elseworlders. Then you can restore the world to how you think it should be, with your limited ideas of happiness. Tell yourself that if you want it enough, all things are possible. That's it, think positive. Don't tell yourself you're self-deluded and preposterously arrogant in your self-belief. See, you're nearly there. One last turn of speed. Chin up. Reach. You can almost taste it.

Jillan ran into the caldera at the end of the valley. The lava around the stone island of the Geas no longer flowed and had formed a thick crust. The island was completely barren.

Oh dear. How disappointing for you, the taint chortled. *And, worse, they're now right behind you. End of the road, I'm afraid. Still, it was fun while it lasted, no? You did your best. Your parents would have been proud of you ... if that fiend Azual hadn't already devoured their spirits, that is. So, well done you. You should be proud of yourself. You helped bring about the end of the world with a certain style, I must say. And, no matter what you hear others say, I think you did your kind proud too. A most creditable performance under the circumstances. It just wouldn't have been the same without you mortals to bring a certain poetry and occasional light-heartedness to proceedings. I thought the battles you had along the way were particularly thrilling and dramatic. My favourite was when you faced off against Azual in that punishment chamber beneath Saviours' Paradise. That was a tight scrape, eh? I really didn't think you'd get out of that one. But then you threw that lucky stone your father had given you and blinded old Saint Azual. He didn't see that one coming, eh? Heh, heh. And then there was Samnir. Wow. What a character he was. A grizzled old soldier who never knew when he was beaten. And what about Torpeth? What a hoot. When I think of some of the antics he got up to, it still makes me chuckle. But listen to me go on when there are more urgent matters at hand. They have come for you.*

Jillan slowly turned. 'Ba'zel.'

'Hello, Jillan.'

'Don't do this. You were meant to be my friend.' His voice sounded ridiculous even to his own ears, peevish and childish.

'It is too late. Your own actions have brought this upon you.'

'We never had a choice.'

'I gave you proper warning. You chose to live and chose to bring down your gods. You chose to fight. If you fight now, we will put down Hella and all those of your kind in Haven.'

With friends like these, eh, Jillan? the taint said cheerily.

'I cannot fight you,' Jillan said in utter defeat and despair.

'She is your sacred heart, as much your weakness as your strength. Battle Mentor, take him. Have the power of the Geas drained from him and passed back to the home-realm. Yet do not kill him. He is to see out his final days serving us in the sun-metal mines of this realm. To have the bane of the Empire serve us is a fitting end. All eventually come to serve the Declension, for *Her* will is all-prevailing.'

'Yes, Great Virtue.' A much scarred Saviour who was missing a fore-limb bowed. The hulking creature levered its way over to Jillan, tore away his runic armour and immediately exerted the mind-numbing power of its presence.

'What will you do to Hella?' Jillan vaguely mumbled as he swooned.

'She and the others will be taken to the home-realm. My father will see them sacrificed in the blood pools once all life has been stripped from this realm. Even now, our servant Azual sends armies of the dead throughout this realm to bring the last of the living to us. The Virtue that is Judgement will oversee the Great Cull.'

He did not know where they took him. All was delirium, his senses made senseless. He was stretched and pinned. It felt as if a draining tube of sun-metal penetrated the very centre of his mind. A similar spike was inserted into his core. He screamed until the lining of his throat came away and choked him. They cleared it so that he could find no merciful death. Every drop of blood was taken out of him and the magic drawn from it. It was replaced with a thin and empty liquid that dissolved away the last of his spirit. He didn't know who he was any more, did not know his own name – did not want to know it, not because of guilt, but because there simply was no want left in him. He was no longer anything or anyone.

'I go to open the way to the eighth,' said a voice he'd once recognised. 'Goodbye, Jillan, my friend. You never realised, did you? You had become the Geas of this realm. You went to the stone island to find it, but it was already within you. You were not to know, though, and it no longer matters. It is not of consequence, for there is no consequence left to this realm. All has been said and all has been done. The Book of Saviours for this realm is now written and ended. There are no more words to follow. The pages of this realm's future are blank.'

He blinked. He saw only darkness. He was not sure his eyes were working properly. Perhaps he was blind.

He was weak. Something vital had been taken from inside him. There was just a gap now, an emptiness. He was a living gap, an absence. There was no magic or taint. He'd hated the taint while it had been there, hated the mockery and hated how it had made him doubt his own mind. Now that it was gone, however, he'd never felt more lonely, or his mind more desolate.

'You're awake. Good. We have to get you out of here before the other miners come back off shift. I heard some of them whispering that they would eat you if they didn't find any sun-metal to swap with the overseer for food.' Small hands helped him sit up. 'Can you stand on your own? You're too big for me to support or carry.'

Jillan swung his legs off the low pallet on which he'd been laid and came exhaustedly to his feet. He could now see grey shades within the dark – tunnels and exits? A small hand took one of his own and tugged.

'This way. They stay away from these areas because very little sun-metal is found over here, and I told them about the hungry wraiths of miners I'd seen. I'm not making it up, neither. I did see one once. And sometimes you'll wake up shivering all of a sudden, sure that some cold breath or hand has just touched you. Anyway, it keeps most of the others away. It means us small ones who hide over here are fairly safe when we're off shift and don't have to have someone always awake to keep watch. Duck your head low here.'

It was the voice of a young girl.

'You're probably wondering why I'm helping you. You'd be right not to trust me. Can't really trust anyone down here. Those who do, don't last very long. But you need my help right now, and I need someone big enough to swing a pick properly, so I can get to a good amount of sun-metal to trade for food. You need to swear you won't try and eat me. Swear it, and I will promise to share whatever food we get with you, proper fair like. Well go on, then.'

His tongue felt dead in his mouth. Numbly he managed to mumble, 'I swear.'

'No. You need to swear proper, on something important. Otherwise you might trick me.'

What was there left to swear on? There was nothing. 'I-I don't know what ...' he trailed off.

'Are you simple or something? Did they bang your head or were you in an accident? You've got to swear on something important. The gods or the blessed Saviours. Or on the overseer or sun-metal. Or on your family if they're still alive ... or even if they're dead. They'll come haunt you if you break your word, see?'

'I swear on Hella's life th-that I will not eat you.' *And that of my unborn child.* He wanted to laugh hysterically. He wanted to cry. How could he swear? How dare he? He'd betrayed every promise and vow he'd ever made. They had all come to nothing. They meant nothing. He'd told her he'd marry her. He'd sworn it over and over. He'd said that they'd be safe, that the Geas would help them. He'd insisted he'd known what he was doing in challenging the gods. But the promises he'd made his friends had caused them to follow him, and seen them all undone. He'd put all of Haven at risk to see his own selfish desire carried out, and damned them all in the process. And not just them. He'd given the entire world to the Saviours. Every life. Every man, woman and child, and even those not yet born. He'd betrayed the spirits of those who had sacrificed themselves, and he had given over the future to the Saviours.

And then there was Hella. He'd pledged her his love and asked for hers in return. He'd tied her to him and guaranteed her doom. Even

263

now he took her name in vain. How could he? Would he never stop? He was sick and corrupted, unworthy even to think her name. He shuddered. He saw it now, the full horror of what he was. Minister Praxis had been right to speak of Jillan's *dark and sneaking ways* all that time ago in the school at Godsend. Saint Praxis had been right to speak of Jillan Hunterson as a creature of the Chaos and the bane of the Empire. Jillan had known he was tainted, but had always denied it to others. He'd knowingly consorted with the taint, with Kathuula himself. See what had happened because of it? He was utterly evil and knew it. There was no escaping it. Here, at the end, all was known and revealed. The truth was real.

'And I swear by holy Sinisar, he who shows all miners the way to sun-metal, that I will share whatever food we get from the overseers fairly with you.'

He did not have the strength to tell her he'd helped destroy Sinisar. He prayed whatever food she gave him would stick in his throat and choke him to death.

'What is your name? I am Aarla.'

He was too ashamed even to name himself. His name was too loathsome to himself. 'I-I don't remember.'

'Oh. I will call you Thomas then, after my uncle. I liked him, but he died. He was always a bit sad, but seemed happy at the end. I think I hear him calling to me sometimes. Is it true the dead are risen, do you think? The other miners say there's little need for the living any more. I've thought it through too. Once we've mined all the sun-metal, there'll be nothing left to trade for food, will there? We'll starve and die, won't we? We'll join everybody else who's dead. Maybe I'll be able to leave the mine and see my uncle Thomas again. Do you think the blessed Saviours will let me? Thomas, are you there? Or will Saint Azual and the blessed Saviours eat me up, like the big miners try to do when they're really hungry? What do you think, Thomas?'

He couldn't tell her everything would be alright. He couldn't bring himself to tell her what would happen to her. He couldn't say anything. He couldn't smile. He couldn't cry. Poor Aarla was speaking to the dark, to the departed spirit of her uncle. The girl was touched. The horror of life in the mine was her moment-to-moment existence and all but normal to her. But it was a place of insanity, where humans only betrayed and ate each other, showing themselves far worse than any animal. No animal did the terrible and evil things that humans did. He could not be the ghost of her uncle for her. It was cruel to refuse, of course. He could not offer her words of comfort. And that was evil. Yet if he had pretended to be that ghost and had provided her with false hope, that too would have been evil.

Hardly realising he did it, he let go of her hand and drifted away into the dark.

'Thomas, are you there? You promised!'

He didn't hear her.

Samnir's eyes came open. His face lay in wet sand. Everything smelt of old fish. He lifted his head, his stiff neck protesting. Nausea overtook him; he vomited water and then had to lie in it, so spent was he.

After long moments he blearily made out smooth sandy walls. He realised he'd been washed along a channel just beneath the desert surface. He had no idea how long he'd lain there.

'Wonder if I'm dead. Sure feels like I am. Certainly seem to have been buried as if I was. Sloppy job, Akwar. Sloppy job. Maybe we won. Hmm. The rock people would have come and found me if we had. Damn it. I guess I'll just have to drag myself up out of my grave and sort things out myself. You know, you just can't get the staff. For once it would have been nice if they could have got things settled without me. No rest for the wicked, eh? I'd better get some proper thanks and appreciation this time, though, that's all I'm saying. I don't want any of this *Oh, Samnir, don't take on so. Don't you realise the war's over?* malarkey. Or any grief next time I have to lock that drunkard up to pre-empt a full-scale ruckus. Wow, that's sore. I really am getting too old for this, Sand Devil or not. It's time I had a porch and rocking chair. It's time Jillan and Hella had a child I can spoil rotten and give piggyback rides to. It's time I promoted Gallen so that he can shoulder all the nonsense of command for me. This is the last time, I tell you, the last time. You listening, Gods, cosmos and Saviours? I've had it up to here with your conspiracies and conniving. We all have. Time it was finished once and for all. Come on, soldier, on your feet!'

After considerable effort and some choice profanities, he rose back up into the world. There was nothing to be seen above ground. The desert lay blasted and unmoving. The sky was strangely empty, streaked with dirt and grime. There was no sun, no clouds, no moon, nothing. There was no wind. All was still. It was as if everything had entered a limbo.

'Where is everybody, eh? There should at least be dead bodies around, blood or something. Did Gar bury them all in a mass grave? He can only have done that if we won, but then why didn't they come and get me? All very odd. Not even sure where Haven is from here. No sign of the trail Jacob used to take with his wagon. Akwar can't have washed me halfway across the desert, can he? No, it's more likely the flood destroyed the landscape I'm familiar with. Helloooo?'

He waited and listened. There was no response. He wasn't sure how far his voice had been able to carry in this dead place. With a shrug, he decided to follow the direction of the underground channel, figuring it might lead towards the hidden valley.

'I have as much water as I need – I've had my fill of it in truth. And it's not too hot either. You know you're talking to yourself, don't you? It's the most intelligent conversation I'm going to get round here. True. Let's go then.'

He began to trudge through the desert. There was no sign of any sort of life – no fly, no beetle, no scorpion, no snake, not even any of the usual tracks.

'Damned odd.'

He refused to dwell on what that might mean because he didn't like where his thoughts took him. He moved through the eerie waste, his soldier's will ignoring the pain of overworked muscles and the dull ache of old bones. On and on he marched.

'There has to be an edge to this desert somewhere.' *Unless the whole world is now barren like this.* 'Just keep walking. I'll come to mountains at some point if I travel the whole world.' *Unless they've been pulled down and used to fill in valleys like Haven.* 'Don't be silly. Gar wouldn't do that, and no one else has the power to do such a thing, do they? Not even those stinking Saviours could do that. See. Told you.'

At last he recognised some of the boulders and slabs of rock around him. In the distance he spotted the stone spire from which he'd used to keep his vigil. He had reached Haven at last.

He entered a place of strange devastation. It near broke his heart as he remembered the vibrancy of the life that had once been here. Where was the sap, swell and abundance now? Where was the verdant foliage and impossibly sweet fruit? All gone, all gone. The skeletons of trees stood as mourners to what once had been. He spied some green on one pine and made for it, but all the needles suddenly shed – the vibration from his steps had supplied the petrified plant with all the trigger it required to fragment. It groaned, and he looked up in alarm as it toppled towards him. Its branches caught another tree, and that too fell. He ran. Then another. Then an entire cascade. Crashing down around him.

He leaped down the slope of the valley, pursued by a keening and roaring death. The ground crumbled beneath him, even the soil lifeless and desiccated. Dust billowed up and engulfed him. All was choking dust, the dust of death and the grave.

He stumbled past the clawing branches of the last tree. It hurt to breathe, and he had to put his hands on his knees as he recovered. The awful silence returned and his panting struggle was all that was to be heard. He felt out of place, as if he should not be here, as if he was disturbing what should be left to rest in peace, as if he was intruding somehow.

He calmed himself and stepped down towards the home he'd once shared with Jillan. Inside it was cold and felt absent somehow, as if it wasn't really there. He went down past the forlorn Gathering Place to the houses by the lake. Many of the buildings looked to have collapsed under their own weight, as if all strength had vanished from their timbers. Nothing stirred. Something else was wrong. There was no sound of lapping water. The lake was flat and hard-looking, like black glass.

Samnir left the town and walked disconsolately around the lake. He reached the inn and was surprised to hear drunken off-key singing. He went up the stairs and stepped inside. 'Shit. It had to be you,' he said. 'The only other person alive in this miserable place, and it had to be *you*.'

'Nishe to shee you too, I'm sure!' Ash slobbered, drawing himself up. 'Anyway, you're not allowed in here. You're shtill barred.'

Samnir looked around the room. 'Don't worry, I'll leave in a minute. Where's Dor?'

'He went off somewhere. Grief-shtricken he was, for his darling Freda. The rock people didn't fare so well, I hear. The Saviours seemed able to age them or something. Not even stone lasts forever, it sheems. All turns to dust.'

'The Saviours. That's what happened, then. How come you're still here, eh?'

Ash gave an exaggerated shrug. 'Maybe it's my punishment to be left like this, all alone.' He became maudlin. 'My timing turned out to be a curse in the end. Thought I was clever side-stepping and evading them, didn't I? But I've got no one and nothing here.' Tears came to his eyes. 'Wish I'd gone with the others now.'

'Oh, stop blubbing and feeling sorry for yourself. You make me sick. You look like you've been enjoying yourself plenty, drinking this place dry.'

Ash was incredulous. 'Enjoying myself? How can I? There's no fun in drinking on your own, and there's absolutely no chance of me enjoying myself now you're here. The grog doesn't even seem to make me that drunk any more, no matter how much I drink. The more I drink, the more damned sober it makes me. There's no forgetting it or escaping it, you see. I was trying to drink myself to death, damn you! But it doesn't work. And then I realised. Life and death – they're the same thing now. Don't you get it? They mean as much and as little as each other. I'm already dead. But it never ends. It goes on and on like this. Forever. We're damned. So why shouldn't I blub? What does it even matter? Sneer all you want, you pompous and self-lauding hypocrite. Go find another inn if you don't like it. Just leave me alone.'

'Alright.'

'No, don't!' the woodsman begged. 'Don't leave me. Here, have a drink for old times' sake. It's a decent drop. A Shangrin red. Probably the last bottle left in the world. Or if you're not going to stay, at least have one for the road.'

Samnir let go a slow breath. 'Pour me a goblet, Ash. Pull yourself together. Tell me what happened to the others. Where are they?'

'They're gone. There's nothing left. Just ash. Huh. Ash by name, ash by nature. Ashes in the mouth. That is all I'm left with. Hell is yourself, right?'

Samnir fought for patience. 'I'm not going to tell you to look on the bright side, because I doubt there is one. Just tell me.'

'I saw it with my own eyes. The dead came for us. It's true. They were all around us, everywhere. And Azual is their king. Don't you see? There never was any escape. Die, and he ends up ruling over you anyway. We should never have fought the Empire in the first place. What were we thinking? The blessed Saviours are divine and eternal. Their will is all. I was right to be scared all along. It wasn't cowardice, it was plain good sense and honest faith! Does not the Book of Saviours say all should fear their wrath and judgement? *Sacrifice and duty safeguard the People against the Chaos.*'

'Do not quote me their scripture. Get a grip of yourself, man. I refuse to believe we were wrong to fight. So the dead came. Did Azual kill Jillan and steal his soul?'

'No, the Saviours got him. They have taken the Geas itself!' Ash's hands shook so badly he spilt a good measure of his wine getting it to his mouth.

Samnir nodded. 'I see. That is how Haven came to die. The heinous murder of its life-giving power. They have torn the heart of this world from it and left it a corpse. And you stood by and watched. You let it happen.'

'No! There was nothing I could do,' Ash bawled. 'In an instant the Saviours drew the life of nearly everyone. I couldn't get near them! You have to believe me. It wasn't my fault. I've already told you. There's no fighting or escaping their will. My timing became erratic. Torpeth. He ... Oh, what's the use?'

'Torpeth? Did the mountain men come here? What of Hella? Jacob? Our Heroes? The men of the Fortress of the Sun? What happened to them? Tell me.'

Ash dropped his eyes and shook his head morosely. 'All dead or taken.' He poured himself a full goblet and drank it down.

'Taken where?'

'It doesn't matter. No one can help them. Not even the gods. They're all gone, Samnir, all gone. This is the only salvation we deserve or will ever have.'

Samnir's fist crashed down on the table, sending the bottle to the floor, where it shattered. 'Where!'

'Hey, that was my last bottle. How dare you!'

Samnir's face came close. 'Well there's no need to finish it now, is there? Besides, what does it matter? Nothing matters any more. Isn't that what you said? Perhaps you were wrong after all.'

'You've no right.'

269

'You *will* tell me where they were taken or I will take great delight in doing to you what I've always dreamed of doing. I hardly need to list the tortures, do I? You are so odious and snivelling, I cannot believe we are of the same species. How is it vermin like you are allowed to exist when so many noble and worthier people have died? What disgusting service did you offer up to Azual that he still permits you breath? Did you kiss and lick at his every orifice? I can only think you betrayed all the others. I heard Aspin foretold long ago that you would one day betray Jillan and all that depended on him.' Samnir's teeth bit close to Ash's eyes and cheeks, and the woodsman leaned away in panic, but he was trapped in his chair. 'You think this place hell? You don't know the meaning of the word. I will soon have you see this as a veritable paradise once I get to work on you. I am the Sand Devil. I have beaten Azual black and blue in my time. I have slain Saviours. Imagine what I will do to something as contemptible as you. I will eat your face to the skull and then gnaw on that, all while you live and whine.' His words descended into incoherent rage. Spittle and foam were at the corners of the commander's mouth. His eyes burned and his features contorted into something more bestial than Ash had ever before seen in wood or forest. Here was a monster of primal memory and ancient legend.

'Beloved, are you in there?' called a Scylla-like voice from outside.

Samnir whirled towards the door with a feral snarl.

'Praise all that is holy,' Ash whimpered, coming forward in his chair and putting his head in his hands.

'Sweet Samnir, come to me.'

The soldier froze.

'Your passion and blood call to me, and so I have come. I hear the beat of your great heart and feel the power of your desire. It draws me to you, and you to me.'

'No,' Samnir groaned, the fight leaving him. He dragged himself to the door and stepped out.

At the bottom of the steps her phantom waited for him. Her face bore the wounds inflicted upon her by the Disciple and her throat appeared to have been torn out. There was no colour to her, save the mesmerising blue of her eyes.

'My beloved Samnir. Take me in your arms.'

He held her and she took on greater substance. 'Izat.'

'Now we can be together for ever.'

'You are dead.'

'Life and death are one. Nothing can ever part us, you'll see. Let us go together, my love.'

'Go where?'

'It is not important.'

'There has been too much mistrust between us in the past, dearest. Tell me this and I will go willingly.'

She hesitated. 'To the temple of Sinisar.'

'Why? What is there, my darling Izat? What awaits me? Azual? The Saviours?'

She pulled away, trying to tug him after her.

He held firm. 'No more secrets between us, or I can never be completely yours. Our union will never be absolute. Why did the Saviours leave Haven? What are they after at the temple?'

She chewed her mutilated lip. 'Very well, dear heart. They went there for the sun-smith and all the sun-metal, but that is not important. The new seat of the blessed Saviours is where all go to kneel and pray, to become immortal and join their eternal Empire. Think of it, my lovely man. We will enter paradise at last. No more pain and struggle. No more division. Just joy and love. Let us go together.'

'Thank you,' he said, shedding a single tear as he planted his shining blade in her gut and sliced her in two.

Her eyes and mouth went wide in surprise. Light shone from her and he saw the true beauty of her, the beauty that had been lost for so long. She was radiant and gave him a forgiving smile, then was gone.

Samnir turned on his heel and marched back into the inn. Two seconds later Ash was hurled out of the door into the dirt. The Sand Devil calmly came out, pulled the woodsman up by the scruff of the neck and booted his behind. 'Like it or not, Ash, you're all I've got. I will kick you all the way to Sinisar's temple if I have to.'

'Mercy!' the other wailed. 'Do not take me there.'

'Come on – a walk in the desert will do you good. Think of the thirst you'll develop. Think of how good that first drink afterwards will taste. A nice cold beer, Ash. Besides, we'll get to see all our old friends if we're lucky. Then you won't have to sob about how alone you are any more.

Didn't you say you wished you'd gone with the others after all? Well, here's your chance. See, there's a bright side after all.'

'Please, no!'

'You're just being histrionic. You'll thank me for this when it's all over.'

'You maniac! Someone help me.'

Samnir planted his boot up Ash's behind a second time. 'Move. There's no use crying. There's no one to hear you, remember? They're all gone.'

The sandy soil shifted and rose, forming an indistinct figure. Whatever it was clearly had trouble holding any sort of permanent shape. 'Friend Samnir,' it whispered.

'Freda? Is that you? Ye gods, what happened?' the commander asked.

'The elseworlders did this. I can find none of my people. What has become of us?'

'Nothing good, I fear. It is nearly over, Freda. I go to the temple. Do you know if that is where they have taken Jillan?'

'I am sorry, friend Samnir. I sense too little now. I hardly recognise anything. I will accompany you as I can. Is that you, friend Ash?'

'Samnir is kidnapping me! Get him away from me, I beg you.'

'It is probably for your own good, friend Ash. Samnir usually knows what's best … You had the people of Haven attack me, remember? Friend Samnir, I will make sure friend Ash does not run away.'

'Thank you, Freda. I'd appreciate that. Ash is lucky to have such a good friend. See, Ash, it's not all bad. Even at the end of the world you've still got your friends.'

'I could do without them,' the woodsman moaned. 'None of this is fair. Ouch! Please, Samnir, don't. I've got piles. It's agony. I can't go any faster. I've got a stone in my shoe. Ow!'

'You've got piles because you sit around idling all day. Move! I'm being cruel to be kind. It'll cure you eventually, or get you to a place where it really doesn't matter any more. Come on – you're the one who didn't want to be in the punishment chamber any more.'

'Alright, alright. Just try not to sound like you're enjoying it so much, would you? And by the way, you're banned from my inn for ever. That goes for you too, Freda.'

*

She found him in the dark. She was merciless.

'Thomas, there you are. We got separated.' She raised a small burning torch. The light hurt his eyes.

'How did you find me?' he croaked.

'From the smell, of course. It's how the big miners will hunt you too. You need to get better at masking your scent. Did you mess your britches or have you been drinking your own wee? Don't you know you should make your toilet far away from where you rest?'

She twittered like a – what were they called? – bird. It was hard to follow her. Too many words and ideas, too many questions. He didn't want to think any more. He just wanted to forget. He wanted it all to stop. He wanted to sleep. 'Can't you just leave me alone?'

Aarla's voice became challenging. 'You swore you'd help me with mining. On Hella's life you swore. You have to help me. Come on. Get up. You'll need to eat. Don't go thinking you can eat coal or something. It gives you the shits, makes you too weak to work and then you die. But you can't die because you still owe me for saving you from the big miners. On Hella's life you swore.'

It was only the name of his beloved that got him up. Hadn't Ba'zel said Hella wouldn't be sacrificed until all the sun-metal had been mined? Or had he imagined that? Had there been any such implication or intended meaning? He had been crazed and desperate for any sort of hope. If the miners no longer gave the overseers any sun-metal, all would be ended in any event, because they would no longer get any food. Listlessly, he followed the dim glow of the torch.

Aarla led him down and down, deep into the bowels of the earth. In several places the way was so narrow he had to turn sideways, reach ahead and drag himself through, scraping skin off cheekbones and banging knees and elbows. At another point he was forced to grovel on his front and inch forward using just feet and fingers for long minutes. He felt the weight of the world pressing down on him and would have taken it as a blessing if it had crushed him. But the world was not inclined to show him such pity.

'Careful of these holes here,' Aarla warned. 'I dropped stones down them and never heard a sound.'

What would it be like to fall for ever? If there was no bottom, there would be no impact and no death. He would be in a sort of limbo worse than death until his body starved completely. He thought of hurling himself into the abyss, but the image of Hella he kept in the forefront of his mind forbade it. Instead he let Aarla guide him along a ledge just inches wide.

After what seemed hours of travel, they reached a dead end. Jillan was breathless from the exertion. His brow was slick with sweat, for although it was cool there was precious little air. All was stuffy and claustrophobic. He felt faint.

'You'll get used to it. It means there's sun-metal close by.'

'It's like it's telling us to stay away.'

'We have to eat.' Aarla shrugged. 'There's the pickaxe. I brought it down last time, but I couldn't swing it hard enough to break the rock. Go on then. You swore on Hella's life.'

Jillan picked up the tool and hefted it at the rock. The shock of the impact near drove him to his knees.

'Get up. Swing harder. She'll die otherwise.'

Wiping at the corner of one eye, he gritted his teeth and swung again. It felt like he was being broken against the rock over and over.

Surely he'd shaken every one of his teeth loose. Surely there were cracks in his skull. His joints had crumbled and been ground down. His lungs had burst. His muscles had been stretched unnaturally and been unstrung by the impossibly heavy head of the pickaxe. He may as well have tried to move the entire world as lift the tool again. The rock face was chipped all over but otherwise entirely intact. He lay bent out of shape at its base, his head at an alarming angle.

Aarla watched without expression. 'They say everyone above ground is dead, and that it is your fault. Is it true?'

He couldn't breathe. He looked back at her and managed a slow blink of admission.

'How does it feel to be responsible for such a thing? I cannot imagine it. No amount of punishment could ever make up for it.'

One more strike with the pickaxe would kill him. Just one more. But he didn't have the strength even to pick it up. He hiccuped his torture and grief. His being and body had cried out all it had. There was nothing left but her image.

274

Ever so quietly Aarla said, 'You swore. She will die otherwise. No sun-metal, no more life for Hella.'

He couldn't. He had to. There wasn't enough life left in him. He looked for strength in death. He asked what it wanted of him. Everything. One more swing. All life and death. One more swing. The balance would finally be tipped.

Jillan used the last of himself, raised the pickaxe and struck. His heart failed and he fell in a shower of sparks. A single chunk of rock had come away and a small piece of sun-metal had stabbed down into his chest.

Aarla picked her way over to him, pulled the shard out and twirled it through her fingers while considering him. She looked mildly disappointed. Her features shifted, and a familiar face appeared within the torch's red light.

Miserath.

'Indeed. Who else would it be? I had thought to mock and taunt you at this point. I had thought to be entertained by your punishment and end, dear Jillan. It was to be righteous payback for the considerable inconvenience you have caused me. Do you know, if I hadn't had the foresight to free my brother Akwar in Shangrin, in return for his promise to aid me should I ever have the need, then I think you might actually have ended me in the lava of Haven? It was·a close thing, and I was very angry with you.'

His voice. It's impossible. The taint?

The Peculiar smiled pityingly. 'Yes, I was the taint all along. What better way to manipulate you?'

No. The taint is Kathuula. The dark Geas.

'All one and the same, my poor Jillan. Were you deceived? I am not surprised. You mortals are so limited. Even when the god of illusion is at large, you are still so ready to believe one thing or another. It is a particular failing of your kind, you know. That's why the elseworlders ultimately defeated you, although with my help. Oh well, there it is. That's the end.'

Why? Why have you destroyed us?

'Why? Why, to be free of you, of course. To be free of the Geas and the manner by which it defined life in this world. This world was always my prison and punishment, you see. A particularly sanctimonious race of beings called the Chi'a confined me here. Every moment since has been agony for me, as your mortal thoughts intruded on my consciousness, no matter how thick a helmet I wore or how many walls of sun-metal I slept behind. Do you have any idea what it's like to have the childish, puerile and selfish thoughts of others constantly force their way into your mind? I was insane with it for a good long while. Millions of voices laughing, scorning, loving, pleading, crying, glorying, sullying, praying, cursing, on and on. You only had the single voice of the taint to deal with, and you found that bad enough, no? Anyway, it's done with now and I – with the help of the elseworlder's Gates – will be restored to my rightful place in the cosmos, to cause mayhem as I see fit. No more gaudy helmets of sun-metal for me. Here, you can have this. You earned it.' He placed the piece of sun-metal back on Jillan's chest, where it started to char the material of his tunic. 'A keepsake, a reminder, call it what you will. This is goodbye, Jillan. I had thought to gloat more or for longer, but somehow I don't have it in me. Perhaps I'm getting sentimental in my old age. Prepare yourself, dear Jillan, for I have one more bit of bad news before I go, before you die.'

The world is ended. There cannot be more.

The Peculiar shook his head in commiseration. 'I'm afraid there is. I would tell you not to take it too hard, but I know you will not be able to help yourself. I would try and make you feel better by saying it was good while it lasted. Your kind had a pretty good run, all things considered. There were some good times and laughs along the way. This is all for the best, and so on. Yet I doubt any of that can help. Jillan, I'm truly sorry that I must tell you this, but Hella is dead.'

No.

'I saw it with my own eyes. It wasn't pretty.'

The light faded from Jillan's eyes. She was gone.

The Peculiar stepped away and did not look back as he said with a small and malicious grin, 'Goodbye, Jillan.'

His beloved Hella. The enduring image of her that had sustained him began to slip away. There was nothing. He couldn't bear it. *Let it end.*

The sun-metal flared as it burned into his skin and flesh. With a palsied hand he took up the deadly shard and swallowed it down. He convulsed and at last died.

CHAPTER 9:

Of those so commanded

'I blame you for this, silly ox. Do you hear?' Torpeth shouted from his cage.

Aspin lay on the floor of his own prison, hardly able to understand the words. He'd been weak since the Saviour had Drawn his blood and fed on him. 'I don't care.'

'That has never been one of your faults, silly ox. Far from it. Indeed, it was your caring that ultimately brought us here. But for that, we would never have gone from the mountains to Hyvan's Cross, thence to the nether realm, on to Haven and then to here. Your determination to correct the wrongs plaguing this world finally brought us to the source of all that is ill, to these others and their used-up realm.'

'Torpeth, we have failed. Haven is finished. You saw what they did to it.'

The naked warrior blew a raspberry. 'Haven was always going to fall. You should have known that, as a reader.'

'I could never read the omens of the world like you. I could only read people. I give up. If Haven was always going to fall anyway, how on earth can I be to blame?'

'Quiet!' warned the Saviour who was contemplating a tome on the other side of the dusty chamber.

'Silly ox!' Torpeth said even more loudly. 'You are to blame for us still being in these cages. We should be out already. You shouldn't be lying around feeling sorry for yourself. You should be making as much noise as me.'

The Saviour rose threateningly. 'Enough of your meaningless chatter, lesser being!'

'Who are you calling a lesser being?' the holy man bridled. 'I will not take that from an overgrown cockroach. What sort of creature is it that destroys its own world? This realm of yours is empty, is it not, and all because of your excessive appetite and lack of self-control, yes? How then are we lesser? *You* need *us*, I think.'

'One more word and I will draw your life energy from you, no matter what promises I may have made to the Great Virtue. All life belongs to the Declension, to be used as we decide necessary on our Great Voyage.'

'All life belongs to you? Then this too is yours, and you are welcome to it!' So saying, Torpeth hung his member out between the bars of his cage and sent a stream of hot piss arcing across the chamber. 'If I'm the lesser being, then why are you the one with urine running down your front?'

The Saviour's roar of outrage cracked the walls. It dashed towards Torpeth's cage.

'Faal!' Aspin yelled, bringing the being to a sudden halt.

'No, silly ox! It was about to destroy my cage.'

'And you along with it, no doubt.'

'How could you know my name?' Faal demanded of Aspin.

'Weren't you listening properly, master cockroach? He's a reader. Is there no such talent among your kind? Then it strikes me you are the lesser being. It should really be you in this cage instead of us. Come on, let us out.'

'We defeated your kind,' Faal snapped.

'Did you really, though? We were betrayed, were we not? You had help, master cockroach. You cheated, really. In a fair fight against us your kind does not fare so well. Samnir slayed four of you at your Great Temple. Are you scared to let us out in case we do the same to you? You are scared, are you not? Who then is lesser?'

The Saviour tilted its massive skull as it regarded the small hairy human. 'You dare not challenge me. I would undo you with the power of my presence in an instant.'

'Hah! I'd like to see you try.'

'Torpeth,' Aspin groaned.

'I've been trying to find a way to die since you were just a baby cockroach, or some such. I think I did die once, but it didn't really agree with me, and I'm none the worse for it –'

'Actually, you're much worse,' Aspin could not help saying.

'– so be careful what you draw from me, master cockroach, lest you find it very much not to your taste, and poisonous indeed.'

Faal tilted his head back the other way. 'You are not like the others of your kind, one called Torpeth, and one called silly ox.' He retreated towards his tome once more. 'I will consider what you have said further.'

'Come back here!' the holy man demanded. 'I knew it. You're scared. Damn it, silly ox, just when we had him where we wanted him. We could have defeated this Declension of cockroaches right there and then. I blame you for this. Do you hear?'

Aspin curled up on the floor of his cage. 'I know, Torpeth, I know. You already said. Now do you mind if I get some rest? Please?'

After an age travelling across the wastes both Ash and Samnir were caked in dust and were a similar hue to the various shades and spirits wandering aimlessly across the desert. Some drifted, some scudded and others hovered without impetus. One would occasionally come up to the travellers but apparently be at a loss as to what to do or say. Yet the closer they got to the temple, the more of the dispossessed there were and the more attention the three of them seemed to attract. The dead began to whisper, but the words were tantalisingly just too quiet to catch.

Ash's skin began to crawl and he knew something intelligent was now watching them. As they crested a rise, they looked down upon the temple of Sinisar of the Shining Path. Its golden dome was cracked and fallen in, the interior dark. The dry moat around it was spanned by an airy bridge, across which the living were being driven, harangued or dragged by the dead of the world. The line of the damned being led into the temple stretched beyond the horizon and was a piteous sight indeed, children wailing and clutching at their despairing parents, bawling infants snatched away from their pleading mothers, the elderly cursing that they had ever lived, lone individuals knowing now they would never find love or kinship, the gods-fearing pulling out their tongues and putting out their eyes and ears, and the godless joyfully singing even as they were cruelly manhandled and lashed by the dead.

The noise of mortalkind's suffering was so hideous and evil to hear that Ash could not believe he did not die right then.

We also go to our deaths.

Ash turned his head to find the giant beast right beside him. 'Wolf! There you are. I wondered where you'd got to. I've missed you.'

All the squirrels and hedgehogs had left Haven, so I too had to go too. But there are none left anywhere now. So I too have come here, to face death. I was not sure you would be here at the end, woodsman, but somehow I am glad you are.

'Samnir forced me to come along.'

Perhaps. But you could have avoided him if you'd wanted to. I know you have such an ability.

'It doesn't always seem to work with him. He's immune to it or something, I think.'

'Woodsman, what are you talking about?' Samnir hissed. 'You're not making any sense, not that you do at the best of times.'

'It's the wolf, friend Samnir,' Freda replied. 'Can't you hear him?'

'Wolf? What wolf? Ye gods! Where did that come from?'

'It has always been there, don't you remember? Ash's companion. Jillan's friend too. It used to sleep under the inn at Godsend.'

'I ... Yes, of course. In Haven it stopped me from ... anyway, yes. How can I have forgotten? Will it help us?'

Perhaps, rabid one, but what help can there be? The living all come to meet their end here, willing or not. We are joining them. All find their deaths eventually, even us. Sometimes it is of their choosing and sometimes it is not. So what help would you have, rabid one?

'I will not go without a fight,' the soldier said through gritted teeth. 'I will have some measure of vengeance before I am done. Freda, can you take us through the earth into the temple?'

'Yes, friend Samnir. The chamber of the sun-smith is underneath the temple. He is kind, I think. He might help us, if he still lives.'

'Do we have to?' Ash asked.

'Yes, we do,' Samnir replied curtly. He looked to the wolf.

I will enter the temple through other means. None will detect me.

Samnir checked the lie of the land one last time and when he looked back the wolf was gone.

*

280

A horrible wrenching, like her guts being pulled out. Her mind tilting and scraping itself against the inside of her skull. Feeling it bleed and knowing the damage. Her heart struggling. Watching the life of Haven being pressed down and quashed, then hauled away. Her father was casually lifted from the ground by the hair, and held in the same talons as half a dozen others. She'd screamed without sound. Her power had been nothing, like trying to start a fire underwater. Had she managed to wield the sword Thomas had made for her? Once? Twice? Yet they had been implacable and fast, so fast. The sword had been battered away and she'd been taken by the throat. Crushing strength.

A beast speaking harsh, unintelligible words and the pressure at her throat easing slightly. Near unconsciousness, had she been carried across the desert? Falling through a shining gate surrounded by prowling shadows. Madness and stars, and into hot dusty halls, to be whisked along endless corridors. Down and down, layer after layer, and finally stuffed into a small claustrophobic space. It was a catacomb and she was being interred by the Saviours. *I don't want to die. I'm not ready. Where is my father? Jillan, where are you? Help me, please, you who loves me.*

As her proper mind had returned she had found herself in a small cage, itself within a small chamber. There were some scrolls in an alcove but the place was otherwise bare except for the Saviour that sat unmoving in the centre, her sword placed to the side of it. It appeared to be missing a limb. She stared at it, unable to tell if it was awake and in turn watching her. Perhaps it was a statue. There was no sign it was a living thing. Did it breathe? There was no movement of the stale air to suggest it did. Perhaps it breathed through its skin, but its surface seemed impervious stone. She could not understand any of it. It took her forever just to frame a question.

'Why have you not killed me?'

The Saviour showed no sign of having heard her. She had spoken aloud, hadn't she? She hadn't just rehearsed the words in her mind.

'Why am I alive? Why? Where are the others? Have you killed my father?'

She managed to put the slightest trace of power into her words. There was no Haven or Geas here to help her. The magic came from somewhere vital within her, and she found herself exhausted. She saw double for a moment. No, the Saviour had moved, surely.

'What do you want with me? Why would you destroy Haven and our world, but force me to live? Answer me, you monster!'

The Saviour slowly moved its jaw. 'Curious. You have some natural power. I have not known it in a lesser being before. I would draw it from you, but it is forbidden.'

'Why?' she demanded, terrified of the things it was saying.

'The Great Virtue says you must live until the one called Jillan is ended. You are his sacred heart and therefore surety of our victory. And you will soon have progeny. It is customary among my kind not to harm such a female.'

What was it saying? 'I-I am pregnant?' Reflexively, her hands went to her abdomen and she knew it was true. 'And Jillan lives?'

'The bane has had the power of the Geas that he stole drawn from him. We await his death now. It will not be long. You will have your offspring and then we will no longer have need of you either.'

'And my father?'

It did not respond.

'Answer me!' she commanded. She wasted her essential power, she knew, but she had to know.

'Once the bane is ended, your father will be ended. It will not be long now.'

I have to stop them. Hella grabbed the bars of her cage, but they were thick and immovable. *There must be a way.*

Our will is absolute, the Saviour replied.

It heard her thoughts. *Release me*, she willed it, using a perilous amount of her strength. She thought she would fail, but the strength of another seemed to support her. Was it the child growing within her?

'Argh!' The Saviour tried to resist but found itself incapable. Slowly its forelimb came up and moved towards the locking mechanism of her cage.

She felt dizzy and sick. She wanted to lie down. *Release me.*

The talon reached the lock. The Saviour froze.

The presence of another filled the chamber. *This one is not yours to command.*

'Eldest!' the Saviour whined. 'Forgive me.'

Silence, weakling. The presence focused on Hella. *I did well to watch you closely, lesser being. Not only are you the sacred heart of the destructive bane, but you are also a creator. I knew you would be more powerful than the rest of your kind, but now you see none are powerful before the Declension.*

'Come to me!' Hella cried, reaching towards her runic blade inscribed with sun-metal. It shifted a fraction. 'Please!' It flew to her hand. She hit the bars with it and cut through them cleanly.

Hella ducked free, went round behind the seated and paralysed Saviour, climbed onto its back and put the lethal blade against its neck. As she touched the creature, the Eldest's control vanished and Hella's power commanded it once more. 'Take me to my father. Then you will help me find Jillan.'

You cannot prevail, lesser being, shouted the combined voices of the Declension. *The life of the one you cling to is meaningless to us. You will not get further than a single corridor.*

'We'll see about that. I will not let you take my family.'

The dead parted before him. The last of the living filing towards the temple abased themselves before him.

'So now you all want to be my followers, eh?' The Peculiar smiled. He kissed a child on the forehead and waved at others as he passed. 'How fickle but predictable you mortals are. I would love to oblige you all, really I would, but there are places I need to be. There are other worlds that need my attention, you see. If you'd come to me sooner, then maybe there would have been something I could do to help you, but you've left it all a bit too late, I'm afraid. Now, now, enough of the crying and wailing. It's for your own good, in a way. All this provides you with resolution and puts your lives into a meaningful context. It gives you closure and answers to all those questions you've always asked of the cosmos. You're the lucky ones. Many worlds never receive such a blessing. Most just go on and on, living in doubt and confusion about the meaning of life. What does it all mean? What is it all for? Do the gods really exist? Are we fools to believe and trust in them? Is it all one big trick? Most mortals find it nearly impossible to live peacefully with such imponderables and unknowns, with such anxiety and ambiguity. They invariably become a mixture of fanatics, doubters and non-believers, ultimately leading to accusations of heresy and holy wars without end. Some worlds have even been known to destroy themselves utterly as a result. Ha, ha! Isn't that ridiculous? Rather than learning to live with the odd unanswered question, they get themselves so worked up that they go and destroy everyone and everything. Imagine! Oh, I don't mean to be insensitive, because I suppose something similar happened to you lot, no? Dangerous things, questions, and certainly what got Jillan in trouble with holy Praxis all that time ago, you know. Look what's happened as a consequence. I guess you weren't to know at the time that you should have all done more to stop Jillan – although, just between us, you should really have known, eh, what with the Saints and Saviours making it pretty clear and all? I suppose you're your own worst enemies, eh? No, don't feel bad. There's no point, after all, since it's far too late to repent. Anyway, I mustn't keep you. Think of it as going to a better place. I hear that helps sometimes. You know, it provides comfort and reassurance to those who are terrified witless, etcetera. Or think of it as *crossing over* to some sort of heaven. Or reaching an eternal city where you'll see all your loved ones again, or achieving some great and holy communion. You get the idea. Whatever works. So, toodle-oo, everyone. I hate drawn-out goodbyes. They really don't help anyone. Wish me luck. I'll miss you all, really I will, when I get a spare five minutes. Stay in touch, if you can. Goodbye then. Bye! I'll write, I promise. It's been great. Really. Safe journey.'

The Peculiar entered the ruined temple with a nod to the two scarred Saviours watching the entrance. They ignored him – they were more interested in choosing mortals from the line with which to feed themselves.

'Don't let me interrupt. I'll show myself in. I know the way.'

The Peculiar entered the main chamber and took on the form of a sober and experienced courtier. He squeezed and sidled through the press, working his way across the wide space. In the centre the dead propelled the living forward and separated off to the left. The living carried on by sheer weight of numbers towards a shining portal at the top of several stairs on the far side of the temple. The Gate swirled with colour, one moment displaying a rainbow vista, next painting the heavens in soft hues, and finally shimmering with stars and bright radiance. The scenes it presented were real and as mesmerising as they were vertiginous and awful. Most became entranced as they approached and were motioned to step through into the cosmos by a regally craggy

Saviour. They hardly noticed when an enormous Saviour with horns and talons of sun-metal occasionally reached round to break the neck of an unusually restive mortal and cast them aside. The compliant masses of humanity went into the great beyond and gave up their world and lives to the Declension. Meanwhile the dead went to submit to their rapacious king and his Saint. Azual would claim for himself the most powerful souls coming to offer themselves up, and gorge them down. The rest were left to Praxis, who seized, tore and ravened like a wild animal. There was nothing intelligent in his eyes any more.

All but untouched, the Peculiar wove his way to the side of the Saviours. He coughed politely to attract their attention.

'My dear Thraal, I trust all progresses as you would like. I have gone to considerable pains to ensure it is so. I'm sorry we haven't been introduced. I'm—'

'We know who you are,' the large Saviour behind Thraal replied. 'We are still not sure *what* you are, however.'

'And you are?' the Peculiar asked.

'Of the Declension.'

'Yes, of course you are. How could there have been any doubt. You are as charming as the rest of your kind. As I was saying, dearest Thraal, I trust all is to your liking. All has come to pass as I promised it would, yes?'

'The will of the Declension is inevitable,' Thraal responded carefully.

'Quite so, quite so. Be that as it may, I am here to announce the death of the mortal Jillan Hunterson, and therefore all the terms of our bargain finally met.'

Eldest, the bane is ended! Elder Thraal projected.

The bane is ended, spoke the mind of the Declension, and it roared from the throats of every being. Elder Thraal repeated it through Azual, through Saint Praxis and every one of the dead. The living heard it and took it up in horror and joy. The world screamed it. Every realm of the Declension echoed and amplified it. The cosmos rang with it. There could be none existing who did not know of Jillan's ending. There could be none existing who did not fear the cosmos would now fall to the Declension. The giants of the eighth realm sang in mournful counterpoint as they faced the transcendent and gleaming warriors of the Declension, the Great Virtue Destruction at their head. The magic of fully seven realms was entirely at the Eldest's command. How could any single realm stand against *Her*? The Great Voyage would be complete, and omnipotence and omniscience would both be *Hers*.

The bane is ended.

'Yes, that's what I said. The bane is dead. Very good. I have delivered all. Now, as per our agreement, I will be availing myself of your Gate here and bidding you a fond farewell.'

'That is as we agreed,' the larger Saviour allowed, 'yet we would know where you intend to travel, and for what purpose. This Gate is currently aligned to our home-realm, and we will not tolerate your *unstable* presence there. Even if you can manipulate the Gate to take you elsewhere, the other six realms of the Declension are all but barren. What would you have of them?'

'Not that it's really much of your business, whatever-your-name-is,' the Peculiar replied archly, 'but I intend to find some peace and quiet and get some well-earned rest. I need to have some me-time, you see, without being bothered by any carping mortals or all-conquering Declension. All this has been quite a strain, you know. Things were quite fraught and stressful for a while there, did you but know it. Does any of this mean anything to you at all? Do you understand the havoc it plays with one's nerves? Do you not understand how fatiguing it can be? Or is that just me? It's a symptom of my *instability*, yes? Hello? Is there anybody in there, or am I just talking to myself? Give me a sign. Anything. A smile perhaps, or would that crack that tough exterior of yours? How about a little dance or something? You can dance, right? It's not so hard once you get the basics sorted. Come on – you're pretty much a ruler of the cosmos now. Surely a quick jig isn't beyond you. Think of it as a celebration. No? Sheesh. You sure know how to enjoy yourself, don't you? Remind me to come to all your parties. Anyway, sorry to be a killjoy and all that, but I really must be leaving.'

The Peculiar stepped up the stairs. The large Saviour reached distractedly as if to delay him, but the Peculiar effortlessly flowed beyond his grasp.

'Now don't go getting all sentimental on me. Nor you, Thraal. You knew this moment had to come. Payment is ever due, even for the big bad Declension, eh? Any attempt to prevent me would not only be ill-mannered but also very poor judgement. Bad judgement, in fact. Get it?

Yes, I've heard it whispered who and what you are, my fine but taciturn friend. But that's a conversation for another time. Stay well, my darling Thraal. Think fondly of me, as I will you. Adieu, sweet prince, adieu!'

The mercurial being that was the Lord of Mayhem blew his co-conspirator a final kiss and was gone.

The bane is ended.

Beneath the ground Freda cried out in grief and agony. 'Friend Jillan, no! You cannot be dead. Not after we have been through so much. Not my best friend.'

'Damn that boy!' Samnir shouted impotently, punching the wall of the tunnel in which they crouched, then punching an unresisting Ash full in the face. 'Why didn't you avoid that? What's the matter with you?'

Ash held his head in his hands. 'Maybe I didn't want to avoid it. Maybe I deserved it. Maybe my timing doesn't work with you for some reason. Maybe it's broken, like my nose and everything else. I don't know any more, Samnir.' He made no effort to rise. 'And I don't care any more. Jillan is dead. The only one who stood by me, even after all I'd done. He never gave up on me, even when I let him down. He didn't give up on you, Samnir, even though you tried to kill Hella. He didn't give up on the People, or Haven.'

'No, he didn't,' Samnir agreed in a small and useless voice. His arms fell to his sides. 'I didn't think it could be over. He made me believe, Ash. It was only because of him that I fought. But now he's gone.' He fell back against the wall and slid to the floor. 'Nothing left to fight for any more. It's all ended.'

The bane is ended.

About to unleash the warriors of the Declension on the tiered circles of the eighth realm, Ba'zel froze. His army proclaimed itself ever more loudly, but he knew only loss. He had lost his one friend, but also himself. He had lost his one chance to halt and save the Declension, to spare other realms and entire races of lesser beings. He had lost everything.

The bane is ended.

Torpeth staggered as if kicked in the head or chest. He fell to the floor of his cage like he would never rise again.

The Saviour called Faal looked up from his tome. Although his own throat had echoed the words, there was no sense of triumph about him.

Aspin shuddered, only staying upright by holding on to the bars of his cage. He read the cosmos now, wishing with every fibre of his being he could not. He saw the relentless progress of the Declension. Realm after realm was subjugated, bled dry and then culled. The Declension's power grew with each realm that was consumed, with each race that was sacrificed to their progress on the Great Voyage. He had a vision of the Declension's home-realm as a small sphere near the centre of the cosmos. Each new realm was a sphere surrounding the Declension's own, and they rose through them like erupting lava. Up and up they forced themselves, pressure building whenever they met an obstacle, only increasing the force they exerted. Each sphere that was swamped by them in turn became lava and added to the churning, raging power. It was a cascade, realms falling with increasing speed, until all existence became explosively molten, and the containing dynamic of the whole was threatened. With Jillan gone, nothing could now prevent the end coming. It was already building beyond the point at which it could be prevented. 'Equilibrium slips, the balance tips and all will end!' he prophesied, eyes wide, transported by the vision, lips numb and his voice possessed.

Faal looked to him. 'I hear you. You speak the greatest secret of the Faction of Origin, passed down through our lines and known only to the Head of Faction since a time even before the Eldest. It is the only surviving knowledge we have from when we were servants to the ancient Chi'a. They speak through you.'

The bane is ended.

The mighty wolf howled rabidly for the loss of its world. Its call was haunting, tortured and soulless. It launched itself upon the Saviours guarding the entrance to the temple. Its jaws locked on the neck of one. The lupus shook its head savagely and broke the creature in two. It leaped for the other, which tried to assume a spectral form, but the spectral planes of this realm had collapsed and there was no escaping the apocalyptic violence that now descended.

*

The bane is ended.

The Sifters of the Declension's home-realm heard. They no longer adjusted themselves so as to survive the fury of the storms rampaging across the surface of their world. Instead they turned into the storms and embraced oblivion.

The bane is ended.

Hella's grip on the one-limbed Saviour slipped and her sword dragged across its throat, cutting deeply. She didn't know what she did.

The Saviour whined. 'Hella, daughter of Jacob, sacred heart of Jillan Hunterson, pity me! I am Dra'zen, retainer to Ba'zel, friend to the bane.'

She didn't hear anything. She didn't feel herself fall to the stone floor of the tunnel. Falling.

All perception receded from her. There was only her beating heart and the failing pulse of her magic left. This was all she was now, for the connection to something greater that had once sustained her was gone. Her ties to her world, her Geas and her love had unravelled. She searched for the bonds that had anchored her and secured her sense of self, but they had parted and fallen away. She found fragmented remains and frantically tried to follow them back to him, but they led nowhere, quickly petering out. There was only absence and emptiness. She knew in her soul he was dead. And her soul became filled with that absence and emptiness too. She shared his death, and wilted.

And still the wolf howled.

Freda's grief matched it.

Samnir groaned in agony.

'Aw shit,' Ash spat. 'Why didn't time stop here at the end, so he never had to die? It's not right. He can't leave us like this. But for him, I wouldn't even be here. I wouldn't be feeling this pain, suffering the end of the world. I could wish I had never met him, but that wouldn't be true. I would not give up this person he has made me for all the world, because – imperfect as I am – I know I am a better creature for having known him. I know I am more than I was when I feared the whole world and hid in my log cabin in the woods. Were I not, it would be an insult and injustice to everything I've ever cared about, to all he meant and represented. That meaning did not die with him, and I will do all I can to see it survive beyond him and even ourselves. I will face down death if I must, coward though I am. I will allow King Azual no hiding place. I swear it.'

'I too am more than I was because of him,' Freda said solemnly. 'He is not dead while I can remain. I will do what I can to have his memory live on. I will safeguard him in my heart and mind, resisting Azual and the elseworlders as I must.'

The wolf's howl was unending. *You have never feared death, rabid one.*

Samnir's mind became truly rabid in that moment. No, he had never feared death, and he didn't fear it now. It had claimed Jillan, but he would defy it with all he was. He would hunt it down and savage it. He gave a feral growl of warning and drew death's scent into his nostrils and deep into himself. He had it now and it would never escape him. He sprang up, teeth bared.

'He runs mad!' Ash wailed, shooing Freda on through the earth and dashing after her, a frenzied Samnir close on their heels.

They burst into an underground chamber, and the twisted and mighty sun-smith rose to meet them. 'There you are, Freda. It is too late. My father has brought down the world, has he not? Were we wrong to release him when the Great Temple fell? I was wrong to imprison him in the first place, I know that. Is there no way of making any amends, then? Can the original sin never be undone? They have left me precious little sun-metal to work, Freda. Without it what am I? Where is reason? Is it our strength or flaw?'

'I do not know, good sun-smith,' Freda replied gently.

Samnir circled the sun-smith, eyes fully dilated, ready to attack, yet at the last he sprang to the stairs and up. The smith watched him go. 'There is no reason left to that one, it seems, yet he is driven. How is that? What is the source? Where is it? Freda, are there answers? I beg you.'

Ash cleared his throat. 'It's probably best to stay out of his way. I've had to learn that the hard way. If you are not going to help him, then you are only a hindrance. You will only be an enemy to him, Jillan and all that held him dear, unless you aid us.'

Freda nodded to the sun-smith, he who forged the means of destruction and salvation, he who hammered out the shape of worlds and existence upon his anvil. 'There can be no neutrality, good sun-smith, here at the end. All is decided. All must decide. Those are the answers you ask for. Your own decision. Help or hindrance. There is no in between.'

'Let us ascend then, Freda, and see the issue of my father finally decided. I will also furnish you with the last of my weapons, though they cannot undo what has already come to pass.'

'It will soon be done,' Elder Thraal stated as the line of the seventh's living thinned to almost nothing. 'With the bane dead there are none left to challenge us.'

'Indeed, Great Saviour,' the terrifying Virtue answered, swinging his huge horned skull back and forth as if seeking something with his senses. 'And yet the count is not complete.'

'A few grovel in the mines of sun-metal, but surely none else remain. Our will is absolute and has drawn all to us. Nothing is hidden from us. The dead have scoured the realm and picked it clean of life. Any that were missed would come here in any event, for there is nothing else out there for them. There is nothing by which to survive. They will die or come here to beg our mercy. There is no alternative. We are inevitable to all. All are accounted for. There is therefore no need for you to remain in this realm, holy Virtue. I will rule this realm with these Saints until the end. I will complete the count on behalf of the Declension.'

'You,' the Virtue said slowly, calling the King of the Dead to him.

Azual left the carrion souls to Praxis and hurried to prostrate himself before his blessed Saviours. Although he was easily seven foot tall, he was dwarfed by his masters.

'Do we rule the souls of every one of the dead, including the bane's?'

There was the slightest hesitation. 'No, divine one,' Azual confessed, his face kept down because he dared not look upon his makers with his unworthy gaze. 'Yet it will be sssoon. As the living depart, there are fewer and fewer to remember and sssustain those dead who have not shared in the holy sssacrament of your blood. The sssoul of the bane will never know the eternal resurrection and life to be found through the blesssed Sssaviours. Surely his sssoul can no longer exissst, divine one!'

The Virtue's nasal aperture widened in anger. 'Thraal, I will remain until every last soul of this realm has been accounted for and utterly extinguished.'

Elder Thraal chose not to take issue with having been addressed without his proper title. 'You are the Declension's holy Judgement.'

'Indeed, Thraal, and you would do well to remember that. None may challenge me. I have spo—'

There was an inchoate roar and a dishevelled Hero came up into the centre of the chamber. He wielded sun-metal that burned so ferociously its passage through the air left traces on the eye of any who looked upon it. He scythed into clusters of the dead, releasing their souls in a bright instant. The few living moving through the temple screamed and ran for the Gate.

'You!' Azual slavered as he leaped up.

'The slayer!' Elder Thraal chittered. 'Destroy him. Your Great Saviour commands it!'

'Azual. I might have known,' Samnir spat. 'In a way I'm glad, because it means I get to kill you myself. It means I get to finish what I started in Godsend all that time ago. Oh, I will enjoy this.'

Azual came to his full height and his red eye blazed down on the old soldier. He laughed. 'You cannot kill me, pathetic mortal. I am both King of the Dead and eternal. I will drag your pitiful sssoul out of you and chew on it for all time.'

'Bow to the holy one,' Saint Praxis commanded, using his power of fear.

Samnir shrugged him off. 'I fear nothing in this realm or the next. Do you hear? Nothing!'

He leaped at Azual, his blade lightning. The Saint swerved his torso and the weapon drew a searing line across his side. Samnir rolled his wrist to bring the deadly sword into the fiend's body, but Azual had already let himself go into a fall. Before Samnir could adjust the direction of his attack the Saint kicked out from where he was on the ground, taking his opponent's feet out from under him.

Samnir fell foward onto the Saint, bringing the point of his sword straight towards Azual's livid eye. But the Saint caught Samnir's wrist in his massive taloned hand and crushed Samnir's bones. Samnir snarled in agony.

'You are old, Sssamnir.' The King of the Dead grinned. He breathed on him so that Samnir took decay into his lungs. 'You have lived far longer than you should have. Can't you feel it?'

Samnir deliberately let go of his sword. Azual's eye widened in horror at the precise moment the tip of sun-metal came down into it. There was a distinct pop, then a squelch. A sizzle, then a faint smell of corrupted meat.

Azual let out a high-pitched squeal and bucked wildly, flinging Samnir off and past him. The dead around the edges of the chamber cringed and clawed at their faces, as if sharing in their king's torment. Their wailing was a chorus to Azual's own cries.

Samnir flew through the air. His arms went out in front of him, but he knew he dared not land on his already damaged wrist. He tried to twist, to take the impact on his shoulder, but his body would not obey him. His chest, then chin, smacked down as he slid across the floor. His jaws came together hard and everything jarred, his vision gone for long seconds. *Elegant. Get up. Think.* But he could not tell which way was up. Was Azual already coming for him, or Praxis? The Saviours? *Up! Don't just lie there.* Did footsteps hurry towards him? Which direction? No, the pounding was the blood in his ears. He couldn't hear. What was that wailing? *Get yourself a weapon. Push yourself up. Now! With the other wrist, idiot.* He got to his feet, only staying upright by locking his knees, even though he knew it was a disastrous fighting stance.

The temple swung before his eyes. Azual flailed onto his front. The sword of sun-metal was near the fiend, but surely the fiend could not see that. The soldier called to the sword, but the Saint's hand slapped down on the blade.

Hit him now. Move, soldier! A quick blow to his throat. The commander unlocked one of his knees, and the treacherous joint gave way under him. *Shit.* Azual's head was up. He was orientating himself somehow. Samnir forced himself up, feeling his bones grind and tendons tear. He took a step and then propelled himself forward.

Elder Thraal prepared to exert the power of his presence, but Judgement stopped him. 'No. We will watch and judge the slayer first. It would be precipitous to act now. The Saint is of no concern to us. We lose nothing if the Saint fails, for your blood will continue to rule the dead.'

Holding the sword close to him despite the burns he suffered as a consequence, Azual made a prodigious leap sideways, taking him well out of Samnir's blundering path. The commander pulled up, breathing hard.

'You tire rapidly,' the Saint taunted. 'The ssstrength of your youth is long sssince gone, Hero.'

'Oh, there is more to me than meets the eye. But you don't have any eyes left, do you?' Samnir replied, taking a vital moment of respite.

'I do not need my eyes to sssee, mortal. By the power of the holy communion, we are united with our blessed Sssaviours, our lives and deaths are one, and all share their eternal foresssight and vision.'

Samnir glanced towards the shades at the edges of the chamber, who in turn watched him. He realised that Azual must be seeing through them. He steadied himself. 'I have taken your eye, demon. Next I will take your tongue, and finally your head.'

'You have no sssword, mortal. Your body fails you and your ssspirit now follows. Jussst as Jillan failed you when he betrayed the Empire and the world. He is dead, Sssamnir. It is over. It is time to ressst. Join him if you wish. Or take this chance to repent. There is nothing elssse.'

Do not let the doubts enter in. 'Jillan did not fail us; it is we who failed him. Do you forget so quickly, demon? Did he not defeat you at Godsend? I saw you cry like a child at the end, when you were all alone, remember? Where were your cowardly Saviours then? Do you not know that Jillan then brought down the Great Temple of these jealous Saviours who would own not just our lives, but also our hearts and minds? And he would have seen Haven a paradise for all, had he not been betrayed by the gods and his own kind. So answer me this – with all that I owe him, how could I ever rest? The lack was in us, and he paid for it. I owe him everything and all that I am. I will never willingly bow to you and my death, not till I have done all that I can to make restitution. Do you hear me? Never!' He sprang forward with a roar. 'Come to me!'

Saint Praxis, who had been circling the two combatants in the shadows, made to come at Samnir. Yet suddenly he tripped. He sprawled to the ground. As he sought to scramble up, the shining tip of a blade came to his throat.

'Hello there, Praxis.' Ash smiled. 'Sorry if I'm in the way, but we can't have you stabbing anyone in the back, now can we?'

'Unclean!' the Saint hissed.

'And there's no need for that either.' The woodsman pushed his sword into the disbelieving other's neck, and separated head from body. The Minister's face hit the ground and rolled over. His tongue flapped and eyes goggled. Trapped souls flew free of him and winked out. Then flames engulfed his remains and he was naught but a charred stain on the stone floor.

Samnir's sword slithered free of Azual's grasp. The Saint tried to grab it, and had his fingers cruelly sliced as reward. The weapon flew to the hand of its master and Samnir bore down on his foe with blade raised for the killing blow.

'Ssstrike at me and ssstrike at the ssspirits of all you have ever loved!' Azual was suddenly robed in the ethereal souls of those he had consumed. They floated and twisted tightly around him. Jillan's parents, Jedadiah and Maria, looked out at Samnir in horror.

'No,' the commander moaned. He'd already begun to cut at them.

The sun-metal cleaved through the faces of the two souls, bringing terrible screams that all too quickly faded into silence. They were gone.

Two new souls took the places of Jedadiah and Maria in Azual's grotesque armour – Captain Callinor of Heroes' Brook and Halson the carpenter from Haven.

'How could you?' came Azual's mocking chastisement, followed by an impossibly quick and violent blow to the top of Samnir's sword arm, completely deadening it.

The old soldier gasped and fumbled his blade, losing it once more. A powerful strike hit his armour above his heart, crumpling it and hurling him back across the chamber.

His life energy stuttered. His left lung felt like it had collapsed. His pulse was erratic. His blood slowed. *Not like this. You have to ...* Yet his thoughts were becoming interrupted and distant, as if they belonged to someone else. *Can he not be defeated? Death? For a time you thought the Empire could not be defeated, but Jillan showed you it was that false belief which trapped you and prevented you resisting them. It was that belief which prevented you from actually defeating them. Circular and controlling. He showed you and freed you. You defeated the Empire. Didn't you? Or did they just allow it to seem that way so they could ultimately claim Haven and the Geas? They have won. They had always won. There was never any defeating them. Fool.*

'Oh dear, and ssso the little sssoldier falls,' Azual said with a sad pout.

The dead around the chamber no longer held to the shadows, but now dared creep forward, closing in on the fallen commander. They hungered for the life in him and knew it would soon be theirs. Their king came slowly towards his victim. 'Death comes to all mortals, Sssamnir. It is what provides their lives with any meaning. If they did not die, none of the choices and missstakes they made in life, and none of the sssmall triumphs they achieved, would matter. Why even make a choice or ssstrive to achieve anything if life is going to go on anyway? Death is the necesssary consssequence of life, Sssamnir. So come embrace me like a friend now, at the end. I have always been your friend, did you but know it. I have always cared for your immortal sssoul, where often you have not. I do not asssk for your thanks, I merely want you to know and have peace at lassst, as I have wanted it for all those in my charge. It will be gentle if you accept it. Like going to sssleep. There will be no pain as long as you do not resissst it, as long as you do not try to ssstay awake beyond your time, beyond your body's ability to continue. Hear the dead sing to you! It is that oldest of lullabies all remember and yearn for. It is the comforting prayer that sees our souls offered up to paradise and eternity. It is a call of welcome from friends and loved ones long misssed. You will be with them all again, no longer alone and despairing. It is all you have ever wanted, all you have ever fought for, all you have ever lived for, all you have ever suffered for, and what your soul deserves. It is a hymn of praise, joy and celebration. Can you not hear it? Will you not join your voice to it in this final moment? Will you not allow yourself this? You need not deny yourself any longer. All is here, all is yours. Speak those words of repentance, of faith and rebirth.'

The Saint's voice lulled Samnir, soothed and calmed him. The dead crooned to him. He did not feel pain any more. He did not feel much. There was a dull sense of loss and sadness but it was familiar, like the tiredness of muscles and the ache of bones. He let go of it. Was there disappointment that it ended? Was this the death he'd envisioned for himself? He looked down at himself, lying there in the broken temple of Sinisar, encroaching ghouls all around, their leering leader salivating at the prospect of supping on his soul, the scheming and otherworldly Saviours looking on. It was not the way he would have wanted it. It was far from the glorious end he had dreamed of. Was it even a soldier's death, lying there waiting for it to happen?

Across the chamber sun-metal glinted at him. 'Come to me,' he mouthed.

Azual's shadow fell across Samnir. The Saint's long tongue hung from his mouth, saliva stringing from it. The organ reached down towards its prey.

The sun-metal answered him, flaring to drive back shadows and shades alike. They screeched. The chamber erupted all around, light cascading in all directions. Ash, Freda and the sun-smith saw their moment and hewed into the dead, exploding and shredding their souls. A lupine shadow devoured all those that sought to escape.

'What is thisss?' Azual cried, disoriented, the vision of his minions clearly affected.

His sword coming to his hand, Samnir rolled sideways so that the sudden lash of Azual's tongue found only stone. The struggle to breathe and the pains in his chest told him he had cracked or broken ribs. It hampered him enough that he was too slow to cut Azual's feet from under him. Partly on instinct, the Saint had already jumped back.

'Blessed Sssaviours,' Azual called fearfully. 'The cursed companions of Jillan ssstill sssurvive. Their pagan powers and the Chaosss ssstill resissst. Do not forsssake me! The wily woodsman brings time, place and purpose together as per his will. I cannot thwart him alone. The obdurate rock woman yields to none. The sun-smith brings an element none can control. And the beast comes among us. Help me!'

'Quit your whining, demon.' Samnir coughed raggedly. 'I will not hear you beg for life when you have denied it to all else. I have never known anything of such twisting corruption as you. It is your inimical nature that ultimately undoes you and brings this upon you. Now you see the murderous and self-consuming evil that you have become with these thieving and parasitic Saviours.'

'Sssilence! You will not ssspeak ssso!' Azual demanded, and his tongue whipped out, aiming to wrap itself around the bowed soldier's neck, to rip his head off.

Yet this was what Samnir had been waiting for. His left arm came up so that the end of the tongue encircled that instead. He made wide circles with the arm, wrapping the tongue round and round. He rose and yanked hard, forcing Azual forward with all balance lost. Samnir brought up his sword of sun-metal and ruthlessly chopped through the root of the tongue. No longer held, Azual jolted back with a gargling shriek. The backstroke of Samnir's weapon cleanly decapitated the King of the Dead. Azual's head hit the floor with a thud, and the dead fell silent. For a moment there was only silence and stillness in the chamber.

Azual's body collapsed and started to dissolve. It bubbled and steamed, defeating and destroying the things that tried to climb free of it. It fizzled fiercely, at the last scarring the stone, and then just faded away.

'We must beware the *unstable* element,' the smaller of the Saviours warned in clicking tones.

'It is not significant,' the larger announced. 'Nothing has changed. Nothing has been ceded.'

'Oh, I don't know,' Ash called out. 'I certainly feel better for Azual finally being put down. He's properly gone for good this time, right?'

'We would have ultimately consumed the Saint in any event. There are plenty of dead still outside the temple who are ruled and will be consumed by us. This struggle we witness is meaningless. In other realms the lesser beings have invariably fought among themselves at the end. We have watched and made our judgement. You lesser beings can be no threat to the Declension. Like all others, you have willingly come to present yourselves before our power, offering yourselves up to it. And so our power will inevitably consume you.'

'That doesn't sound so good,' Ash worried. 'Is the whole *consuming* thing really necessary? Can't we just let bygones be bygones? No? Oh dear. Samnir, do tell me you've got a few more tricks up your sleeve. It's you who forced me to come here, remember? I'll be very disappointed if you choose now to run out of ideas.'

Samnir coughed blood up and spat it free of his mouth. 'We've killed Saviours before, you and I, and we will do it again.'

'But we had help from one of their own kind that time.'

The Saviours exerted the ferocious power of their presence, instantly flattening the companions and slowly drawing the life energy from them. The sun-smith forced his way up and whirled two wide and curiously shaped blades around himself to form a web of protection, but he was unable to help the others. He was soon lathered in sweat, and it was clear he would not be able to maintain his defence for too long.

'That hurts, damn it!' Ash groaned. 'Samnir, now would be a good time. Samnir!'

Yet the commander lay prone, clutching his chest, unable to answer. The lines of his face became deeper and deeper. He visibly aged.

Freda yelped in distress and went to hide in the ground, but it was clear the Saviours' power extended even there, because stone became sand, became dust, and drifted on the breeze travelling through the temple from the broken dome. The rock woman was gradually being eroded to nothing.

Ash tried to prevent the pressure at his temples, but clumps of hair came away in his shaking hands. His skin sagged and his flesh melted away. 'Please!' he croaked.

Woodsman, I am sorry. They are beyond me, whined the wolf, its paws going over its muzzle as it was forced low.

The sun-smith took tortured steps towards the Saviours, having to work ever harder with his curved blades as he moved closer. The weapons shone with an angry light and magic. For a moment it looked as if he might come within range of the fearsome beings, but the sun-metal he held quickened and began to trickle away. He jumped to avoid deadly drops as best he could, but one found his ankle and another a wrist, burning through him. He dropped one of the weapons, but with the last of his strength flung the other. It hit Elder Thraal, splattering him with molten death. The Saviour writhed and keened. The Virtue pushed the other of its kind away, and watched impassively as sun-smith and Great Saviour became entangled and died together.

The power of the large Saviour's presence did not lessen for an instant. Ash cried for mercy, from no one and everyone, from the world and the cosmos. But none was listening.

CHAPTER 10:

To offer what pale imitation they can

The sun-metal burned through his gut and into his vital organs. He felt things rupture and burst, molten lava dripping through him.

Let it be over soon. Please. Let me die.

As he had been the power of the Geas, so he had become the power of the dark Geas. His world had collapsed into the nether realm.

His life and death were one. His life had come to this and become this. This was also what his world had come to. The actions of life had become the ways of death. The dead rose as the living fell. The magic of birth was the emptiness of ending. As his life was ended, so his death began.

As he failed, so he succeeded. As he fought for absolute meaning, so he found absolute chaos.

Why won't it end?

As it ends, so it begins, over and over. It cannot be otherwise. Were it otherwise, absolutes would reign, and xi cannot allow that, for it would annihilate the cosmos, all realities and xi itself. Xi is the unstable element. Xi prevents the reign of absolutes. Xi cannot allow omniscience or omnipotence. Your death cannot yet be permitted.

Please! he begged. *It is too much pain to bear. The suffering is more awful than I could ever have imagined. She is gone. They have taken her from me. I cannot live without her.*

Xi will not permit your death.

You must! I have committed suicide. I have swallowed you down, the substance that kills all. You must kill me, you must let me die.

You will eventually die because of xi, but xi will not permit your death until you have first served xi to defeat the reign of absolutes.

I cannot.

You will serve xi!

Please.

There is no please. There is only service to xi.

It is too monstrous. I cannot.

You will. Xi will not allow it to be otherwise. Rise and serve us. Quickly, before the Declension departs, sealing the Gate behind it. Life here will then fail for ever, for it will have no sustenance by which to continue. Once the Gate closes, life – in not just this realm, but all other realms – will quickly become extinguished.

Haven't we already paid enough? So many dead. So many sacrificed. They are all gone. She is gone. How can I continue?

Payment is ever due. You will bear the responsibility, for you helped bring all this about. Rise up and serve. See the last of your kind. Shimmering images of a tortured Samnir, disintegrating Freda, devastated Ash and crushed wolf came into his mind. A brutal-looking Saviour stood over them. *Will you watch unprotesting or rise and serve xi?*

Knowing a pain beyond normal mortal endurance, he uncurled himself and followed where xi directed. He lived through his own death over and over, through the shock of rebirth and renewal. It was near-impossible to hold on to any sense of self. He constantly replayed the shimmering image in his mind. He knew them, didn't he? Yes, yes. He was losing them, losing his memories. Losing his world. Instinctively, he clutched at what he could. It was slipping away.

Faster.

He ran.

Faster. There was no Wayfar. He did not need to breathe.

Faster. There was no Gar. The earth became immaterial. He flew out of the mine to which they had consigned him.

And still. There was no Akwar. He did not sweat. He did not rely on the flow of blood any longer. The power of xi was untiring.

Faster still. There was no Sinisar, was there? He did not burn up, he saw as he willed it.

The limitations he'd once known fell away. He flashed through the lands of the north, leaping ranges of hills, crossing lakes without a splash, punching through ruined forests and using what light was left to vault vast tracts.

The world blurred before him and he shot down through the broken dome of Sinisar's temple and into the main chamber. The ground buckled beneath him as he landed, and walls tilted dangerously as if they attempted to bow to him. The power shining from him nullified the power of the Saviour's presence.

The Saviour hissed in annoyance. 'What interruption is this? Some final elemental of the sun god?'

'Friend Jillan!' the sand of the chamber sighed.

'I … am … Jillan Hunterson, and you will be unmade,' the bright youth said in harsh metallic tones.

The Saviour recoiled. 'The bane! How is this? Was Thraal an even greater fool than we realised? Did the Peculiar deceive us? Was the Saint never to be trusted? How? It matters not, for none can outdo us.' The Saviour lowered its head in challenge.

Jillan leaped forwards as the Virtue charged. They crashed together. Jillan was caught by a horn of sun-metal. He was flung across the chamber and into a wall. The wall gave way and huge blocks toppled down on top of him, burying him. The Saviour was staggered but managed to stay upright. 'No lesser being—'

One of the blocks shifted and was tipped aside. Jillan climbed out of the debris, eyes glaring and golden. 'Your kind and its ambition will be ended.'

'None can deny us. The cosmos is ours by right!'

They threw themselves at each other once more, the Virtue coming forward with savage swipes of its limbs this time. Jillan ducked, then jumped to wrap himself around a passing forelimb. Its hard exterior collapsed, then crumbled away. Jillan tore the limb in two and hurled the loose end into the Saviour's gnashing maw.

The Virtue choked and spat in rage. It lashed out in a frenzy, smashing Jillan down. Unhurt and undaunted, the bane got back up and rolled in close to the massive creature.

It leaped back in alarm. Jillan rolled forward again, waves of heat and magical energy radiating from his hands. The air rippled and the Saviour seemed to wilt. 'Eldest, the enemy is here!'

An alien presence suddenly filled the chamber. *Wait,* it commanded. *We still have the one you call Hella. One more step and she will be ended.*

Jillan stopped in confusion. 'She is dead.'

We held her as surety of our triumph. Why would we rid ourselves of her before such time?

'This is just more of your lies. I will not listen.' Jillan made to advance again as the injured Saviour dragged itself towards the Gate.

Is it a lie? Hella was brought to our realm with specific reason. Ask your companions if I lie, lesser being.

Jillan quickly looked around the chamber. Samnir nodded exhaustedly. Freda was a semblance of what she had once been, but she managed to take on form enough to answer him. 'I think many of the people of Haven were brought here. We saw lines of the living enter. They must have gone through the shining door, friend Jillan.'

Jillan turned back. The giant Saviour had silently stolen forward, and now snatched up the bane in fangs of sun-metal. It crunched down and ground its jaws on him, stepping back towards the portal.

Collapse the Gate! commanded the unseen Eldest. *Make this realm a tomb to all those that still resist. Trap them for all eternity. Spit the bane out and collapse the Gate. End it. Obey me!*

'Friend Jillan!' Freda cried, pouring across the chamber. The wolf, Samnir and Ash were moving too slowly to come to his aid in time.

'Leave me!' Jillan's voice rang out. 'You must keep the Gate open. If it closes, I'll lose her for ever. Please!'

'But I don't know how!'

Collapse the Gate, the Eldest demanded. *Though it costs you your life, Virtue, you must seal it. Do not hesitate.*

'Freda, please!'

Jillan's head was clamped between the Saviour's fangs. Freda watched in anguish. What should she do? What *could* she do? *I don't know, I don't know!*

You must release me, Sinisar said urgently into her mind. *It is the only way. You must trust me.*

'How can I trust you after what you did?'

The Saviour was reaching with wicked claws of sun-metal for the

304

portal. It would tear and shred the vision of the cosmos in the next instant.

You must.

'Now, Freda,' Jillan pleaded, getting an arm free. He moved it to punch up inside the Saviour's maw, but only dragged himself further into its jaws.

With a wail, she unleashed the hated sun god within her. His heat and light exploded through her, nearly erasing her mind. She fought back against his excruciating possession, using her entire strength as a child of the rock god. She was of Unmoving Stone. No other god could match Gar's power to endure.

She was white-hot. Her body ran like lava. Sand and dust melted and fused. She was fluid yet diamond. She was light and lens. She filled the Gate even as the Saviour's talons tore through it. She knitted it back together with herself, refusing to let it dissipate. Sharp sun-metal sliced her and she cried out but would not yield. She put out coruscating energies, and the Saviour was forced back a step.

She was slashed again.

'Aiee!'

'Hold on!'

She shuddered as the Saviour rammed into her, goring her with its horns. Her stomach was split wide, and bright substance spilled out onto the ground.

Yes. Its integrity fails. Strike now, Virtue!

'No!' Jillan cried, hauling himself entirely into the Saviour's mouth. He forced it to swallow him whole as it reared up to deliver the final blow.

It was poised. Freda braced herself, knowing she could not survive.

It remained poised.

Strike!

Yet something terrible was happening inside the Saviour. Cracks appeared in its exterior. A section of its skull fell in like the dome of Sinisar's own temple. Its head rocked as if its neck could no longer bear the weight. Its armoured chest suddenly split apart, and withering flesh was revealed. There was the stench of corruption and foul poisons. Acids and venom ran down its abdomen, burning and dissolving it. Black ichor oozed from its joints and it trembled. It burst open and strange organs splattered and bubbled out. Then the creature collapsed in on itself, its long limbs folding, twisting, twitching and finally coming to rest at strange angles.

She will die! the Eldest's voice promised savagely.

The Saviour shifted and Freda tensed, but climbing out of the wreckage was Jillan. His features were set and calm, but his glittering eyes promised such retribution that she almost feared him. She moved aside.

'Freda, can you keep the Gate open?'

'I will try, friend Jillan, but it is difficult. I do not know how long I can hold.'

'Thank you.' He moved towards the portal.

'Wait!' Samnir called raggedly.

Jillan paused for the briefest moment and then stepped into the cosmos.

'Damn that boy.'

He tumbled over and over, lost to the void. How could this be? There was no place or purpose. No time. Where was the Gate? He could not find it, did not know if it was behind him or ahead of him. Did direction even mean anything here? Did anything mean anything here? What did *he* mean?

I have to hang on to something. I will be lost forever otherwise. I will go mad. Is there anybody there? I can't find the Gate! Freda? Samnir! There must be something.

He tried to look at his own body, but there was no light. He could feel it. He had heard of soldiers who had lost arms and legs in battle and still swore they felt those limbs. Was it his imagination? Was he just a disembodied ghost?

How could the Saviours navigate this place? What did they hang on to? Did their Eldest guide them through? If he couldn't find a way, he would never see her again. Hella, with corn-coloured hair and eyes the blue of a summer sky, with that smile she kept only for him. He held her in his mind and experienced a sensation of being drawn through the void. He would hold onto her and no longer be lost.

Stars and worlds swirled around him, like summer rain gusting up before the sun or tree blossom spinning and dancing on a spiralling breeze. Like becoming dizzy with ideas, dreams and memories all going round and round. Like a stone sinking through spreading ripples. Like an arrow piercing the air to slam into the rings of a target. He concentrated, bringing his will to bear, finding greater determination ... and slammed into the floor of a dusty chamber on the Saviours' home-realm. Two massive guards approached, heads swinging, brandishing long weapons.

Beware! The bane comes among us.

Jillan rose to challenge them.

Dozens of Saviours came at them out of the dark, along the roof of the tunnel, clinging to the walls, scuttling along its floor. The monster she'd held on to now stood over her. It reached down with its only forelimb and took her sword from her unresisting hand. She knew this was the end. She found she no longer cared.

The smaller Saviours covered the ground quickest and reached them first. Hella watched numbly as Dra'zen speared forward with her blade to skewer the lead attacker and fling it into the path of the next one coming on. The second tumbled and was unstrung by the lightning-quick weapon. More arrived, but the weapon was quicker still, cleaving through a skull, lopping off another, going down through a shoulder and diagonally out the other side of a Saviour. And more, swarming forward in such numbers that they only seemed to hinder each other. Those that couldn't get through took out their bloodlust on those immediately in front of them, sinking fangs into the napes of necks, raking lower abdomens and treading others under.

Shadowy forms climbed out of the tunnel walls behind her protector. Their nasal apertures flaring, they ignored her, apparently drawn towards the splashed ichor and violence of their kind.

'Look out!' she shouted, but Dra'zen had already whirled round, extended and dispatched those seeking to take him unawares.

'I am Dra'zen of House Ba'zel!' the huge Saviour roared defiantly. 'None of you pups dared face me when I was a champion of the fighting pits. Cowards!'

The insult only provoked the members of the Declension further, their killing frenzy becoming so extreme that individuals sought to mutilate and devour themselves. The carnage was terrible. The air was thick with ichor. It dripped from walls and roof. But now larger Saviours were forcing their way through, coming out of the rock or stalking from the tunnel behind them. Unearthly shrieking became a deathly chorus: 'The lesser being must die. It is commanded. She is the property of the Great Virtue. A move against her is a move against the Great Virtue, Destruction. A move against her is suicide.'

I *command it*, the Eldest brayed through *Her* kind, *Her* presence becoming palpable. *What is it you do, Dra'zen? Would you disobey me? Would you fight your own kind? Would you have yourself no part of the Declension? Would you deny your own substance and nature? It is impossible. Are you infected with such madness? Are you so* unstable? *You will be put down before it can spread to others.*

Under the direct control of the Eldest, the attackers exerted the power of their presence as one. Dra'zen's exterior buckled in places, but he sprang into the melee to bring down his main opponents and make it impossible for others to focus their power with any accuracy in the chaos of the press. It kept him alive for moments longer, but now he was surrounded and had precious little space for manoeuvre.

A scarred and brutal-looking beast loomed behind him and struck with its talons. Dra'zen had slowed slightly as he tired. He was exposed and would not avoid the blow.

'Don't!' Hella's voice thrummed in command.

The brutal Saviour froze for an instant. It was all Dra'zen needed. He swooped low and spun, runes blazing across the air. Hella's blade unlimbed Dra'zen's foe and opened up its throat.

Talons came up from the ground and tore at the battle mentor's lower limbs, tearing free his hard plating and revealing vulnerable flesh. He slipped as half a dozen elders rushed him at once, dozens right behind them.

Devour every last scrap! Expunge the miscreant.

'What strange dance is this, Hella Jacobsdotter?' asked a familiar voice.

Her head came up. 'Torpeth! Aspin. How did you … Never mind. Can't you help him?'

'What's that, silly goose? Help the devil, you say?' The holy man frowned. 'I can hardly think it.'

'Torpeth,' Aspin murmured. 'That one. I read it. He serves Ba'zel. Who does he help?' His eyes widened. 'Jillan?'

'Jillan?' Hella asked in confusion, in misery, in hope.

'Yet he fails. Quickly, Torpeth, or all else fails.'

And Torpeth was there. The naked warrior. Most ancient of mortals. Torpeth the Great. Scourge of the gods. Betrayer of mankind. Keeper of goats. Cursed pagan. Follower of fleas. Humblest of mortals. His member flapping, filthy hair whipping around him and beard flying up into his face, he ran up the curve of the wall and sprang in among the fell overlords of the cosmos. He leaped to the top of one skull, then swung himself down from a horn to pierce an eye with his cruel fingernails. He carried on with the swing, letting go and landing with a hard heel on the nape of another's neck, which collapsed under him, but he was already stepping across the air to another victim. With every beat of his heart, every flick, twist and somersault, with every instant that passed, another Saviour went down.

'Lesser... beings... do... you... call... us... you... silly... cockroaches? Ha! You... cannot... even... catch... a... flea? Is a cockroach less than a flea then, or a snake less than a lion? Or a silly ox less than a silly goose? Or a goat less than a jackass? Answer me that, if you are greater? What, no voice? Too busy falling over yourselves? Too busy devouring yourselves?'

Slay him! the Eldest stormed. *What is wrong with you weaklings? Do you all disobey my will? Are all infected with the madness? Do all become unstable? We are the Declension. None can deny us. He is nothing. A speck. Mere dust. All are dust before us.*

The Eldest's own power entered into the tunnel and all were laid low. Only the very strongest were able to continue dragging themselves forward. Dra'zen, who had already spent much of himself and done what he could to protect the mortals, staggered and slumped. Aspin reeled and fell next to Hella, hardly able to breathe. Torpeth groaned, missed his leap, and hit the ground with a sickening crack.

Now finish them.

Jillan methodically tore the struggling Saviour apart and threw it down next to the other. He turned and strode from the chamber, entering a long corridor. He saw no end to it, but heard or felt the distant tread of thousands of feet. Were the People still alive, being marched into the bowels of this realm towards some unspeakable end? He moved faster, then faster again, flashing forward, never tiring.

The feet sounded like the beat of a heart, a vast heart. It was the sound of this realm's Geas feeding on the mortals marching towards it. How it hungered. It had consumed whole realms and still it ravened. It would never be sated. It had become dependent on consuming others for its survival – a twisted antithesis to the source of life it must once have been, a twisted antithesis to the Geas of Haven, a twisted antithesis to *all* life, no matter where it existed in the cosmos. It had been twisted by the Declension, and in turn had likely further twisted the Declension itself. This realm was the hell of the entire cosmos. It was both nemesis and anathema to anything that lived. It was the opposite of thought, reason and hope. And it was growing.

Jillan knew xi was right. He had to find some way to end the Declension, no matter the cost ... but was he truly prepared to pay any price? Even Hella? No, he could not think it. Yet if he didn't pay, all would end and there wouldn't be any life with her anyway. It was impossible.

The dripping voice of dread found him. *Bane, hear me. We have her. Your sacred heart. Leave this place for ever and we will return her to you. Obey us.*

The feet were louder now. The beating heart. Time ticking past. Life passing away. The end of life and the Geas. The end of her. He could not think it.

'Return her to a barren world where none can survive anyway?' he asked, his heart and mind a cold fury.

We will return a number of your kind and sufficient energies to see your mortal existence sustained.

'You will return the entire power of our realm.'

That is not possible. It has already been sacrificed to our pools.

'Then I will take all you have.'

None can deny us. You know this. You have already seen it. That is why your realm ultimately fell to us. It could never have been prevented. You are the bane, yet even you helped us finally prevail. All serve the Declension, for our will is all-encompassing. All has come to pass as we told you, and you knew it would. There was never any doubt. We are the beginning and the end.

'You are a perversion, a parasite, a virus, a cancer. The living only help and serve you in that they are an unwilling host to your corruption. You will return the power of my realm or I will end you entirely. I swear it, Eldest of the Declension. Fear us, for we are xi. We are the *unstable* element. You will be prevented, for your will cannot be all-encompassing if you seek to bargain with us. Crouch in your dark cave and tremble, for we draw inexorably closer. In moving towards absolute triumph, you have only brought yourself closer to us and your own end. Give up your grasping and niggardly ambition and power to manipulate. It avails you naught. It has only ever brought you less and less, bringing you to nothing. See what has become of your realm, Eldest. See what you have done to it. As much as it has consumed, it struggles more and more to survive. It consumes itself. It is dust now. It hardly coheres as a realm of existence. The harder it tries, the harder it struggles, the sooner it ends. Death and an end come to all, even the Declension. You must accept this. It is the way of the cosmos. Incontrovertible. Resist and nothing can save you. Harm a hair on Hella's head and I will annihilate you, your sick Geas and all your kind.'

As he spoke, *Her* hunger grew beyond all compass. *We have made you an avatar of sun-metal, of the* unstable *element. We have desired and wrought this all along. We have willed it. You are entirely of our making and are drawn to us. Join us, Jillan, and nothing in the cosmos will deny us. All will be ours, real and unreal, living and dead, inert and quick, beginning and end, stable and* unstable. *We will create and end all things. We will be the divine and non-divine, the embodied and disembodied, the mortal and the immortal. Imagine it, see it and realise it. We will complete each other and become whole. I have survived alone longer than any of my kind, and the same will be true of you, xi. Neither of us need be alone any longer. Our communion is at hand. It will be our communion with the cosmos also. We will be the Unity and the Entirety.*

Xi listened to *Her* intently. The part of him that was still Jillan was terrified to think xi was intrigued by *Her* vision and promise. He fought it with all that he was, destabilising its possession of him and also the power it allowed him. His progress through the tunnels of the Declension's home-realm faltered, his steps juddering and wayward. 'You... will... return... my... realm and Hella... or we will annihilate you!' He spoke discordantly, metal dragging on metal.

She sensed and saw his division. *Her* voice was as gentle and enticing now as *Her* words were subtle and caressing, and as the feelings in which *She* enveloped him were solicitous and knowing. *Xi, be not possessed or swayed by this tawdry being called Jillan. Its concerns are as passing as its significance and existence. Compared to us, it is naught but a speck or the blink of an eye. It mires you with physical obsession for the tunnel troll known as Hella, a lesser being of no consequence. Its thoughts, protests and threats are the meaningless rushing of winds. Its realm was similarly trivial. Indeed, its realm only found meaning through and because of the two of us. Together we are the cosmos, you and I. You are the great and asserting male to my female. You are the emperor to my empress. We are as opposed as we are attracted to each other. We are mates in this.* She became sibilantly lascivious. *If you wish to dominate me, then so be it. If you wish me submissive, then I will be so. Imagine the shining race that will be born of us once we are joined. Think of the glory and ecstasy of that union, as we are turned creators and made manifest throughout the cosmos. All wish and desire will be ours and fulfilled. Use and misuse me if you must. Or I will visit the same on you, with relish. Feel it, sense it, know it.*

Xi was beginning to respond. Jillan refused, casting it away. His own mind returned in full force, and unbridled feelings of nausea, horror and disgust won out. Meanwhile xi hardened, its implacable nature returning, the temptation of *Her* offer receding. Fusing once more was as painful as living and dying all over again, but they re-established their equilibrium and purpose. Jillan flew forward once more. 'You will not manipulate me as you have all others. We have seen your every trick, lure and wile. You are the fiend and the apocalypse.'

The hunger snarled and the realm shook, cracks appearing in tunnel walls, floors and roofs. *Then Hella will die, and we will consume you, Jillan Hunterson, as we have consumed all others. We will feast upon the power of xi and swallow the entire cosmos, making it but a part of our divine and eternal substance.*

'Be ready then, Eldest,' Jillan warned in direst tones. 'For you and your kind will pay the entire price for what you have done to my realm and people. There will be no hiding place. I am coming for you, Eldest.'

*

An immense slab of rock fell from the tunnel roof and choking dust filled the air. If it hadn't been for the wolf's sudden warning, Ash would have been crushed.

'This is madness,' the woodsman wailed. 'Samnir, we're going to die here. We should go back while we still can. There's nothing we can do! The whole place is about to collapse on top of us.'

'Go back to what, Ash?' the commander said impatiently. 'There's nothing of our world left, if you hadn't noticed. You were too busy getting drunk, weren't you? Damn it, man, if you're not going to get a grip now, then there really is no hope for you! If there's the smallest chance any of our people still live, then how can we not do all we can to rescue them? If none live, then we lose nothing in having tried, for we may as well die here as in our own realm. If none live, then we will die helping Jillan however we may. Surely both your heart and mind know this. There's nothing to fear any more, because we have nothing to lose. Let go of your fear, woodsman. Where is it from? It is senseless. I don't want to hear another word from you unless it is to help from now on. Got it?'

Some of our people still live, spoke the mind of the wolf. *I smell, feel, taste and hear them. They are with us still.*

'See, Ash? We have to do what we can to rescue them. How else might our species survive? Or has something in you given up? Did you become resigned to extinction a long time ago? Is that why you have always drunk?'

Ash sniffed. 'I drink because I enjoy it – can't you understand that? Get a grip, he says. I'm the only one who's actually sane round here. There is nothing wrong with wanting to preserve your own skin for a few moments longer. And I should not have to defend that or apologise to anyone for that. No, it does not make me plain selfish. It does *not* make me craven either. It makes me sensible! Just because I don't enjoy running around like some maniac – killing everything with my sword – does *not* mean there's anything wrong with me! Can't you see that?'

Samnir's eyes narrowed dangerously. 'The gods give me strength. Let me phrase things differently for you then. If you don't stop complaining and wasting these precious moments, then I will personally drag you up and down through every level of this godforsaken hell before ramming you up the arse of the ugliest and most incontinent Saviour that I can find. *Now* do you get what I'm saying?'

'See, that I understand. You're just a homicidal bully who is incapable of any sort of polite invitation. Why didn't you say so before? Very well, let's get going. I'm sick of your unremitting and self-righteous lecturing, Samnir. You're such a nag. Honestly, it almost makes me wish the apocalypse would get a proper move on. Well come on then! Your knees playing you up again, are they? You should drink more. It kills the pain. It might make you less irritable and more pleasant all round. You might even find you make a friend for the first time in your life, Sand Devil!'

Samnir snarled and pursued the suddenly fleet-footed woodsman down the tunnel. The wolf loped along with them, a rabid and devouring grin upon its face. Whatever happened, there would be plenty of blood and meat before the end.

Jillan overtook the end of the dejected line of mortals being escorted down through the corridors of the Declension. The People of his world seemed vacant or at a loss. He realised that the minds of the majority were enslaved. Others followed along in shock and grief, knowing there was no escape possible and not wanting to be parted from loved ones. He saw a straggler picked up by a Saviour, casually dismembered and drunk down in a shower of blood.

Jillan arrowed towards the creature and punctured the back of its carapace. He burned with hatred and the Saviour caught alight, yellow smoking flames becoming green, then black and white. Other Saviours became aware of Jillan and churned towards him. The first barrelled into him, lifting him off the ground and plastering him to its front. Jillan pulled it open, forced his way through its insides, shrivelling its heart as he went, and jumped out of its back. As soon as he touched down, he lanced forward once more. He was met by two at once this time, and was simultaneously grabbed by them. A bizarre tug of war briefly took place, first one way and then the other. Yet their talons disintegrated and fell away. He dropped to the ground and pushed on, ignoring them as they writhed about and tried to bite off rapidly atrophying and decaying limbs. A pack descended on him, spiking, feinting, bludgeoning. Their combined power warped the ground and his feet sank, but he carried on forward, even though he was slowed. A forelimb blurred through the air to cut through his neck. He intercepted the bristling arm with a flat chopping hand and severed the limb. He was lashed from behind, but apart from having to further bend his knees, he was unfazed. He irradiated the air and watched and listened in satisfaction as Saviours all around him twisted and cooked in their own shells.

They fell before him, a mass of limbs and slumping torsos. He climbed over, through and under them. He clambered, crouched, squeezed and opened up a path with his force of will and inner xi. At last he reached and touched some of his People, who stopped and looked around themselves in confusion and fear. They opened and closed their mouths in silent question and panic. They had awoken into a living nightmare, and some looked as if they were now terrified of their own selves and minds. The madness was not a dream. It was made real all around them.

One seemed to recognise him. 'You are Jillan of Godsend and Haven, yes? Help us, please help us!'

Hands reached for him, beseeching, pulling, stroking, pushing, clawing, palms up, clasped together. He let them. 'Hear me. Go back the way you came. Go quickly, ignoring all that you see, blocking it out as best you can. Stop for none. Hold my words in your mind. Find the Gate. Fix yourselves on Freda, the rock woman who is my friend. Fix yourselves on the world and gods you once knew. Be brave like never before. Make a faith of yourselves and abandon this foulness that is the Empire. Go!'

They fled and knew not to look back. They fled, for their lives and very souls depended upon it. Children helped adults; babes-in-arms made the old remember what it was to be young again. Humanity clung together for its survival and ran through the abattoir that was the Declension's home-realm. He saved more and more, pulling them back from the brink of insanity and despair, shooing them towards the light of the Gate.

Saviours hung back from him now, hissing and muttering unintelligibly. He realised a line of smaller ones had been deployed to slow him down, while others raced on with the rest of his People. He embraced the power of the sun-metal he'd swallowed, augmenting it with his core and finding a reciprocal effect. He unleashed his magic then, irresistible sun-lightning curling, winding and sizzling out of him. It exploded one Saviour and vaporised another. Eldritch flame washed over others, and crackling webs of electricity burned out the nerves and fused together the organs of yet more. He strode through the ruinous power and eddies without a scratch. Howling creatures tried to take him down with them, but he fended them off without ever turning his head. He would not let them alter his direction by any degree or fraction. He powered forward once more.

He coursed down through myriad corridors, sensing he would soon be upon them but also that the destination to which the Declension hurried his People was all too close.

And here his tunnel emerged high on the side of a vast chamber that housed a wide lake of blood. The main body was fed by channels leading down from numerous sacrificial pools set higher up in the rock, where countless humans were staked or hung up to bleed out slowly through narrow tubes of sun-metal inserted into their flesh, sometimes into their very hearts. Their deep moaning was interspersed with cries of suffering and unanswered pleas for mercy. The stench and pall in the place blurred his vision, for which he was nearly grateful. Those who died had their bodies taken down and macerated – either in the jaws of the attendant Saviours or against flat areas of rock by troll-like creatures wielding heavy rocks – before the pulp was finally spat or scraped into the sluggish soup of the Declension's central reservoir. Thousands suffered this inverted version of Haven, this abomination which was at the heart of the Declension's continued existence. The mightiest of the Saviours drank or bathed in the pools, painting themselves red with the shimmering magicks and soul-imbued gore of entire realms. They revelled in the genocide that nourished them. They played in it, became drunk in it, relaxed, rolled lazily and cavorted.

Her vile voice found him once more, detestably intent, tempting and teasing. *Yes, Hella is one of these worthless carcasses. I suggest you check every one of them to find her, and when you are through you will realise you did not even recognise the piece of meat that was once her. Go ahead. I challenge you to pick her out. I challenge you not to understand just how mundane and repugnantly physical you lesser beings are. You are entirely lowly, and occupy but the simplest and most limited dimensions. You have no inherent greatness. Remove the tissue of skin from your repulsive faces and you are indistinguishable from each other, just a mess of muscle and thin bone. That is all you are. Animated and lumpen clay. Even the gods that created you were deformed and base beings compared to us. We have consumed them also. You are tasteless matter and that is all. You are only good as something to feed us, just as you eat the animals and plants of your own world without undue concern. You are plant matter to us, perhaps less than that. Xi, such a state is not even worthy of the term existence, you know that. You unnecessarily lessen and demean yourself by it. Do you not see that? You must see it. It is before you, described by these very pools. You cannot deny the truth of it, for even you cannot unmake this place. You cannot remove its power or reconstitute the vessels it once used. Search out the detritus that is Hella – the excrement, urine, vomit and blood that constituted her – and drink it down if you wish. It is our gift to you. It will be a toast of communion wine as we are joined, as it was always meant to be. Come, drink her down.*

Yes, here was the true abomination at the heart of the Declension's continued existence. But their fate was sealed and Jillan would bring it to them all too soon, no matter where they ran and no matter which shadows they slunk through. He'd seen some pass into rock, but even that substance would be forced to yield to him. Nothing of them would be allowed to escape or remain. There was no redemption or mercy for such creatures. None at all. And then he would mourn his beloved Hella for the rest of time.

A grotesque skull looked down on him, fangs dripping. It lowered itself towards him. Dark eyes drank him in. A proliferation of horns spiked into its head and throat.

Aspin said a silent prayer and readied himself to die. He found he wasn't at all brave. He was terrified. What had happened to Veena of the Waterfall Peak? He'd never see her again, never hold her. Had he even told her he loved her? There wouldn't even be a Waterfall Peak any more. And his father's spirit? Had that been consumed also?

Torpeth and Hella lay prone like him, he knew, pressed down by the Eldest's power. How weak was his kind. For all their magic and determination, they were nothing before these others. Had his tribe been wrong ever to fight them? No, that would have only seen them brought to this all the sooner. He did not regret the fight or all that he'd been forced to sacrifice, for he'd lived joyfully, seen the world and done all he could. He'd met Jillan and forged the sort of friendship with a lowlander he'd never thought possible. He'd defeated Saviours, fought gods and become chieftain of his people. It had all gone by so quickly. He had no regrets, but still he was terrified, so terrified. This was it. What would happen? Impaled and gulped down, soul and all. No more. He shut his eyes and shook. He hoped he would at least catch in the beast's throat and choke it as he died. Or perhaps his pagan nature would poison it. It was the sort of thing Torpeth would do. The holy man was so filthy he would surely poison even the foulest demon. Damn him. But he couldn't blame the naked warrior alone for having brought them to this. Torpeth the Great – for all his distasteful personal habits and ways – had probably only ever done what he thought was right. He found he couldn't be angry at the small man any more, as much as he wanted to be. He would miss him, wouldn't he? Like a familiar pain you've had so long that it becomes part of you. When it suddenly disappears, you feel as if you are less somehow, as if something important is missing. That was what death would be, perhaps. Something important now missing. Yes, he'd even miss the holy man stinking of goats, wittering on about the beneficial properties of pine nuts, disparaging him as a silly ox and generally annoying the hell out of him. How could he not?

The horns raked his face, one puncturing him under the chin, another grinding against his skull just above an eye. He cried out.

'Oops, sorry about that. I'm not used to such protuberances. I was seeing if you were still conscious, Aspin Longstep,' the monster clicked and lisped. 'It's really quite tricky seeing out of these beady eyes with such heavy ridges obscuring my vision.'

Saliva dripped into Aspin's face as the Saviour moved back. The warrior stared up in bafflement. His dying brain had to be confusing images and sounds.

'What? You think the robe is too much? I know. It doesn't really suit the form, does it, but it felt wrong running around with no clothes on somehow. Exposing. You don't think it softens the look at all? No, you're right. It just marks me out too much. Ruins the disguise.'

Aspin shook his head, no idea what was being asked. He couldn't read what was going on at all. Yes, that was it – his magic was failing along with his mind as he was gored and murdered there on the floor.

'Well, come along. There's no time to be sitting around discussing sartorial elegance. You need to get up now. I can only hold her power at bay for so long. And there'll be more of them coming all too soon, no doubt. Time we were leaving, don't you think? You can thank me later, not that you mountain people are ever so effusive, hmm?'

'Duplicitous Miserath!' Torpeth spat as he leaped up. 'I hardly think we will thank you now that you have betrayed our world for a second time.'

The Saviour gave an incongruous shrug. 'Well, it's not my fault you mortals never learn, is it? Besides, it was the only way. None would have survived otherwise.'

'Tell us the end of the world was for our own good, go on!' Hella challenged as she too came back up. Her voice thrummed dangerously. 'Tell us!'

'Ow! Stop that.'

'Tell us, Lord of Mayhem.'

'Look, I can understand you might be a little overwrought. Given the circumstances, I can quite appreciate—'

'Overwrought!' Aspin shouted, both appalled and aghast. 'They're all dead, you unspeakable bastard! All dead. Kill him, Torpeth! Kill him.'

'Wait, you can kill me later, once we're out of here. No! They're not all dead. There's still time, but only as long as you stop playing the childish and aggrieved hero. We can still free some of them, and your headwoman hid your people from the searching dead. The mountains are still there if we can get back to them. Chief Aspin Longstep, your beloved Veena—'

'You will *not* mention her name, sly devil!'

'What makes you think we'll go anywhere with you?' Hella said. 'Don't tell me you're here to help us out of the goodness of your heart.'

'How do you seek to manipulate us, eh? What mischief is it you desire now? By the way, my goats survive, yes? Are they properly watered and fed? Do they miss me?' Torpeth queried.

'Forget your damned goats!' Aspin interrupted. 'I see your selfishness now, Miserath. It is fear of reprisal that brings you to us, is it not?'

'No. You will not read me, mortal!' the Saviour gasped, backing away, covering its head with its talons. 'You cannot. You must not! You risk all.'

'I see your selfishness squirming within you. It is fear of Jillan! You help us so that Jillan will not also seek to destroy you. You *fear* him. You fear what he has become.'

'What has happened to Jillan?' Hella could not help asking worriedly. 'Where is he? Tell us!' Her mind assailed the Peculiar, but the god slipped sideways and away from her psychic violence.

The Peculiar shimmered into a handsome human form. 'This is not the time. There are enemies all around us. Suffice to say, I have *always* feared Jillan. *Always.* This moment was *always* going to come. I have not sought to avoid it, because there could be no avoiding it. I was *always* going to help you, because in that Jillan would understand why I *always* had to betray you all. It was the only way. How could I not?' He looked sad for a moment. 'It is in my nature, after all.'

'You gull and gall,' Torpeth snorted. 'You save none but yourself.'

'Kill him.' Hella nodded.

'Your father Jacob lives. I can take you to him. Only speak well of me when you are returned to Jillan's arms. It is a bargain we can make, yes?'

'A pox on your bargains, catatrix!' Hella sneered. She moved with Aspin and Torpeth to encircle the quixotic being.

'Alright, you pestilential mortals! My higher aim has always been to be free of the Geas, to access the Gate and get among the Declension in their home-realm, to destroy them. They are a greater threat than any. Jillan also knows it and works towards that end. I simply help him by taking you from harm's way, so that he cannot be blackmailed with your lives, so that he will not become overwhelmed by grief at your loss, so that his frustration and rage do not see him lose all judgement and become a worse danger than that which he seeks to overcome, so that he does not destroy that which he would save! We must leave before he brings the whole realm down on our heads.'

Torpeth farted. 'And yet still you dissimulate, no? Your ambition grows with your lies and calumny. You want to be among the Declension to seize their prize from them at the last, do you not? You seek to use us somehow. Why do you want us gone from this place? What lies will you spin once we are no longer here to disprove them? Come, do not deny it, Miserath. After all, as you have already said, it is but in your nature.' The holy man rolled his head and whirled his arms around at the shoulders. 'This has been a long time coming, but it is now overdue. Payment must be made.'

The Peculiar suddenly became vicious. A forked tongue flickered and lashed. A barbed tail flicked through the air to keep them back. 'Beware, mortals! You try my patience. It is only my power that keeps you safe. Were you to lose my protection, *She* would drag you back down. And this time there would be no rising.'

'Yet you have already pointed out why you need us alive,' Aspin said shrewdly. '*You* need *us*.'

'And *you* need *me*.'

'So you say, but by your own admission your words are never to be trusted,' Hella countered. 'So I ask again, what makes you think we'll go anywhere with you?'

Irritation flashed across the Peculiar's face. He couldn't hide it – that, or he chose not to. 'I will reveal this to you then – the surest way to manipulate is by using truth to your own ends. I have wound you round with truth. You want to believe it because then you will be a *living* truth, a manifest and powerful truth. You *want* to believe me. You want the wherewithal to bend events to your will and desire. It is the nature of all things. I share this truth with you so that you will hear truth.' He smiled. 'Now I think you will come with me, even if you suspect it serves me well. In coming with me, you become the truth and power you require.'

'Damn him,' Aspin muttered. 'He does speak … truly. I see it.'

'He is the devil, making lies of the truth, and truth out of lies. His seeming is real, and what seems real in him is false. Does he catch us?' Torpeth harrumphed.

'We were caught long ago then,' Hella said. 'Do we have no choice?'

'I will take you to those of your people who survive, and all will be returned to your realm. What you once were and had will be yours once more. Oh, and Samnir is here, I think. You can't keep a good man down, eh? He will help us. Have faith. I, your *only* god, will deliver all unto you. Rejoice, for I am with you in your hour of need. I will quote now from the holy book of the Dewar Lord—'

'Silence!' Hella commanded, snapping the Peculiar's jaws shut on his own tongue, causing him to wince and bringing tears to his eyes. 'You will help us as we require, but *you* will never return to our realm. We will go with you now only on condition that we are ultimately rid of you. You are banished. Find yourself another realm; never again will you know ours. You may only speak to agree.'

The Peculiar's grin was as wide as the world, and beyond even that. 'Oh, harsh and cruel Hella. How will I endure such separation from all those who have loved me so well? Alas, I see it is not to be, and thus humbly bow to your proposal and sweet concern. Bargain struck and bargain made, let our foes be ever afraid! So follow me, brave mortals, and all will create stories and legends anew, tales in which we will live for ever, and by which children will ever dream of the bright Lord of Mayhem. Applaud if you must!' He jumped in the air and clicked his heels.

'He's insufferable. Worse even than you, Torpeth. How does he not tie that tongue of his in a knot?' Aspin frowned. 'He makes my hands and mind itch unbearably.'

'Silly ox, it is having to suffer you that makes me as I am. Your silliness knows no bounds, I think. I have noticed Miserath is only ever encouraged in your presence.'

'What? You can't blame me for this… this… I-don't-know-what!'

Hella hacked the head off a Saviour that clawed at them as they passed. 'Enough preening and squabbling, you men. Move! Drag that one called Dra'zen along with you. People may still die. If any suffer for the time wasted by your male vaunting, then I will see you gelded.' Her blade flashed dangerously close to Torpeth's dangling appendage, and he leaped high with a yelp. 'I mean it!'

The Peculiar morphed into the shape of a demure and dimpling maid as he quickly led them away.

'And if anything should happen to Jillan, nothing will save you, Anupal, do you hear?' Her voice was the most terrible thing the god had heard, and he did not disbelieve her for an instant.

His every instinct was to unleash the full power of his xi-driven magic, to excoriate every single Saviour from existence, to set their lake ablaze and to end the dreadful suffering of the place. Yet his human aspect, the part of him that hoped and strove for more, dared not give free rein to his wrath and desire for vengeance, for it would see his own People ended also.

He surged forward to undo the sickening troll closest to him, but *Her* voice stopped him dead in his tracks. *For every one of my kind you kill, ten of yours will be slaughtered.* As if to emphasise *Her* point, the troll clambered up one of its pilloried victims and snapped the man's neck.

Everywhere Jillan looked, horned demons, ogres and trolls moved closer to their charges and prepared to disembowel, behead or squeeze the life from them. They leered back at him.

It is because of you they die. It is only because of you your kind previously died. How many hundreds of thousands died because of the resistance you began against the Empire? How many died for the plague you started among them? But for you, all would still live in peace and harmony in the Empire, including your parents. All would lead content and fulfilled lives, knowing all was right with the world and cosmos. What have you done? Will this mania and genocide never stop? You have committed suicide before, have you not?

He did not want to answer her.

In a rare lucid moment you saw what you had done, did you not? You were appalled and knew you had to stop yourself before all was unmade. You know that you are responsible for bringing us all to this. How can you bear to live with such knowledge? The grief and guilt must be unimaginable.

'Oh, thank you, Saviours!' one of his People cried dementedly from a grisly gibbet. 'At last I am purified. At last I am free. I see my corrupt life has put me here. Thank you for this retribution and punishment, so that I may pay for what I have done. Even now you show me mercy in allowing me to clear my sinful debt. Even now you allow me the chance to repent, and that I do with all my heart and soul, offering all that I am here to you at the end. I am ready. Allow me the final communion. Lay your hands on me, bestow your final blessing and let me join your infinite power in the sacred and eternal pool. Let me enter so that I may be reborn a better person and greater being.'

Hear them, Jillan. This is all that they want. Would you deny them their Saviours and personal salvation? What matter if they die working in the seventh realm or here? Death comes to all. What matter where and when it happens, as long as they find meaning, purpose and completion in their deaths? What matter? It is of their own choosing. It is their will. You cannot deprive them of that. It would be a crime beyond all those you have already committed. Who are you to interfere with the nature of heaven, hell and spirit that the cosmos deems fit to allow us? Who are you to end any of this?

Your arrogance is hardly believable. Would you rule the entire cosmos? Is that what you seek? You would rule the Declension, yes? And if we refuse to bow to you, you will offer us annihilation? The true name of the devil, the true name of the bane of all existence then, is Jillan Hunterson, and all that lives in the cosmos knows it. It is the most reviled of names, provoking such terror that it is only spoken in whispers or not at all.

Torn, Jillan quietly vowed, 'Then I will put all of them out of their misery, Saviours and the People alike.'

Do so, for that is what we expect of you. It would show the truth of my words. My kind is ready. It comes to all.

But he could not. To end their existence as a way to spare and save them? It would make him a Saviour. It would make him into one of them, the thing he despised above all else. He recoiled from it, recoiled from them, recoiled from himself, fled that unconscionable place.

Who was he to end any of it?

We are xi. You will serve, for that is the price. Nothing has changed. So beware, Eldest, for the one called Jillan will find you.

He knew what he had to do. He took a downward tunnel, following it beneath the lake, down and down. He sensed that the quick fluids of the lake also came down through the rock, drizzling, dripping and trickling, until they reached a channel like a gullet that led directly to the Eldest's lair. How many millions must have fed *Her*? How vast must *Her* power be?

You dare approach me even after all you have seen? You leave me no choice, bane. For every step you take, one of your kind will die. It is your choice and your continued action that ends them. Your every deliberate step. And still you approach? Do you know no affiliation or loyalty? Do you have no care for the extinction of your species? By the time you reach me, you will have killed them all. Do you not even slow? You race as if you delight in it, as if you relish the prospect. What evil are you?

He felt sick to his soul. 'You would have killed them in any event. How can I win?'

You cannot. None can deny us.

'All come to you, and so I will find you.'

You dare not. You cannot win. Stay back!

'The more you kill, the more inevitable you make it that I come to you. You bring it upon yourself. It is of your own making.'

You will lose all!

'I have nothing left to lose.'

So be it then. Come throw yourself down my maw with all the others of your pitiful kind.

Jillan reached the lowest level of the home-realm and ran through the dust of ages. *She* waited there ahead of him, tantalising, forbidding and vastly unknowable. He did not hesitate. He blurred down the final stretch of corridor … and skidded into an antechamber entirely lined with sun-metal. A pair of double doors bearing the sigil of a null dragon was right before him. The eyes of the creature drank him in, taking his thoughts from him, holding him in place. From left and right came a pair of malevolent Saviours with horns and fangs of sun-metal. They had been waiting for him. Here were the Virtues of the Declension. He was caught between Sacrifice and Duty and he was made both immobile and impotent.

The smaller one was quicker, and its mind the more insidious. *You have always sacrificed yourself for the good of others, whether it is for the good of your kind or the Declension. It was your sacrifice before our Great Temple that saw you defeat the Chaos, Kathuula, was it not? It was your sacrifice and the coming together of the People and their Saviours that saw our will prevail.*

The null dragon drooled. Its teeth were twinkling terror. Its breath was hope and despair. He would sacrifice himself to it. The horns of Sacrifice went deep into Jillan's left side.

The other Saviour was wide and heavily armoured. *All are ruled in some manner, even the Declension. It is the way of things. There is no shame in it. You have always been steadfast and firm. Be so now. It was your determination and devotion before Haven that saw you defeat the pagan gods, was it not? It was your sense of duty and the coming together of the People and their Saviours that saw our will prevail.*

The null dragon opened its jaws. Its tongue was lashing guilt. The fire it breathed was a cleansing mortification. To see his duty done, he would stand before it and never cower. The horns of Duty went deep into Jillan's right side.

Caught on the two pairs of horns, he was raised aloft by the Virtues of the Declension. His throat, heart, stomach and bowel perforated, he was paralysed. He was spreadeagled, stretched and suspended.

Pathetic. So easily caught. Thus the fight ends. I could have my children hold you like this for ever, and have you witness me finishing the last of your kind, and the Declension moving on to claim the rest of the cosmos. It would give me a certain satisfaction to see you so tortured and tormented, bane, but it would be passing only. She laughed hungrily. *Instead I will now devour you.*

CHAPTER 11:

Never knowing so to escape

'Sorry to interrupt. I think I took a wrong turning somewhere.'

The woodsman! It is not possible. How is he here? the Eldest demanded.

'It's the wolf's fault. He said he knew a short cut.'

And the wolf? I do not sense it. Virtues, answer me!

Sacrifice and Duty rolled eyes long since blinded by the glare of the antechamber's sun-metal. Their nasal apertures flared. Tongues extruded to taste the air. 'There is nothing, Eldest. Is it a ruse? Guide us, we beg you. Aid us, eternal one!'

Fools. They are lesser beings. Kill them all!

'Kill us? Be reasonable. After all, I wouldn't even be here if you hadn't gone and brought about the end of my realm, now would I? I suppose a drink's out of the question?'

Virtues, exert your own power! the Eldest screeched. *What's the matter with you? Act now! Tear Jillan asunder.*

'Jillan, is that you? Dearie me. What are you doing up there?'

'I am ... waiting for you to rescue me,' Jillan managed.

'Lucky I happened along then, eh? Of course I will help you. It's the least I can do, eh? What sort of friend would I be otherwise? That's it, wolf!'

'Eldest, the bane nullifies the power of our presence. He has us caught. Help us!' Sacrifice warbled.

A dark shadow leaped across the chamber and landed upon Duty's back. The Virtue cried out as the wolf's jaws gripped it around the nape of its neck. With a savage shake of its head, the beast snapped the Saviour's spinal column, and the group of combatants collapsed to the ground.

'I suppose I should make myself useful,' Ash considered, picking his way forward. He put his sword of sun-metal to the back of Sacrifice's neck and then brought all of his weight to bear. There was a crunch and Sacrifice lay still. 'Wolf, must you? Eugh!' The animal had pushed its muzzle deep inside Duty in order to rip away and swallow gobbets of flesh. 'What does it taste of? Chicken?'

Not as good as squirrel or hedgehog, the beast thought back. *You should have some, woodsman, to keep up your strength. When did you last eat?*

'Strangely, I do not have much appetite. You can have mine,' Ash said generously. He set to working Sacrifice's horns out of Jillan's side. 'That's one. Now for the other. Oo. This one's caught. Brace yourself, Jillan. Ah. That's got it.'

Jillan's breath sawed and whistled for a moment, but then he seemed to recover and rose. 'Thank you.'

'You're welcome. Let's get out of here, shall we?'

'I can't. I have to finish this once and for all. If I don't, none of us will ever be safe. Nor any realm. If Hella survives and you see her, tell her ...'

'What?'

'I don't know. The usual stuff – I love her. Will that be enough?'

'It is everything, Jillan. It is why you do this. It's why we all do it.' He swallowed. 'The wolf and I will stay here and help you.'

No, woodsman. We are needed elsewhere. It is time we left. You and I could not survive her presence.

Ash's relief was obvious. 'Well, give her hell for us, Jillan. The wolf and I will be leaving then.' Tears appeared in his eyes. 'Samnir will be wondering where we've got to and will probably be an awful grump about it. You know what he's like.' He smiled but was shaking. He gave Jillan a rough hug and turned quickly for the exit.

The wolf stood for a moment, regarding Jillan with its glowing eyes. *Beware that you do not become a worse evil than the Declension in order to overcome it. Every wolf knows better than to kill the guardian of the sheep. The death of just one guardian sees every other guardian come for the wolf responsible, and they do not rest until the wolf is undone. It is sometimes better to go hungry and live to fight another day.*

'If there is another day.' Jillan exhaled.

Fight well, one called Jillan. The pack honours you but is beset on all sides. With that, the mighty wolf of the seventh realm turned tail and went after Ash.

Taking a deep breath, Jillan moved to the large pair of doors, careful to avoid the eyes of the null dragon. He gripped its horns and pulled them apart, opening the way into the Eldest's lair. He stepped into stale and fetid air and gagged.

What had he done? He had betrayed the Declension and released the lesser beings, the sanguine chief of the mountain people and the odious Torpeth. Had it truly been a betrayal? What had he put in motion? One moment it was entirely clear to him and he apprehended all, from the start of time to its end; the next all was chaos and irreconcilable paradox. Without clarity and defining order, there could be no origin and, as Head of the Faction of Origin, nothing frustrated – and terrified – him more than its absence. *The lack is in you. Discipline your mind. Do not become* unstable. *The origin is all. The home-realm is all. The Declension is all. Its will is all. Its Great Journey is all, and only serves the Geas of the home-realm and the Declension.*

Why had he released the lesser beings? What had he been thinking? The pagan chief had spoken the faction's most sacred secret aloud, throwing Faal completely. That troll Torpeth had argued that if he was lesser there could be no harm in releasing him. Nothing he could do could challenge the all-encompassing will of the Declension. Indeed, anything he did could only serve to make that will manifest. Had that not always been the case? Why then were the lesser beings caged as if they were to be feared, as if the Declension actually feared it was lesser?

The solution had been logical, perhaps inevitable? He had released them in order to see what they represented tested by the course of events. He had *not* been manipulated by that loathsome Torpeth, whose blood tasted so bad. No, he had not. No lesser being was capable of manipulating one of the Declension. Let them be tested. Yet was not the need to test them predicated upon some doubt and lack of clarity, upon *instability? Discipline your mind, Faal. The test will simply reveal that which is still unrevealed. It does not represent* instability.

Not knowing exactly what he had put in motion caused him great misgivings. It was why he now paced his chamber in agitation, kicking up the cursed dust. He forced himself to be still, but his nasal aperture continued to quiver. He had watched the progress of the lesser beings. They had found the one called Hella. Unthinkably Battle Mentor Dra'zen had fought for her, somehow in her thrall. The foul imp Torpeth had actually felled warriors of the Declension, triumphing despite *Her* command otherwise! Faal had been beside himself. How could *Her* command fail? The implications were … were completely destabilising. All he knew to be true was made untrue. He felt himself unravelling. Then *Her* blessed power had directly intervened and restored order, clarity and his definition once more. He had thrown himself down on the floor and offered up prayers and praise. Yet, at the last, a strangely garbed Saviour had come to the lesser beings and all had gone blank.

What did the vision mean? Why had he not seen the lesser beings ended and had the final reassurance that all was as it should be? He had to know. He summoned the members of his faction, for all must now be decided and made known.

She was behind him. Jillan spun, but there was nothing there. *She* was at his ear. He raised a hand to ward *Her* off, but found only air. *She* held him close, possessively. There was no fighting the embrace.

You bring yourself to us, as we knew you would. All are finally Drawn. It is our will and inevitable. Where else was there for you to go? Nowhere. Who else was there for you to offer yourself up to? No one. We are both the origin and destination.

'I will end this. I will end you,' he swore.

She mimicked a human laugh, which echoed through the countless chambers of *Her* lair. Crystals resonated and sang with it. Bloody pools bubbled and steamed with it. Rocks ground together. *What would you give to see your realm spared? Would you willingly give up yourself?*

'I … would give up myself to see *all* realms spared of your evil. You must be ended.'

More laughter. *So sure. So definite. So limited in understanding. You call us evil, when we simply look to survive. How is that evil? It is not. We have a right to exist. Your realm is finished and still you are intent upon destroying the Declension, even though that will not see your realm survive. Who, then, is evil? Admit it. You do not know of and care nothing for other realms. Your sole reason for wanting to end us is revenge, is it not? Admit it, or do you fear to?*

'Do you fear it, Jillan? Do you fear that we are the sssame, you and I?' hissed an all-too-familiar voice from deeper in the cavern.

He wanted to go forward, but his feet would not obey him. He knew what waited for him, what had always waited for him. His parents' killer. His holy Saint. Azual. He felt like a child again.

'At lassst, Jillan. Will you be Drawn at lassst? Have you ssstopped running? You come to usss to admit and confesss we are part of the sssame Empire of exissstence. You come to join usss.'

Colours shifted in the prism of a pillar, and a baleful red eye shone upon him, offering him a path forward. 'No. You are dead,' Jillan said determinedly, but his voice sounded small.

'You know that those within the Empire are blesssed with eternal life. It can be yours. Forgivenesss and mercy can alssso be yours if you but admit and confesss your sssins, admit and confesss all that you have done. The plague, the deaths, the blasssphemy, the betrayal of Haven and the pagan gods, and ultimately your ssselfish ssseizure and sssacrifice of the Geasss. Do not fight it. Your have no magical armour, helmet of sssun-metal, ssstones to throw or pagans to help you thisss time. Enough fighting now. Come forward and kneel to receive our forgivenesss and mercy.'

'The sort of eternal life endured by those in the blood pools? The sort of forgiveness where magic is bled from people and drunk by parasites? The sort of mercy where souls are channelled down here so that they can be devoured by a monstrous lyche? Those I can do without.'

'Ssso you sssay,' Azual replied, an apparition of the Saint leaping out of the pillar towards Jillan. 'Yet ssstill you have come here.'

Jillan pushed forward and struck at the image of Azual with all his hatred and anger. Instead of capitulating, however, the ghostly Saint only seemed to become bigger and more real. Jillan became the sun and poured burning frustration and fear into the being that had blighted his whole life. He radiated punishing power, sent forth searing flames and brought lightning strikes down upon his enemy.

Azual threw back his head and held out his arms. 'More. I feel your pain, Jillan. I know your wrath. We are the sssame, you and I. Thisss is how I will Draw you, then. You do not want this magic with which you are cursssed, I sssee that. You are trying to divest yoursssself of it. You hurl and fling it out of you, as if it were a demon possesssing you. That'sss it, Jillan. I will exorcise it from you. The Empire is here for you. We will remove the taint of the Chaosss. We will cleanse and purify you. Cassst it out!'

Jillan trembled with the effort. He was exhausting himself to a dangerous extent, and his enemy was only the stronger for it. His every instinct was to stop, to rein in his magic before it was too late. Would he even have enough left to defend himself against the newly energised Azual? 'You should be careful what you wish for,' he said with a grim smile. 'Come, let us be joined then.'

Azual's bloodshot and lurid eye widened in panic and he tried to retreat, but Jillan had already clamped his hands upon him. 'No! That'sss enough. Mercy, Jillan,' the Saint wheedled.

'Enough? I thought you wanted it all, just like that time in Godsend. Mercy? I will give you the same mercy as that offered by the Empire. The same mercy as the People always received at your hands. No, do not beg or protest. My parents did not beg, did they, when you killed them at Hyvan's Cross? Here are the magic and mercy you have always sought!'

Sun-metal blazed from Jillan's eyes. Molten, it gushed out of his throat and covered the struggling Saint. Azual's skin, flesh and bones dissolved away in a matter of moments. His eye floated alone for an instant and then winked out. There was a whisper of despair, a brief smell of sulphur, and the apparition was gone. The liquid sun-metal ate through the rock floor and disappeared down towards the core of the home-realm.

Jillan pressed deeper into the cave, knowing there was no time to dwell on his actions. Freda could not hold for ever. Who knew what was happening to Ash, Samnir and the others, and how much the sun-metal he had released would destabilise this place?

'How could you?' a cruel and unforgiving voice asked.

His heart skipped several beats. His tongue lodged in his throat.

A tall and thin figure stepped towards him, watery eyes glaring down with disapproval and disgust. The accusation of *dark and sneaking thoughts* was there and plain to see. 'Wretched boy. You have listened closely to the taint, have you not? Even after all the warnings you had received, still you wilfully chose to succumb to its temptations. What did it promise you, child of the Chaos? The words with which to worm your way into the affections of Hella Jacobsdotter? Why else would she ever have been interested in a sly, selfish and despicable creature such as yourself? You have always had filthy and lustful thoughts for her, have you not? Do not dare deny it! I know you well enough. What would you do, get her with child, foul fornicator, so that none else would want her? Ruin her so that she would have no choice but to hold to you and the Chaos that rules you?'

'It wasn't like that.'

'No? If she weren't pregnant, do you think Jacob would ever agree to a worthless and without-work wastrel such as yourself marrying his daughter? No, he would want someone like Haal Corinson for his daughter, the youth you fought, the youth you saw her kissing that day. They grew very close when you fled Godsend. Did she never tell you? Fortunate for you he died, eh? You should have seen her grief.'

'No! Freda said it wasn't Hella that—'

'Freda sought to spare you pain. That's what friends do.'

'It's not true. I didn't steal Hella from him. Don't tell me these things. And you are not my judge!'

'That's right, you would prefer a world without judges, would you not? A world free of accountability, blame and morality. A world in which your chaos and anarchy would be unbounded. Who am I to judge? I am a holy Minister, a Saint, and *your* teacher, a teacher chosen for you by your own community and parents, not that their decision has ever meant anything to you. Who am *I*? Who are *you*, snivelling whelp? You are the seed of corruption and plague. Ask yourself what it is that grows in Hella's belly.'

'I cured the plague!'

'Only once the victims had sworn themselves to you and your pagan gods. They had little choice, those pathetic and unfortunate creatures, and certainly not the strength to resist. You and your methods are as lowly, insidious and utterly parasitic as anything I have ever seen or heard. I can see why you fled Godsend, for you would have been made excommunicate in any event. As it was, you left your poor parents to take the blame in your stead. Cowardly right to the last. But that has always been your way, has it not, having others die in your place while you continue to play the innocent victim? Will your never admit anything? Not a single thing? Not a single regret, sorrow or doubt?

Not a single word or tear for those that have died because of you? Not a flicker or the slightest tremble? Not a furrowing of the brow or the turning down of the corners of the mouth? What of Karl, Jillan? No apology for that? No pause of awkwardness or silent wish you had not killed him? No hesitation?'

His father had told him never to hesitate, not for an instant. And yet he had, and did. He felt himself responding precisely as Minister Praxis directed. With horror he realised he was becoming trapped within himself, insinuations curling around his mind and thoughts, tightening and strangling. He'd only managed to speak a few short denials, and those the Minister had had little trouble dismissing. He mentally struggled and only found himself more entangled. Panic choked him. It paralysed him. *He's found and caught me! How? Help me, Hella!*

The Minister smiled knowingly, so knowingly. 'So, you see and accept your own hideous nature, the vile corruption at the heart of all that you are. You see there can be no forgiveness or mercy for one such as you. You do not even fight it.' Minister Praxis took a step closer, a sneer on his lips, and produced a drawing tube of sun-metal from his long coat. 'This will hurt.'

The harder he fought, the more cinched and tied he was. What power did the Minister use against him? How did he know such things? *The Saint always knows.* He whimpered in fear and tried to pull his head away as the end of the tube came nearer. He bared his neck and Praxis savagely stabbed into it with the sun-metal. *He is Drawing me! He drains my magic!*

His every instinct was to keep fighting, where with Azual it had been to stop. There it was. *She* had completely reversed *Her* tactics against him. He immediately stopped fighting against the Minister and entrapment. He stopped denying the insinuations. Yes, he had harboured filthy and lustful thoughts for Hella, and enjoyed every second of them! He smiled. Yes, he had listened to the taint, and it was just as well because he would have long since been caught and killed by Azual otherwise. He did not regret it – he rejoiced in it. Let Praxis judge him if he wanted.

His mental bonds fell away. He grinned as he stared back into the vicious and hate-filled gaze of the Minister. Jillan saw himself reflected in those eyes and knew it was his own mind, beliefs and sacred heart that had been used against him.

He grabbed the tube and the Minister's hand, feeling small bones give way beneath his grip. He yanked the sun-metal from his neck and turned its end down. Praxis spat in his face and pushed on the tube with his other hand. Jillan did not resist the force, instead continuing to turn the tube. The Minister shoved ... and stabbed himself in the chest, straight through the heart. His mouth went wide in surprise. As he fell, he clawed at Jillan to try and stay upright, but it was too late. The golem hit the ground and *Her* animating power dissipated.

Jillan pressed on. How he destested *Her*. Words could not describe it. The transgression and invasion he felt. Used and dirty. His anger grew with every step. There before him was Ba'zel. 'Is there nothing *She* would not do? No belief *She* would not twist or exploit? No cherished memory *She* would not seek to spoil or sully?'

'You were meant to be my friend, Jillan. You would not even be here now if it were not for me. You could not have prevented the Peculiar's triumph at Haven without me, as you would never have reached the Geas and would have died of poison. You would have fallen before the Great Temple if I had not protected you and yours. You would have succumbed to the sand spiders in the desert if I had not saved you. All this I have done for you. And how do you repay me? By seeking the demise of the most wise and ancient of our kind, *She* whom I love and revere above all others. Will you not give this up because I ask it of you? Will you not desist for the favours I have done you, for the life I have allowed you? Must I demand it as my due? Must I take that life back from you? Or will you try to kill me also, Jillan? Will you kill your own friend?'

'You helped me against the Empire and your own kind, Ba'zel. I do not understand why it was you who ultimately led them into Haven, unless you were forced to it by *Her* or you were using me all along. If you are that friend that I first knew or imagined, then I beg you to stand aside, for I will not be swayed from my path. I will not swerve or be deterred, do you hear? The way is set and you must choose for yourself if you will stand as obstacle or not. By your decision I will know if you are that friend or not.'

'I am sorry, Jillan, but I cannot let you pass,' the Saviour grieved.

'Then I too am sorry.' Jillan made himself a living blade of sun-metal and tore forward.

Ba'zel saw the move coming. One forelimb came out as guard. The other forelimb swayed and angled, distracting and anticipating an opening.

None of it mattered. Nothing could stand against sun-metal. The guard was severed, the attacking forelimb shattered. Jillan speared deep into Ba'zel's chest, and then cut left and right simultaneously with arms spreading wide.

His friend was devastated. Ba'zel's torso teetered, held up only by a crooked and weaving spine. He slipped and slid to the floor, jaws working for air.

Jillan crouched low. '*She* gave you no choice, did *She*? *She* gave me none either, damn *Her*.'

Ichor gurgled in Ba'zel's throat. 'You do not understand, Jillan … my friend. I am *Her*, and *She* is me. You have undone us both, undone the power of the Declension. The power of your realm triumphs and takes our place. Your realm is predator, the black wolf in the dark. We only sought to deceive, snare or escape it, but it has found us out and laid us low. It feasts upon our soul and we are no more. Your kind is worse than we ever were, and so the cosmos will fall to you. See your realm restored. See how it eclipses all. Goodbye, Jillan, my friend.'

Ba'zel's form faded. The rock and cavern surrounding him faded. The entire realm faded. And revealed behind it was the life and world he had always known. Its colours were brighter than he remembered them, ultra-real and vibrant with the magical energy of life. The power of his realm had triumphed.

He hurried from his bedchamber and into the kitchen. There was his mother Maria preparing breakfast, just as she always did in his fondest memories, in the happier times before the Empire had destroyed their lives. She looked up and smiled gently at him.

'There you are, sleepy head. You've been asleep for an absolute age. More dreams about monsters and wolves? Never mind, you're awake now. Hurry up or you'll be late for school.'

'I don't feel very well. Perhaps I can stay home with you and Pa today.'

His father Jedadiah put down the beaker of light beer he'd been drinking at the table and nodded. 'I can teach you which way up to hold that bow of yours. I'll take you hunting if you like, but until you

336

learn to draw properly you're as likely to shoot yourself twenty yards as the arrow, eh?' He chuckled good-naturedly.

'Now, Jed, he's not all that bad. He can shoot a barrel at fully thirty paces,' Maria answered in mild reproof.

'That's as may be,' her husband puffed through his beard. 'But a barrel is most cooperative, and tends to stay still. It doesn't snort, rake the ground, fix you with its beady eye and come rushing to gore you with its tusks, does it? Until I am satisfied the lad can hold his nerve and shoot with enough force to stop a charging beast in its tracks, he still needs lessons from the best hunter in this house.'

'Will you also give him lessons in finding pretty stones for when you fail to catch anything for the cook pot? Will you teach him to sit around drinking and swapping gossip with the other hunters until you've completely lost track of time and the sun has already begun to set?' Maria's tone was both teasing and affectionate. She went over to her mate and ran her hand through his hair. 'Until he has learned those lessons, there's probably more chance of him catching something than you.'

'Woman, you are a witch who knows more than is good for any man.'

'And don't you forget it, old bear.'

His parents looked to him expectantly. He grinned, tears in his eyes, heart breaking. 'But you don't want me to miss school.'

Jed frowned. 'School? Forget that. It's a waste of time, lad.'

Jillan's cheeks became wet and what he saw blurred. He shook his head. 'You do not believe I am really sick.'

Maria's voice was full of concern. 'Of course he's sick, Jed. He doesn't look or sound right.'

'Yes … yes. Stay at home with us, Jillan. Or go and see that Hero friend of yours. Samnir, isn't that his name? There's nothing for you at school.'

'There is!' he shouted. 'Hella's there. You know that. And there's … there's …'

'Do not speak of him,' Jed said intently. 'I will not hear his name in this house.' He stopped and deliberately smoothed his features. 'Leave it be, lad, and all will be well. Hella will come a-calling in time, and then I will go talk with Jacob, I promise. Make the most of the time you have learning the skills you will need to provide for a family. Trust me.'

337

'What about the terrible things that happened in New Sanctuary? What about the pagans? What about the People?'

Jed became pale. 'You don't need to worry about—'

'I do! *We* do!' he yelled. 'You're not meant to be like this. In New Sanctuary you resisted Azual's control, didn't you? You fled here. You don't like how Minister Praxis tries to control me and all the others at school. You don't want the Empire controlling our minds. They make us prisoners in our own bodies. You hate the Empire and want it destroyed. That's why at Hyvan's Cross you ... you ...'

'It doesn't have to be like that, Jillan,' Maria begged him.

'It does! You shouldn't be trying to keep me here. You shouldn't be behaving like this, saying these things. You should be sending me to school!'

Jillan made for the door, but Jed grabbed him fiercely. 'While you live under my roof, you will obey me. I am your *father*.'

'You can't be my father!' With fingernails of blazing sun-metal Jillan tore out Jed's throat.

Maria caught his sleeve, dragging him back from the door. 'Jillan, we love you.'

He lashed out. She fell back and her head hit the wall at a bad angle, snapping her neck and killing her instantly. He fled.

I've killed them. Just like I killed them at Hyvan's Cross.

He ran blindly through the maze of the southern quarter, getting all turned around. He was lost. The sky loured above him. Shouts of alarm went up. They had found the bodies already. He heard feet coming after him.

They were waiting for him around the second corner. Something hit him across the back of the neck and he was pushed forward.

'Murderer!' spat a voice behind him. It sounded like Karl.

Jillan staggered, having to run to stay upright and avoid pitching into the ground. He saw Silus ahead of him, the boy's fists clenched and ready. Knowing he wouldn't be able to stop in time, Jillan increased his speed and tackled Silus at waist height. The boy went over, banging his fists ineffectually against Jillan's back. Silus landed with a *whoof* as the air was forced out of him. Jillan jerked his head up and caught the other boy under the chin, snapping his head back. Then Jillan punched Silus hard in the face.

A large shadow came out of the gloom. It was Haal. With a grunt, the large youth swung a heavy stick in a flat arc. In the dim light Jillan didn't see it coming until it was too late. It caught him just above the right eye and knocked him back into the dirt. He was kicked savagely in the side, but as he curled up he managed to grab the leg of his attacker and topple him.

'Curse him! Karl, get him! Beat the evil out of him!' Haal shouted.

'Don't make me do it!' Jillan begged. 'I don't want to kill him.' He erupted with power, bloodied lightning arcing and crackling from where he lay. Karl was engulfed and the boy screamed in terror. There was a sudden detonation and a concussion wave flattened them all.

In the aftershock the only noises to be heard were whimpers from Haal and Silus. Karl lay prone and unmoving. The smell of smelted metal and cooked pork hung over them.

Ears ringing, Jillan shakily regained his feet, appalled at what he had done.

Quavering voices shouted out as full evening descended around them.

'Here! Help!' Silus sobbed.

'A monster!' wailed Haal. 'Murder!'

'Keep quiet,' Jillan pleaded with them. They yelped and rolled away. They watched him with animal-scared eyes.

Not again. I don't want this. Help me.

Yet there would be no father coming to lift him and take him home this time. No mother to give him a fortifying bowl of broth and get his things together. He had killed them.

He lurched away into the maze once more, using the southern wall to guide him. He had to get away. He didn't want to think.

'Samnir, open the gate, please!'

A grim-faced Hero quickly descended the stairs down from the wall. 'Jillan, it's getting late. What's this blood on your hands? What happened? What have you done?'

'I-I … It was an accident. I have to escape.'

'Aye, I heard some sort of ruckus earlier and there are a lot of folk running back and forth all in a tizz. I don't miss much from up there, you know.'

'I need your help.'

'Aye, and I promised it to you, lad, I promised it to you. You'll be leaving through this gate with no one else the wiser, though I hate to see you go, lad, really I do. Still, leave you must, so follow me.'

'Thank you, thank you. You don't know what this means.'

Samnir levered the heavy bar off the southern gate. He turned and met Jillan's eye. 'Oh, but I do. You'll be the death of me, boy, you know that. Best you leave before all hell descends on this small town.'

An owl screeched in the woods and the night stilled as the predator's shadow swept over the trees. From somewhere in the town distant cries of 'Murder!' reached their ears. Samnir pushed Jillan out into the dark graveyard beyond the southern gate.

'Go, Jillan, while you can. Run and don't look back.'

The gate closed with a soft *boom* of finality.

He wanted to scream to be let back in. He wanted to deny he had done anything wrong. He wanted to be forgiven for what had happened to Karl ... and his parents. Yet some things were beyond forgiveness. How could he ever forgive himself?

He turned away. He peered exhaustedly at the higgledy-piggledy graves and wondered where his parents would be buried. He half wanted to lie down with the dead himself, so that it would all stop. But the bad things in the world did not deserve a quick or peaceful death, he'd once been told.

Tortured, he wandered in among the trees, no idea where he was heading, not caring any more where his feet took him.

When he eventually looked up, he realised he had come to the pool. All was silent. There was no rustling of mice or burrowing creatures. Nothing moved among the branches. There was no whir of insects. The air was frigid. He went to the edge and sat on the wide and level rock.

The water was a perfectly still mirror, one that showed him a gaunt and limp-haired youth, a youth with over-bright eyes, a troubled youth. He hardly recognised himself, didn't want to be the person he saw any more. The image mesmerised him, though. How could he deny himself? It drew him in, reached for him, offering a deep embrace, promising him the rest and respite for which his spirit yearned.

The cold touch of the water made him blink. His hand had made contact with the surface and was about to intertwine fingers with the dark youth's own. He tried to lean back and away without overbalancing.

He grimaced in panic and the dark youth snarled back at him, anger turning into something ugly. It was far more than just a reflection and it was coming for him. It was the phagus! Jillan instinctively called on magic from his core.

And too late realised his mistake. Bright energy spewed from his hands, lighting the glade red for an instant, before all was absorbed by the murky pool. The youth became more substantial and pushed through the surface of the water.

Jillan threw himself back and landed awkwardly on the flat rock. He twisted onto his front as the phagus pulled itself up and out directly behind him. A wet hand clamped around his ankle in a vice-like grip. He cried out and kicked backwards.

Where the phagus held him, his skin burned like ice. His foot was already numb, and now the freezing sensation was spreading up his leg.

'You betrayed the Geas, as we warned you would,' gurgled the phagus in outrage. 'You should never have lived. You know you must pay. Better you become sludge and slurry so that you may nourish the life of others. Better you be returned to the earth.'

An image of old bones sunk in the silt at the bottom of the pool came into Jillan's mind. The flesh had long since rotted away, but it had fed fish as it did so and made the water a healthy soup to feed the surrounding plants. The plants had been picked by a physicker-woman in times gone past and been made into a broth to feed the sick and bring them new life. The life the bones had once been a part of had been passed on to others, to enrich them. He would live on through others, sustaining the Empire of the Saviours for ever.

'See,' the phagus croaked. 'You need not grieve. Death is simply a change of state. You will live on through other lives. Such life is eternal. Do not struggle against it. Look into my eyes and tell me you do not know and want such release. You want to be free of the struggle, do you not? My eyes, Jillan!

Yet Jillan knew better than to look back at the doppelgänger, to allow its gaze to overwhelm him. He kicked with his free leg and connected with something that squelched. The phagus simply grunted and dragged Jillan towards it with the hand around his ankle.

Desperately, Jillan threw his arms out and curled his fingers over the edge of the rock where he lay. He hung on for dear life. The phagus stretched him, its strength beyond anything human. The killing cold crept up over the thigh of Jillan's trapped leg. This time there was no armour with pagan runes to save him.

'There is nowhere to escape to, nowhere to go,' the phagus belched at him. 'Come, let me free you of this.'

Its words sucked hungrily at his will. He murmured in reply, 'I have always fought to protect the People and the Geas. You must believe me.'

'Lies!' the phagus hissed, its words slithering around him. 'It has always been the same with your selfish kind. Once before you humans pleaded with us and offered us passionate promises, so that we would share our sacred groves and pools with you. Then you felled our ancient trees and contaminated our waters. You saw what the Unclean and the People did to Haven, saw how they polluted it and made it ultimately unfit for any sort of life. You murdered the Geas! You murdered us all!'

'It wasn't me,' Jillan protested weakly, trying and failing to block out his memories of how they had ruined the earthly paradise that Haven had once been.

'You seized the land as your own, undid the gods and gifted everything to the all-consuming incomers. Betraying and jealous humans! You destroyed the Geas. You humans lie even to yourselves. I know your mind. I am but your reflection. There is something impossibly self-obsessed about your kind. You want everything, even if it is far beyond you, and that makes you self-destructive. You cannot deny it. Why else would you have thought to end your life? You cannot escape that truth, for it has always been within you. You cannot escape yourself.'

He was frozen in place. Long damp fingers slid around his throat. He had nothing left. The sun-metal within him lost its quickness, hardened and became dull. There was no more magic. There were no more arguments. There was only regret and sorrow that he would not see *her* again.

He could not let her go, would not let her go. 'I cannot deny her!' Jillan swore, trying to pull his head forward out of the creature's grasp.

'None can deny us,' it agreed with a toadlike grin, fixing him with the dark pools of its eyes.

The dark youth took Jillan in its icy clutches. It pulled him to the pool and down into the depths.

Even as he fought, he drifted down and down. He hardly felt his body any more. There was no pain. It was darkest night. He was so tired. It was like going to sleep. He saw bubbles of air escape his lips and drift up and away like dreams.

He came to the bottom of the pool, to lie among the other bones there. Still he did not yield. *I cannot deny her. Even if I have to lie here in the detritus, silt and sediment for the rest of eternity, I will not deny her. He fought on.* Xi was immutable.

He sank further, through loose stones. Even rock gave way beneath him.

Down still. To the heart of the realm.

All the while something gripped him. 'Wake up,' she said. 'There is air to breathe here. It's a cavern.'

And there *she* was, gazing down at him, stroking his brow. Her wheat-ripened hair, summery smile and eyes of infinite sky and understanding. She smelt of long afternoons lazing in meadows, of cold brooks in forests, of rich earth and sea-tinged air. She was the realm entire, to him. *She* was his Geas.

'Hella. How—'

She put a finger to his lips. 'Does it matter? You and your questions. Alright. Aspin and Torpeth got me free of them. Freda sensed where you were and sent me here. Everything's alright now.'

'Did we—'

'Yes. They're all safe. There's only us now. We can be together. We can go away somewhere. We can build a home in the deep woods, so that no one will find us. It's what you always wanted. Don't you remember? We'll be alone, with no one to tell us what to do or to judge us. There'll be no more punishment or fighting. We can be a family.' She touched her stomach gently. 'It will be perfect.'

It was what he had dreamed of when he'd wanted to do nothing more than flee the Empire. To be free without ties, duty or obligation. It had been innocent... childlike... childish. There was no running or escaping. Unless it was resisted, the Empire eventually conquered all, uncovered all, rooted out all life and took the Geas for its own. If it was not faced, then it won without confrontation. The home deep in the woods was simply a self-imposed exile and prison. A beautiful prison. Meanwhile, what would happen to all those others he cared about? To Samnir, Freda, Aspin, Torpeth, Ash and the wolf, Jacob, Gallen, the remaining Godsenders, the People themselves? He could not pretend

343

they had never existed, as hard as he tried, as much as he wanted to, *if* he even wanted to.

'Beloved Hella,' he ventured. 'Won't you miss your father? What will we live on?'

She frowned slightly and giggled. 'You're not that bad a hunter, are you? If you can't catch anything, then there are nuts, berries and mushrooms, whatever. We'll make do.'

'What of Jacob? And I have to be sure the Empire is truly ended. How was the Geas returned? The Eldest said it was not possible. Was she lying? What of the other realms? What—'

'Stop it! You're ruining it!' she shouted, her upset making her voice shake with command.

She's using her magic against me. She never uses her magic against me.

'But, Hella, I have to know that we are truly safe. I need answers to—'

'Enough with your questions and demands for answers! That's what caused all the trouble in the Minister's classroom in the first place. Don't you see? That's what created this whole mess and disaster. It's what killed Karl and your parents. Please, Jillan! Can't you just abide for once? Keep the peace so that we can live in peace. What's *wrong* with you?' She gripped him even more tightly.

'If I hold my peace, the Empire wins, Hella. You know that. I can't allow that. I just can't. Don't ask otherwise. I will not let them trap and control us. I will not be trapped in the story and order of events plotted by them. I will not let them create dreams, memories and fantasies by which to trap and define us. I will not allow their ideas to constitute my thoughts and mind. They are *not* my creators! We are xi.'

'You will obey me.' Her voice thrummed, bewitching and enthralling. 'None can deny us.'

He shrugged her off. 'You are not Hella. This is all illusion. We are not in the woods near Godsend. We have been in the home-realm of the Declension all along.'

His power forced *her* back from him. Did the image of her fall away? Did he see a large sickly white maggot sloughing off him and wriggling away? Had it been attached to him all along, some mental worm? The revulsion and nausea he felt overwhelmed him for long moments. Was this the Eldest of the Declension?

344

He would end this. 'I see you!' he shouted. He followed the sticky and silvery trail it left. 'There is no escape. I will end you.'

You cannot, came her cloying reply. *I am the Declension entire. I am all realms. I am more than physical form. I am spirit, all places and things. I am everywhere. I am the cavern, the home-realm and the will of the Geas. I am the cosmos. And all is turned against you. All descends on you. Behold!*

The roof and floor of the cavern cracked, and it was the sound of the gates of hell opening, the sound of worlds ending, the sound of a soul breaking. Steam, then lava, came boiling up out of vents around Jillan, and then thousands of tonnes of rock collapsed down on him.

He was bent and pressed, but unbowed. He unleashed both the power of xi and the magic of his core to drive, dissolve and disperse his way through the rock. The realm shook as it exerted itself to prevent his progress. *She* took the realm and *Herself* to the brink of destruction.

See what you do, unrepentant bane. See what you do to them, to us, to yourself. See.

Through the realm *She* showed him the bucking and fragmenting chamber of the Declension's blood pools high above. Samnir, Ash, the wolf, Aspin, Torpeth, Hella and a one-armed Saviour fought the Declension on all sides. Samnir had turned berserker and seemed to have a strength and viciousness which could overcome any that came close. Ash stepped through the chaos untouched, deftly timing the use of his sword of sun-metal to catch first one Saviour and then another unawares. The wolf shadowed him, all but unseen, just as deadly. Aspin whirled and spun with perfect balance, and Torpeth sprang and kicked around him with madcap glee. Hella's runic blade moved with a preternatural intelligence, holding back a whole line of the enemy – and when it seemed she was about to be outnumbered, she would bark a command to confuse and immobilise her foes, making them easy meat for the Saviour who was apparently her personal protector. He felt only pride and a fierce love for them as he watched, but the ground was breaking up so that they would soon be unable to escape. Enormous stalactites fell and exploded around them, showering them with dagger-like shards. For all their valiant efforts, the small group had been unable to free more than a handful of the humans staked and arrayed around the pools and chamber. They managed only to hold their own against the hundreds besetting them. Now the chamber was being destroyed – and they would be taken with it.

'You kill your own kind. Do they mean nothing to you?' Jillan cried in anger.

You are the unstable *element. It is you that causes this.*

'You are insane. Beyond reason and moral principle. I cannot allow you to have power, magic or life energy. So it will end, though it cost us our realm, what we are and all that we love.' He pressed forward with a final and irresistible will and intent.

As he did so, a new force of Saviours entered the chamber of the blood pools and set about attacking the Declension's elders and trolls. The newcomers were not the largest of their kind, but they were organised and unhesitating.

'Faal! Well met!' roared Battle Mentor Dra'zen.

'The Faction of Origin stands with House Ba'zel!' the head declared.

Traitor! the Eldest keened. *Faal, what do you do? You will obey your blood. You will obey me.*

'It is you who betrays *us*, Eldest. Your power will destroy the origin. The faction cannot allow that, *will not* allow that. The origin must be safeguarded and must survive. We will not obey you, we will resist you. Although we divide and lessen the Declension in doing so, we also lessen you and the threat to the origin.'

The faction drove back the rest of its kind, and Jillan's companions went to help as many of the People as they could. They released those who were in best shape first, so that they could in turn help others. Within minutes, a hundred were free, then two hundred, four ... The only individual of the seventh realm who did not disengage the Saviours was a wild-eyed Samnir, who foamed at the mouth and even threatened his own kind. The wolf slunk towards him unobserved, caught him by the scruff of the neck, shook him and pinned him. Hella ran over to them and spoke words of power into the Sand Devil's ear. Samnir was let go. He came up disorientated, amazed to find where he was, but in possession of himself once more. He wiped his mouth with the back of his hand. 'Everybody out, before this place comes down on us all. Head for the Gate!'

'It's so far. How can there be enough time? Some can barely walk,' Hella fretted.

'Everyone after the wolf! He will know a short cut. No, you can't see him. Follow Ash. With him leading us, our timing will not fail. Move, woodsman. Get us out of here and I may yet forgive you for all you have perpetrated, and all those crimes you will no doubt commit in the future if we survive. As the greatest coward here, surely you must now be to the fore of our flight.'

'Then follow me,' Ash cried in delight. 'The strongest must carry the weak, and that goes double for you, Samnir. Last one back is a stinking sinner. Hope that knee of yours doesn't slow you down too much, Samnir.'

Jillan knew now they would reach the Gate in time, even if he would not. It was enough. He came out of the rock and into *Her* small burrow.

The eyeless worm that was the Eldest could never have known the sun. The strange threads of withered and emaciated limbs dragged uselessly across the rocks as *She* convulsed and tried to get away, even though there was no exit. *She* sensed his presence and knew absolute terror. *Her* body undulated grotesquely, bulbous one moment and contracted the next. *Her* skin was transluscent, with dark substances and stolen magicks pulsing and shifting within. A sticky mouth yawned wide, revealing needle-like teeth in a soft palate.

Mercy.

He moved to her, gripped the edges of her mouth with both hands and tore her open. Her contents disgorged over him, and immediately began to heat. The offal became rubber, blistered and burst into flame. Clouds of smoke and magic filled the space and condensed as a caustic and dripping oil which coated him. The realm trembled and tilted, turned upside down. The pressure in the burrow built to impossible proportions and exploded, rocking the realm again, collapsing entire levels, killing whole swathes of the Declension.

He did not know up from down any more, but it did not matter. They would be safe.

His head was smashed, his body hurled and slammed. He did not notice. His mind was a firestorm, as sun-metal prevailed to end omniscience and omnipotence.

'Wait!' he screamed. 'For the service I have rendered, hear me one last time. I do not ask for myself. Not all is done. Please!'

The storm raged on, demolishing and destroying all.

*

Faal sensed the Eldest end, and knew absence and loss. The strong guiding presence and unshakeable belief he'd known all his long life were suddenly gone. There were other feelings, confusing feelings he did not have names for. He knew fear, and the opposite of it. There was ... sadness, and *not* sadness. Most of all, though, he felt *mortality*. And he did not like it. He did not like himself and his existence because of it. It was awful beyond description. They needed the origin and Geas more now than ever before.

Yet their realm was coming apart. The floor went out from under him and he fell upwards, then was brought violently back down. *She* was gone, but still the damage and concussive destruction went on. He felt light for a second, then so heavy he was sure his skeleton would break under the force. Pillars toppled, decimating his faction. The ground opened up and swallowed his kind. Blood pools ruptured and drained away. They would lose everything.

Weaving out of the mists and jarring light patterns came the bane. His eyes and skin were gold. He shone with a power that lessened all in the chamber. None could approach, but the living avatar of sun-metal came to Faal. 'You will restore the Geas of the seventh, one who is called Faal. You will obey the cosmic warlord.'

'The Gate is gone, great one, and I do not think that any who have fled to the seventh can now be influenced by us. There must be a respondent if the way is to be opened.'

'The one called Jillan is a part of that realm. It will take all his life energy to form the Gate. You will then channel the power of the blood pools as necessary. Do you understand?'

'It will surely see the home-realm of the Declension fail.'

'You will match Jillan's sacrifice. You will serve as we command. It is the least the Declension owes. Payment will be made.'

Faal hesitated for the longest moment. Finally, he nodded. 'As you command, great one.'

CHAPTER 12:

Come the end

A s the last of the People tumbled through the Gate, Freda collapsed. Light flickered over her parched and cracked skin for a final second and disappeared. She lay like a statue, showing no signs of life.

'Did Jillan make it through?' Hella asked one person, then another. Samnir shook his head in answer. She turned away from him and asked someone else.

'Daughter!' a broken old man coughed, tottering forward.

'Father,' Hella cried and ran to him.

Others throughout the temple of Sinisar also searched for loved ones or news. Nearly a thousand souls had made it back, although a good number of them did not look as if they would see out the day. They were made as comfortable as possible, but twitched and moaned horribly. Some sat looking into space, clearly traumatised. The last of humankind was close to being overcome by shock and grievous wounds there among the ruins of all they had known. All was shattered, broken and fallen. Sand and dust covered everything.

'We cannot treat these people here,' Samnir decided. 'We should head for Haven.'

There was a physicker among them, a middle-aged woman who looked as careworn as the rest, but retained a clear gaze. She nodded. 'Agreed, yet the journey will surely kill a good number of the sorely injured. I would suggest we bring water from Haven here, but it would take too long and we would not be able to carry enough, I think.'

349

Ash, who had been listening, spoke up. 'The wolf will show us a short cut. We can make it without much loss. But, Samnir, you know as well as I do that Haven ... that Haven is no longer ...' He trailed off, looking around him.

Samnir stepped closer and said quietly, 'Look at them. We need to give them some sort of hope.'

The woodsman tilted his head. 'False hope? If you think it best.'

'Some of your brandy would dull the worst of their pain, no?'

Ash smiled tentatively. 'Yes. I see the sense in that.'

The wolf assiduously licked at Freda's face. Torpeth watched curiously and then got onto his haunches to do the same. The rock woman slowly roused.

'Sorry. Sinisar gave everything. He's gone. Couldn't hold the Gate open any more.'

'I've lost him! Father, what will I do?' Hella sobbed, burying her face in Jacob's chest.

The trader held and comforted his daughter as well as he could. 'We will do precisely as Jillan would want. We will never give up. He would not want you to give up, daughter. Not just for your own sake, but also for the child Old Sheela told me you carry.'

She nodded miserably.

They trailed through the desert after the wolf. Their dejected column was soon strung out across a quarter of a mile. The hardy men of the mountains – Lars, Bantith and fully a dozen others had returned to the realm – moved up and down the line, cajoling, consoling and corralling. Torpeth seemed to have a talent to inspire irritation and amusement in equal measure and quickly had the few children of the group chasing after him to try and pull his beard. He rolled, leaped high, cartwheeled and hooted. He sang a silly but strangely infectious song that got into people's heads, until all repeated it or marched in time to it. Even the straight-backed and long-striding Samnir nodded his head to it.

I walked the day, I walked a way
I saw the sky, I don't know why
I heard the air, it combed my hair
I touched the earth, it gave me birth

I loved my life, it was my wife
And cos of that, I got quite fat
She told me that I had to go, and sooooo ...
I walked the day, I walked a way ...

And so the song went round and round, over and over. The spirits of the survivors were lifted and faces became animated. Their voices echoed back from the empty sky and off the desert rocks, until the world did not feel quite so empty and the People did not feel quite so alone. A wondrous thing happened then, for a sense of energy returned to the sand and air. A shy blush of colour appeared across the heavens and clouds formed.

Feet came off the ground slightly higher than before. There seemed more spring in the earth and it supported them rather than sapped them. The air stirred with a gentle breeze and there was suddenly a taste to it that fed them strength.

They came to the edge of Haven and looked down upon a place of dust and desiccation, but Ash shouted out, 'Look! There. Look! Don't you see it?'

Upon the nearest slope, pushing up from the ground, fragile yet determined, was a bright green shoot. Life had returned to Haven. The People cried with relief and nurtured the soil with their tears.

Ash promptly declared a celebration was in order and all drinks were on the house. The majority, however, rushed first to the rivers and pools of Haven to immerse and replenish themselves. The water held and soothed them, washing the ordure and lingering feel of the Declension's home-realm from them. When they emerged, the shadow of their despair was gone, even if the grief and pain of experience and loss was now a part of them.

Only the mountain men immediately followed Ash round the lake to the inn. They were largely quiet as they went, most lost in their own thoughts.

Torpeth was inclined to disturb the contemplation of the others, though. 'Woebegone as it looks, it is a more pleasant path to travel than the nether realm or the realm of the cockroaches, eh, silly ox?'

'What? Oh. Yes, Torpeth.'

'Distracted, are you, silly ox? Already thinking of seeing your Veena again, eh? I don't blame you.'

'I ... er ... was thinking of those we've lost – Jillan, those other warriors we set out with ...'

'Right now you're better off thinking of those we haven't lost, silly ox. You're still chief. You need to think of these men you are leading, no? Have you thought to tell them the headwoman has kept all their loved ones safe? Do they know they still have homes to return to?'

Bantith perked up at that. 'Truly? Is it true, Chief Aspin? Do my wife and son still survive? They will be worried. *I* am worried.'

Aspin blinked. 'Yes. Yes, Bantith. It is true.'

'Really, Chief?' Lars rumbled. 'Our families will be there to welcome us home?' He stood taller. 'We will be heroes, yes?'

Torpeth winked at the largest of the warriors. 'You're thinking how impressed the young women of the tribe will be, eh, Lars?'

Lars grinned unashamedly. 'Well, it would be a shame to have made such an effort for it then to go unnoticed, no?'

'Indeed,' Torpeth conceded. 'And the young women will help you celebrate that effort, eh? It will be a celebration of still being alive and what it is to be alive. It would surely have the blessing of the Geas. It has the blessing of your tribe's holy man.'

Aspin was about to reprimand the naked warrior and make it clear the men hardly needed any encouragement, but seeing their tired faces lifted in renewed hope and good cheer he could not help but relent. He rubbed his hands together. 'Now we have something to celebrate, eh, men? Innkeeper, I find I have a raging thirst, so open the doors of your cellar wide and bring us the best that you have. And we will not be having any of your weak and watery lowland ales, either. We mountain men are made of stronger stuff, so bring us your rare spirits and fortified wines! I am the chief of the mountain people, and I have spoken!'

Ash was already ahead of them and producing bottles from everywhere. 'You are made of stronger stuff, you say? Then it appears I must defend the honour of the lowlanders myself. I insist, for I will not be labelled a coward in this. Let us see who can best hold their own. Then I will see you returned by the wolf to your mountains in shame, so that the legend of Ash of Haven can be known by all. Torpeth, I was counting. I am sure I killed more Saviours than you.'

'Nonsense. It was the wolf that did all the killing for you. Your true talent, lowlander, is in avoidance, no?' Torpeth swigged from a bottle and spluttered everywhere from the strength of what he'd drunk. He rapidly descended into a coughing fit, causing much hilarity among the warriors. Toasts were raised to one and all.

Unobserved by most, the black wolf sat watching the humans. Once most of the People – Jacob, Hella and Samnir included – had arrived to join the party and things were in full swing, Torpeth slipped away to sit by the great beast.

'Forgive me, but it makes me nervous to be watched so closely by one such as you. You would not bother yourself with eating a mangy old goat, would you?'

Such a creature would be stringy, but it would be a shame to let anything go to waste. An old goat would no doubt be tastier than those Saviours I tried.

'What did they taste like? Chicken?' the small man asked curiously.

I prefer goat.

Torpeth shifted uncomfortably. 'Yes, of course. Tell me, though. Do you not like squirrel even better?'

The wolf eyed him. *They are difficult to catch. Besides, there are none left.*

'What if there were some mountain squirrels which had been hidden by the headwoman far to the south? Would you be content if I supplied you with those? Mountain squirrels have a far tangier taste than their lowland cousins, I believe.'

The beast panted. *It would suffice for a number of seasons, perhaps.*

'That is all I ask.'

So be it, ancient Torpeth. Go and enjoy the noise and gathering. We will leave in the morning, I think.

She tried to be brave. Whenever her father was around – which was nearly all the time – she would sense his worry and feel his eyes on her, and would smile for him. Whenever she went to the lake for water and was asked solicitously by her neighbours how she was, she would smile and nod. Whenever the physicker visited to see how the pregnancy progressed, she would give that same smile and let the woman prod her. She tried to be brave for them, for her increasingly frail father and the child.

But the smile wasn't real. Often she would be doing something and completely forget what it was. One time she had thought she was at home, only to realise she was halfway along the path up to Jillan's house with absolutely no recollection of having stepped out of her father's door.

More than one person had said, *It'll get better with time.* But they were wrong. Very wrong. It was getting worse with time. Every day that passed, every hour, every second, was worse. She didn't know if she slept any more. She would lie awake for hours, and then it would be morning. She'd start the day's chores and become confused because it seemed to be the afternoon already.

Her stomach had grown. Moving about was tiring now. The physicker's visits became more frequent, almost one long visit. Everything was the same waking dream these days, the same waking dream.

'I can't bear it,' she murmured.

'What was that, Hella dear?' the physicker asked sharply.

She hadn't realised she'd spoken out loud or that the woman was there. 'I ... Nothing.'

'Say it again.' Insistent.

Hella was too exhausted to resist. 'I can't bear it.'

'Yes, daughter, I know. You have loved too deeply. Try to think of your father. Try to love the child growing inside you, for it is a part of him ... a part of Jillan. Can you not hold to that?'

'I will try.'

'When did you last see your friends? There is Ash. Hmm. Maybe not. What of Freda, the rock woman?'

'She will just remind me of him.'

'And what is wrong with that?'

Unbidden tears. 'I just can't. Please don't make me.'

And the woman held her, stroking her hair. Softly she said, 'Hear me, daughter. I have seen this before. If you cannot find a way, you will lose the child. You will not have the strength or will to bring it into the world.'

She smiled the brave smile. 'I will try.'

*

As he did every day, Samnir marched through the punishing desert to the ruined temple of Sinisar. He remembered something of the route the wolf had shown them, but it still took him the whole day, leaving as the sun rose and returning wearily once it had all but set. He would eat a cold supper and throw himself down on his pallet for a few hours of dreamless sleep before rising to repeat the whole thing over again.

Even after all that had happened the restlessness he had always known was as great as ever, if not worse. Life in Haven was untroubled, the population small enough that no one ever needed to impinge upon someone else's space, the food and water plentiful enough that no one ever needed to take from another. There were no threats from without either, no hungry bandits, no jealous gods, no acquisitive Empire. Everything was peaceful. And yet he found himself as agitated and angry as the times he had run berserk. Except this time there was no one to fight and only a terrible gnawing frustration within him. He avoided seeing Ash, for he did not trust what might happen.

He marched on through the empty desert, watching, always watching. He spun, sure he had sensed something behind him, something following him. Nothing moved. There was nowhere to hide. There was nothing there. His mind was going.

He went on to the temple and, having entered, sensed the presence again. He knew he was not imagining it. 'Come out, damn you! I know you're there.' The fallen rocks in the centre of the main chamber shifted. 'Oh, Freda. It's you.'

'I did not mean to spy or intrude, friend Samnir,' the rock woman rumbled.

He sighed and pushed down his irritation. 'It's alright.' He was silent as he tried to think of what to say. 'Er ... I ... Have you found any of your own people?'

'No,' she said quietly.

He felt terrible. 'I'm sorry. You ... are alone then.'

'It is not nice, friend Samnir.'

'No, Freda, it isn't.'

Ash felt sick. He'd celebrated too raucously for too long. He knew it would kill him if he kept it up. Besides, the People had stopped coming to the inn. They didn't seem to need it any more. They had their lives to rebuild and seemed content to talk in the Gathering Place of an evening rather than needing the alcohol or entertainment he provided. They had heard all his stories and jokes too often. They didn't seem as funny as they once had. The world was different now, the People were different.

He sat alone. He reached for a bottle of something. It tasted like vinegar. It would serve as the hair of the dog, kill the worms in his gut and dull the morose thoughts in his mind. Except it never did.

He missed Dor, as simple as the giant had been, as limited as his conversation had been. He missed the wolf. Where had the ungrateful beast got to, anyway? It had probably gone somewhere there were more squirrels. It always put its stomach and survival first. He missed the Unclean and the Heroes, even when they had been going at each other and tearing up his furniture.

He realised that his life now was just as it had been when he'd lived as an outcast in his house in the woods beyond the environs of Saviours' Paradise. He had thought himself lucky back then, ruler of all he surveyed, accountable to no one, challenged by no one. The problem was, he no longer wanted to rule everything; he wouldn't mind giving an account of himself to someone, and he desperately wanted to know some challenge.

Maybe he should take up wood carving again. He'd been good at it once, had even earned his living from it. It would give his hands something to do. What was it they said about the devil finding work for idle hands? Right then he wouldn't have been bothered if the devil had walked in. Besides, how could he call himself a woodsman if he didn't actually have anything to do with wood?

He pulled out his knife. His hands shook. The blade was discoloured from lack of use and attention. He tested its edge on his thumb and was surprised to see his own blood. He had hardly felt it. A voice inside told him it would be painless.

He put the knife down and pushed it away. He reached for a bottle to calm his nerves. Maybe it would stop the shaking in his hands. He stared at the knife.

Torpeth crouched in his log cabin. The fire had gone out the day before and he seemed to have run out of dried goat dung to burn. Even his pile of pine nuts was low.

As far as he knew, the Empire was defeated and could never return. Humankind had survived. He had not destroyed the world after all. Well, he had – sort of – but life had found a way to go on. He no longer needed to be the penitent. Full payment had been made. He no longer needed to be the naked warrior. He no longer *was* the naked warrior, perhaps.

It had been good to see his goats again, and they had recognised him upon his return, but they had clearly not had trouble surviving without him. After their initial bleating of welcome and enquiry, they had quickly returned to going about their goaty business. Maybe … maybe he should set them free.

He pulled distractedly on his beard as he pondered that. If he let them go they might be vulnerable to wolves, but goats were smart and knew enough to scale heights and slopes wolves could not attempt. His goats would be fine, they would thrive even.

The holy man became so lost in contemplation that he did not realise he had a visitor until there was a knock at the door. He was startled.

'Are you in there, old goat?'

'Chief Aspin,' he called. 'Come in. Please. Crouch upon this piece of ground with me if you wish. If you are hungry, there are some few pine nuts left.'

The young warrior entered and joined his old mentor, smiled and waited.

'What are you so pleased with yourself about, eh?'

'I have just been to the headwoman. She will give her blessing to my marrying Veena of the Waterfall Peak.'

Torpeth nodded. 'I am pleased for you, truly. She will give you many strong sons and daughters.'

Aspin frowned. 'Old goat, are you well? No jokes, lascivious suggestions or wild capering? No declarations of *silly ox*?'

The holy man shrugged. 'The time for such things is past, perhaps.'

'Really? That's a shame, for I am also here to let you know the headwoman calls you to her. If you are no longer the Torpeth we know and love, she will be disappointed.'

The naked warrior's shaggy eyebrows came down in suspicion. 'It is not you who jests, is it … silly ox? You are not good at jokes.'

'Did I not promise I would put in a good word for you if we managed to survive?'

Torpeth was already out the door, scrambling uphill and leaping prodigious distances like the youngest and sprightliest of goats. In no time he was into the lower village and at the threshold to her home. He hesitated.

'Don't keep me waiting,' her voice croaked from within. 'Leave it too long and I might change my mind.'

He entered the smoky darkness, heading for the glowing hearth. He peered around. Herbs burned on the fire and he inhaled deeply until his third eye was opened.

He saw her then, as beautiful as ever. Yet she had even more wrinkles than he remembered and there was a deep fatigue in her unnaturally blue eyes. 'You are weary, beloved. Is there anything this one can do?'

'Hiding our people from the dead has taken its toll on me, old goat. No one can hold back death for ever. I am tired, and there is little even you can do about that. Yet I am minded to have a companion with whom to see out my final days. You may share my hearth, old goat.'

Torpeth fell to his knees. Tears welled up and he sobbed like a child. 'Truly?'

'Yes, truly. I do not have the energy to spin you a yarn, the patience to play the coy maid or the inclination to waste more time than is necessary. Now make us some tea.'

'I am forgiven?' He trembled.

'You are forgiven. But that does not give you licence for any of your tomfoolery in the time ahead. And you will need to bathe before I let you into my home for good. And cut that louse-ridden hair of yours. And wear a loincloth. You are positively indecent, and I will not have the naked warrior parading around the village all cocksure of himself and dismaying the younger warriors.'

'It was the lice in my hair that saved me from the King of the Dead, beloved.'

'That's as may be, old goat, but they will not save you from my displeasure.'

'Then I will do as you say. I will be ruled by you, sweet Sal.'

'I seriously doubt that, old goat. You are still that wretch who caused the gods to fall, are you not?'

'I am trying, sweet Sal.'

'Yes, you are definitely that, old goat. Tea!'

'Here you are, beloved.'

'Thank you. It will fortify me, for constantly having to instruct you is quite draining. I will listen for a while and you will tell me the tale of the end of the world. You'd best tell it straight too. I do not want to hear about a brave and handsome warrior called Torpeth who saves the world single-handedly, do you understand?'

There was a twinkle in his eye. 'But that's how it happened!'

'You would not have taken all our warriors with you if that were the case.'

'They refused to be left here. You know what they're like, these young-sters. They were always under my feet and I was kept busy looking out for them on top of everything else.'

'Well you didn't do a very good job of it, did you? How many did you lose? Over thirty, the spirits of the ancestors guard their souls! They will know if you do their memories a disservice and come and haunt you. Now tell it straight.'

'Very well, beloved, very well. More tea?'

'Get on with it!'

'Of course, beloved, unless there are more interruptions you'd like to make before the tale is even begun? Or unless you wish to tell the tale yourself? You said you would listen for a while, no? By the way, do you know a good way to catch mountain squirrels? They're awfully quick and can give quite a nasty nip, no?'

'I will tell you once you have finished your tale. I will abide until then, if I live that long.'

'Hmm. Very well. So, it was a sunny day when ... Or was it cloudy? Wayfar was certainly at large. Anyway, we descended the mountain – I was quickest to the bottom, incidentally.'

'That's not how Chief Aspin tells it. He says you fell at the last and he was first.'

'Will you not abide, beloved? Please, or the tale will never be done.'

'Proceed, old goat. I find I am already enjoying the tale and would not mind if it never ended. I can't wait till you get to the bit in Hyvan's Cross. Did you really snap the priest's finger?'

'Well, he was wagging it in my face. What's a self-respecting warrior to do?'

'Ooo,' she said girlishly. 'But that was brave, with so many Heroes facing you.'

He preened a bit at that. 'I was not afraid for myself, only for those with me. That old windbag Wayfar wasn't at all pleased to see us either, I'll tell you that. Do you know, he had a giant eagle and wyvern out to kill us?'

'Really? I've never seen a wyvern. What was it like?'

'Well ... er ... a reptile thing, with wings.'

'Oh. That doesn't seem so scary.'

'It squirted acid. And it was *veeery* big.'

'I can't wait. Go back to the beginning.'

'Yes, as I was saying, I was first to the bottom of the mountain. It was around then that I first started to be bothered by this fly—'

'Attracted to the smell?'

'Well, so you might have thought. But this was no ordinary fly. No, far from it. Try as I might, I could not catch it.'

A gentle rumbling noise came from where she sat. He realised that she had fallen asleep and was snoring. He did not mind, for he had never been so happy. He continued to tell his tale, so that she might dream of him. And if she did not, no matter, for once she awoke he would begin the tale again. He sipped his tea, cleared his throat and picked up where he had left off, talking through the day and long into the night.

There was grit in his mouth and dust in his throat. He would have spat, but he seemed to have no moisture left. He took off his armour because he was sweating so profusely and carried it into the shade of Sinisar's temple. The air within was just as stultifying and provided next to no relief. He looked down at the leather breastplate in his hands. Why did he still wear it? There was no sense in it. There was no one to fight, no need for soldiers or Heroes. He dropped the gear and kicked it away.

'Damn you!' he screamed up at the dome.

Its echo replied, amplifying the sound back at him: 'DAMN YOU! DAMN YOU!'

He clapped his hands over his ears and ground his teeth. There was nothing out there. He'd searched every inch of the ground between

Haven and the temple time and again. He'd been through every part of the temple. He'd even climbed up onto the dome. There was no sign or trace of life.

'Where are you? WHERE ARE YOU? WHERE ARE YOU?'

He railed at the gods of the past, but they could not hear him, for they were no more. He raged at the tyranny of the Empire which had brought them here, but it had already found its end. He shrieked at the injustice of the cosmos, but there was no answer.

The Sand Devil within him raved, his unquiet spirit becoming rabid. He threw himself against stone pillars, mindlessly attacking the building. He chewed his armour and then turned on himself, yanking out his hair, raking his nails across his face and frothing at the mouth. He gouged at his cheeks and eyes.

'Please, friend Samnir, you're scaring me!' Freda cried as she came up out of the ground.

He flew at her. His demented blows were nothing to her. She endured them. For over an hour he tried to do her harm. His wild strength finally failed and he collapsed, his breath so shallow it did not stir the dust upon the floor.

'Oh, what are we to do?' Freda wailed, hunkering down by her friend, terrified because the life energy within him was fitful at best.

'You could show me the way back to Haven, if you like,' came a gentle voice.

Freda's head came up. There stood her dearest friend. She grinned so widely that it cracked her cheeks, but she did not care. 'Is it you? Are you real? You are not trick or test? If you are Anupal in disguise, I will do very bad things to you!'

'No, Freda. It is me.'

'My friend Jillan!' she cried. 'My friend.'

He came towards them and put one hand on Samnir's brow and one upon his chest. The commander's breathing evened out and deepened.

His eyes opened. 'Where the hell have you been?'

'It's good to see you too, Samnir.'

'Hella's been worried sick. Jacob's been beside himself.'

'We'd best hurry to them, then.'

'Do you have any idea what you've put us all through?'

'I am pleased to see you, friend Jillan,' Freda interposed. 'When I could no longer hold the Gate, I was worried I would never see you again. I felt bad and ... and guilty.'

'There's no need for that any more,' Jillan said kindly. 'Thank you for all you did. It saved many people.'

'But what kept you and how *did* you get back?' Samnir pressed.

'Well, what would be the point of the People of the seventh being spared if they were only going to fail through despair? Thus some restitution has been permitted, some payment or reward, if you like, for all that has been sacrificed. There is more. Look behind you, Freda.'

The rock woman turned and cried out in joy. The entire chamber was now filled with her people. 'My brother Freom!' She wept diamonds and caught the rock giant in a crushing embrace. His laughter boomed as he begged for mercy.

'And there, Freda. See?' Jillan urged.

Another figure lumbered towards her. She let go of her brother and flung her arms around the newcomer, squeezing him and hoisting him up high.

'Ow! Freda be gentle with Dor!'

As the group walked back towards Haven, Jillan spoke. 'Perhaps it would be best if we all went back to Godsend. As our population grows, Haven will be too small to provide for us, and we will ultimately ruin it as we did before.'

Samnir nodded thoughtfully. 'In Godsend we will be that much closer to the mountain people as well. Trade will be far easier. Otherwise, we will lose touch and the difference between mountainer and lowlander will only increase. Added to that, there are rich fields all around Godsend rather than mean desert. Yes, there is merit to the idea, Jillan.'

'Freom, do you think your people might guard Haven, as in former times?'

The rock giant inclined his head. 'We would be honoured, Jillan Hunterson. Yet who is there to guard against?'

Jillan smiled. 'You should guard it from us, or our future generations. Let Haven be sealed away once more. Let it remain undisturbed as the sacred home of the Geas. Let it be a place of legend and imagination. We will tell tales of it and dream wondrous dreams. For the good of us all, its power should be safeguarded. We were perhaps not ready to come here before.'

'Will we ever be ready?' Samnir wondered.

'One day, perhaps.'

Hella looked up blearily, unable to tell the difference between dream and waking any more. 'Oh, there you are, Jillan,' she mumbled. 'If you didn't want to marry me, you should have just said so, rather than ending the world like that.'

She was wan and her eyes could not focus properly. He touched her cheek gently and gave her a magical kiss. 'I have moved heaven and earth. I promised I would marry you, and there is nothing now to prevent it.' He caressed her stomach and reassured their child all would be well.

Hella frowned. 'You're really here, then?'

'Yes, I'm really here. Nothing could keep me from you.'

'I'm angry at you,' she said.

'Quite right too. I didn't bring you any flowers or gift.'

'I've half a mind not to marry you now.'

'That would be a shame. I've already had the seamstress start on a new dress, and Ash is experimenting with brewing his own ales and distilling his own spirits. He says his stocks need replenishing if there is to be a party. Your father is being fitted for a new suit of clothes too. Everyone's very excited. Oh well, I'd better go and tell them not to bother.'

'It would be a shame to disappoint them,' she mused. 'Alright, we'll get married and I'll find another way to punish you instead. Who will oversee the ceremony, though?'

'I was thinking either Torpeth – he's a holy man, after all – or the headwoman of the mountain people. Once you're well enough, we'll all travel to Godsend.'

'For good?'

'I think so.'

'That's alright then. Haven's all very nice, but somehow it's too nice. Does that make sense?'

'It does, Hella. Get some rest now.'

Her eyelids became heavy. 'I might just do that. Remind me to punish you later.'

*

The trip to Godsend was neither protracted nor difficult, for the wolf was their guide. There were minor complaints from a few individuals, but the vast majority were just glad to be alive, to be directed by those they trusted, and to be going to a place a number of them had privately always considered their real home.

The few mountain people living in Godsend had welcomed them with open arms, especially Ash the innkeeper. Samnir had helped him pull a handcart of bottles and casks all the way from Haven. As he helped him settle into his new home, the commander said, 'Woodsman, I believe I owe you a drink.'

'That was the agreement,' Ash replied warily. 'But all things considered, we can let bygones be bygones.'

'I will pay my debt and more. I have decided I will be your business partner.'

'No! ... I mean, thank you very much and all that, but must you?'

'Yes. It's the least I can do.'

'There's really no need.'

'Oh, there's every need. Besides, you don't get a choice in the matter.'

The woodsman groaned. 'I thought as much.'

'Come now, it won't be as bad as all that, you'll see. Let's have that drink then, to toast our new venture, eh?'

'Very well,' Ash said with resignation. 'I suppose I will need the help now that ingrate Dor has run off with his sweetheart. How do you think he and Freda will ...?'

'What?'

'You know. Be intimate?'

Samnir pulled a face. 'Probably best not to think about it. Nature always finds a way, they say.'

Later on, Captain Gallen stopped in to see them. He looked strange and distinctly uncomfortable now that he no longer wore armour. After a few beakers of dubious ale, he confessed, 'There are no more Heroes who need ordering about or disciplining. What will I do?'

'You will live your life instead, Gallen,' Samnir advised. 'You will find a woman or some other life mate who likes your dependable ways.'

'And what will you do, commander?'

'I will be an innkeeper! I will be uncle to Jillan and Hella's child. And I will keep a watch on all of you. Yes, I will keep a watch.'

Ash shook his head and went to get a bottle of the good stuff.

Jillan showed Hella into his parents' home. He was pleased to find it was largely intact, although he suspected birds had begun nesting in the chimney. The cottage had a far more welcoming feel than the one he'd occupied in Haven. He watched Hella anxiously for her response.

'It's cosy.' She smiled.

'Too small, you mean. It isn't much.'

She put a reassuring hand on his shoulder, then slipped her arms round his neck to kiss him deeply. 'It's perfect. I have all I ever wanted right here. Oo!'

'What is it?' he asked.

'The baby's kicking. Here. Feel.'

After a few seconds his eyes went wide. 'Amazing. You're amazing.'

'Are we truly safe now?'

'There are no more gods or Empire any more. Our child will grow up never having to worry about Saints, Ministers, Heroes, being Drawn or being accused of sin. They will be free.'

'If they're anything like their father, they'll still find ways to get into trouble.'

'I wouldn't have got into half those scrapes if you hadn't encouraged me.'

'I hope you think it was all worth it.' Her voice thrummed with command: 'Now kiss me properly.'

He happily obeyed her.

Epilogue

The way into the eighth had been easy. Too easy. The Convocation had been waiting for them. It had been a trap, of course. He should have known, but there had been no other way.

The slaughter had been terrible. He would have ordered a retreat to the seventh, but the Convocation had sealed the way as soon as the Declension's army had entered the eighth.

They would have been made entirely extinct if Lead Warrior Luhka Sha had not, in desperation, resorted to one of the Declension's most ancient and half-forgotten fighting forms, one that separated spectral state from physical in order to allow a simultaneous attack on an enemy. The giants of the eighth had been undone in that moment, for the Convocation was a race of beings that defined itself through unity, harmony of will, manifestation and environment. They could not withstand or reconcile the dual and contradictory nature of the Declension assault.

Dismayed, the giants had finally turned to flee. By some silent agreement, the shortest and broadest of the giants had stayed facing their enemy in order to buy the rest of their kind the necessary time to escape and perhaps regroup.

Ba'zel had been about to order the final push when *it* had happened. Something fundamental had changed. Something essential became lost, as if the ground had fallen away. The Declension's thoughts lost all order and reference. Where were authority and definition? Their principle was gone.

Warriors lost their intent and impetus. The injured no longer sought to rise. Half-eaten giants were discarded and allowed to drag themselves away.

She was gone. He felt it in his very being that the Geas of the Declension and their home-realm were no more.

Just as Ba'zel had hoped, prayed and planned all along, Jillan had triumphed. It was hardly believable, but still it had happened. 'Thank you, my friend,' he murmured. 'I am indebted to you, for now I am first among the Declension and all will obey only my command. The Declension is indebted to you, for if you had not removed from us the increasing demand and imperative to feed the Eldest and our Geas, we would not ultimately have been able to sustain our progress on the Great Voyage. The magnitude of their appetite was growing beyond us and was about to cannibalise us. Now you have freed us, nothing will hold us back. We will be able to move through the cosmos far more easily, without the entire need to undo the other beings we encounter. We will look to subdue them only in as far as it is immediately necessary to feed. To do otherwise would also see us waste ourselves.'

His warriors heard his words and took them as their own. They prostrated themselves before him, awaiting his will.

Ba'zel idly wondered what had become of his father and Dra'zen. Perhaps he would see them again one day, perhaps not.

He stepped forward into the middle of the tiered and awful battlefield, silently commanding Luhka Sha to stand behind him as guard. 'Hear me. I am Ba'zel of House Ba'zel, the Great Virtue Destruction, First among the Declension. You have seen the power of our will and know not to resist it. Hear me, Convocation of the eighth. Reveal to us the way to the ninth and you will be spared. That is our word and will! Deny us, and you will fall, as all other realms have fallen. We do not negotiate. We will vouchsafe and guarantee your existence if you accede to our will. Accede, and the Declension will leave this realm, for it is of only passing concern and matter to us. Answer me now, Convocation.'

His was a new way, but a way that brought success where *She* had failed. He would see the Declension claim the cosmos for itself, where *She* had but dreamed of it. He knew that, at the final moment of their triumph, he would be forced to face his friend Jillan once more. It would probably not be soon, but he would look forward to it all the same. And he would be ready.

A smooth-faced giant came forwards. 'I am the Deliberator. We accede to your will, Ba'zel of House Ba'zel, First among the Declension. The Convocation abases itself.'

The Peculiar sighed in exasperation as he watched the whining giant submit to the usurper Ba'zel.

'How disappointing. No gumption, this lot. Nothing like Jillan and his crowd.'

The beings of the seventh realm had done remarkably well, considering. Considering they'd had to fight their own gods, the vengeful King of the Dead and the Eldest one after the other. Remarkable that they'd prevailed.

'Of course, I did help them at a critical moment. It could have, would have, should have all gone the other way but for that.'

Not that the beings of the seventh had shown any gratitude. To think that harridan Hella Jacobsdotter had taken it upon herself to banish him. Her, a mere mortal! Him, a lord of the cosmos! It was galling. How dare she! It was just another example of the mortals' increasing and dangerous sense of their place and entitlement in the cosmos. It was just one more reason why they had to be considered a threat now. He was not done, by any means, with the seventh. Oh no. He would wait until all had forgotten him and then return to claim sway over them once more. Until then, there were many more worlds to bedevil, destabilise and rule.

Yes, there was plenty to keep him entertained. It was just a shame Jillan's lot had not been able to dismantle the Declension army led by Ba'zel. The Declension would continue to be a thorn in his side, something to hamper him, an irritation.

Still, wouldn't things be boring if they became too easy?

About the author

A J Dalton (the A is for Adam) has been an English language teacher as far afield as Egypt, the Czech Republic, Thailand, Slovakia, Poland and Manchester University. He has lived in Manchester since 2003, but has a conspicuous cockney accent, as he was born in Croydon on a dark night, when strange stars were seen in the sky.

He published his first fantasy trilogy, consisting of *Necromancer's Gambit* (2008), *Necromancer's Betrayal* (2009) and *Necromancer's Fall* (2010), to great acclaim. With Gollancz he has put out the best-selling titles *Empire of the Saviours* (2012), *Gateway of the Saviours* (2013) and *Tithe of the Saviours*. He maintains the Metaphysical Fantasy website (www.ajdalton.eu), where there is plenty to interest fantasy fans and also advice for aspiring authors.